Killing Harry Shaw

W H Bowers-Elliot

Copyright © 2024 W H Bowers-Elliot

All rights reserved. The author claims the right to be identified as the author of this work in accordance with the Copyright, Designs and Patents Act. You may not copy, store, distribute, transmit, reproduce or otherwise make available this publication or any part of it in any form or by any means (electronic, digital, optical, mechanical, photocopying, recording or otherwise) without the express written permission of the author. Any person who does any unauthorized act in relation to this publication may be liable to criminal prosecution and civil claims for damage. Licensing requests: contact the author at whbowers-elliot@proton.me

DISCLAIMER

This is a work of fiction and the author's invention. Excepting references to known whistleblowers and security service programs in the public domain, the events and characters are imaginary. Any resemblance to real events or people, living or dead, past or present, is purely coincidental.

ISBN: 9798340792426

Front cover image and design by SSW
Back cover image of Benhall GCHQ © Crown Copyright 2022.
Sailing image courtesy SSW, modified by GenSwap AI

In memory of the real Harry Shaw, who died at sea.

"The story they don't want you to read, with hush-hush revelations that no UK publisher would touch! To hell with it, I thought, self-publish and be damned!" — W H Bowers-Elliot

1

In the pit of his stomach, he sensed danger. A tense, hollow feeling. But why?

Harry Shaw sat alone in the cockpit of his classic sailing yacht, Ariana. Thirty feet of wooden perfection, built in the 1960s of the finest Burma Teak. A gentle breeze blew from the west, bringing with it a swell that rhythmically lifted the boat every twenty seconds or so. Harry's eyes had become accustomed to the darkness, so he could clearly make out the line of the horizon between sea and night sky.

He had just completed his regular lookout duty by carefully scanning the sea all around his vessel, as far as the horizon, in all directions. He concluded that his yacht was entirely alone, with nothing but empty sea for three miles in any direction. He could see no threat of collision, so what was his gut feel trying to tell him?

The nearest vessels were behind him, to the south. A line of dim white masthead navigation lights was visible just above the horizon, about six miles distant. That was the endless stream of ships heading southwest down the English Channel, their destinations unknown. No problem there.

Next, Harry checked on his wife and kids, sleeping down below in the main cabin. Looking down through the open companionway into the darkness, he could make out the faint outlines of his wife Miranda and his two children, George and Charlie. All three were fast asleep, tucked up in their sleeping bags. His son was making quiet snuffling noises. "They all look peaceful," he thought.

Could it be some problem with the yacht's sails or rigging?

Harry pushed the tiller away and let the yacht turn towards the wind until the sails started to flap a little. The boat slowed down to a crawl. He lashed the tiller and, grabbing a torch, he clambered on to the port side-deck with practised ease. From there, he completed a slow circumnavigation of the yacht, examining the sails, halliards, sheets, and other ropes.

He felt the tension in each of the seven taught wires that supported the long wooden mast. He looked up to where the masthead navigation light was displaying white, red, and green in each appropriate sector. Everything appeared in perfect order.

Returning to the cockpit, Harry worked the handle of the hand pump that would empty any water from the bilges of the boat. After two strokes to prime the pump, it became harder work as his efforts lifted water four feet up a pipe to spurt overboard. After six more strokes he was pumping air. The bilge was dry again. "So, we're not sinking," he told himself. "I must be imagining things — don't be stupid — relax."

Returning to his helming duty, he altered course to fill the sails with wind. The yacht heeled a few degrees, accelerated back to cruising speed, and headed north once more. To improve his mood, Harry looked up at the celestial light show. There was no moon to illuminate the night sky and reduce the relative brilliance of the stars. The reward was that pinpricks of bright light filled the entire sky, billions of stars tightly packed together. He gazed at the endless galaxies, receding to millions of light years away. There were so many that in some areas of the Milky Way there was no visible space left between each star to identify the black void that separated them. Harry pondered how such an awesome sight is available to only the fortunate few who travel to remote locations to find dark skies, or climb high mountains, or go to sea.

His intention was to make landfall at Lulworth Cove, on the Jurassic Coast of Dorset, between Weymouth and Swanage. Around seven in the morning, he would wake his children as they approached the seemingly unbroken coastline of cliffs. And then, when close, an opening would appear. The yacht would sail through a narrow entrance to reveal a little horse-shoe bay that would encircle them, with hills and cliffs curving protectively around pristine waters. Harry pictured their wide-eyed wonder as they took in the scene, formed at the end of the last ice-age. All in all, this trip had been perfect sailing, a vacation that his young children would never forget. He began to relax.

"I'm a lucky man," he murmured, as the cool night air brushed against his face, filling his lungs with the scent of sea and freedom. This trip meant more than just relaxation. After years where business came first, this was a chance to strengthen the bond between himself and his family. "Four weeks," he thought. "No distractions, no business calls, just us. Being unemployed has its benefits!"

Harry had recently been fired from his role as CEO of the software company he founded, eleven years previously. There had been an acrimonious disagreement between him and the new owners of the company, which culminated in a boardroom bust-up and his swift departure.

He was a healthy forty-seven-year-old, relatively wealthy, with time on his hands and the freedom to choose a new career path. But that could wait. Right now, he was relishing quality time with his family. Then, Harry's mind drifted to his father, John Shaw, a retired naval officer. How proud his dad would be to know that the next generation of Shaws were being introduced to the sea and sailing. Then Harry recalled his father's wise words, "At sea, those who are cautious live longer than those who are careless."

That set his nerves on edge again. He started to repeat his sweep of the horizon, from ahead to the starboard beam to astern, where he stopped. What was that?

He was convinced that he could discern a little patch of total darkness, directly astern of Ariana. It was a black void amidst the otherwise shimmering, starlit sea — an anomaly that shouldn't be there. "Odd," he voiced his "Odd," he muttered to himself, earnestly staring astern. Was the spot growing? Yes, it did appear to become slowly larger.

Harry knew that on a night like this the surface of the sea is not black but just visible. The starlight bounces off the moving water, scattering light in all directions to illuminate the surface of the sea and the crest of each wave.

A patch of nothingness, an absence of reflected light, indicates the presence of some dark object. For example, once, at night, Harry had spotted an unexplained black patch ahead and at once altered course. By doing so, he narrowly avoided colliding with a container. Tons of metal box had been mostly submerged, floating low down with one corner just above the surface of the sea. It must have come loose and fallen from the deck of a container ship, probably during a storm, hundreds of miles away. If Harry's yacht had collided with that container whilst sailing at full tilt, it could have holed the hull below the waterline.

"Focus, Harry," he told himself as he stood up to improve

his view. Scrutinizing the black void, he reasoned: "I know the horizon is around three sea miles away, so whatever I am seeing is a little over one mile behind me and it seems to be getting closer."

He glanced back at the cabin, considering whether to wake Miranda and the children. But then, to distract him, the wind gusted, causing Ariana to heel and veer off course, which forced him to return to his helming duties. He steadied the yacht, narrowed his eyes, and returned to studying that dark patch astern of the yacht.

It continued to slowly grow, now revealing itself to be more than just a trick of the light, or a figment of his imagination. As it was drawing closer, it was taking on a definite shape. Harry recognised the unmistakable silhouette of a powerboat. A matt black powerboat. It was on course to collide with them. And there were none of the obligatory white, red, and green navigation lights that a motor vessel should display. The eerily stealthy boat was slowly coming closer.

Why no navigation lights? Was someone trying to hide their presence as they approached his yacht? "Damn it!" He said as reached for the powerful torch, clicked it on and aimed the beam at the white mainsail. "You'd have to be asleep to miss that," he thought, hoping against hope that the approaching boat would see them and veer off course.

"Miranda!" he called down the companionway.

"Eh — yes — Harry — what's going on?" His wife's sleepy voice drifted up from below, followed by the groans and murmurs of the children as they awoke.

"Get up, put on lifejackets and wait for instructions." Harry had switched into masterful skipper mode, when he would issue commands clearly, concisely and in such a way as to brook no discussion. "There's a boat approaching, and I don't like the look of it." His family stumbled about in the cabin below, following his orders.

Harry could now discern a sharper image of the powerboat. It was low in the water with a long-pointed bow. As he watched, the craft accelerated towards them. He could now hear the growl of powerful engines and see white spray thrown aside as the vessel approached at high speed. At about fifteen metres away, it suddenly stopped.

All was silent for a moment. It was then that Harry saw what looked like a couple of metal balls coming towards him just above head height. One was going to land in the sea. The second metal object was arcing through the air straight at him, glinting faintly in the starlight. Harry instinctively ducked as it passed over his head, missing him. For a moment he was convinced it was a metal golf ball.

His thoughts raced as the object disappeared down the open hatchway into the cabin below. He could hear it rolling around the wooden floorboards. His daughter Charlie yelled, "Mummy!" Miranda bent to pick the thing up with the intention of throwing it overboard. His son George had the same idea, and as they bent down, they bumped heads and fell. Time was against them.

The evil little device exploded, the report shattered the quiet night, sounding like several shotguns fired in unison. The world seemed to stop as the shockwave momentarily shook the wind from Ariana's sails and made Harry fall to the cockpit floor, the realization dawning that the object had been some sort of miniature grenade.

"NO!" Harry yelled. His anguished howl carried over the

empty sea until the wind and waves swallowed the sound. A horrifying truth was settling upon him that his wife and children must be dead.

He stood once-more, defiant, with a desperate fury rising within him. That's when a searchlight blinded him and he heard the crack, crack, of a firearm, and heard a sound like 'fwit' as one bullet passed his right ear, and then a searing pain on the left side of his head as another found its target. He felt his head being spun around on his shoulders like a top. But that was only a fleeting sensation. The world tilted and Harry collapsed in the cockpit, darkness swallowing his vision as he passed out.

In the wake of the destruction, the yacht Ariana seemed relatively unperturbed. The sturdy cabin roof, designed to withstand the force of crashing waves, had remained intact. The yacht, with no hand on the tiller, turned gently towards the wind until her sails started to flap. And then her bow turned away from the wind, so that she slowly pottered along a see-saw course with the sails repeatedly flapping then filling, heading northwest.

The growl of the powerful engines reduced to a burble as the powerboat pulled alongside the yacht. Two men, dressed in black from head to foot, faces smeared with camouflage cream, stepped aboard with SIG P226 pistols held at the ready. They had thrown a modern version of the Dutch V40 golf ball grenade; a measured and contained instrument of death, lethal within a radius of about four metres.

The men checked the cabin and saw the remnants of three dead bodies, two of which had been children. They spotted a gentle little stream of blood pumping rhythmically from Harry's head wound, staining the teak grating of the cockpit floor. "He's alive," said one of the men.

"This isn't right – not what we were told," declared the other before he called back to the powerboat, "Pass the first-aid kit."

2

Harry Shaw stirred from a dreamless sleep. He noticed the sterile scent of antiseptic. He blinked several times, trying to adjust his vision to the bright overhead lighting. His mind felt like a foggy morning, the details obscured. The devastating scenes at sea failed to resolve into a coherent picture, leaving him feeling empty and confused.

"Mr Shaw," a soft voice broke through, drawing Harry's attention to the woman standing at his bedside, clad in a crisp white coat. The doctor's intense brown eyes regarded Harry with a mixture of concern and curiosity.

"Where am I?" Harry croaked, his throat parched and sore.

"You're in Dorset County Hospital, in Dorchester," the doctor explained as she pushed a pair of large tortoiseshell glasses up her nose. "I am Doctor Teresa Camilleri. You've been through quite an ordeal."

"Ordeal?" Harry repeated, struggling to recall what had happened. It was then that he noticed a powerful pulsating throb at the left side of his head and a band of pain across his back.

The doctor interpreted Harry's grimace. "Ah, yes. You were found unconscious on your yacht. You came out of surgery two hours ago and now you're in a private room. We've removed some small splinters of wood from your back. And you sustained a head injury. The surgeon told me that a large wooden splinter must have grazed your head, knocking away some scalp and a small fragment of bone. It must have been quite a blow; a serious concussion. We shall keep you here for a few days."

"Head injury?" Harry asked, frustrated that he couldn't recall his immediate past. He pictured a disjointed image of sea and stars, but it dropped from his consciousness, like sand slipping through his fingers. "What's happened! Why am I here? Have I lost my memory?" The beeps of the heart monitor started to speed up alarmingly.

"Take it slowly," the doctor advised, placing a hand on his shoulder. "For now, you must rest. We'll do everything we can to help you regain your memory. All your questions will be answered but, right now, you should rest."

The doctor increased the amount of sedative dripping into Harry's vein through a canular. Harry watched her checking another machine attached to him by wires and tubes. He lay back, stared at the bright ceiling, his mind a whirlwind of questions.

He clenched his fists, willing himself to remain conscious and to remember. Some fleeting glimpses came and went: the caress of a warm breeze on his face, the salty taste of sea spray, the steady rhythm of waves lifting the hull of a yacht. "Of course, Ariana, my yacht."

He wasn't entirely sure if he was awake or dreaming. The image of his old boat sailed towards him, emerging from a sea fog. He felt exhausted and gave up on trying to think about anything as he lapsed into sleep.

Doctor Camilleri quietly slipped out of the room, leaving Harry to rest. She paused to look back at him through the small window in the closed door. He was lying on his right side with his handsome tanned face turned towards her. A thick cushion of dressing on the left side of his head covered his wound and made it look as if his head was swollen out of shape. He appeared lean, fit and yet vulnerable. She found him attractive, but at that moment she was not sure why.

Earlier that day, she had been working a shift in the Accident and Emergency Department. A dirty green helicopter, not the usual bright yellow air ambulance, had landed on the lawn outside. Harry was unconscious when two big military looking men wearing grey overalls carried him inside. They quickly said that Harry had been injured at sea, which explained his waterproofs and the blood-stained bandages wrapped around his head. She started to examine her new patient and turned to ask for more information, but the men had moved away to stand at a distance. Next, the Chief Executive of the Hospital appeared and was in earnest conversation with the two burly men. Teresa was focussed on examining Harry, issuing instructions to nurses to check his vitals and cut off his clothing so she could fully assess his injuries.

Then, something most unusual happened. A senior surgeon appeared next to Teresa, summarily pushed her aside and took over, telling her that she could move on to another patient. Within a couple more minutes Harry was gone, wheeled away towards the operating theatres.

The previous year, Teresa had volunteered to work a month at the Al-Shifa Hospital, in Gaza. There, she had treated two patients with bullet-wounds. Her first look at Harry's head-wound had convinced her that a bullet had grazed Harry's skull. He was incredibly lucky to be alive. That knowledge, combined with the unprecedented level of executive attention, which Teresa had never before witnessed, added up to something very suspicious.

On the spot, she decided to volunteer for a few extra shifts in the medical wards where she usually worked. That way,

Harry would come under her care, and she might have the opportunity to satisfy her curiosity.

She realised she had been standing outside Harry's room for some minutes, lost in thought. Her mind returned to the present and she turned to leave, only to find herself face to face with the guard. "Who posted you here? Who do you work for," she demanded.

The massive man looked down at her impassively, and quietly replied, "I couldn't say Miss."

It was pointless asking for more information and so she strode off down the corridor to attend to other patients.

In his room, Harry was drifting in and out of sleep. His mind was working in overdrive, grasping for details of what had happened. It was so annoying. His brain refused to cooperate. He knew the information was in there, deep in his memory, but it was refusing to obey his command and resurface. Eventually he fell into a deep sleep.

He awoke in the late afternoon to find a golden sun was filtering through the venetian blinds and casting thin strips of light on the walls. She was there again. That female doctor. She made her way around his bed, checking the speed of a drip and then a machine which clicked every minute, as it pumped into Harry a little cocktail of drugs.

Harry thought that if he could only remember everything, there would be no excuse to keep him here, tethered to this darned hospital bed. His memory held the key to his discharge. Unfortunately, every time he tried to recall his wife and children, his head throbbed with an incessant pain, which only abated a little when he stopped trying to remember.

Doctor Camilleri could see the strain on Harry's face and

guessed what he was thinking, or rather trying to think. "Memory loss is quite common after a traumatic event. Most patients recover their memory fairly quickly."

"Is that supposed to make me feel better?" Harry snapped; his voice strained with exhaustion. He immediately regretted his tone, but the words had already been said

Teresa regarded him with sympathy, "Your mind is healing, just as your body is. I believe you will remember."

Harry looked around the room and eyed the door, feeling a powerful desire to go through it. As it stood ajar, he noticed the burly guard stationed outside. The man felt his gaze and turned to glance between him and the doctor before turning his head to look away.

"Why is he there?" Harry asked, suspicion in his voice.

The Doctor hesitated for a moment. In truth, she wondered the same, but she simply repeated what she had been told to say. "It's just a precaution, Mr Shaw. People want to ensure your safety while you're in our care."

"People? Safety?" Harry repeated. "Right," he muttered, unconvinced. He wanted to ask more, but the machine clicked, another pulse of drugs passed down the tube and into his veins. He just had time to wonder whether that clear liquid included a sleeping draft as, with a resigned sigh, he closed his eyes and gave in to the seductive pull of sleep.

♦♦♦

What had he been dreaming about? Ah yes — his yacht. In his dreams, his boat was moored alongside a quay that was packed with holidaymakers who were strolling along, admiring the various craft, and wishing they too could sail away. In this dream, an old man stopped in his tracks to gaze at the craftsmanship of the wooden decking and the varnished teak cockpit. He chatted with Harry about the days when boatbuilders used spokeshaves, chisels and copper rivets instead of spray guns, glass matting and resin. Had anyone looked, they would have noticed that Harry was smiling in his sleep.

And then his dream switched to being at sea. A steady breeze filled new white sails and Ariana heeled over to the wind as she punched through waves. Spray was flying over the cabin roof and soaking his wife and children, seated in the cockpit, screaming and laughing with joy, eyes bright with excitement.

But then, that idyllic scene changed. The sun disappeared behind dark, threatening clouds. A storm was approaching fast. In his mind's eye, Harry saw a black sky. Thunder crashed directly overhead, followed by bolts of lightning that struck the sea all around the boat, making the water hiss with steam. Relentless waves battered the yacht, and his children looked at him with terrified expressions. A massive wave rolled over the cockpit and his children were carried away, followed by his wife, Miranda, who was clawing at the side of the yacht, desperate not to be sucked into the foaming turmoil. As she went, he heard her cry, "Harry!" It was as loud and insistent as reality. He reached out, desperate to save her, felt her wet clothing slip from his grasp, and watched as she vanished beneath the chaotic waters. An empty cockpit. No children. They were gone in an instant. His dream broke.

He was clutching wet sheets, soaked from his perspiration. "Miranda!" He bolted upright in bed, drenched in sweat and panting heavily. "George! Charlie," he shouted.

At that moment of waking, Harry's recall of the past two days returned like an unwelcome bolt from the blue. It was as if a door into part of his memory had burst open so that the painful memories came charging out of the door in vivid colour, with cinema surround sound making an explosion in his head which hurt like hell. The awful truth.

"Mr Shaw." A nurse rushed into the room, in response to his shouting. Concerned by the tortured expression on his face, she bent over him. Her voice brought him fully back to the present. And then Doctor Camilleri arrived. She was there again, a reassuring presence. She calmly guided him back down onto the pillows. "It's alright. You're safe."

"Safe," he echoed, his voice hollow as the details of his nightmare receded.

"Were you remembering?"

He nodded in the affirmative as he closed his eyes. Harry spent the rest of that evening repeatedly playing a video in his head. He relived the ordeal at sea in all its gory detail. He would quietly sob himself to sleep, exhausted, only to wake a few minutes later, when he must endure the events again and again.

At one point he was retching in his sleep, then vomiting, which caused a minor panic as nurses rushed around cleaning him up, checking him over and hoping he hadn't beathed any vomit back into his lungs. Eventually, the doctor on night-duty administered a full syringe of hydromorphone, even more powerful than morphine. After that, Harry passed out for a full seven hours.

3

Next morning, Harry accepted something light to eat and lay propped up in bed, prodding the edges of the dressing on the left side of his head to test how painful it felt. The painkillers had not only dulled the pain but also fogged his mind. He was fighting to stay awake. He needed to stay alert so that he didn't miss the next visit from a doctor, or anyone who might answer some of his questions.

He was in danger of drifting off to sleep when the door opened, and a tall figure stepped inside. Shiny silver hair gleamed under the ceiling lights above a lined, tanned face. Below the face, Harry observed his attire: a navy-blue Dunhill double-breasted blazer, a perfect white shirt, and a striped regimental tie. His grey trousers sported knife-edge creases that ran down a fine worsted material. Harry thought his visitor looked like a retired army officer who had just stepped out of his gentleman's club in London. The man stood at the foot of the bed and regarded Harry with a stern expression, which did not put him at ease.

"Mr Shaw," he began, "I am Commander Adrian Forbes of MI5," his voice cold and authoritative.

"Good God, why are you here?"

"We need to discuss the incident that took place on your yacht." He paused while Harry adjusted his position, pushing himself more upright. Now he was alert and totally focussed on his visitor.

As he spoke, Forbes began to pace back and forth in front of Harry's bed. "There was a grave mistake made by our intelligence services. Your yacht was misidentified. It was believed to be carrying terrorists who were heading for a cruise ship anchored in Weymouth Bay. Later that morning, King Charles was due to arrive by helicopter, after which he would inspect the new low-pollution engines, a British invention."

Harry's heart raced. His grip tightened on the bedsheets as he struggled to keep his composure. "Are you telling me that my family has been killed because of some — mistake?"

Forbes stopped pacing and looked Harry straight in the eye, "Our special forces were dispatched to neutralize the perceived threat. They approached from astern of your vessel, where sailors rarely keep a proper lookout. When they were close enough, they fired a type of fragmentation grenade, designed to kill those in close proximity. And then you fell in the cockpit. When they boarded your yacht, they expected everyone to be dead."

Here was definite proof that Harry's overnight nightmares were not fantasy, but fact. Again, he started reliving the event as he ducked the metal golf ball, followed by his children's screams, the explosion, the blinding searchlight, the muzzle flashes and the searing pain in his head. Harry's eyes were darting around, and he was twitching.

Forbes's cold, factual description was heartless. This man was standing there calmly saying that it was all due to some error. Harry found it difficult to control his mounting anger. He took a breath to steady himself as, incredulous, he asked, "Are you telling me that my wife and children are dead because someone couldn't tell the difference between terrorists and a family on holiday?"

After a pause, Forbes quietly replied, "Unfortunately, yes." And then, to Harry's amazement, Forbes added that, "I understand your anger Mr Shaw, but we cannot undo what has been done."

Those dispassionate words were too much for Harry. His vision blurred as tears welled up in his eyes and he sobbed his heart out. The room felt suffocating and the throbbing pain in his head returned with a vengeance. He wanted to scream, to rage against the world that had taken everything from him. But all he could do was lie there, weak, and powerless.

Forbes waited for several minutes, until Harry had composed himself. He expected another outburst from Harry but instead he quietly asked, "How did you people make such a catastrophic mistake?"

Commander Forbes's face remained impassive. Harry wondered whether the man was masking his feelings or simply heartless. He suspected the latter.

"Mr Shaw, in this line of work mistakes can be costly. We strive for perfection but sometimes even our best efforts aren't enough."

"Tell me what happened after the grenade," Harry demanded, his voice wavering but determined.

"Very well," Commander Forbes said, as he began pacing back and forth again.

"For God's sake man, stand still!" shouted Harry, "It hurts me to keep turning my head."

Forbes stopped moving and explained, "The special forces team boarded your yacht, expecting to find dead terrorists. Instead, they discovered... they discovered your family."

Harry shouted, "So my wife and children have been murdered by the very people supposed to protect us!"

"Indeed." Forbes added quietly as he looked at Harry with

a flicker of sympathy. "It was a grave error. Your family should not have been caught in the crossfire. The state will, of course, consider you eligible for compensation."

"Compensation!" Harry scoffed, his heart pounding in his chest. "You think money will appease me? You think money can wash away the blood on your hands?"

"Mr Shaw, I understand your pain, but –"

"Understand!" Harry let out a mirthless laugh, "How could you possibly know the agony of losing everything you hold dear? I need to know. How did this happen? How could you mistake my yacht for a terrorist vessel?"

"I'm afraid the details of our intelligence gathering are classified."

"Classified," Harry hissed, his eyes narrowing.

Forbes's voice took on a softer tone. "I understand your need for answers, but if you want to know more, then first you'll have to sign the Official Secrets Act. It is a formality that allows me to be more forthcoming — I have the document prepared." Forbes reached inside his jacket and pulled out a sheet of small print on stiff grey paper.

Harry tried to study the document before him, but the words seemed to swim before his eyes. "I guess that if I sign this, it will prevent me from revealing what you tell me?"

"Yes."

Harry hesitated. Years of experience negotiating business contracts told him to stop, read through twice and think carefully. But this was different. The thought of signing away his right to speak about this tragedy was a bitter pill to swallow, but the hunger for truth overruled the caution with which he would normally treat an important document.

"Fine," he muttered, snatching the pen from Forbes's hand,

and scrawling his signature.

"Very well, Mr Shaw." Forbes added his own signature as witness and deftly pocketed the document. He nodded at Harry in approval and a slight smirk played across his lips, just for a moment, unnerving Harry.

Forbes opened the door and beckoned to someone waiting outside. "Allow me to introduce Professor Jeremy Hall, from GCHQ, our country's intelligence, security and cyber agency."

A thin man with a bald head and sallow complexion entered the room, his eyes darted around as he assessed the scene. He reached out, offering a hand to Harry, who shook it limply, his gaze never leaving the professor's face.

"Mr Shaw," Professor Hall began slowly, enunciating each word with precision. "May I offer my sincere condolences. I am so sorry for your loss."

Harry did not respond but looked expectantly at the Professor.

"I am from GCHQ. Our mission is to keep Britain safe by monitoring various threats: cyber, criminal, terrorist, and others."

Harry's mind stood to attention as he listened intently to Hall's explanation.

"Your yacht was identified as carrying terrorists who represented a foreign power, a country with malign intent towards the United Kingdom. That assessment was based upon information gathered by our monitoring systems," Hall continued. "We had second and third sources which all confirmed the plan. It was all very convincing, which is why GCHQ alerted the armed forces."

"Then I must ask AGAIN, how did it all go so wrong?"

Hall replied carefully, taking a deep breath. "The only explanation for the incorrect identification of your yacht, and the subsequent tragedy, is that our system had been hacked. We suspect that a foreign power was behind this, presumably with the intention to kill King Charles if they were lucky, or at the very least to embarrass our government."

The revelation struck Harry like a punch to the gut. His family had been collateral damage in a twisted game of international espionage.

"Professor Hall," Harry said, his voice quiet and as menacing as he could manage in the circumstances, "I expect you to find those responsible for this hack, and to make them pay. In fact, I will do all I can to help. I cannot simply do nothing. My family has been snatched away, destroyed, and I have to do something about it."

Hall hesitated, his eyes flicking left and right. The professor was weighing Harry's sincerity and determination against the risk of involving a civilian in such a sensitive matter. Finally, after what felt like an eternity, he gave a slight nod.

Forbes rushed to interject, "Mr Shaw, you have signed the Official Secrets Act, but that doesn't make you part of our intelligence services. Professor Hall is heading the investigation into this matter at GCHQ, and I assure you no stone will be left unturned."

Meanwhile, outside the hospital room, Doctor Camilleri had been watching the exchanges through the window. She had seen the strain on Harry's face. Her heart wrenched with worry for her patient. His emotional state was precarious enough without these mysterious men pushing him further.

Resolutely, she moved to open the door and intervene, but the security guard barred her way.

"Let me pass," she insisted, "that man needs medical attention."

"Sorry Doctor," the guard replied, his expression impassive. "I have my orders."

Inside, Forbes, Hall and Harry continued their conversation, their voices hushed.

"Mr Shaw," said Forbes, his tone brooking no argument, "You must keep this entire incident a secret. You cannot reveal any of what we've discussed here today. If you do, you'll be arrested, tried, and imprisoned for a very long time."

Harry's jaw tightened as he absorbed this ultimatum, feeling the weight of his government's duplicity. He felt betrayed by Forbes, Hall, the special forces and his own government. To expose the truth would mean sacrificing his own freedom; to remain silent would be to acquiesce to a coverup. It was a cruel, impossible choice.

"The press has already been informed," continued Forbes, "newspapers and TV received a press release explaining that there was an accident aboard your yacht. It was a gas explosion caused by a leak on the gas line to the cooker in the galley. By pure chance, there were troops on exercise in the area who quickly came to your aid."

"How can you live with yourselves?" asked Harry in disdain.

"Sometimes," Forbes replied solemnly, "we must all do what is right for the greater good."

Harry scoffed at this hollow justification but knew he was powerless. "Fine; I won't say anything." He glared at Forbes and Hall. "Now get out — both of you."

Hall hesitated for a moment before handing a business card to Harry. He took the card which held only Hall's name and phone number.

"Contact me if you need to," Hall said quietly, meeting Harry's gaze with an inscrutable expression

As they left, taking the guard with them, Harry heard Forbes reprimand Hall. "The idea is to keep Shaw at arm's length, not to encourage him."

The door clicked shut, sealing Harry in silence. A few seconds later it opened again. Doctor Camilleri rushed in; her face etched with concern. She quickly checked Harry's vitals, noting the rapid pulse beneath her fingertips.

He stared at her, his thoughts a mix of gratitude and despair. But even as he yearned to confide in her, he knew that he could not. He nodded to himself silently, accepting the heavy burden of permanent secrecy.

The doctor's eyes softened with sympathy, but she said nothing. Her silent presence beside him was a comfort. "Thank you, Doctor — for everything." And then he added, "I can't quite place your accent."

"I come from Malta," she replied.

"Ah, yes, I remember now. I lived there for a while as a child.

She nodded, her eyes glistening with unshed tears as she gently replied, "You're not alone Harry. Remember that." As she left the room, he watched her go, thinking how much he appreciated the ministrations of such a caring woman.

He couldn't rest. His mind raced, replaying the tense confrontation with Commander Forbes. That man was repugnant. Harry clenched his fists, knuckles turning white at the memory of the smug satisfaction that played across Forbes's face when he'd obtained Harry's signature on the Official Secrets Act. It was clear now. That had been his main objective. He had come with the purpose of silencing him to maintain the pretence of an accident at sea.

Harry's gaze wandered to the entrance door where the security guard had stood. A pawn, like him, in the cover-up of state murder.

"Damned bastards," he slowly muttered under his breath, venom lacing each syllable.

And then there was Professor Hall. In stark contrast to Forbes, he seemed genuine, even remorseful. He spoke with precision and clarity, his words measured and thoughtful. There was something about him, an air of sincerity that Harry found himself drawn to, despite the circumstances.

"Perhaps the professor will genuinely look for answers," Harry mused, fingering the business card that Hall had handed to him before Forbes had chided him for doing so. He might be helpful in the future.

As the day wore on, Harry's resolve grew stronger, fuelled by the desire for truth and justice. He mused, "I can hardly believe it, just two days ago, under that magical starlit sky, life was full of happiness and promise."

He closed his eyes and allowed himself to be swept away by the thought of his wife's gentle touch and cuddling his children. But those moments of respite were fleeting, replaced by a growing desire to avenge their deaths. "I can't wait to get out of this place."

◆◆◆

Harry awoke in the early afternoon, disturbed by the sound of shuffling feet. He looked up to see his father, John Shaw, coming through the doorway with a worried expression on his face. In one hand was a walking stick and in the other a bunch of grapes.

Harry noticed how the knuckles of his father's once-strong hands had become gnarled by arthritis. That nasty disease had transformed his father into an old man before his time. As he walked towards the bed, he lent on the walking stick, to help keep him upright.

"Harry," John said softly, his voice tinged with concern. One of his knees audibly protesting as he approached. "How are you feeling?"

"Tired and a little confused," Harry admitted, his eyes downcast. "I lost my memory for a few hours."

A realisation suddenly hit him. He couldn't tell his father what really happened. He was forced to go along with the lie about a gas explosion killing his family. The idea that forever more he must lie to everyone, even his father, settled upon him as a heavy responsibility. He must have shown his inner distress upon his face because his father said, "Frankly Harry, you don't look so good. Shall I fetch a nurse?"

"No thanks Dad, it was just a wave of temporary pain. I get them now and then. It is already passing." Harry lied, realising how quickly he was becoming an accomplished liar. How he regretted having signed that damned Official Secrets Act.

John nodded, pulling up a chair next to his bed. "The doctor told me about your memory loss and said that it usually returns quite quickly." The old man placed the grapes on the bedside table and sat down with a wince. "In the meantime, perhaps I can help jog your memory."

And then John's eyes filled with tears, "I'm so sorry for your loss, Son. It's so unfair. Miranda, George, Charlie. All gone."

They both sat there in silence, apart from the sound of sobbing, for what seemed ages, until a woman burst through the door noisily, carrying a tray of tea and biscuits and chattering about what a lovely sunny day it was, as if all was right with the world. She left the tea on the bedside cabinet and sensing the tension, she quickly withdrew. Her tea trolley clinked and rattled as she set off down the corridor.

"Please, tell me something about recent events," Harry implored. "What about my work. I need you to confirm the details?"

"Alright." John took a deep breath. "Do you remember selling your software company, BankApp Ltd., about a year ago?"

Harry furrowed his brow, trying to sift through the jumbled fragments of his memory. "Right — yes — no — I think so."

John leaned forward, "I'll tell you anyway. After you sold the company, you stayed on as CEO. The new owners wanted to start using AI to speed up the creation of new apps. You were against that idea."

Harry's eyes widened as a flicker of recognition sparked within him. "Yes," he murmured, his pulse quickening. "I remember arguing with them about it. I mean, you can't have bank customer's money handled by an app that may contain elements of code that our programmers would not fully understand and therefore not be able to support."

"Exactly." John's face softened, pride shining through

the worry. "You always had a strong moral compass. And that's what made your company reliable and trustworthy. It was one of the reasons for your success."

As Harry listened to his father, more pieces fell back into place. "Thank you, Dad," Harry said, his voice thick with emotion.

"I'm ready for more now Dad. I want to hear everything."

"Well, Harry, you didn't just take issue with the new owners wanting to use AI. You fought them tooth and nail."

A vivid image of a heated boardroom meeting flashed through Harry's mind, with table thumping and raised voices, frustration on both sides boiling over. He remembered standing his ground, his passion for quality driving him to fight for what he believed in.

"Banking apps are different from other software," Harry continued, the words flowing more easily now, "There's so much potential for fraud and theft if the programming is flawed."

John hesitated for a moment, then sighed. "They fired you son; you are no longer CEO. You're currently unemployed. But you did get a generous severance package," said John, trying to add something positive.

The room fell silent once more as Harry stared at the ceiling, processing this latest information. His memory was coming together like shards of glass that were slowly reforming into a mirror.

After some time, Harry remembered the hurt of betrayal and the foolishness of anger. Unemployed? That's why he had time for a vacation with his family.

"Ah, the sailing holiday," he murmured, his voice thick with emotion. "Miranda and I decided that as I was unemployed, it was a great opportunity to enjoy more family time..." His words petered out.

"You wanted to give your kids the world. You introduced them to the thrill of adventure and the self-reliance that comes from cruising in a small boat." The old man choked back tears.

With a reluctant nod, Harry leaned back against the pillows.

"I can see you need a break, Harry," his father whispered, upset to see the distress on his son's face which was unusually pale and sweaty with dark circles under his eyes. The drugs, combined with the emotional stress, had exhausted Harry again. He wanted to talk more with his father, but he just couldn't keep his eyes open. The effort was too much.

As soon as he was sure that his son was fully asleep, John Shaw quietly left the room, emotionally drained from trying to keep a tight rein on his own feelings of grief.

He slowly walked towards the end of the corridor, but then an overwhelming feeling of loss burst through. He collapsed onto one of those rigid plastic chairs that line so many hospital corridors. If those seats could talk, they would tell many stories of despair, heartache, hope, relief, the full panoply of human emotions. For about ten minutes, Harry's father sat there alone until he had regained sufficient control to head home.

4

A salty breeze wafted through the open window, proving the sea was only a short walk from the old red-brick house. Harry sat in an armchair, nursing a cup of tea, gazing at the flagpole on the front lawn. Elaborate wire rigging supported it, making it appear like the mizzenmast from an old sailing ship. That was the last relic from the days when his father's house had been a home for senior ship's officers, stationed at the nearby Warsash School of Navigation.

His father had purchased the house many years earlier. It had been a wonderful home for Harry. As a teenager, he had roamed for miles along the coast. And later, George and Charlie had spent weeks here during the school holidays, enjoying more freedom to play outdoors than he would have dared allow them in London.

Looking through the window, Harry could see across the heathland to the shingle beach, and then across one mile of sea to the Isle of Wight in the distance. "Harry," his father's voice came from the kitchen, "Would you like more biscuits?"

"No thanks Dad." His father was using every opportunity to feed him more calories and fatten him up. Harry was surprised how much weight had fallen from his body during his two-week stay in hospital.

Returning home to his and Miranda's house in Brixton was out of the question for now. The memories there were too raw, too vivid. So, Harry was happy to accept his father's invitation.

Harry took another sip of tea as his mind wandered towards his dead wife and children. "Your mother always loved this view," his father said, entering the living room and taking the seat opposite him. "She'd sit here for hours, watching the ships go by."

Harry looked into his father's eyes, searching for some of the strength he needed. "Dad, how did you... How did you cope when Mum died?"

His father hesitated, and then replied, "Time, Harry, time, and patience. The pain has never gone away completely, but over time I have learnt to accept life as it is and to carry on. You will do the same. You'll find that you're stronger than you think."

"Am I?" Harry wondered aloud. "I hope so."

The lies forced by the cover up of his family's slaughter, and the sting of how Commander Forbes had so easily tricked him into signing the Official Secrets Act, were eating away at him. Harry found it especially painful that he couldn't share the truth with his father, who had lost a daughter-in-law and two grandchildren.

And another thing gnawing away at his conscience was the problem of well-meaning friends and wider family. They would keep on trying to contact him. He couldn't handle their clawing sympathy. He had become adept at sidestepping conversations, leaving his father to handle all his phone calls, which often placed John in awkward situations.

Harry had stopped reading WhatsApp messages altogether. His phone lay on his bedside table, battery flat, and good riddance to it. He wondered how spies could maintain a life of permanent subterfuge without it eating away at their souls. He was finding it impossible to live a normal life whilst being unable to talk honestly about the attack on his yacht. He could never relax in case he accidentally revealed something that he should not.

He scanned the track in front of the house, where a man caught his eye. He didn't fit the usual scattering of dog walkers and couples who passed by. This man was not wearing relaxed country clothes but a city style of raincoat. He was alone, alert, too focused. To Harry, he stuck out like a sore thumb. The man glanced towards the house and the window. It sent a shiver crawling down Harry's spine. Could MI5 be keeping an eye on him?

"Who's that?" he muttered, half to himself.

"What's that?"

"Nothing Dad," Harry lied.

"Look, you can't keep bottling everything up inside, it'll tear you apart."

As they sat there, father and son, bound by grief but separated by secrets, Harry couldn't shake the feeling that the raincoated man was watching him.

Early the next morning, the sun cast a golden light across the heath. Long shadows made the swaying grasses glow as they danced in the wind. Harry trudged along the shingle shore, the rhythmic crunch of his footsteps grounding him in the moment. He turned to face the sea breeze, cold and invigorating.

"Great day, isn't it?" his father said, struggling to keep up with Harry's pace as they walked side by side. The lines of pain that occasionally showed on his father's face were evidence of the arthritis that tormented his knees. Harry knew his father had taken a couple of Codeine tablets before setting out, yet the old man never complained.

Harry nodded, managing a half-smile. "It's a good day."

He hesitated, then added, "Thanks for coming with me, Dad."

"I wanted to; I enjoy our walks, and the fresh air does us good."

There was a prolonged period of silence. Harry was lost in thought, pondering the forthcoming funeral, which he was dreading. His father was quiet because he was wondering how to broach a subject that was concerning him. Eventually, he found the right words.

"Harry, I've been thinking about what happened on your yacht," he began, his voice serious. "And I have to say that the story of a gas explosion doesn't ring true."

Harry's pulse quickened. He had hoped his father wouldn't pry into the matter, but he should have known better. John was too experienced to easily be deceived.

"Look," John continued, "you're a conscientious skipper, a qualified Yachtmaster, and you maintained that boat in perfect condition. A major gas leak? I don't think so. Not credible." John looked down as he waited for an answer.

Harry didn't want to lie to his father, but he couldn't say the real cause of the explosion was a grenade. He opened his mouth to speak but couldn't find a suitable obfuscation. As a result, he just turned red in the face and looked away from his father, who continued.

"I'm not going to push you for the full truth, but whatever happened, just remember that you don't have to shoulder the burden alone. I'm here for you."

Harry swallowed hard, an emotional lump forming in his throat. "Thanks Dad," he whispered, his voice thick with emotion. "That means more than you know."

A week passed. Slowly, Harry was recovering his energy until one morning he awoke feeling a new determination to start living again, to get on with life.

"Morning," John greeted him as Harry bounced into the kitchen with an air of enthusiasm. The smell of freshly brewed coffee and toast filled the air as he sat down at the scrubbed wooden kitchen table.

Handing Harry a plate of scrambled eggs on toast, John launched into what was on his mind, "You're not doing yourself any favours by staying cooped up here with me, an old man. You should get away, take a break from — all this."

Harry listened intently, relieved to hear his father voice the thought that was already on his own mind.

"Get away from it all, take a vacation, leave the country for a while. A change of scenery would do you good."

Harry found the idea extremely attractive. He wanted to escape his own paranoia about MI5, and the suffocating cloud of sympathy that he felt all around him. "Any ideas on where I might go?"

"How about Malta," John suggested with a hint of nostalgia in his voice. "It's remote enough to provide a complete change. And remember how much you loved it when we lived there, when the navy stationed me at Valetta?"

Harry remembered the sun-drenched, honey-coloured buildings, the sparkling turquoise waters, the father and son adventures. It was Malta where Harry learned to sail, in a corner of Valetta harbour. He remembered the sense of adventure. As he tucked into his breakfast, his mind drifted back to times when, with friends, he would head off to explore the battlements and the ancient narrow streets of Valetta. It seemed idyllic, an ideal refuge.

"Malta. Yes. You're right. It's just what I need."

5

The day of the funeral dawned cold and grey, with a thin veil of mist wafting across the cemetery grounds. Harry and his father were standing outside Lambeth Crematorium, shifting around, partly to keep warm, but mostly because they felt anxious about the ordeal ahead.

Harry looked up at the soulless brick buildings which he thought an example of 1960s architecture at its worst. Two flat-sided, flat-roofed, windowless, square boxes comprised the chapels. They appeared to have been dropped onto the land without care. He stared at this place designed to process funerals with rapid efficiency and thought how Miranda would have hated this whole event.

"Harry," his father placed a hand on his son's sleeve. "It's time."

Three black hearses, whisper quiet, approached and then rolled to a slow stop in front of them, their gleaming black bodywork shone despite the gloom. The coffins inside, one for his wife and one for each of his children, were shiny black with chrome handles, as stark and funeral as could be.

"Here we go." John nodded towards the entrance as he did his best to hold his emotions in check.

"Let's get this over with," Harry replied, as they fell into step at the head of the sombre procession, following the polished black coffins into the chapel.

As the procession entered, the chapel filled with an instrumental refrain of Tina Turner's 'Simply the Best.' Harry winced at the choice made by Miranda's parents; she had never cared for the singer.

After they sat, in the pause before the ceremony started, Harry scanned the room, taking in a sea of solemn faces and watery eyes. He briefly noticed Doctor Camilleri. It had never occurred to him that she would attend. She was a vision of composure, dressed in black, sitting upright at the rear of the chapel. Their gazes met for a moment.

"Let us pray," the vicar intoned, his voice resonating with practiced solemnity. "For our dearly departed sister, Miranda, and Harry and Miranda's children, George and Charlie."

"Miranda was a woman of great faith," the vicar continued, "a loving wife, a devoted mother..." And so on. Harry tried not to listen, not out of callousness, but because it might break his resolve so that his emotions would take over and he would be unable to hold himself together. "... they brought joy and light to all who knew them..." The ceremony passed by quicker than seemed respectful. "...and finally," said the vicar, his voice tinged with sadness, "we commit their souls to the loving embrace of their Heavenly Father. May they find eternal peace in His presence."

"Amen," the congregation murmured, and a hush fell over the room, the only sound the noise of the vicar closing his Bible. "Let us depart in silence and reflection," the vicar instructed.

Harry thought, "He could have mentioned the need to hurry because another funeral will want to use this chapel in less than five minutes time!" Then he admonished himself for inappropriate thoughts.

Subdued music accompanied the three coffins as they began their solemn journey behind the curtain. It was Vera Lyn's 'We'll Meet Again.' Harry's jaw clenched, the song's sentimentality grating against his nerves. Miranda's parents had again chosen a soundtrack for a stranger. How little they really knew about their daughter.

"Harry," murmured a familiar voice, bringing him back to the present as he stood near the chapel's exit. One by one, friends and family stepped forward to offer their condolences, eyes swimming with sympathy.

"Thank you," he whispered to each person, shaking hands, nodding robotically. Their words were a blur, warm yet of no real comfort. With each touch, he found it more difficult to maintain his composure.

"Such a tragedy," sighed Aunt Mabel, her grip surprisingly strong for her years. "You've been through so much, Harry. You're in my prayers."

"Appreciate it," he mumbled, forcing himself to meet her gaze.

"Harry, I'm so sorry." It was James, an old friend from sailing days gone by. He grasped Harry's hand firmly. "If you ever need to talk, or just get out on the water again, give me a call."

"Harry!" Miranda's father, Mr Parker, raised his voice to cut through the air like a serrated knife, shattering the fragile atmosphere. "This is all your fault!"

There was a stunned silence as Mrs Parker added her own words, spat with venom. She trembled with anger as she made her accusation, "Our daughter and grandchildren are gone because of you!"

"Miranda trusted you," Mr Parker shouted, standing close in front of Harry, and look where that got her. You killed them on that damned boat of yours."

"Enough!" Harry shouted back, before he could stop

himself, his fists clenched by his sides. He knew they were grieving too, but their allegations were more than he could bear. "I loved them. I cared for them," he mouthed, but behind his tears the words were barely audible.

"Come along Dear." Mrs Parker tugged at her husband's arm. Her face twisted as she looked Harry up and down in disgust before she turned and strode away, dragging her husband along, leaving the crowd in silence.

For a while, all the mourners stared at Harry. His father was about to stride after the Parker's and tell them a thing or two, but Harry grabbed his arm and held him back. Harry wanted to turn and run but he was rooted to the spot. Anger, guilt, sorrow, and pain filled him as he looked down to hide his distress.

"Harry?" A soft voice with a Maltese accent broke the silence. He looked up to find Doctor Teresa Camilleri standing before him, her brown eyes radiating empathy. "I'm so sorry for your loss."

"Thank you, Doctor," he forced a weak smile. Her presence was like a balm on his raw nerves.

"Please," she continued, her hand momentarily touching his arm, "if there's anything I can do, don't hesitate to ask."

"Thank you, Doctor," Harry repeated. As she walked away, he watched her retreating figure, feeling grateful for her support. Once again, she had been there to help him at a time of need.

Harry thought, "God, I've got to get away from all this!" But then, a much darker thought crossed his mind. There was one crucial thing he must do, a personal obligation to fulfil before leaving England.

❖❖❖

After Teresa left the funeral, she slipped into the blue Skoda Fabia that she had recently bought, her first new car. She steeled herself for the long journey home, 128 miles from London to Dorchester. It would take her at least three hours, with much of the time in heavy traffic.

She would not normally take time off work to attend a funeral for the relatives of a patient, but Harry was an exception. Whenever she was with him, she could feel the attraction. And she liked to hope that was a two-way thing. No, that was going too far. Harry had behaved impeccably, but she dreamed that one day he might feel the same way about her.

The cityscape of London gradually gave way to green countryside as Teresa turned onto the M3 motorway heading southwest. She settled into the inside lane, matching her speed with the flow of traffic, allowing her to think back to the funeral, with the sombre faces of Harry's friends and family. And she recalled that she had received some cold stares from Mr and Mrs Parker. It was as if they knew what was in her mind.

Those images swirled through her head, and she found herself gripping the steering wheel more tightly than necessary. She tried to relax.

She thought that Harry didn't deserve that tirade from Miranda's parents. And then she reflected on how so little about him. She believed his head wound was a graze from a glancing blow by a bullet. But then, perhaps it wasn't. The surgeon told her the cause was a flying splinter, and that she shouldn't have such fanciful ideas.

Teresa pondered the presence of the security guard outside Harry's hospital room. And there were his official looking visitors, the obviously secret conversations, the raised voices, the horror of hearing about the gas explosion aboard his yacht.

Teresa suddenly noticed in her rear-view mirror that a massive juggernaut was tailgating her car. Lost in thought, she had slowed down. In irritation, the driver flashed his headlights at her. She dragged her concentration back to her driving, but soon her mind was drifting again. Eventually, she came to a decision. After she arrived home, she would go online to investigate Harry Shaw and see what she could learn about him.

"Oh Harry," she said aloud, as the windscreen wipers beat rhythmically against the rain spattered glass, "why am I so drawn to you?"

"Pull yourself together woman!" she chastised herself, "You're going to cause an accident if you don't concentrate on your driving."

She indicated right, pulled across two lanes of traffic to the fast lane and accelerated to seventy miles per hour.

After leaving the hot little Skoda in the driveway, Teresa entered her small but cosy house, tossed her coat on an armchair, opened her laptop, and searched for the phrase *Harry Shaw*. She resolved that if he came up trumps and what she learned was good, then she would pursue a relationship with him. If he fell short, then she would try to forget that she had ever met the man and move on.

6

A few days later, the weather was dry and sunny. Harry was not thinking about Teresa one little bit as he inched his car towards the entrance to the secretive Special Boat Services (SBS) headquarters situated in Poole Harbour, nestled discretely alongside Dorset Lake Shipyard. The few unmarked buildings blended seamlessly into the general look of industrial units.

On the westerly breeze the air carried the familiar scent of a boatyard: mudbanks, seaweed, paint, polyester resin and diesel fumes; a reminder of countless hours devoted to maintaining his beloved yacht, Ariana.

The thought of seeing his boat again brought back the torture of losing his wife Miranda, their son George, and daughter Charlie — all gone in an instant of violence.

"Hello?" A curt questioning voice came out of the speaker at the entrance gate.

"I'm Harry Shaw," he looked fiercely into the security camera, "I'm expected."

"Park your car over to your right and wait by it," the voice instructed. Harry complied and steeled himself for what comes next.

As he leaned against the warm metal of his car, his gaze drifted towards the expanse of Poole Harbour beyond the shipyard, missing the freedom and peace he once found sailing with his family.

A shadow fell across Harry's vision, jolting him back to the present. An unsmiling, bulky man stood before him, his long hair at odds with his otherwise military bearing. He wore black overalls, the fabric stretched taut over his formidable biceps.

"How do you do, Mr Shaw?" the man said, his voice devoid of warmth. He offered no introduction, only a steely gaze.

"Fine, thank you," Harry replied, thinking that was a ridiculous thing for him to say in the circumstances.

"Follow me." The man turned on his heel and walked towards the heart of the shipyard. As they passed between the buildings, Harry's thoughts wandered to his father, John Shaw. The retired naval captain had always been there to offer support at times of crisis. Right now, Harry longed for his father's steady presence, but he knew this was one duty he must accomplish alone.

As they rounded a corner, he stopped dead, and he felt his chest tighten. There, hidden out of sight behind a large structure, stood his beloved yacht, Ariana.

"Here she is," the man muttered, gesturing towards the boat. "I'll leave you alone for a few minutes." He turned and walked away, leaving Harry standing in front of his yacht.

He took a deep breath and looked up at Ariana, now standing on her long, lead weighted keel, held upright by supporting legs within a large steel cradle. Once a symbol of freedom and adventure, the wooden vessel had been reduced to a crime scene, an emblem of loss. On dry land, the waterline was about level with Harry's head; he recalled how it would dip below the surface as the yacht heeled to the wind and powered through waves.

As he walked around the boat, he looked up and was surprised to see that the yacht looked just as always, undamaged. But then he noticed that the glass in the small round portlight windows of the cabin were smashed. The jagged edges glinted in sunlight, hinting at the violence that had occurred within. The glass shards were still mostly hanging in place, not blown out by the explosion. Initially, that surprised Harry, but he reflected how that glass was laminated and over fourteen millimetres thick. His little 30-foot boat was very tough, designed to cross oceans and withstand severe storms.

Taking a deep breath, Harry climbed up the three notches cut into the rear edge of the rudder. They were there to help someone climb out of the water after swimming, or falling overboard, but now they provided an impromptu ladder. He climbed into the cockpit where he stood on the familiar teak grating, noticing the brown stain from his own blood, which set his heart pounding in his chest.

"Miranda... George... Charlie." Harry reverently spoke their names, then paused for five whole minutes, holding a private funeral service in his mind, remembering the good times, thankful for having shared part of his life with them, and wishing them peace in the afterlife, should there be such a thing. That memorial over, Harry moved on to the second reason for being there.

With shaking hands, he slid open the hatch to the cabin and looked down into the dim interior. The sight that awaited him was too much to bear. The once pristine space now bore the scars of the explosion that had claimed the lives of his family.

"Damn you," he whispered through gritted teeth, staring at the wreckage of what was once his family's sanctuary. He forced himself to take in every detail of the carnage. As his eyes adjusted to the dim light that filtered through the broken glass, he found himself looking down at a battlefield.

The sleeping bags where his family had slept that night lay in tatters, shredded fragments scattered across the cabin like coloured confetti.

"Good god," Harry whispered, his voice wavering with the awfulness of the sight before him. It was as if a mad animal had gone berserk. The white painted and varnished teak woodwork was scratched and scarred with deep gouges and splintered edges. In one place it looked as though someone had taken a sandblaster to the wood; in another, it seemed as if a maniac had been hacking away with a knife, each blow fuelled by blind rage and hatred.

Harry couldn't tear his gaze away from one small sharp metal shard, embedded in the wood and glittering like a deadly diamond. His mind began to piece together the puzzle, slowly forming an image of the weapon responsible for the carnage.

The little golf ball that flew over his head must have been a fragmentation grenade – something designed to explode with a carefully controlled force, sending hundreds of razor-sharp projectiles in all directions with cruel precision. His heart ached with the thought that his family had been subjected to that brutal, destructive force.

"Enough," Harry said aloud, steeling himself against the nausea and a wave of grief that threatened to pull him under.

His eyes shifted to the white cabin ceiling, and his breath faltered as he saw the deep brown stains that were unmistakably blood. He followed the trail of ruin down to where the foresail had been tossed onto the cabin floor, a white shroud covering the horror and devastation that lay beneath it. His stomach churned violently, threatening to expel its contents, but he fought back the urge to vomit. This was no time for weakness; he had a purpose here.

"Get it together," he muttered under his breath, standing up and breathing deep. With determination, he pivoted towards the aft locker in the cockpit. He pulled it open and rummaged through its contents until his hand found the familiar shape of a one gallon can of outboard motor fuel. It felt heavy, which meant it must be full.

He unscrewed the cap of the fuel can and emptied its contents into the cabin, watching as it splashed over the shredded cushions and soaked into the discarded sail. The fumes filled the air, stinging his nostrils.

Without giving himself a chance to hesitate, Harry took out the box of extra-large matches he had in his pocket. He struck a match, waited a second until it was burning brightly and threw it into the cabin. Instantly, with a whom, the petroleum gases exploded, and a fire burst into life, beginning to consume the evidence of that appalling scene.

"Goodbye," Harry murmured. And with that, he turned away from the increasing flames.

The acrid scent of burning paint, polyester sail and upholstery filled Harry's nostrils as he clambered down from the boat, the heat already strong enough to sting his face. His heart pounded. He turned his back on Ariana, his legs a little unsteady, and started to walk away, forcing himself not to look back.

"Hey! What the hell's going on?" The unsmiling SBS man's voice cut through the crackling of the fire. He stood there with a scowl, looking ready to pounce on Harry.

Harry faced the man, his eyes cold and resolute. "That's a funeral pyre," he replied, his voice steady despite the turmoil within, "Finishing the job that you guys started!"

The SBS man's eyebrows shot up in surprise, but he said nothing more. Harry thought he saw sympathy in his eyes. Perhaps the man's brusque manner had been a defence against his own feelings of guilt. As Harry walked away, the flames became a blazing inferno. The cabin roof was now on fire and black smoke rose towards the sky, an orange glow reflecting off one of the aluminium clad buildings.

He slid into his car and headed for the exit barrier. For a moment, he thought they wouldn't let him go, but the barrier lifted. As he accelerated away down the narrow road, he felt a weight lift from his mind. Now, he was more ready to accept that, despite his grief, he must start to live again. His next destination was Bournemouth airport.

7

As a child, Teresa had been teased and bullied by classmates at her school. Her academic success, her caring nature, her mild-mannered approach, and being the only child to wear spectacles all added up to her becoming a target for the school bully and her little gang.

One day, Teresa arrived home with a cut over her left eyebrow, a puffed eye and a bleeding nose. That was the last straw for her father, who insisted she attend Brazilian Jiu-Jitsu classes. A few months later, with her newfound ability to defend herself, Teresa's life at school had improved. She had started a lifelong journey along the road to acquiring a high degree of competence in the martial arts.

Being of an academic bent, Teresa borrowed books from the library in Valetta. Some of the books she wanted to read were not available in libraries, especially those which revealed the points where one blow could disable an opponent, or even prove fatal. She had to seek out suppliers of those books and have them posted to her direct, arriving in plain brown wrappers that intrigued her parents.

Her study opened her eyes to the difference between the external martial arts such as Jiu-Jitsu, Karate, or Wing Chun and the internal systems and lesser-known arts. Those preached unity of mind, body, and spirit, plus developing one's instinctive reactions. She even researched some of the more esoteric styles with names that most people would have trouble pronouncing, such as Taijiquan, Baughan, Xinyuan, and Dachengquan.

After Teresa became qualified as a medical doctor, she

moved to England to work in the National Health Service. By now, she was no longer interested in attending group classes where everyone copied the teacher and robotically performed staged movements. Teresa wanted to experience the real thing, up close and personal. She found a dojo in Fareham, Hampshire, which practiced a modern variation of Kung Fu. She went there frequently when not working. There, she learned the old way, in one-to-one lessons.

It was a place where students, if accepted, would learn how to protect themselves from attack whilst, with aggressive intent, they disabled their opponents. She was mastering the unsavoury realities of ending a fight quickly and decisively.

The other students were an interesting bunch, including a keen teenager, a lawyer, an estate agent, various other men and one soldier who was serving in the SAS. He came whenever he was not away on tour, doing something secret in the Middle East or elsewhere. What he did at work was never open for discussion.

Teresa enjoyed the camaraderie of this disparate bunch. Occasional accidents were inevitable. She carried a small scar in the middle of her forehead. She learned how to master whole-body power, as did the other students, with unfortunate results. She had suffered a broken rib when another student accidentally delivered an over-enthusiastic punch. The guy was most apologetic because everyone respected the code. They were there to learn how to harm others but not each other.

During her most recent grading examination, Teresa was tested on covering her centreline and controlling her fear as she repeatedly moved towards an instructor who poked and prodded at her with a long wooden pole.

On the business-end of the pole was a hardwood knob the size of a golf ball and wrapped in leather. It could deliver a very painful blow at real fighting speed. Physically, psychologically, and emotionally, advancing on that pole was an exhausting experience. Initially, her arms and legs felt like jelly as she closed in. Over time, she conditioned her mind to remain calm and focussed. A strike from that pole caused a panic in students which either paralyzed them or made them overreact, leaving them wide open to be hit repeatedly.

If, during her exam, the instructor managed to penetrate her defence once and strike her head, body, or other key area, it would be an automatic failure and a painful reminder to get it right next time.

With a whirl of movement, she deflected and re-deflected the weapon, focussing intently on her adversary as she advanced towards him looking for the clues that betrayed the direction of the next attack. Teresa passed her exam.

The day after the funeral, the first light of dawn illuminated the dew-speckled leaves in Teresa's back garden. She stood motionless amidst the overgrown foliage, her breath misting in the crisp morning air. Her long deep brown hair cascaded down her back over a loose T-shirt.

To the casual observer her actions, or rather inactions, would look somewhat strange. She stood silently with her feet positioned about shoulder width apart, and toes facing forward. Her knees were bent so that she sank about ten centimetres below her full height. Her pelvis was tilted carefully to a certain angle, as if to sit on an invisible chair.

Her back was naturally straight, with her neck and head

stretched upward and perfectly aligned with her upper spine. Her arms were raised to just below shoulder height, and her elbows were out and sunk, as if she was holding a large balloon out in front of her. There was no balloon, but her hands and fingers were motionless in the pose that would gently hold a balloon if it were there.

After a few minutes of holding this stress position, an observer would have noticed how the effort required to hold this stationary pose was changing Teresa's shapely form. The smooth feminine shape of her arms and legs were now showing powerful, clearly defined muscles that betrayed her strength. Her baggy sweatshirt was hiding the six-pack of her immensely strong torso.

This was her daily standing exercise. Her teacher taught her this pose and explained that she must hold the position, remaining perfectly still and calm until her body relaxed and her mind would let go of all thoughts. She was to maintain the correct posture until exhaustion. Her mental endurance would be tested. After time, her body would sink lower as she relaxed into the posture. Eventually, the muscles would start to shake, and she would experience what could only be described as a 'liquid pain' shooting up and down her legs.

When, for the first time, her face betrayed that she now understood what he meant, her teacher laughed fit to bust, "Excellent Teresa, now hold that for as long as possible."

Standing practice was one of the secrets of Kung Fu that Teresa had learnt. The many hours of effort holding this stance gradually strengthened the core muscles and tendons in her body until she possessed a power that one would have thought impossible from such a small frame.

"Be still," she whispered to herself as she settled into her statuesque pose. She usually devoted this break in routine to developing inner calm through meditation. But today, instead of emptying her mind, the image of Harry Shaw fought for her attention. His face was dominating her mind to the point of distraction.

"Focus," she admonished herself again, her quiet voice mingling with the rustle of branches swaying gently in the breeze. She decided to give in and let her mind return to the events of yesterday. After driving home from the funeral, she had spent the evening searching the internet for information about Harry.

At thirty-five years old, Teresa's body clock was compelling her to find a partner and start a family. She couldn't help but feel a sense of urgency in her desire for male companionship and her own children. And Harry's face was fast becoming synonymous with that image of her future.

"Perhaps I am being too hasty?" she asked herself. She had always been cautious when it came to matters of the heart. Was the physical desire she felt for him leading her astray?

Teresa recalled the details of the conference website she found after Googling "Harry Shaw."

The 'Application Development Platforms Conference' had taken place in San Francisco and Harry had been one of the guest speakers. Her searches revealed that he was a well-known industry figure. His reputation as a leader in the software industry had paved the way for him to address an audience of eager developers and innovators.

Harry's speech was entitled 'The case against using Artificial Intelligence (AI) to develop software.' There was a link to watch a YouTube video of him. She had clicked through and watched for thirty minutes, studying Harry's face and listening carefully.

Most of the jargon flew straight over her head. However, she could understand the gist of his arguments. He made his case fluently. He logically explained his reasoning against the use of AI when the resulting apps would be used in sensitive areas such as banking, personal records or the security industries. She could hear the restrained passion in his voice, the conviction with which he argued not only the practical case against AI but also the need for ethical boundaries in technology.

She thought back over the past weeks. After spending time with Harry in a hospital ward, seeing him at the funeral, and now scrutinizing him at work, she was falling for a man who is sincere, honest, and principled.

Is it possible? she pondered, her thoughts weighing the likelihood of sharing a future with him. It would have to be a two-way street. Would Harry be interested in her? Could their relationship work? And then the obvious point about timing. It was only a month after Harry lost his family. She thought to herself, "Now is definitely not the right time for me to declare my interest!"

Teresa had now been standing motionless for twenty-five minutes. She was dragged back to the present as the effort began to really take its toll. Her olive skin glistened all over and her sweatshirt was soaked with sweat. A close observer would have spotted how hard she found it to remain motionless. The pain mattered less these days. She had become inured to the sensation. This time she endured for another five, long, painful minutes.

"Enough," she murmured as she took a deep breath,

straightened up, relaxed her limbs, carefully stretched, and warmed down while she consciously considered the world around her, grounding herself in the reality of the moment.

Her mind flip-flopped between two alternative decisions. On the one hand, forget Harry and move on, and on the other, follow her desires and pursue a relationship with him. But then she wondered, "Is there such a thing as love at first sight? I barely know the man."

The magnetic pull she felt towards Harry won the day, just as emotional love always drowns out rational thought. There was also the question of why. She now wondered if it was not Harry himself, but his grief and suffering that attracted her. She had always been drawn to helping vulnerable people. This was all a conundrum that she could only solve by getting to know Harry better.

That's when she made the decision that would change the course of her life. She resolved to try and spend more time with him. And, although Teresa might not admit it to herself, she wanted to be available when he eventually looked for female solace.

"Harry Shaw," she whispered, her words a promise to herself, "let's see where this goes."

Later that day, the sterile environment of the hospital cafeteria made an impersonal location for the very delicate conversation Teresa had on her mind.

She sat at a corner table, her untouched sandwich before her. That morning, at her office computer, she had tapped into the hospital records and extracted Harry's personal and next of kin information. The din of clattering dishes and hushed conversations barely registered in her ears as she took a deep breath, pulled out her phone and dialled

Harry's number.

The phone rang once, twice, three times, before reaching voicemail. This was the third time she had called and not left any message. "Harry might be avoiding calls, especially from an unknown number," she reasoned. "Perhaps he would be staying with his father?"

Her heart pounded in her chest again as this time she tapped the number for John Shaw's landline. As she dialled, she rehearsed again, for the umpteenth time, what she would say.

"Hello?" came the gruff old voice on the other end.

"Mr Shaw? This is Doctor Teresa Camilleri. I treated your son, Harry, at the hospital." Her voice was steady despite the nerves that tensed her stomach and restricted her breathing.

"Ah, yes, Doctor, how can I help you?" John replied, his tone polite but guarded.

"Actually, I was hoping to speak with Harry," Teresa admitted, her fingers unconsciously twisting a loose strand of her hair. "Is he available?"

"Harry?" John hesitated, his concern palpable through the phone. "He's gone abroad, I'm afraid. He needed some time away after everything that happened."

Teresa's heart sank, but she pressed on. "I understand, Mr Shaw, but it's quite important that I speak with him. Can you tell me where he is?"

John was silent for a moment, clearly wrestling with his desire to protect Harry's privacy and the anxiety he sensed in Teresa's voice. "He's in Malta," he finally relented. "However, he told me he intended to switch off his phone and ignore it for a couple of weeks, at least."

"Malta?" questioned Teresa, surprised at the coincidence

of Harry choosing her own country as a getaway.

"We lived there for a couple of years, when I was stationed there in the Royal Navy."

Teresa thought she must not squander the opportunity, so she pressed on.

"Could you tell me where he is staying. Perhaps I could have a note passed to him. And then he could choose whether he wants to hear from me?"

"I'm not sure," John replied hesitantly.

Teresa blurted out, "I promise you; my intentions are sincere."

There was a long silence. John had seen how Teresa looked at his son. Almost against his better judgement he decided that some female contact might be good for Harry.

"He's staying at the Grand Harbour Hotel in Valetta." And after a pause he softly added, "Harry could use a friend right now, and — do treat him with care please Doctor."

"I will," she vowed.

As they ended the call, Teresa stared at her phone, the knowledge of Harry's whereabouts was both thrilling and daunting. The gears in her mind began to turn as she began plotting a chance meeting in Malta.

With a renewed sense of purpose, she stood, her chair scraping against the hard floor as she left her uneaten sandwich behind. How fortuitous that Harry had chosen to hide away in her homeland?

For the first time in her life, Teresa decided there was such a thing as fate. A newfound belief was directing her thoughts and actions. Destiny awaited her in Malta.

8

At Malta International Airport, Harry Shaw stepped out of the arrival terminal, squinting as the brilliant Mediterranean sun glared down. He breathed in the fresh air, remembered the childhood scent of hot earth, but then coughed as he inhaled a whiff of aviation fuel, which reminded him of countless business flights.

He spied the bus stop ahead, where a modern green and white coach with sleek lines and tinted windows awaited passengers. On a whim, he decided to take the bus. "To the Valetta Bus Depot," Harry told the driver as he entered. He chose a window seat and settled in, gazing out at the passing landscape.

The scenery reminded him of childhood, when he would regularly travel on those ancient British Leyland and Bedford buses that were shipped to Malta after they retired from service in England. Those boneshakers were older than Harry! These new models lacked the character and charm of their predecessors, but riding a bus rekindled the spirit of adventure that he associated with the island.

Although getting away from England had separated him from the need to speak with relatives and friends, it had not stopped his thoughts from often returning to his late wife and children, and the unjust condemnation he received at their funeral when Miranda's parents had loudly blamed him for their tragic deaths. The thought gnawed at him, but he felt the need to put those thoughts behind him, at least for a while.

The front of the bus dipped, and the airbrakes hissed as it

came to an abrupt stop at the terminus. Harry disembarked, turned towards the Tri Tritoni fountain and wheeled his suitcase past the tourists and along narrow streets, grateful for the shade provided by the tall honey-coloured buildings. The wheels of his suitcase clattered over the irregular shaped stone paving as he puffed his way uphill towards the Grand Harbour Hotel.

Perched high up on 'Tri Il-Batterija', the view was indeed grand. Harry paused to gaze across the harbour to the commercial quays on the opposite side. Malta's historical importance was there for all to see. The ancient golden brown limestone harbour walls rose majestically above the water, unchanged since the 1700s. He imagined the bustling harbour as he had seen it in oil paintings, crammed with sailing ships from every corner of the Mediterranean.

Today, the harbour looked comparatively bare, with one cruise ship and two enormous white superyachts that looked very out of place. "Probably Russian oligarchs," thought Harry.

Harry tore his gaze away from the harbour and turned to walk across the street and enter the hotel. He at once felt a sense of renewal growing within him, as if Malta held the key to his future.

"Welcome to the Grand Harbour Hotel, Mr Shaw," the receptionist greeted him warmly, her smile genuine.

"We've had a cancellation and I've taken the opportunity to upgrade your booking to a room with a view of the harbour." The receptionist handed him the key with a smile.

"Much appreciated, thank you." He accepted the key, his mood continuing to lift as he considered the prospect of waking up to the splendid view.

The following morning Harry rose before dawn, eager to witness the sunrise from amongst the opulent arches, fountain, and terraces of the Upper Baraka Gardens, created in the seventeenth century for the sole pleasure of the Knights of St John. Skipping breakfast, he set off through the quiet streets. The sun began to climb from the horizon, casting warm hues over the ancient city and bringing with it a day of hope.

From an open window somewhere nearby, music could be heard. The chorus of a familiar Beatles song was being shared with all in earshot:

Good day, sunshine,
Good day, sunshine,
We take a walk,
the sun is shining down...

"That will be my earworm for today," thought Harry as the repetitive chorus locked itself in his consciousness. Watching the sun rise, and feeling the radiated warmth, he set off to explore Valletta on foot. He ambled through the narrow streets, enjoying watching the town begin to come alive. The rich aroma of fresh coffee called to him as he walked past the Café Castille, so he stopped for a simple breakfast on the pavement outside.

The relaxed format of his day continued. He walked many miles, criss-crossing his path amongst the network of narrow streets. For the first time in years, his phone was not in his trouser pocket but in his hotel room, the battery flat, unable to interrupt his thoughts with emails and messages. For the entire day, he immersed himself in the beauty and history of

Valletta, accompanied all the time by his internal juke box playing g*ood day, sunshine…* Harry not only walked miles but also repeatedly descended to sea level and climbed back up again to the heights.

By late afternoon he was surprised at how tired he felt from his exertions, so he returned to his hotel room where he threw open the windows to let in the welcome coolness of the sea breeze. The only problem he had was that grief was proving to be a determined and insidious enemy. Every time he relaxed, whenever his mind was not already filled with some distraction, he would find himself drifting back to contemplating his lost family.

That was occasionally comforting, but mostly stressful. The positive memories kept on morphing into the pictures and sounds from the awful night when he lost them. In his room, he sobbed quietly, hoping nobody could hear, until he fell asleep and snoozed until dinner time.

After dining in the hotel, Harry plucked a novel from the bookcase in the resident's lounge, climbed the stairs to his room and retired early to bed. That night, for the first time since 'the event at sea' he slept soundly.

The next day, Harry decided to restart his daily routine of jogging before breakfast. He pounded the streets, navigating the circumference of the area that was at about the same altitude as the hotel, about three hundred feet above sea level. After three laps he resolved to find a longer route for his morning run.

Surprised by how out of condition his body was, he spent the rest of the day lounging about the hotel, allowing himself to rest and recharge. He read, sipped coffee and then tea and chatted idly with other guests who included a fair number of retired and elderly Brits.

After dinner, feeling guilty about his idleness, Harry stepped out of the hotel to find the sky looked like a watercolour painting, awash with subtle hues of orange and pink as the sun began to dip towards the horizon. He made his way through the winding streets, down to the old fort of St Andrew's Bastions, where he gazed across Marsamxett Harbour at the many yachts and fishing boats.

The sun sank lower, and the water darkened from its daytime sapphire to an inky blue-black. The lights from Sliema, the town across the water, reflected on the surface to brighten the scene. "What a beautiful evening," he said quietly to himself.

"Indeed, it is." An elderly man standing nearby nodded at Harry with a warm smile. Another solitary figure, they exchanged pleasantries before the man continued on his way, leaving Harry to his thoughts.

After some time, he set off back up the stairways and through the narrow streets. He spotted Cockatoo's little backstreet bar tucked away in one alley. The happy patrons spilled out on to the street and Harry pushed his way inside, drawn by the convivial atmosphere. As he sipped his cold beer, he observed the patrons, their laughter and chatter creating a lively atmosphere.

He couldn't help but notice a young couple who were quieter than the rest — their affectionate gestures, the soft laughter, intimate conversation whispered in each other's ears, the frequent physical contact between them. The man tenderly brushed a strand of hair from the woman's face, and something stirred deep within Harry.

The couple noticed that he was watching, so he quickly

looked away and drowned the last of his beer, suddenly feeling very alone.

"Another Cask Lager, Sir?" the bartender asked, snapping Harry out of his reverie.

"No thanks." He left a generous tip on the bar and hastened back to his hotel and bed.

9

Harry had settled into a daily routine: morning run, breakfast, walk, lunch, relaxing afternoon reading, dinner, evening stroll, beer at a bar, and back to his hotel for, hopefully, restorative sleep.

It was his sixth day in Malta. He was on the mend, feeling fitter in mind and body. Invigorated, straight after breakfast he strode out of the hotel, turned left, and set off at a brisk pace.

"Oof!"

Harry collided with a woman walking in the opposite direction, towards the hotel entrance. Their bodies met with an unexpected jolt, and Harry instinctively reached out to steady her.

"Doctor Camilleri?" Harry said, taken aback by the sudden appearance of the woman who had cared for him in hospital.

"Mr Shaw," Teresa replied, her cheeks flushing pink with embarrassment. "I'm so sorry, I wasn't watching where I was going."

For a moment, they stood there, locked in an awkward silence as passers-by navigated around them. The tension was palpable. Teresa just looked up at him from her close position and smiled. He felt unsure how to react.

"Err," said Harry, "what a surprise."

Teresa stood there, looking at him with a self-conscious glow. Harry shuffled from foot to foot. He felt the need to fill the silence and heard himself saying, "Would you like to join me for coffee?"

"Yes, I'd love that. I know somewhere nearby, and please

call me Teresa. We're not in hospital now."

They walked side by side in awkwardness, down a street where the morning sun cast long shadows, so that one side of the street felt quite cold and the other warm. "Malta is my home," said Teresa as she trotted out her prepared lie, "and I am here visiting my parents."

They arrived at a small café tucked away in a quiet alley. Harry took in the scene with wrought-iron chairs and tables, starched pink and white chequered tablecloth, vibrant bougainvillea, and gentle background music. He thought to himself, "She's chosen what looks like a romantic French café."

Seated across from one another, sipping their coffees, Harry looked at the doctor properly for the first time, analysing what he saw. She had a perfect olive complexion framed by shiny long brown hair, full lips, large eyes which sparkled mischievously behind big spectacles. The tortoiseshell frames were of an intelligent shape, if such a thing were possible, and they perched on nose that was a little too small for such large frames. She was neither tall nor short, somewhere between petite and shapely. She sat straight backed as she spoke. As he listened to her, he found the accent charming. Altogether, she was extremely attractive.

His mind returned to what she was saying. "My family owns a farm in the north of the island. The land includes ancient olive groves that have been in our family for generations."

"Really?" he replied, genuinely interested, "That sounds wonderful."

Teresa's face lit up as she told him about her elderly

mother and father and her older brother, who also lived on the farm. She told Harry about their animals and crops and the olive trees of which she was so proud. She described the gnarled trunks and silvery leaves, the arduous work of harvesting the olives and pressing them into oil.

Their conversation moved on to exchanging questions. How was he feeling now? How often did she visit home? How well did Harry know Malta? How long had she been living in England? And so on.

After three cups of coffee and two pastries, fuelled by caffeine, sugar, and growing familiarity, the voices became louder, the conversation quicker, the bodies more relaxed and occasional laughter was heard by the young girl waiting table.

That waitress had a hobby. She would observe the couples who visited the café and invent stories about their relationships. In this case, she created a fairytale where a beautiful young woman found her prince charming. The problem was that the prince never noticed her. Somehow, she must make him appreciate her charms, so she took him to a café where she mesmerized him with her wit and wisdom. She captivated the prince, and they lived happily ever after.

In this case, the waitress was not too far wide of the mark. The beautiful woman was entrancing the prince, but it would be a long time before he was ready for her. The prince had been living happily until an evil ogre had killed his wife and children, and it was going to be months or even years before he became available.

And then the tone changed. Teresa took a deep breath and looked into Harry's eyes. "I need to be honest with you," her face serious. "I spoke to your father before coming here."

Harry's eyes widened slightly, surprise in his expression. He was torn between feeling that she had invaded his privacy and being grateful for the distraction of her presence.

"I called your father, and he told me where you were staying," Teresa confessed, her gaze never leaving his. "I wanted to make sure you were okay," and then another pause while she plucked up courage, "And I also wanted to see you again." Her cheeks once again turned pink as she looked him straight in the eyes and waited for his reaction.

After a moment that seemed an eternity, Harry cautiously replied "Thank you." It seemed a daft thing to say, but he couldn't immediately think what else was appropriate. He looked at the tablecloth for a while, gathering his thoughts. The silence made Teresa think she had blown it; permanently ruined her chances.

Eventually Harry added, "I'm glad you're here and I am very pleased to see you. I am extremely grateful for the way you cared for me in hospital. However, I must be honest, I'm not ready for a new relationship just yet. I hope you understand."

Teresa nodded, her expression a little crestfallen. She quickly recovered herself and spoke the words she had already prepared for this situation. "Of course, Harry. I'm not expecting anything from you. I just hoped to spend time with you. To help if I can. And perhaps you would like me to show you some more of Malta?"

"That would be great," Harry replied, with a smile of relief.

And so, Teresa had achieved her first goal. They would get to know each other under the pretext of her showing Harry her homeland. She felt elated that her plan appeared to be coming to fruition, but Harry's response about not being ready for a new relationship was tempering her excitement. The phrase, 'proceed with caution,' came to her mind.

Meanwhile, Harry was contemplating Teresa. "What a woman! Refreshingly honest and sincere. Knows what she wants. In other circumstances, I might be tempted."

They set off, with Teresa leading the way. She was a knowledgeable tour guide and soon in her stride. She pointed to a flag, fluttering above a building.

"The cross you see on the Maltese national flag comes from the time when the island was ruled by the Knights Hospitaller and a dependent state of the Kingdom of Sicily. The island was at a crossroads in the Mediterranean, making it a strategic target. There have also been Ottoman cultural and architectural influences, not to mention the French, British, Byzantine, and Arab rulers at various times in history."

She led him to a side chapel in St John's cathedral where bars separated the congregation from a small ornate altar. "The bars and gates between us and this chapel are solid silver. When Napoleon's troops invaded, the Maltese painted the gates black so the French wouldn't realize it was precious metal. At the time, Napoleon was short of cash. He plundered all the churches, stole their gold and silver, and melted it down into bullion. No person ever revealed what was under the black paint. We Maltese have always been united in proudly protecting our island's possessions and culture."

Teresa radiated national pride as she spoke, which Harry thought an admirable quality. "We Brits could learn a thing or two from the Maltese about having pride in our nation and our achievements," said Harry.

Lunch came and went as the hours flew by. Eventually, they ended the afternoon in a quiet corner of the Argotic Botanical Gardens, where the scent of jasmine filled the air, mingling with the refreshing breeze that swept in from the nearby harbour.

Teresa plucked a delicate blossom and twirled it in her fingers, sniffing the exotic scent, "These are my favourite gardens," and continuing her role as tour guide, "at one time it was illegal to create a garden on any property in Valetta, to conserve water. These gardens were the sole exception."

She flicked her head so that her long hair fell down her back and then held the flower up for Harry to smell. As he did so, she commented, "The Roman's thought the scent of jasmine an aphrodisiac."

She looked Harry in the eye and emitted a naughty giggle. "I must be getting home. I have borrowed my brother's car, and I must return it by 6 o'clock."

As the sun started to dip toward the horizon, casting a warm glow over the ancient limestone buildings of Valetta, they stood before her brother's car, a shiny new silver-grey electric Mazda.

Harry opened the driver's door for her and said, "Thank you for an enjoyable day. It has given me some relief from the black thoughts that so often invade my head. I really appreciate your kindness."

"Thank you for allowing me to share it with you." Her brown eyes searched his face for a moment before she slid into the driver's seat. "I'll be staying with my parents, at their farmhouse in the northeast of the island."

Harry nodded, "Drive safely, okay?"

"Of course." She smiled, reaching up to touch his arm briefly before closing the door.

Harry jumped back in surprise as the electric car started to silently move. Teresa laughed through the windscreen as she manoeuvred the vehicle and set off along the narrow street.

As the car pulled away, Harry raised a hand in farewell. He couldn't deny the connection he felt with her, but the pain of losing his wife and children was a raw wound that refused to heal. But then, this newfound companionship was a light relief. The car soon disappeared around a bend, swallowed by the city's labyrinthine streets.

Back in his hotel room, freshening up before dinner, Harry was smiling to himself, rejuvenated by his day, and ready for more human interaction. He found his phone and plugged the charger into a socket. "Tomorrow, I'll check my messages and call Dad to see how he is getting along."

10

Reflected light from a golden sunrise penetrated the thin voile curtains, bathing the hotel room in a warm light, Rembrandt style. Harry awoke just before the digital clock on the bedside table blinked 6:00 AM. He swung his legs over the side of the bed, yawned, stretched, and smiled to himself, recalling the previous day with Teresa.

"Another day, another run," he muttered, as he moved about quietly, pulling on running shorts and a t-shirt.

Grabbing his key card, he left the room, softly jogged down the hallway towards the stairs, the familiar surge of adrenaline lightening his mood still further in anticipation. As he stepped out into the crisp morning air, he paused a moment to take in the scene before him. The early morning sun was painting the underneath of sparse clouds in pink and gold hues and casting a warm coloured light along the streets.

As he skipped down a flight of steps past a small Sicilian bar, Harry passed an elderly man sweeping the pavement outside. He was there every day. "Morning," Harry smiled as he ran past him. The man looked up and returned the greeting with a nod as he called after Harry with, "Gawde l-ġirja tiegħek."

Harry had no idea what that meant, but it seemed a friendly greeting. He continued downhill towards Boat Street, where he would begin to circumnavigate the old town at sea level.

Yesterday, for the first time in weeks, he had genuinely enjoyed himself which had recharged his batteries and lifted his spirits. He ran past the doorway of a commercial bakery, the aroma of freshly baked bread increasing his desire for breakfast. The city was slowly awakening, life was resuming, and he felt part of it.

As he rounded a corner, he spotted a man looking his way and scowling. Not everybody, it seemed, felt as happy as him. On reflection, had he seen that man before? Yes, he had, but he could not recall where. Never mind. Not important. He ran until he was back at the steps where he had descended to Boat Street. Steeling himself for the long climb back up to his hotel, he started to attack the challenge of those steep stairs, which he did with maximum effort. He was panting and struggling for breath as he marched through the hotel lobby, unable to do more than nod to the receptionist's greeting.

After a shower and shave, he entered the hotel dining room and gorged himself on fruit, yogurt, a warm croissant, and coffee. Then he took his final cup of caffeine to a window-side table in the lounge, where he picked up a magazine to glance through as he listened to the sounds of the vibrant city below drifting in through the open window.

His thoughts returned to Teresa, a kind doctor, a supporter at the funeral, and yesterday a charming tour guide. He had seen parts of Valletta that he would have otherwise missed, and their conversation had been stimulating. However, he was wary of forming any attachment. After some thought, he decided he would make no effort to contact her.

He soon became bored and returned to his hotel room, where he picked up his phone and replied to the many messages from friends and acquaintances who wished him well. He smiled as he tapped out replies, grateful for their support.

With a final swipe across his phone screen, even his email inbox was clean and up to date. He had replied to every social media message and now felt relieved at having got on top of his digital life.

Next, it was time to call his father. He looked forward to speaking with him. He was about to make the call when his phone lit up and began to vibrate. An unknown number flashed across the screen. He usually let those calls go to voicemail, but this time he answered.

"Hello?" he said hesitantly.

"Harry? It's Teresa." Her melodic voice put him at ease.

"Ah, Teresa. Thank you for being my tour guide yesterday. I enjoyed the break from my own company."

"You're welcome, Harry. Would you like to meet again tomorrow? I could show you more of the island."

He hesitated for a moment, only a moment, because inside he knew that he really wanted to see her again. "Absolutely, thank you."

"In that case, I'll pick you up from your hotel around ten. See you then. Enjoy today!"

"You too; take care."

As the line disconnected, Harry contemplated another day alone. The positive vibes generated by his run were replaced by a returning feeling of emptiness. He stood alone in the quiet hotel room, gazing about as he contemplated how best to occupy himself. He lay back on the bed, staring at the ceiling fan as it made its slow revolutions. Again, as tended to happen when he was not engaged in doing something positive, his mind returned to the black events on his boat. A single tear escaped the corner of his eye, tracing a path down his cheek. Feeling the need for support, he remembered he was going to call his father.

With resolve, he sat up, grabbed his phone, and tapped the speed-dial for his father's landline. The old man owned a mobile, but it might be in a pocket somewhere, inside a jacket, behind a closed door, upstairs. The landline was the most reliable way to reach his father.

"Hello?" came the familiar voice.

"Hi, Dad," he began, "how are you?"

"Harry!" John exclaimed, surprise and joy evident in his enthusiastic response. "I'm fine thank you." And then his voice dropped a tone, "But how are you?"

His father's evident concern caught Harry off guard. It opened the floodgates. He found himself pouring out his loneliness, his sorrow, how he was suffering from the frequent flashbacks to the loss of his family, the funeral, the tirade of blame by Miranda's parents, seeing the site of the slaughter on his yacht, his personal memorial in the cockpit, and the funeral pyre that he ignited.

And then Harry covered the more practical aspects of his arrival in Malta, the warm welcome by the hotel staff, and how he had enjoyed being a regular tourist in Valetta.

His father listened attentively, giving Harry the space that he needed to voice his thoughts. John Shaw knew all too well the pain his son was experiencing.

As he spoke, Harry began to feel the weight on his chest ease. "Thanks for listening Dad," he said softly, his voice catching with emotion. "I... I just needed someone to talk to."

"I'm here anytime you want to chat," John replied.

"And thanks for suggesting I came to Malta. The change has helped occupy my mind with something new to cheer me up. Speaking of something new, I saw Doctor Camilleri, you know, the one who cared for me in the hospital. Yesterday, she took me on a sightseeing tour of Valetta."

John cautiously asked, "You've found her company helpful, then?"

"Yes," Harry confided, "she's kind, intelligent, and seems a very caring person."

He heard his father take a deep breath, weighing his words carefully. "It sounds like she's been a great support for you, Harry. So, did I do the right thing in telling her you were staying at the Grand Harbour?"

"Yes," Harry replied without hesitation.

"I'm glad you've found someone to connect with. It's important to have people around us who care and understand." And then John added, "Just remember to be cautious with this new friendship. You've been through so much already, and I don't want you to get hurt again."

"Thanks Dad," touched by his father's concern. "I'll keep that in mind." And after a pause, "I've told her I am not ready for a new relationship. I can't even imagine being with anyone else after losing Miranda and the children."

John advised, "There's no rush or expectation when it comes to moving on. You take all the time you need to come to terms with your loss. Just remember that it will help to let people in. You may find comfort in making new friends."

Harry blinked back tears, grateful for his father's unwavering support. His throat was, again, tight with emotion, "It's a relief speaking with someone who understands."

"And remember, Harry, you can call anytime, alright? Take care of yourself, Son. I love you."

"Love you too, Dad."

With a click, the line went dead, leaving Harry in the stillness of the hotel room, the silence broken only by the sound of distant seagulls. The conversation had been heavy, charged with emotion, and yet there was a sense of catharsis in having vented his feelings.

He trotted down the stairs to the lounge, ordered a cappuccino, and chose a comfortable seat with a view outside. He picked up the glossy magazine lying on the table and flicked through the pages. He came across an advertisement for some over-expensive watch. The photograph showed a tanned, silver haired male model wearing a dark blue blazer. Harry was at once reminded of that awful man, Commander Forbes, who had taken advantage of him when he was at his most vulnerable, tricking him into signing the Official Secrets Act. Then his mind ran through the details of the tense meeting with Forbes and Professor Hall, including the explanation of how his yacht had been mistaken for a terrorist vessel.

Harry's brow furrowed. The Professor had claimed the erroneous conclusions about his yacht being a terrorist threat were cause by a hacker tampering with the information stored on the GCHQ computer. Allegedly, someone had hacked into their computer and planted false data which incorrectly made his boat appear to be transporting terrorists on their way to either kill King Charles or to at least embarrass the government.

In the hospital, Harry had believed that explanation, but now he was not so sure. He was thinking that it could be as they stated, but what if someone had targeted him and his family with the objective of having them all killed. That was equally implausible. Or was it?

"Was that possible? Who would do such a thing?" he asked himself. "And another thing, how did they know exactly where my yacht was, some twenty-odd miles from land in the English Channel?"

Then, a crucial detail surfaced from his memory. His yacht was fitted with the safety feature of an Automatic Identification System (AIS), which regularly transmitted the vessel's identity and position. AIS recorded his vessel's port of departure, course, position, and speed. Harry had that technology fitted because it should increase his safety at sea. He knew that most big ships monitored AIS all the time, so they would be aware of Harry's yacht's presence, even if they didn't spot the little thirty-foot vessel among the waves.

The other safety feature of AIS was that in a worst-case scenario, if his yacht were in distress, the rescue services could gather valuable information to help in their search. But in this instance, it could be that the very tool meant to protect them had led directly to their downfall.

Anyone with internet access could visit the AIS website and see his yacht as a little point, crawling across their computer screen. But why had GCHQ paid such close attention? He left his half-finished coffee and returned to his bedroom. He fished his laptop out of his suitcase, grateful that he had brought it with him, thinking, "Where do I start?" and then he typed into the search bar: UK government tracking of ships and yachts.

As the results loaded on the screen, one search result stood out as especially interesting. He read the summary about the website, which stated that, "The Joint Maritime Security Centre (JMSC) is the UK government's centre for maritime security. It monitors maritime security threats and enables cross-government coordination to deliver a whole-system response to mitigate them."

Harry clicked on the link and on their home page he read that, *The JMSC collaborates across all Government agencies including the Maritime and Coastguard Agency, UK Border Force, Home Office Police, Marine Management Organisation, National Crime Agency, the Royal Navy – other collaborators dip in and out as required.*

Harry was thinking that those 'other collaborators' would no doubt include GCHQ, so they could easily have tracked his yacht. He felt angry at the thought of state surveillance putting him at risk. But none of this satisfied his core question of how the false information got to be on the GCHQ computer. If it were not a hacker, who could have placed it there, and why?

Harry decided to keep digging for more information. He wanted answers, but it was already lunchtime, and his stomach rumbled in protest at having been ignored for so long.

In the hotel dining room, he observed the other guests as he ate. He wondered if any of them ever thought they might be under surveillance by their own government. As he prodded the starter on a small plate, eggs and anchovies, he wondered what other information about him the spooks at GCHQ might be collecting.

"Excuse me, is this seat taken?" A prim, professional looking woman asked, gesturing toward an empty chair at his table.

"Please, join me," he replied, trying to keep his mind from wandering back to his unanswered questions.

"Thank you," she said as she settled into the seat opposite him. "I'm Lucy."

"Harry," he responded, offering a polite smile before returning his attention to his meal.

"Are you here on holiday?" Lucy inquired, as the waiter delivered his second course, which was a sardine salad.

"Something like that," Harry answered vaguely, not wanting to reveal too much. "And you?"

"Business trip," she explained. "It's been lovely, though. Malta's such a beautiful place."

They exchanged small talk about the tourist sights they had seen. Lucy spoke with clipped efficiency. Harry could imagine her in some position of senior responsibility. It was that thought which made him wonder if Lucy was really an MI5 officer sent to spy on him." But then he almost laughed aloud as he reprimanded himself for such crazy, paranoid, ideas. He finished his meal with a final bite. Without asking, a waiter placed a small glass cup of espresso in front of him; the hotel staff knew him very well by now.

Harry sipped his coffee, the powerful bitter liquid invigorating him. He was ready to continue searching for answers. He bid goodbye to Lucy and returned to his room, ready to delve further into the murky waters of government surveillance.

He settled into the plush armchair and perched his laptop on his knees as he typed *GCHQ surveillance of citizens* into the search bar and hit enter. The volume of contentious search results that appeared before him astounded Harry.

His eyes were at once drawn to one item, where a bold newsfeed headline proclaimed: *Europe's highest court of human rights rules that GCHQ used bulk interception to unlawfully breach citizens' rights...*

"Blimey," Harry muttered under his breath, clicking on the link. He had always considered himself a loyal citizen, but the thought of his own government encroaching on his privacy made his stomach churn with indignation.

Further down the list of search results, Harry found an article from a UK newspaper, The Guardian. He read that Britain is an *Intelligence Superpower, rivalling even the United States*, a fact that at first impressed him, but then the article went on to reveal that GCHQ had placed data interceptors on fibre-optic cables carrying internet data in and out of the UK.

"Good grief, spying on the internet itself," he said aloud to an empty room. His pulse quickened as he absorbed this valuable information. But then, it seemed so clever. Why try to hack into individual computers when it was so much easier to hoover up all the information as it passed along a cable? At first, he found it hard to believe that his own government would spy on the internet traffic of all the citizens of the UK. It was only after he found the same information repeated on several newspaper websites that he eventually accepted it as true.

Harry visualized invisible tendrils snaking around the vast network of fibre optic cables, vacuuming up all the passing information.

He typed in more searches, and soon learned that tapping into all those cables enabled GCHQ to access enormous amounts of global internet data. One newspaper article revealed the codename for this operation to be *Tempora*.

"If I can learn this so easily, what other horrors am I going to discover?" Harry thought, rubbing his temples as he tried to process the enormity of what he'd just learnt.

He paced the room, his mind in overdrive. Surely, he reasoned, if GCHQ were tapping into international internet traffic, it is no leap to assume that the United Kingdom's internal backbone of fibre optic cables was also being hacked by government.

He then searched for the website of GCHQ itself to see what they had to say about themselves. On the home page, he read that, "We are the UK's intelligence, security and cyber agency."

Harry knew that his email provider was located in Australia, which meant GCHQ would see every email that went back and forth between him in the UK and the provider's server. "They can read my every email," he indignantly exclaimed aloud. His next search about citizen surveillance told him that the major source of data about a person comes from their smartphone, which is permanently connected to the internet and constantly sending and receiving data.

He picked up his own phone and examined it. Now, he saw the device in a completely new light. There were the social media apps. And, of course, his location. Oh yes, and recently, instead of a credit card, Harry had started using his phone to make purchases. Now he was entering an area where he had specialist knowledge, due to his experience in writing apps for banking. He thought, "But all my internet browsing is encrypted," which he knew was indicated by web page addresses which started with the acronym HTTPS, standing for Hypertext Transfer Protocol Secure.

His next search engine query was, *Can I decrypt HTTPS traffic?* Harry expected the answer to be a flat no, but instead he found a host of websites that explained how to do so, including one that advertised software called *Wireshark* which allegedly made it easy. Harry reasoned that if a private individual could decrypt another person's browsing traffic and see the contents, then surely, with all their expertise, government agencies would be able to routinely read everyone's email, web searches and the identity of all the web pages they visited.

He sat back and contemplated how access to all the information that passed out of his phone and through the internet would create a detailed picture of his life. GCHQ could easily see what interested him. His business emails would reveal how he earned his living. The photos he took on his phone were automatically uploaded and stored somewhere in the cloud: all those snaps of his wife and children, some of which were on his yacht. And there were details about all his online shopping, which accounted for almost all of his purchases.

And then there was his online banking. He knew that banks make extra efforts to encrypt the traffic between themselves and customers, which he had previously thought to be totally private. Now he wasn't so sure. Whether from his phone or his laptop, GCHQ might be looking at all the money in and out, and his savings. Somehow, he felt especially hurt at the thought that his financial situation might be an open book. Telling the taxman how much he earned was okay, but revealing absolutely everything was going too far, an unacceptable invasion of privacy.

Harry sat in his hotel room and quietly seethed. He realised that the searches he was engaged in making right then were being snaffled as his browsing entered and exited the UK. In his mind's eye, he visualized the data leaving his phone, travelling through the air to the nearest phone mast, being relayed to the fibre optics, where it suddenly accelerated to the speed of light, and then he saw it passing the GCHQ receptors as it entered the UK, where the Tempora program would snatch a copy of his data so that someone could, if they wished, observe what he was up to in real time.

Next, Harry's mind reversed the process, changing his attention to what arrived on his phone. There was the newsfeed that Google judged would interest him, based upon what they already knew about him. There were also the many interactions with friends and family, his business contacts, and so on. GCHQ would be able to build a picture that placed him at the centre of a large web of people.

Thinking of how his own digital life affected others, he remembered that he had recently installed a video doorbell at home, which continuously uploaded the view of his front garden and the road in front of his house, recording all the comings and goings of everyone who passed by.

His brain was now working at top speed. He started thinking about all the other devices that recorded his activity and sent it over the internet. There was the cash machine where he occasionally withdrew bank notes. And what about all those CCTV cameras on streets and in stores? The vast majority of those passed their video data through the internet on their way to be viewed at remote locations or stored in the cloud.

Harry then thought about the increasing prevalence of vehicle number plate recognition cameras. Back on his laptop, he soon discovered from the Metropolitan Police website that about thirteen thousand ANPR cameras recorded over fifty million number plates moving past them each day.

All that would mean, for example, that his last car journey with Miranda to their local supermarket could have been observed. As he walked into the store, passing the security camera, someone at GCHQ could be commenting upon the baggy shorts he was wearing that day. Harry laughed at the thought of someone wasting their time in such a way, but funny it was not!

No, it couldn't be. Perhaps GCHQ did have the ability to snaffle all the data about him, but surely, they would not have sufficient staff available to observe or analyse his exceptionally large digital footprint! To keep tracks on him, let alone every citizen would be a gargantuan task beyond even the government's ability, wouldn't it?

Harry was reminded of George Orwell's book, *'1984.'* In 1948, Orwell had created a fantasy government, led by Big Brother, who watched every aspect of citizen's lives. That all-seeing eye pried into their every actions.

Now, seventy-odd years later, Harry fictionalised a situation where hosts of people, all working at GCHQ, stared at computer screens to watch his every move as they noted what he did. All those people, watching and assessing his movements and asking themselves if they should report Harry to a higher authority.

He recalled the film, *The Truman Show*, with that poor man who was totally unaware that his life was broadcast on television, every intimate detail made into a soap opera. That ridiculous image relaxed him a little.

He couldn't imagine doing without his laptop and mobile phone. Life without them would cut off friends and family and become very inconvenient. But now he looked at them both as instruments of surveillance, tracking him. A chilling thought entered his mind. His searches during the past hours would reveal his train of thought. The people at GCHQ could easily know that he was investigating them. Might that lead to consequences for him?

Restless, he paced back and forth in the confines of his hotel room, his fingers raking through his blond hair. He looked out of the window at the sea. And then another thought surfaced, the oceans. Another quick search revealed that the first telephone cable across the Atlantic was laid in 1858. Since then, the number of cables had mushroomed. By contrast, laying cables across the vast Pacific Ocean from America to the far east was a much more expensive and difficult undertaking. The result was that, with fewer connections bridging the vast expanse of the Pacific, a substantial proportion of global internet traffic funnelled through the UK.

Harry reasoned that GCHQ had access to not only the digital lives of British citizens, but also an extensive portion of the world's population. He looked at his laptop computer and wondered whether Malta escaped their surveillance. He searched for a map of all the undersea internet cables. There was a detailed one available at the BBC website, which he studied with interest.

There were hosts of cables running along the bottom of the Mediterranean, carrying data back and forth, connecting to the shores of the various countries that bordered the sea. Following those connections, Harry concluded that much of the internet traffic from Malta would pass through the UK on its way back and forth to America. Many of the search results from his activity had been websites in the USA, so GCHQ would have a clear picture of what he was doing today, should they be interested.

Harry freshened up and went down to dinner. Afterwards, he took a brandy from the bar into the lounge, where the hotel had laid on evening entertainment in the form of a film. Tonight, they were showing a recent version of Michael Caine's old spy film, *The Ipcress File*.

"How appropriate," thought Harry. He enjoyed the film, drank a little too much brandy and retired to bed looking forward to the next day, when Teresa would show him some more of Malta. He smiled at that thought, "Now there's something to look forward to!"

11

Teresa said she would collect Harry at ten. He thought she was the type of person who would be punctual, so five minutes before the agreed time he was outside the hotel and gazing across Grand Harbour to the high walls of Fort St Angelo. The Royal Navy had occupied the medieval fort for many years, including when his father served there, and his family lived in Malta. He smiled as he looked down on the waters where his father had first taught him to sail. It was a magical time, filled with boys' adventures.

The quiet hum of Teresa's brother's electric car brought Harry back to the present. Her deep brown hair cascaded over her shoulders as she leaned across the seat to open the passenger door for him. A radiant smile greeted him. She was wearing a dark green linen trouser suit, which complimented her Mediterranean olive complexion. Harry thought she looked splendid.

"Morning Harry," Teresa greeted him, "I hope you're ready for a day of adventure."

"I sure am! I've been looking forward to it."

As he settled into the comfortable leather seat beside her, Teresa tapped her fingers on the steering wheel before turning to face him. "I've planned something special for today," she explained, her eyes twinkling with mischief. "We're travelling some distance to a place I think you'll find very interesting."

"Really?" Harry raised an eyebrow, curiosity piqued. "Where are we going?"

Teresa chuckled softly, shaking her head. "Ah, that would

be telling, wouldn't it? You'll just have to wait and see."

"Alright, I'll play along," Harry conceded with a laugh. He switched the subject of conversation. "Did you have a good time yesterday"?

"I was helping on my parent's farm. My father and I were tilling a field using our old tractor, ready for drilling seed, which is planned for tomorrow. I enjoy driving the tractor when I get the chance."

The car silently cruised along the winding road leaving old Valetta and down to sea level, along the coast road, passing the yacht marina to their right. The faint scent of seaweed might not be to everyone's taste, but Harry loved it. He gazed at the rows of white motor and sailing yachts, with a scattering of brightly coloured old wooden fishing boats called Luzzu. They were traditional sailing boats featuring high bows with painted eyes, one each side. He knew those eyes to be an ancient Phoenician tradition, said to represent the eyes of the goddess Osiris, there to watch over the fishermen at sea.

Teresa interrupted his thoughts, "So, what did you get up to yesterday?"

He hesitated for a moment, weighing his words carefully. "Well, I spoke with my father," he began, and then paused, unsure if he should continue.

"Ah, I hope that was a comforting conversation. How is he?"

"It was, yes, and he is fine, thank you." He took a breath before continuing. "Afterwards, believe it or not, I spent my day researching governmental spying on UK citizens. It's a topic I am becoming very interested in learning about."

"Really!" Teresa's eyes widened in surprise. "What

prompted you to explore such a subject?"

"Nothing specific," Harry lied, squirming inwardly. He couldn't reveal that his real interest was the result of the attack on his boat, bound as he was by the Official Secrets Act.

"It just sort of...caught my attention." A half-truth was better than none, he reasoned. He wanted desperately to have sincere relationships with people, as he always had in the past, but now he was forced to lie, and he found it exceedingly difficult.

"Interesting," Teresa mused, her gaze briefly flicking towards him before returning to the road. Harry was not listening anymore. His mind had been whisked back to a discussion with his daughter. She had been six years old at the time and wise beyond her years. When asked if she was telling the truth, she replied, "The truth is easy, but life is difficult." Back then, that nugget of wisdom floored him and now it returned as a painful memory, knotting his stomach.

The car rounded another bend, revealing the view on their right of Manoel Island, sitting in the centre of Valetta's second harbour, Marsamxett.

Harry tried to bring his focus back to enjoying this day with the captivating Teresa Camilleri. Like his daughter, she was also an astute woman who, after a few moments asked, "Is there something more to your interest in government surveillance?" She didn't wait for an answer but continued, "If you'd like, I could introduce you to my cousin Nicole. She's an internet security expert and might be able to help you with your research."

Harry glanced at her, impressed by her perceptiveness. "That would be most interesting. Thank you, I'd love to meet her."

"Okay." Teresa pulled over to the side of the road, took her smartphone from a trouser pocket and dialled Nicole's number. As she spoke to her cousin, Harry couldn't help but feel a pang of guilt for not being entirely forthcoming about his reasons for delving into this subject.

"Nicole says we can come over for coffee right away," Teresa announced as she ended the call. Her enthusiasm was infectious, and Harry found himself eagerly anticipating meeting her cousin. They agreed to abandon their original plan to visit the secret destination and set off towards Nicole's apartment.

As they drove, Teresa chatted animatedly about Nicole having studied in California for her master's degree in computing science and artificial intelligence. Harry listened with interest, grateful for the opportunity to learn from someone with such expertise.

Soon, they arrived outside the apartment in Sliema, an impressive modern building overlooking Marsamxett Harbour. "Come on," Teresa urged, leading him towards the entrance. "Let's go meet my brilliant geeky cousin."

"Wow, Nicole must be doing well for herself," he thought as he took in the impressive structure before them. He looked up at the tall building, clad in polished stone and sporting a large entrance door with a cluster of bell pushes under a speaker grill and a door security camera.

They were soon inside and Teresa made the introductions.

"Harry, this is my cousin, Nicole Cassar," Teresa gesturing towards a tall, gangly woman with short dark hair cut in a very controlled bob. She was wearing a grey, expensively cut outfit and large, black-rimmed glasses, which added to a very business-like appearance. "Nicole, this is my friend Harry Shaw."

"Nice to meet you, Harry," Nicole said warmly, extending her hand for a firm handshake."

"Please, make yourselves comfortable while I brew some coffee," Nicole said as she disappeared into the kitchen. Harry looked around the large room, noting the high-end furnishings and the original paintings that adorned the walls.

"Your cousin certainly has good taste," he commented, examining an oil-painting that depicted fishermen sailing a Luzzo through stormy seas, loaded down with a catch of fish, and heading for the safety of Marsamxett Harbour.

As they settled into the plush seating area, Harry hoped that Nicole really could shed more light on the shadowy world of government surveillance. The scent of freshly brewed coffee wafted into the room as she returned carrying a tray with three steaming mugs and a plate of almond biscuits.

"Actually, Harry, I first want to offer my condolences," Nicole began, her dark eyes filled with genuine concern. "While you were on your way here, I did a quick search online and I came across a newspaper report about your yacht suffering a gas explosion at sea. It must have been a harrowing experience. I'm so sorry to hear about your loss."

Harry's chest tightened at the mention of his family, but he managed a small, grateful smile. "Thank you, Nicole. It's been a difficult time, but I'm trying to move forward."

The sun's golden rays spilled into the room, casting warm patterns on the polished wooden floor, and softening the austere lines of the minimalist furniture. Harry found the simplicity of the furnishings, and the effective soundproofing of the large, triple glazed windows created an air of calmness.

Surrounded by two confident professional women, Harry felt slightly unsure about how he would approach the question of learning more about GCHQ, the Tempora program and, even more importantly, the possibility of hacking into GCHQ's computers. He decided to let the conversation flow until he felt it was the right moment to ask direct questions.

"The reason we're here is this," Teresa interjected, sensing Harry's discomfort. "I told Harry about your expertise in cyber security, and he's eager to generally learn more about government internet surveillance."

"Ah, yes," Nicole nodded, adjusting her glasses. "Well, I work from home as a self-employed consultant. I have corporate clients in several countries. My main goal is to help them keep their data secure from potential threats, so government cyber security is not my specialism. However, I do know something about the subject. Today, I won't start work until this evening, when I have an online meeting with a client in the USA, so we can talk for as long as you wish."

"Sounds like fascinating work," Harry commented, taking a slightly noisy sip of his coffee, savouring the bold, spicy flavour.

Nicole noticed him tasting the coffee like a pro and explained, "It's Old Brown Java, my favourite. But, to internet security, it can be quite complex at times. However, I find it rewarding when I've helped a client protect their valuable information."

"Nicole," Harry began, his voice hesitant yet determined,

"I'd like to learn more about how government internet surveillance programs operate, such as Tempora."

"Okay." Her eyes narrowed in thought as she started her explanation, "I expect that I can predict some of your questions, so how about this? I think it will be easiest for you to get a clear picture, if you let me explain things in my preferred way."

"Fine, how about you treat us like a couple of clients and give us an executive briefing?"

Nicole laughed and said, "You sound like a CEO Harry. Okay, here goes."

"Nowadays, governments gather vast piles of information from digital surveillance. Then, as a second stage, they sift through the data to extract the few significant morsels of intelligence. There are two western superpowers in the great surveillance game, namely the United States and the UK. Israel would come third in this league table. I know less about the activities of the Russians and China, so I'll focus on the UK and US. They share data and there is a high level of cooperation between them. For example, you would find Americans working on secondment at GCHQ in Cheltenham and Brits working at the American National Security Agency, the NSA.

"There is also an alliance called the *Five Eyes*, which includes Canada, Australia, New Zealand, the US and the UK. That sounds like an arrangement between equal partners but, the reality is that most of the infrastructure for the world-wide internet was constructed by the US and remains owned and maintained by them. The main reason for the Five Eyes agreement is that it legitimises the US spying on the internet traffic in those partner countries. In return for that permission, the NSA shares some of the information gathered."

Harry and Teresa sat forward in their seats, listening intently as Nicole got into her stride.

"The UK and US also have agreements with other countries. For example, I was saddened in 2014, when Iceland gave the NSA permission to spy on their internet traffic. Up until then, Iceland had been a bastion of personal privacy. And then, only recently, the US and EU agreed to share data under what America calls the Foreign Intelligence Surveillance Act. Malta is part of the EU, so I feel certain that the NSA, and thereby GCHQ, have access to the internet within Malta. But in any case, back in 2014, documents became known which showed that GCHQ was already tapping the internet traffic between Malta and Italy."

At this point, Nicole paused and looked for a response, but her audience remained quiet until Harry offered a supporting comment. "This is excellent Nicole. Clear and concise. Please, carry on."

"Now, let's move to considering legislation. Each country has laws which protect citizens' private information. At least, that's how it used to be. Current legislation that appears to protect people will also contain clauses that legalize a government spying on its own citizens. And, to understand the complete picture, you often need to look at how several laws work together."

Looking at Harry, Nicole continued, "In the UK, for example, there is the Surveillance Camera Code of Practice, the Investigatory Powers Act, the Data Protection Act, the Data Retention Regulations, and others."

"However, governments often overstep the boundaries,

and spy on ordinary citizens. America and Britain have been caught exceeding their legal powers. My teaching point so far is that Britain and America spy on internet traffic worldwide. We learn about these things on the rare occasions when an employee of the security services disagrees so strongly with their employers' activities that they leak documents. Doing that requires enormous courage, because of the consequences for them under the Official Secrets Act in the UK, or The Espionage Act in the US. Those whistleblowers are either heroes or traitors, depending on your point of view."

Harry interjected, "I presume you are referring to Edward Snowden. I found his name associated with the Tempora program?"

"Yes Harry. And Katherine Gunn, who worked at GCHQ. She revealed that the US asked GCHQ to bug private conversations of diplomats at the United Nations to find out how they might vote on a resolution about the prospective forthcoming invasion of Iraq. As an aside here, note that GCHQ in Britain could intercept conversations taking place thousands of miles away."

"WOW," exclaimed Teresa.

Nicole continued, "And there was Chelsea Manning, who passed something like seven hundred thousand documents to Wikileaks, even including incriminating video recordings. Chelsea is the only whistleblower to serve time in prison. President Obama shortened her thirty-five-year sentence to seven years."

Teresa was fidgeting in her seat, feeling uncomfortable about what she was learning. She announced that, "When I have some spare time, I am going to search for more information about Gunn, Snowden and Manning,"

"There's plenty of fascinating stuff about them online," offered Nicole, before she continued with, "Would you like to hear about some of the secret programs that the US and UK would rather you didn't know about?"

"Absolutely." Teresa jumped in. Harry laughed and added, "Sounds like fun."

"Well," said Nicole, "You'll have to wait until I've freshened up the coffee."

"Tease," shouted Teresa, "This is as frustrating as TV adverts spoiling a decent programme!" She followed Nicole into the kitchen, where she was quizzed about her relationship with Harry.

He was oblivious to that discussion, because he went off to use the bathroom, after which he paced up and down, looking out across the harbour, making a mental list of what else he wanted to learn from Nicole. Most important to him was the question of whether anyone could hack into GCHQ's systems and change data. And what information does GCHQ collect about civilians? And, if they collect masses of data about people, how on earth could they find the time to analyse it all?

When the three were once more settled around the coffee table, Nicole brought the meeting to order and continued…

"Harry, you mentioned Tempora. For Teresa's benefit, it was a program where GCHQ tapped the undersea fibreoptic internet cables that connect the UK to other countries. They collected a copy of all the data that passed by and stored it for a rolling thirty days whilst they analysed it, looking for whatever might interest them. Inevitably, they were also tapping all the cables onshore as well. That was ten years ago now."

Harry became animated as he added, "It's so clever. Why try and hack into computers here and there, when you can collect everything that travels between every device without anyone knowing? The only thing I cannot understand is how they could expect to look at all that data, let alone analyse it to discover the few things that really matter."

"I'll come to that later," said Nicole. "Now let's move on to *PhotonTorpedo*. This was an American program where the NSA grabbed all the user data from MSN Messenger as people sent messages between each other. MSN Messenger later became Windows Live Messenger, then Yahoo and Facebook Messenger and currently is called Skype. I mention that because it illustrates how the NSA and GCHQ have targeted people's textual communications for at least twenty years. By now, I expect they can intercept all social media traffic."

"This is much more intrusive than I thought possible!" said Teresa, "What next?"

"OpticNerve," replied Nicole. "That was a program that intercepted video calls and captured a webcam snapshot every five minutes, which was then matched to personal information and stored."

"Anymore?" asked Harry.

"Oh Yes!" exclaimed Nicole. "Muscular was a program run jointly between the NSA and GCHQ which collected over 180 million surveillance records. WindStop and Incenser dwarfed that by gathering over thirteen billion records.

"You might have heard of Prism, a program used to allegedly tap into the German Chancellor's phone calls. On a lighter note, I know the NSA were collecting data about people via the Angry Birds game on smartphones. It's good to enjoy some light relief when considering this stuff. Some of the spying efforts have wonderfully silly names, like Black Foot, Boundless Informant, and Cheesy Name, which was to do with accessing documents that governments and business thought they had safely encrypted, and there was also FlatLiquid and FoxAcid. And there's more..."

Teresa raised her hand and demanded that Nicole stop. "I can't get my mind around the scale of all this."

"Okay," said Nicole. "So far, I'd like you to accept three definite facts. One: GCHQ and the NSA between them continuously spy on the data that travels through the internet. Two: their reach is worldwide, which means they can follow your activities wherever you go. Three: they can grab not only text, but also sound and images."

There was a moment's silence, then Harry asked. "We've heard about the spies gathering massive amounts of data; how much do they collect? How and where do they store it? And how long do they keep it?"

"Okay," replied Nicole, "What I am about to tell you is almost certainly going to shock you. Do you want the unabridged version, with all the proof, or the quick explanation?"

Harry answered, "You've shown us that you know what you're talking about, so let's keep it short."

Teresa nodded in agreement.

Nicole looked serious, took a breath, and started...

"Edward Snowden's documents revealed that both GCHQ and the NSA collect everything. Over twenty years ago, the NSA started collecting absolutely everything they could lay their hands upon with the intention to keep it forever. Edward Snowden referred to a 'full take,' which means that they collect everything that passes along the internet cables. I'll list a few things that affect the three of us: our car's identity and location from every number plate recognition camera, video of us from CCTV and security cameras, including privately owned outdoor and indoor security footage, the location of our smartphone at all times, call logs for every phone conversation, all text messages and data about all our cloud uploads. Our smartphones reveal a tremendous amount. All the information about everything that leaves or arrives on your phone is collected. And new cars, such as Teresa's brother's, transmit telematics, which includes such information as location and speed, braking effort, rate of acceleration, g-forces, oil level, and even tyre pressures!"

The two looked aghast, but Nicole was in her stride…

"And consider your home. Phone locations reveal who is at home with you. Your smart TV reveals much of what interests you. The smart light switches tell when you switch out the lights and go to bed. Google Nest or Alexa communicates with their relevant clouds. If you upload your photos to the cloud, you help identify faces and places with names. You no doubt make web searches and use online banking. All that information passes along cables which are tapped into. The data can be collected, stored and, if required, analysed."

"How could they possibly store all that?" asked Harry. "It would mean they are duplicating the amount of data stored by all the cloud servers in the world."

"It's held in various locations across the planet. Some

military bases have cavernous underground communications centres with banks of servers. In America, according to Snowden, they built one data centre that could hold all the metadata about all our lives in perpetuity. Think of that. A baby's first scan in the womb, through to the record of his or her death many years later. They no doubt have squirreled away all they have about us three, gathered over the past twenty years. And, again, according to Snowden, they created a secret search engine designed specifically to efficiently search through the ever-increasing database of peoples' lives. That was named *XKEYSCORE*."

"I can believe that it would be possible to store all the metadata, text takes up little space, but the video and photos?" Harry looked disbelievingly at Nicole.

"Well Harry, you remember the Tempora program you started asking me about? At that time, they were keeping data for a rolling thirty days. I believe. I say 'believe' because I don't have the proof that GCHQ and NSA hold their 'full take' for a limited time, say a couple of months, but the associated metadata is held forever, providing a permanent record of our lives."

Teresa frowned. "Can we take a break while I try to absorb what you have said. And after that, will one of you please explain, what on earth is metadata!"

Nicole and Harry smiled benignly at Teresa who left the apartment to take some fresh air. While she was gone, Nicole asked Harry about his previous experience of technology, and he told her a little about the company he founded and the software they had written for banking apps. The two were still locked in animated conversation when Teresa returned, looking a little more relaxed and ready to continue.

"Let's get to it! I'm ready," exclaimed Teresa. "Metadata. What is it."

This time, Harry took the lead. "Metadata is a small amount of textual data that describes and identifies the data itself." Teresa repeated his words to herself and said, "I still don't get it."

"It will soon become clear. Let's create some metadata now. Please take out your phone and take a photo of Nicole." Teresa did as he instructed. Nicole posed elegantly until at the crucial moment she stuck out her tongue.

"Now," instructed Harry, "Look at that picture on your phone. The file that contains the picture is the actual data, but there is more available. Tap the option to look at the information about that photo. You will find some text that tells you the name of the file itself, the GPS location where you took the picture, the time you clicked the shutter, and it also stores the unique identity number of your phone, the shutter speed and other camera settings, what camera app you used, and more. All that information is the metadata which describes the data itself, the photo."

"Nice example," complimented Nicole.

"I understand that, but how else do I generate metadata," asked Teresa.

Nicole spoke quickly, "Almost everything generates some metadata. Your internet searches carry info about your computer including its unique identity. And your search generates more metadata as it passes each server along the way to every web page you visit. And you're generating metadata just sitting there. Your phone frequently 'pings' a signal which is picked up at the nearest phone mast which identifies that your phone wants to remain connected. The metadata includes the unique identity of your phone, where the signal is coming from, etcetera. That information is collected by your phone company, who is required to disclose it to government agencies, and so it ends up at GCHQ. So, right now, they could know that we three are sitting here. Hopefully, they are not listening, but they could if they wanted to."

The atmosphere in the room was now subdued but Harry was pleased with how much he had learnt. He thought now was the ideal point at which to take a break. He looked up, smiled broadly, and suggested, "Anyone for lunch? I'm paying."

"I would like to continue this discussion later," Nicole said, "But for now, fresh air and lunch sounds ideal."

Teresa concurred, "There's a local restaurant that I would like to show Harry."

"Lead the way," Nicole chimed in, her enthusiasm apparent as she rose from her seat and grabbed a light cotton coat as they passed through the hallway and out the front door.

As they left Nicole's modern apartment, Harry marvelled at the juxtaposition between the world outside, carrying on as usual, and the technical labyrinth they had just been navigating. A gentle sea breeze was blowing, which, together with his love of the outdoors, reminded him of his passion for sailing and made him think he should get back on the water before too long.

"Where are we going?" Harry asked, his curiosity piqued by the prospect of discovering a new culinary gem.

"Tora, my favourite sushi restaurant. I think you'll love it."

As Teresa navigated the car along the busy streets of

Sliema, Harry stole glances at her. She exuded an aura of serene confidence, both in her driving and in her demeanour. Her compact athletic body sat bolt upright as she focused on the road ahead. She obviously took her driving very seriously. In fact, thought Harry, Teresa appears to achieve a high standard in all she does. He couldn't help but admire her, even as he mourned the loss of his wife.

"Almost there," Teresa announced, breaking into Harry's thoughts. Nicole leaned forward, "I love this place."

They found a parking space opposite the restaurant, which looked to be situated on a platform jutting out over the sea. It was a stark white building with tinted glass, projecting an air of cleanliness, which Harry found a relief, because when it came to eating raw fish, he always chose the venue carefully.

Settled inside, they discussed their favourite morsels of sushi and sashimi, twirled their wooden chopsticks, and started to eat. Sushi, with its many small portions, suited eating and conversing at the same time, so they chattered away companionably.

Nicole volunteered some of her experiences living in California and explained that she enjoyed her freelancing lifestyle.

Harry thought it sounded ideal. "Who wouldn't prefer to work in such a location as this?" It was the first time since the new owners of his company fired him that Harry had contemplated his eventual return to work. Doing what? And where?

Soon, the animated talk between Teresa and Nicole, who were obviously close friends, dragged him back to the present. Nicole looked directly at Harry. "So, how exactly did you two meet?"

"Ah, well," Harry began, hesitating for a moment as he searched for the right words. "It's a bit of a long story but suffice to say that Teresa was my guardian angel during a particularly difficult time in my life."

Teresa blushed at the compliment, her cheeks taking on a rosy hue. "I wouldn't go that far," she demurred, "but I'm glad I could be there for you when you needed it."

Later, back in the apartment, Teresa restarted the conversation. "We were talking about metadata. For example, now I presume that Daniel's car would upload to the cloud the details of our journey to the restaurant and our three phones would identify where we chose to eat, that all three of us were together, and how long we stayed there. And GCHQ and the NSA will already have that information."

"Precisely," answered Nicole, who continued, "And you could add that when Harry paid the bill using his credit card, they would learn who paid the bill and how much our superb meal cost."

Harry jumped in, "Nicole, could we move on to discuss how it is possible to analyse this mind-blowing amount of data that is being collected about us?"

"Okay, well, this is the cleverest part." Nicole became visibly excited as she warmed to her subject. "Artificial Intelligence."

She paused for effect and allowed that announcement to sink in before continuing, "AI does all the legwork. In 2021, Jeremy Fleming, then the Director of GCHQ, revealed they were deploying artificial intelligence. From my degree studies, I know they were amongst the first in the world to develop and deploy AI, starting almost forty years ago, back in the 1980s, when semi-intelligent software was called an 'expert system.' All those years ago, they were using computers to analyse enormous amounts of data. An expert system would not only look for exceptions that people considered possible, but also for patterns and anomalies that nobody had foreseen."

"Since then, increased computing power, processors that can conduct hundreds of thousands of concurrent operations, have combined to make AI possible. Today, the available evidence points to GCHQ and the NSA using the most highly developed artificial intelligence in the world."

"What exactly does it do," asked Teresa.

"Well, AI can trawl through the data at high speed. In a few seconds, one computer can do work that would take thousands of people months to complete. And it does the job much better than humans could, because the AI can find patterns and coincidences that humans would not have even thought to look for, enabling it to identify even the most obscure threats. And consider this, AI can translate between languages quickly and accurately. It can piece together the significance of different conversations in many languages, identify people using speech or facial recognition. It can compare information gathered from CCTV, videos, social media, all the different types of information we've spoken about. It will be looking for any suspicious activity. Then, it will apply reasoning to select what is relevant to report to its masters. This is not science fiction. It is happening now. Who knows, given the power of modern super-computers, the most sophisticated AI may be close to becoming a sentient being, theoretically, a living brain within a computer."

Harry thought, "But that doesn't explain how or why AI thought my boat was carrying terrorists?" He asked, "Is it okay with you if we leave the subject of AI and move on?"

Nicole and Teresa nodded agreement as Harry launched into the question that had dominated his mind all day, "In your professional opinion, Nicole, would it be possible to hack into either GCHQ or the NSA?"

As Harry posed the question, he tensed. He was acutely aware that if it was impossible to hack into these organisations it would mean that Commander Forbes and Professor Hall had been lying to him about a malignant hacker being the cause for the attack on his boat.

Nicole pursed her lips, considering her answer. She had noticed the change in tone of Harry's voice and guessed this was, for some unknown reason, especially important to him.

She chose her words carefully. "Anything is possible. However, breaching the security of GCHQ or the NSA would be incredibly difficult and potentially dangerous, because as soon as they knew you had tried, they would be after you. It would require a very high level of expertise, and considerable resources, which only a few governments would possess."

"You're not ruling it out completely?" Harry pushed further, his eyes locking onto Nicole's as he searched for the truth.

"No, I'm not," she admitted, "but I must stress the sheer monumental challenge."

Nicole's gaze flicked back and forth between Harry and Teresa, "You see," Nicole began, "In 2016, allegedly, a group called 'The Shadow Brokers' claimed to have infiltrated an elite hacking unit within the NSA called the Equation Group. A few taster files and images of the stolen software was released, which appeared to be legitimate. Allegedly, they had stolen cyber warfare tools that the US was using to hack into other countries systems. It was very embarrassing for America at the time."

"However," Nicole continued, "most newspapers did not report the event, bowing to pressure from the US government. There were suspicions that The Shadow Brokers were a group working at the behest of Russia. You could find some information available on the internet but little from attributable sources. And most experts think it more likely that they grabbed a copy of the malware from outside of the NSA, rather than penetrated the organisation's firewalls."

"In conclusion," Nicole summarised, "My personal opinion is that it is possible the NSA has been hacked, but most unlikely." She continued, "And I do not think that GCHQ has ever been hacked. You see, you can't keep these things totally secret. Such a momentous event would generate chatter amongst people like me, and there has been none."

Harry nodded solemnly; his jaw clenched as he processed this information. His mind raced with thoughts of what Forbes and Hall had told him. If GCHQ was impenetrable, then the story they had woven about the attack on his yacht was nothing more than an elaborate lie. But why attack him anyway? What purpose would it serve?

At that moment, Teresa, who is nobody's fool, was thinking there was more to Harry's interest in this subject than he was revealing. However, she decided not to voice that thought for the present. Instead, her eyes wide with concern, she asked "I have just thought of something, Nicole. Surely, when my internet browser shows a padlock in the address bar and says my connection is secure, that means nobody can intercept what I do, right?"

Nicole looked at Teresa as a parent might look at a child, not wanting to spoil their innocence, "Unfortunately, Teresa, that symbol means the traffic between the website you visit and your browser is encrypted, but the web pages you visit and your identity is held in metadata, which is not protected. Furthermore, when it comes to government surveillance, they can easily decrypt that type of internet traffic."

Teresa tried again, "So, Nicole, when I see all those adverts for VPNs, should I pay to subscribe? Would that prevent others from getting at my stuff?"

"Yes, and no. Choose your Virtual Private Network service carefully because some of them will store your information and use it to earn money for themselves. You raise an important point, and I'd be happy to recommend a secure provider."

Nicole looked serious as she continued. "It's strange. Many people will pay good money to secure their home from intruders. They will lock the back door carefully every night to prevent a burglar stealing a few possessions. Yet, they will leave several internet back-doors wide open and be reluctant to invest a small sum to secure their online lives. I find that crazy, when you consider that major organised crime syndicates employ expert hackers to instal ransomware, and they use bots to gather information about people, so they can steal their identity and every penny they own. The days of free internet are over. It's time to cough-up and pay for proper online security."

Harry laughed, "I can see how you sell your cyber security consultancy Nicole. Another time, you might advise us on what we should be doing to protect ourselves online."

"I'd be happy to. And no charge. You need to consider VPN, private browsing, secure and encrypted email and who to trust with your cloud storage. It requires a little technical understanding, but I'd love to help."

She ended with, "Let me summarise. Governments collect masses of information about us and, although we can reduce that, we can't altogether stop it. However, we can easily reduce our exposure to criminals. We can reduce the impact of the many information leaks that take place at the companies from whom we buy. And we should stop giving away every scintilla of information about every minute of our lives to the big tech companies we rely upon, such as Microsoft, Apple, etcetera. I respectfully suggest we have been too trusting of them. They possess more confidential information about us than our doctor."

"Thank you, Nicole," Teresa said quietly, "Today hasn't turned out as I expected. I have learnt so much, but I'm not sure that I wouldn't have preferred to remain ignorant."

Harry asked, "Nicole, you seem to know quite a bit about hacking. How did you come by this knowledge?"

Nicole smiled, and with a touch of pride colouring her voice, "Five years ago, when I was studying for my master's degree at Stanford University in California, I developed an artificial intelligence hacking bot as part of my research project.

Putting it simply, I created software that in computing jargon we call a bot, short for robot. My bot roamed the internet looking for servers with security weaknesses. I first taught it some basic hacking techniques and then it used artificial intelligence to improve its hacking ability to access servers, gather information, and transmit that information back to a server that I established for the purpose."

"An AI hacking bot?" Harry repeated, chuckling to himself at the thought of Nicole being a secret hacker. He felt a frisson of excitement. "I didn't realise that was possible."

"Thank you, Harry." Nicole smiled, clearly pleased by his respect for her achievement. "But it's not all positive. My bot was so successful that it scared me. I soon shut down the server and did all I could to make sure nobody would ever trace my experiments in AI back to me."

"I have mixed feelings about AI," Harry explained, "On one hand, I recognise the incredible advances in areas like medicine, with new antibiotics, cancer diagnosis, and so forth. But on the other hand, I share the concerns of many experts that an AI could become sentient and, potentially, a malevolent force."

Teresa listened intently, her attention flicking between Harry and Nicole.

"Those concerns are valid," Nicole acknowledged. You may remember that in the summer of 2022, Google fired a software engineer who claimed that an unreleased AI system had become sentient. My understanding is that it will be some years before any AI starts to think like a human being."

Harry sighed, "It's a double-edged sword, isn't it? So much potential for both good and bad." He asked, "Did you see that news report that an out-of-control AI could lead to the extinction of humanity." He paused for effect, allowing the gravity of his words to sink in.

"The article quoted experts who support that view," Harry continued, "Sam Altman, one of the fathers of AI, Elon Musk, Dario Amodei, Demis Hassabis, and others." And then, seeing the expression on Teresa's face, he added quickly, "Of course, there are other experts who say those dire warnings are overblown."

Nicole had convincingly answered Harry's core question about whether anyone could hack into GCHQ, and so he felt it was time to leave. "Thank you for your hospitality, Nicole. It was great meeting you. And thank you for sharing some of your knowledge. Now, I need time to digest all this information."

As Teresa drove him back to his hotel, she turned briefly and looked at him seriously. "You know, Harry, I'm wondering if there is more to your interest in GCHQ than you are revealing. I won't ask, but if you want to share, you know I am here and I would be discreet."

"Mmm." Harry avoided giving a straight answer, "Thank you for introducing me to Nicole. I hope I haven't spoiled your day out?"

"Tell me Harry, I found some of Nicole's revelations hard to believe. Yet, you didn't question anything she said."

"I made a head start yesterday, and much of what Nicole told us is already available online and in newspaper articles. Regarding the rest, I shall search for confirmation, but I am confident that what Nicole revealed is at least ninety percent known fact and the remainder is reasonable assumption."

"It was a day of unwelcome discoveries for me," said Teresa. "I would like to do something to stop this intrusion into my privacy. Soon, you may read in a newspaper that I have been arrested for smashing all the CCTV cameras on the island."

They both laughed and then Teresa suggested that tomorrow she could take Harry to her surprise destination. They agreed, and as she dropped him outside his hotel door she insisted, "Be ready tomorrow at ten!"

"Aye, aye, Ma'am." Harry replied as he saluted before sprinting up the steps to the hotel entrance.

12

It was the following morning, and Teresa was driving Harry out of Valetta into the countryside. Harry looked at fields all around which appeared to have been blasted dry and brown by the relentless sun.

The scene reminded him of all the southern Mediterranean countries that he had visited during summer. It looked bare and dusty, so different from the green fields of England. And yet he knew that Maltese farms must be highly productive, because the shops and markets were stacked high with locally produced, colourful and delicious fruit and vegetables.

Sitting in the driver's seat, Teresa was making progress along the dual carriageway of Route 7, heading north, cutting across the heart of the island. She glanced over at Harry, noting that his time in Malta appeared to have done him some good. The sun had bleached his blond hair even lighter, and he sported a healthy-looking tan, which improved his otherwise slightly care-worn demeanour.

She caught his eye and smiled. "Let's forget about that conversation with Nicole yesterday," she suggested, with her soft and melodic voice, "Today is a new day, and I want you to enjoy it."

"Agreed," he replied, nodding. A day without concerns would be most welcome.

Teresa's eyes twinkled with mischief. "I still won't reveal where we're going. It's more fun that way."

Harry chuckled, intrigued by her playfulness. "Fair enough, Doctor Camilleri. Lead on."

As they made their way northwards, the imposing city of Mdina came into view on their left. One of the bastions of the 16th-century fortifications jutted out, an acute point in the massive stone walls, like an arrowhead aimed at them. Teresa explained that the catholic military order who once ruled Malta, the Knights Hospitaller, had constructed those immense walls.

"Mdina is truly magnificent," said Teresa. "There's so much history there, dating back over four thousand years. Walking the walls is like stepping back in time. The city was once the country's capital. It's known as the Silent City because cars are restricted within the city walls. The Phoenicians built the original city, the Romans added more, then the Arabs, and finally the Normans. Each conqueror left their mark, which has made the city really special."

Soon after Teresa finished her brief history lesson, she turned left. The smooth dual carriageway was replaced by a narrow road with a potholed surface that was bordered by old stone walls. There were no painted road markings, and Harry found himself bounced around as Teresa navigated the rough surface, swinging the car left or right to avoid a particularly large pothole.

"Is this a shortcut?" he asked.

Teresa laughed, "Not really. I always come this way. Most of the roads in Malta are like this, narrow, winding, and full of character."

"Character, huh?" Harry chuckled, starting to relax as he grew more confident in Teresa's driving ability. "I suppose that's one way to describe it. It's very narrow, and I notice you mostly drive down the middle of the road."

Teresa laughed, replying, "In England we drive on the left.

In Europe we drive on the right, but in Malta we usually drive on the shaded side of the road." She winked at Harry, who laughed at her light-hearted way of telling him that she felt very at home in her native land."

Despite the bumpy ride and the proximity of the knobbly stone walls, Harry relaxed and took in the picturesque scenery. The charming little villages they passed looked frozen in time, with few inhabitants to be seen.

"Look at this guy," Teresa said, slowing down and pointing ahead towards a grey-haired farmer coming towards them. He was sitting atop a rusty old tractor pulling a wide trailer piled high with brightly coloured nectarines. A plume of dirty diesel smoke puffed out of the ancient machine's vertical exhaust, matched by a trail of tobacco smoke blowing from the old man's enormous pipe.

He was looking at the fields to his left, perhaps containing his own crops, hogging the narrow road, oblivious of their presence.

"Look…?" Harry began, but before he could finish saying 'look out,' Teresa swerved onto a farm track on their left. The car came to an abrupt halt, dust billowing around them. The farmer continued without so much as a glance in their direction, the scent of diesel fumes lingering in the air.

They sat for a moment in silence.

"Bit of a close call, wasn't it?" Harry said, trying to calm down. "Your quick reactions just saved us."

"My brother would never forgive me for damaging his beloved car," she said, smiling, with her cheeks flushed by adrenaline. "Some of those old drivers can be a — challenge!" With that, she put the car in reverse and manoeuvred back onto the road, continuing their journey.

Fifteen minutes later, they arrived at the ferry port at the north of the island. Teresa parked the car and turned to Harry. "We're taking the ferry to visit somewhere on the island of Gozo."

"Really?" They left the car, purchased their tickets, and fifteen minutes later they boarded a ferry,

Standing on the deck of the little ship, Harry gazed out over the water, revelling in the experience. He enjoyed standing like a human gyroscope, erect and steady, despite the deck rolling and pitching beneath his feet. He felt more alert, more alive as he scanned the sea, which was a bright blue with occasional waves topped by white horses; galloping, tumbling over to disappear in the trough before the next wave.

The ferry cut through the choppy sea, sending spray from its bow. He turned to Teresa, who stood beside him with a drawn pale face. "Is this a gale?" she asked, gripping the railing tightly and swallowing hard.

"Goodness no, this wind is about force four," Harry replied, raising his voice over the sound of the ship's noisy engine. "Perfect for sailing my old yacht, Ariana. A day to enjoy the sun and to make real progress."

Teresa merely replied, "I might be sick."

Harry gestured to the tiny island of Comino they were passing but Teresa wasn't interested. "It will help if you look at the horizon," Harry suggested, "and flex your legs to stand vertical instead of leaning against the rail."

Fortunately, the ferry reached its destination before Teresa's condition worsened, and she breathed a sigh of relief as they disembarked onto the solid ground of Gozo. "I've arranged for us to hire bicycles. It will be fun, and I've been wanting more exercise."

"Okay, I'm up for that," Harry agreed, "let's get to it."

At a small bicycle hire shop that smelt of rubber and oil Teresa asked for the two bikes she had ordered, and they were off. Teresa led the way, climbing through the narrow streets of the small town. Harry followed close behind, looking up at the tall houses that crowded both sides of the road, their balconies adorned with colourful potted plants and occasional laundry hanging from clothes lines that spanned the street from side to side. Away from the sea breeze, the heat was rising and Harry realized this was going to be tiring if they were to cycle more than a mile or so.

As they left the town, they passed a small industrial estate with low buildings gleaming in the sunlight. Soon, fields stretched into the distance, dotted with the occasional stone farmhouses. Fortunately, thought Harry, a following wind was urging them forward.

Ahead, Teresa was pedalling fast, setting a cracking pace. Her shapely figure was hidden beneath her baggy blue linen shorts and pink blouse, but Harry could still discern her athletic proportions. With a mixture of admiration and concern, he wondered how long she'd be able to maintain such a pace, especially given the continuous climb as they headed inland. He was beginning to pant more than a little, despite maintaining a level of fitness that exceeded most men of his age, his middle-age, he reflected.

"Are you sure you don't want to slow down a bit?" he called out, trying to sound casual.

"Where's the fun in that?" Teresa replied, her laughter carrying on the breeze. "Besides, I want to make sure we have plenty of time at our destination." Harry shook his head. He would simply have to try and keep up.

After a while, they cycled into the outskirts of Victoria, the capital of Gozo. The fields gave way to warm coloured limestone buildings which lined the streets. At first, they were modern constructions, but the use of the local stone had created a sense of ageless charm, only broken by passing a McDonald's nestled amongst the traditional limestone facades.

Teresa led Harry to Independence Square, where throngs of people gathered at tables under wide umbrellas, enjoying an early lunch. Lively chatter filled the air.

"Will this be our lunch stop?" Harry inquired, scenting the tempting aromas that wafted towards him.

"Actually," Teresa replied with a mischievous smile, "I have something different in mind."

He followed her to a small sandwich shop. Inside, the air was cool and filled with the scent of freshly baked bread. Teresa asked for bottled water, baguettes filled with local ham and goats' cheese, plus two ice-cold bottles of the local Hopleaf Pale Ale.

"Trust me," she assured him, "You won't be disappointed."

They pedalled on, and the limestone buildings gave way to open fields. Ahead were low-lying hills. Teresa suddenly picked up speed, her deep brown ponytail flowing behind. Harry, caught off guard, pedalled hard to keep up with her sudden burst of energy. Soon, he could feel the burn in his thighs. She glanced back, flashed him a grin, and pushed on even harder. "Keep up!" she called out.

After five more minutes of exhausting work, Harry was relieved when they slowed down and pulled over beneath the arches of an old aqueduct that bordered the road. Its crumbling stones stood tall against the backdrop of the brilliant blue sky. They dismounted, found some shade behind a pillar, and sat down with the cool stone to their backs.

"Was this built by the Romans?" Harry asked, studying the tall columns and graceful arches.

Teresa laughed loudly; "No Harry, this was built by the British in the nineteenth century. It fell into disrepair after the island was fitted with piped water."

"Ah," Harry replied, slightly embarrassed that Britain had left its mark on so many of the islands in the Mediterranean. They ate voraciously. Harry found the light beer paired very well with the ham and cheese, and he let out an appreciative sigh as he took his last swig. No sooner had they finished eating than Teresa sprang to her feet and insisted they continue. "Just fifteen more minutes until we arrive."

The final stretch of their ride led them to an imposing church that seemed to rise from the flat land around it like a phoenix from the ashes. The elaborate stone building looked as if it had been transplanted from a city centre and dropped in the middle of nowhere. The design was of an ancient style, yet the walls were so clean and pristine that it could be recently constructed, creating a strange mixture between timelessness and modernity. They dismounted their bicycles and Teresa spoke quietly, and reverently, as she explained, "This is the Basilica of the National Shrine of the Blessed Virgin of Ta' Pinu. I come here whenever I feel down or in need of inspiration."

"Wow," was all Harry could think to say. They parked their bicycles and entered the church.

Teresa covered her head with a thin scarf, in a gesture of

respect. She stopped, faced the altar, bobbed down and crossed herself.

Harry's gaze wandered around the interior, taking in the details. The first thing he noticed was an old woman dressed in black, bent with age, diligently mopping the already spotlessly clean floor. Her movements were slow and deliberate, each stroke accentuating the atmosphere of devotion.

The lantern windows high above cast a warm light on the pale-coloured wood of the pews and reflected from the stone walls, bathing the interior in a diffuse warm glow. Harry felt relaxed in this place, as if he might belong there.

Teresa nudged his arm and spoke in hushed tones, "There's a room I want to show you. I'll leave you alone in there while I pray."

"Okay, lead the way," Harry replied, curious about where he was going.

She guided him to a side room. "This is The Room of Miracles."

Harry immediately saw that the high walls were covered in tightly packed picture frames, hundreds of them, each telling a story of hope and healing.

"Take your time. Read some of the stories if you like. I'll see you later." She slipped away and he was alone in the smallish room, excepting a woman at the far end, engrossed in reading something on the end wall.

He walked slowly around, amazed by the tangible sense of hope that emanated from the framed stories and the various artefacts collected there. Much of the text was written in Maltese, but amongst them were other languages, including English.

There were hundreds of convincing stories that spoke of healing and hope. Each picture frame held a newspaper cutting or a letter of thanks that described a miracle. He traced his fingers along the glass covering one newspaper article that told the story of a blind woman who had regained her sight after praying at the shrine. The photograph showed her beaming face as she looked out at the world anew.

He paused before a pair of rustic wooden crutches accompanied by two pictures of a boy. In one photo, he was leaning on the sticks, his legs bowed, and his face full of pain. In the other, he was running at a school sports day.

There was a heavily scratched motorcycle crash helmet and an accompanying story about an injured teenager. His mother and father had been told to expect the worse. The young man's injuries were too extensive for him to survive. His parents came to this church and prayed to the Blessed Virgin to save their son. Against all odds, he had miraculously recovered. There were so many stories that, if one were multilingual, it would take at least an entire day to read them all.

Harry noted the number of nationalities represented. Pilgrims had travelled from every continent, united by a belief that prayers offered in this basilica would heal them or the people for whom they prayed.

High up on the walls, Harry spotted several sets of white knitted babies' clothes, their accompanying messages too far away to decipher.

As he took in the irresistible evidence of modern miracles, he was drawn to consider his current state of grief over losing his family. Although religion had never played much of a role in his life, something about this church and this room stirred within him a newfound openness to the possibility of divine intervention.

"Could it be?" he mused, "Is there a higher power? Have I been missing something all these years?"

With cautious steps, Harry made his way back to a pew near the entrance to the room. He lowered himself onto the wooden bench and, gathering his thoughts, he began to pray for the souls of his wife Miranda, and children George and Charlie. And then he prayed for the strength to make the remainder of his life meaningful. As he whispered his heartfelt words, a sense of peace washed over him. Nothing had changed except that he, for the first time, felt at peace with his situation. Life had been cruel, but he was alive. He could never forget them. But he could live on, striving to find a way to make his life worthwhile, and to give to others what he would have given to his family if they had lived on.

Afterwards, he left the church and stood alone, his eyes taking time to adjust to the glare of the sunlight. He leant against the stone wall by the entrance door, his mind empty as he experienced a rare feeling of inner calm and peace. He wondered, "This must be what meditation feels like."

When Teresa joined him, she also looked more relaxed and peaceful. She smiled at Harry before saying, "You know, in Malta and Gozo, there are three hundred and fifty-nine churches. That is one church for every 675 people. And on Sundays, they are mostly full."

Harry looked down at her. "Thank you for bringing me here."

Her eyes searched his face, looking for a change in him. As they walked towards their bicycles, she observed that Harry seemed to stand a little taller, his posture less weighed down.

She felt hopeful that the Blessed Virgin Mary would guide him through his healing journey, which was what she had been praying for inside the basilica. "Are you ready to go?" she asked, mounting her bicycle.

He nodded, swinging his leg over the bike frame. The powerful afternoon sun beamed down on them as they pedalled away from the Basilica, leaving behind the serenity of the church, and heading back towards the ferry.

The journey back to Valetta was uneventful, save for the atmosphere of tranquillity within the car. They pulled to a stop outside the Grand Harbour Hotel, and Harry turned to Teresa. "Again, thank you for taking me to the basilica. It was a revelation."

He wanted to show his gratitude. And he wanted to prolong his time with Teresa. "Listen, I know you must return this car to your brother. Are you in a rush? If not, would you like to join me for dinner?"

Teresa hesitated, then she pulled out her phone and called her brother. After a brief exchange in Maltese, she hung up and turned to Harry. "My brother Daniel said it's fine if I return the car a little later. I'd love dinner."

"Very good," he replied, "Can you suggest somewhere?"

"I think you would like Palazzo Preca," Teresa suggested, "it's run by two sisters who serve good Maltese food."

"Sounds ideal," Harry agreed. They set off at a leisurely pace through Valletta's ancient streets, walking in companiable silence, as friends will sometimes do. They arrived at the restaurant a little early for dinner, being only six o'clock in the evening, but the staff welcomed Teresa warmly and gave them a table at the front window.

From outside the restaurant, passers-by looked in at the

handsome couple on display. People would pause to look. Some stopped to read the menu on the wall outside, and slowly the restaurant began to fill. Harry felt a little on show, a temporary advertisement, but that was unimportant compared to his rare sense of contentment. His wife and children may be gone, life as he knew it destroyed, but in this moment, he could still find some happiness.

They started with Salmon Gravlax, in truth more Swedish than Maltese, washed down with a dry white wine. Their talk drifted from this to that, passing the time chatting about nothing in particular. For the main course they chose the traditional slow cooked rabbit, partnered with a rich red burgundy. By now, the alcohol was working its wonders and they laughed and joked.

Teresa asked about Harry's sailing experiences and then she entertained him with amusing anecdotes from the hospital. She commented on how she found it strange that, when under stress or in pain, so many British people started cracking jokes. "I realise it's a British way of coping. The worse the situation, the funnier you Brits become!" They both laughed again, as Harry admitted that he often chose humour to release some tension.

And so, the effortless conversation continued until the clock struck nine. Harry reluctantly glanced at his watch. "I suppose we should be heading back," he said, taking a generous tip from his pocket.

"Yes," Teresa agreed, "I should return the car, but I've had too much to drink, so I'll just call a taxi to meet me at your hotel."

Stepping into the cool night air, Harry couldn't shake the feeling that they were being watched. He scanned the shadows, searching for the pair of eyes he could feel scrutinising him. There, in the distance, stood a man whose face stirred a vague memory. Could it be the fellow he saw scowling at him during his morning run?

"Is everything alright?" Teresa asked, noticing his furrowed brow.

"Yes, it's just — never mind. Let's walk."

Wanting to show Harry more of Valletta's beauty, Teresa guided him along Old Theatre Street - a narrow, pedestrianised alleyway lined with quaint shops and, on the right, a picturesque square. It was dark with only an occasional streetlight providing pools of light between deep shadows.

"This area is really stunning," Harry commented, admiring the ornate architecture that surrounded them. Teresa beamed with pride as they continued.

They approached a section of the street where a building loomed overhead, with closed shops on one side and curved arches on the other. The area was unlit, with not a soul to be seen. The dark enveloped them and the air was thick with the scent of jasmine, wafting from a hidden garden somewhere.

As they approached the arches on the right, Teresa started to say, "Look at this square…" when a figure leapt from behind one of the arches, a few paces ahead of them. "Pedofelu!" the man screamed as he charged towards Harry, brandishing a long kitchen knife.

In that split second, Harry's heart skipped a beat and he tensed. He barely had time to process the situation before Teresa, with extraordinary speed, stepped in front of him to face the attacker.

To Harry, time seemed to slow. It was like watching a Kung Fu movie. In front of him, Teresa dropped into a low and steady posture. Then, with a fluid movement, and at great speed, her left arm shot up and outwards, deflecting the assailant's knife-wielding arm to the side. And without pause, her right arm shot forwards. Teresa's clenched fist hit the centre of the man's sternum, sending him sprawling onto his back and gasping for breath. Without a moment's hesitation, she sprang forward. With an animal-like intent, she stamped on the man's wrist. Her foot slammed down with her full body weight behind it. The noise echoed down the stone-paved street, along with the sound of the knife clattering across the paving stones. The man lay on his back, with his mouth wide open, gasping for breath, like an injured goldfish.

The sudden commotion caught the attention of a couple approaching from the other end of the street. Their eyes widened in horror, and they turned and fled, their footsteps echoing into the distance.

"Stay down!" Harry barked at the attacker, holding the man firmly to the ground as he struggled to rise. Teresa, panting from the tension and exertion, knelt beside the man and began questioning him in Maltese.

"Pedofelu," was the only word Harry could discern, repeated several times during the rapid-fire exchange. Teresa shouted at the man as she lambasted him in Maltese. The man shouted back. At one point he looked at Harry and spat towards him, but Teresa pushed the man's face sidewise, so he missed.

After a long exchange between them, the words slowed, and the tone became more one of concern than anger. Harry looked at Teresa, searching for answers.

"Let him go, Harry." Her voice was definite, commanding.

"No way! I'm going to call the police."

She looked extremely frustrated by that and almost shouted at him, "That would be a bad idea; it would cause problems for you."

Harry hesitated, his instincts very much against letting the assailant walk free. But he accepted Teresa's instruction. With a wary nod, he released his grip on the man, who scrambled to his feet.

"Here, take this with you," Teresa said in Maltese. She picked up the knife and held it out, her expression unreadable. The man hesitated, his eyes darting between the weapon and the woman before him. Eventually, he took it.

"Go," Teresa ordered. The man stumbled away, sobbing, and cradling his injured wrist, disappearing into the shadows.

"Are you okay?" Harry asked, still reeling from this shocking turn of events.

She nodded, but her eyes did not meet his.

As they watched the man go, Harry felt a mixture of relief and confusion. He turned to Teresa, searching her face for an explanation. Her long hair was a mess, covering her shoulders. She stood legs apart and erect, more like a warrior than the gentle doctor he knew.

"Are you sure it was right to let him go?" he asked. "He obviously wanted to kill me."

Teresa sighed and glanced down at her hands, which were trembling. "I know it's hard to understand, Harry, involving the police would definitely make matters worse." She met his gaze, "I'll explain later. But right now, I need to think about what just happened."

Harry nodded, his mind racing with questions. As they walked towards the hotel, he felt a returning sense of vulnerability, an unease that began when his yacht was attacked and had only just started to ease, but now...

"Thank you," he said, breaking the silence. "For saving my life."

Teresa looked at him coldly. "You're welcome, Harry."

"Are you some sort of Kung Fu wizard?" he asked. "And how did you become that strong?"

"Martial arts have been my hobby for many years, and the power comes from Chi. I'll explain one day. But right now, I don't want to talk."

As they left the alleyway, Harry spotted a CCTV camera pointing at them. "He didn't choose a very smart place for his attack. The video record may be useful if I decide to go to the police."

They continued in silence. When they reached Harry's hotel, Teresa turned to him and firmly said, "I want to go to Nicole's, now!" The taxi that Teresa had ordered was waiting, the driver impatiently standing by his car and looking at his watch. As they drove, Teresa called Nicole and, turning away from Harry, she spoke rapidly in Maltese.

The taxi driver drove quickly, with Harry and Teresa swaying in unison as the car turned corners, almost adding another scratch to one ancient limestone wall near Nicole's apartment block. The atmosphere inside the cab was heavy with tension, a sharp contrast to earlier that evening.

Harry studied Teresa's profile. There was a secretness in her call to Nicole that unsettled him. "Who was that man?" he asked again, his voice imploring.

Teresa just stared out the side window, her jaw clenched. "I'm not going to talk about it right now."

"Come on, Teresa, you can't keep me in the dark like this," Harry pleaded.

"ENOUGH!" She shouted, turning to face him, her dark eyes flashing with anger. You'll have to wait."

Taken aback by her sudden outburst, Harry retreated into himself.

As the taxi pulled to a stop, Nicole was outside waiting. Harry, got out, quickly paid the driver, turned to enter the apartment, but the door snapped shut in front of him. Excluded and confused, he sucked in the cool night air, trying to calm himself.

He waited — and waited, the silence broken only by the hum of conversation from people enjoying themselves in bars along the sea front. After fifteen minutes, he glanced at his watch again, and unable to contain his anxiety, he rang the doorbell and glared at the security camera.

A couple of minutes later, the door buzzed open as Nicole's voice came from the speaker. "Come on in Harry."

"Thank you," he murmured, stepping into the subdued light of the lobby, and making his way to the apartment.

He found Teresa sitting on a sofa, her eyes distant. She looked up at him and offered a weak smile that didn't quite reach her eyes.

"Please, take a seat," Nicole gestured to the chair opposite Teresa.

Harry sat down as Nicole launched into an explanation. "Harry, the man who attacked you... he kept shouting Pedofelu." In English, that means paedophile."

The word paedophile hit Harry like a punch in the gut,

shocked to the core. "No way," he choked out, shaking his head emphatically. "I'm not... I would never..."

Teresa's gaze remained locked on Harry, as if she were interrogating him.

"Then why?" Harry asked, his voice cracking with emotion. "Why was he so convinced I am a...?" His voice petered out as he couldn't say the dreaded word.

Nicole spoke slowly, weighing her words carefully, as she explained that the man, a vigilante, had been driven to violence after an unspeakable tragedy involving his ten-year-old daughter. A tourist had raped her. And the man had left Malta before he could be identified and arrested.

"His daughter?" Harry repeated.

"Yes," Teresa replied, her eyes welling up with tears. "That's why he's so desperate for vengeance. He is intent on exacting revenge by killing a paedophile, and anyone will do. You are the first that he has found."

Anger and frustration boiled up within Harry. He exploded out as he shouted, "I REPEAT. I AM NOT A PAEDOPHILE." He could hardly speak as he quietly added that, "I respect and protect children. I would never do anything to harm a child. This is so unjust, so ridiculous!"

Nicole shifted in her seat, tapping away at her laptop. "I did some digging, and I found your name and photograph on a website called paedosnearyou.com. According to that website, Harry, you are listed as a convicted paedophile."

He felt the blood drain from his face. He shrank back into the armchair, staring blankly ahead. Why me? The question echoed through his mind. "Can you show me?" he croaked, dreading the sight but needing to see for himself.

Nicole turned her laptop screen towards him. There, in

stark black and white, was a photograph of Harry accompanied by the damning caption: 'Paedophile Harry Shaw has recently been released from prison and was last seen in Valetta, Malta.'

A bitter laugh escaped his lips, "This can't be real. It's not possible."

Teresa's voice trembled slightly as she spoke. "Harry, I found it hard to believe that you could be a paedophile, so I asked Nicole to check whether the website is genuine."

Nicole nodded in agreement and added, "The website has been in existence for several years, but I examined the code, the HTML, on the page featuring you. That page was uploaded a couple of weeks back." She paused as she looked at Harry with concern. "When I searched for information about you the other day, I didn't spot it."

Nicole and Teresa watched him in silence, their expressions difficult to read. The room settled into an uncomfortable hush. Eventually, Harry took a deep breath and turned to Teresa. "Tell me more about what you discussed with that man?"

Teresa's gaze dropped to the floor as she started. "His life has been a living nightmare since his daughter was raped. I tried to convince him you were innocent, but he wouldn't listen. I warned him that if he approached either of us again, I'd report his knife attack to the police."

She bit her lip, a flash of worry crossing her face. "You may not have seen the last of him."

Harry's mind was racing. Who could have set him up like this? What did they hope to gain from ruining his life? And, most urgently, how could he clear his name? He looked from Nicole to Teresa and back again to Nicole. "Will you help me get to the bottom of this. If this lie took hold, it would destroy me."

Nicole said, "I'm going to contact the owners of paedosnearyou.com and find out how and why the page appeared. And I'll do my best to have it taken down."

"Thank you, Nicole," Harry said, grateful for her support. But he couldn't shake a nagging fear. He looked at both women. "Do either of you still suspect me? Be honest with me." His eyes darted between the two, searching for any hint of doubt or suspicion in their expressions.

There was a moment of hesitation before Teresa spoke up. "Harry, we trust you. We know you're a man of principle and integrity. We believe you're innocent."

Nicole nodded in agreement. "We're on your side. We'll do everything we can to help you clear your name."

Relief washed over him, but Harry thought he spotted a glimmer of uncertainty in Teresa's eyes. Attempting to shift the conversation, he turned to her and asked her a question that had been on his mind since the attack. "Teresa, how did you learn to fight like that? I've never seen anything like it, except in movies."

Before Teresa could respond, Nicole interjected with an amused smile. "Harry, my cousin here has been practicing the martial arts ever since she was a little girl who was bullied at school. Within our family, her nickname is 'Bruce,' as in Bruce Lee, after the famous Kung Fu film star."

Teresa's cheeks flushed and she couldn't suppress a grin. Uncomfortable laughter filled the room, momentarily breaking the tension. The antique clock on the wall chimed eleven. Teresa glanced at it with a serious expression. "I must go." She rose from her seat. "I'm feeling completely sober now, so I'll take a taxi back to the hotel and then drive my brother's car home."

When the taxi had arrived; she said a simple goodnight as she quickly disappeared through the doorway. With Teresa gone, Harry turned to Nicole. "There's something else I want to ask you."

"Of course." She adjusted her glasses as she studied him intently. "What is it?"

"If you manage to contact the website owners, and assuming they accept that their site has been hacked to create the page about me, could you please try to discover who the hacker might be?"

Nicole nodded solemnly, understanding the importance of the request. "I'll do my best. You have my word."

"Thank you," he whispered, relieved that Nicole was an ally.

She crossed the room to her desk, picked up her phone, and arranged a taxi for him. Soon, the vehicle pulled up outside her apartment, its headlights cutting through the darkness to find the pair waiting outside.

"Harry," Nicole said, squeezing his arm reassuringly. "I'll call you tomorrow to let you know if I have received a response from the website owners."

As he slid into the backseat of the taxi, the driver attempted to strike up a friendly conversation, but Harry was in no mood for small talk. He simply shook his head at the eyes in the rear-view mirror, unable to muster the energy for pleasantries. Each passing streetlight cast a fleeting glow on his face, the alternating light and dark mirroring his inner turmoil.

The taxi dropped off Harry and, instead of going inside the

hotel, he crossed the street to lean against the wall and look out over the harbour. This spot was becoming his favourite place to think.

♦♦♦

At her parents' farmhouse, Teresa parked her brother's car and, emotionally drained, walked towards the front door. It was past midnight so she pushed open the heavy wooden door and stepped in as quietly as she could.

A hushed voice asked, "Where have you been?"

Her brother, Daniel, emerged from the shadows, his hands on his hips and his eyes narrowed in disapproval. "You promised you'd return the car earlier."

"I've had a difficult evening," she replied, her voice quivering slightly. "I couldn't possibly explain everything right now. We'll talk about it tomorrow."

"Your promises mean nothing these days," Daniel retorted, crossing his arms. "You're always chasing after that man as if he's the only thing that matters. You're not a teenager anymore."

"Please, Daniel," Teresa pleaded, close to tears. "Just let me go to bed. We'll discuss this in the morning."

But her brother's disapproving gaze bore into her, his words striking a nerve. An argument erupted, their voices becoming louder, despite their best efforts to remain quiet.

"Stop talking down to me!" Teresa snapped, her anger boiling over. "I'm thirty-five years old! I'm not some silly little girl!"

"Could've fooled me," Daniel retorted, "you're acting like a lovesick adolescent, running around all hours of the night for that man. What happened to the responsible, independent woman you used to be?"

Teresa's hands clenched into fists at her sides, her frustration palpable. "You don't understand, Daniel. I've had an exceedingly difficult evening."

"Difficult or not, it's no excuse for your behaviour!" he shot back.

The sound of a door creaking open cut through their argument. Their father, bleary-eyed and frowning, walked into the room, woken by the commotion.

"What on earth is going on out here?" he demanded, his voice gruff with sleep.

Tears welled up in Teresa's eyes and rolled down her cheeks as she hurled the car keys at her brother. "You're an idiot, Daniel!" she cried, her voice breaking. "I'll never borrow your car again!"

With that, she stormed off towards her bedroom. The resounding slam of her bedroom door punctuated the tense atmosphere left in her wake.

Their father sighed, shaking his head as he looked at Daniel. "One day, you two will grow up and act your ages." With those words, he turned and retreated to his room, leaving Daniel alone, regretting his words and immensely worried about his sister.

13

For once, Harry had forgone his morning run. He wanted to avoid the possibility of meeting his vigilante attacker. He also planned to skip breakfast in the hotel dining room. He was worried that fellow guests might look at him and see a paedophile.

He brewed instant coffee using the facilities in his bedroom. The taste was awful, and he poured it down the wash basin. He stood and toyed with the gold wedding ring on his finger, rolling it between his thumb and forefinger, thinking about his wife and children, as he waited until a car rental company might be open for business.

Eventually, it was eight o'clock. "Alright," he muttered to himself, taking a deep breath as he reached for his phone. "Let's start taking action."

He called a local car rental agency. "Good morning," came a cheerful voice from the other end of the line. "Car Rentals Malta, how can I help you?"

"Hello, I'd like to rent a car for the day, please," Harry replied, trying to match the man's enthusiasm. They discussed the model and arranged for the car to be delivered to the hotel. It was all so quick and easy.

"May I have your credit card details for payment?" the man asked.

Harry rummaged through his wallet and pulled out a credit card, providing the necessary information. A few silent moments passed before the agent spoke again.

"Sorry Sir, but this card seems to have been declined."

"Declined?" Harry frowned, feeling a sudden unease

settling in his chest. "That shouldn't be possible. I'll use another one."

He gave the agent the details for his second credit card, only to be met with the same response. Panic bubbled within him as he tried his third and final card, only to have that one declined as well.

"Is there a problem with your payment system?" Harry asked, his voice edged with frustration.

"Apologies for the inconvenience, Sir, but our system is working fine for other customers. Perhaps you should contact your bank?"

"Alright, thanks," Harry said through gritted teeth as he hung up.

He stared at the useless pieces of plastic in his hand. This couldn't be happening, not now, when he needed to see Teresa and be sure things between them were alright. He gripped his phone tighter, convinced that this was no coincidence; he was again being attacked. This made three times, the attack on his yacht, the knife attack last night and now this financial attack.

Determined to get to the bottom of this, he decided to reach out to Nicole. Her cybersecurity skills might provide a lifeline. With purpose, Harry grabbed his jacket and left the hotel, walking at speed to the taxi rank at the bus terminal.

Twenty minutes later, after paying the taxi fare in cash, Harry stood outside Nicole's apartment building, a cool breeze ruffling his hair. He steeled himself as he looked into the door entrance camera, pressed the buzzer, and waited. After a few moments, Nicole's voice crackled through the intercom. "Yes? Oh! Hello Harry."

"Nicole, I need your help again."

"Come on up." The door buzzed open, and Harry stepped inside.

Nicole was waiting at her front door, her large, black-rimmed glasses perched atop her nose. She was not her usual smart self. Her hair was dishevelled, and she was wearing a sloppy joe track suit. Harry apologised for turning up so early, and uninvited.

Nicole explained her appearance by saying she had been up extremely late last night, trying to get the web page about him taken down.

"Some good news Harry," she volunteered, "That website about paedophiles responded to my enquiry and I have not long finished speaking with them."

"Oh, really. Thank you," said Harry, reassured by her commitment to his cause.

"Firstly, they accept that their server had been hacked and the page added without their knowledge. Secondly, they have taken the page down and deleted everything relating to you from their server."

And then she explained how the website owners had, at her insistence, done their best to track down the IP addresses used to upload the page, but without success.

"Harry, the trail of IP addresses is broken," she explained, her voice tense. "This means the hack came from a clever source."

"Before we go further," Harry started, rubbing the back of his neck, "I just want to say thank you for getting that awful page removed. I was thinking I would have to hide-away from everyone."

Nicole waved off his gratitude with a flick of her wrist. "No problem. The website owners were more than happy to remove it once they knew what was going on."

She studied Harry's face, observing the taught lines of stress, "Tell me, what's happened this time?"

"Now there's another problem. My credit cards have all stopped working, and I think it's another attack. And that means someone is out to get me, coordinating these events."

"Really?" Nicole furrowed her brow, her fingers tapping against her thigh in thought.

Harry explained his experience with the car rental company, and then Nicole shrewdly suggested, "Let's just double check that, shall we, before we jump to conclusions."

And so, Harry used Nicole's laptop to try and make an online purchase at Amazon. His cards were all declined, one by one, as before. The problem confirmed, Nicole fell silent as she considered Harry's predicament.

Eventually, she turned to him and suggested, "Potentially, I think you're receiving a full-on digital attack from a high-level expert." She paused again before adding, "And, very cleverly, the paedophile web page motivated someone else to make the attack, which I'd describe as a digital attack by proxy."

Harry agreed with Nicole's conclusions and, although he didn't voice his opinion, he was becoming ever more convinced that all the attacks may be originating from within GCHQ.

"So, what can I do?" asked Harry.

"Frankly, I'm not sure what to suggest right now."

A tinkling sound from Harry's phone drew his attention. It was a new email. His heart rate quickened as he looked at the subject line, which was blank. And then he looked for the sender's email address, which was also missing. He opened the email and read it aloud, "Don't mess with me." Those four words were all the message contained.

"Don't mess with me," he repeated, looking up at Nicole's questioning expression. He handed the phone to Nicole, who squinted at the screen, and as she did, an identical message arrived via SMS text. Harry's pulse raced as the phone tinkled again, announcing a WhatsApp message. The third message echoed the same chilling words, 'Don't mess with me.'

Nicole eyes widened in disbelief, "Someone's hacked all three platforms. And they've coordinated these messages to all arrive at the same time. I've never seen anything like this."

As, together, they stared at the phone, all three messages vanished, gone from Harry's email in-box, text messages and social media, leaving no trace they had ever existed. Harry instinctively looked around, feeling that some all-seeing power was watching him.

"Whoever's doing this is a very high-level expert," Nicole whispered. "We're talking of an immensely skilful hacker with unprecedented access, maybe even at government level, the security services, or perhaps even a cyber warfare agency."

Harry's thoughts went back to his very unpleasant meeting with Commander Forbes and Professor Hall, back in the hospital. He was now convinced that there was a connection.

"Nicole, I must find this person and stop them. I can't live like this, constantly looking over my shoulder, waiting for the next attack."

Harry stared out of the window. It had started raining and drops streaked down the glass as he contemplated his next move.

"There's someone I can contact who might know what's going on," Harry said hesitantly, aware that he was treading on dangerous ground, due to the Official Secrets Act that he had signed. "His name is Professor Nicholas Hall."

"WHAT!" Nicole's eyes widening behind her large spectacles. "Do you mean THE Professor Nicholas Hall?"

"I guess so," said Harry, "Why?"

"He's a world-renowned expert on artificial intelligence?"

"That makes sense," Harry replied, thinking how parts of the puzzle were beginning to come together. From his wallet, he pulled out the white business card the professor had given him, listing only his name and a phone number.

"Wow," Nicole breathed, clearly impressed. "Why do you think he might be able to help?"

"That's complicated, Nicole, but I am going to see if he can."

"Before you do," she added, her expression turning serious, "you should make sure your money is safe. If this attacker is as skilled as we think, he or she could target your bank accounts next."

Harry's heart skipped a beat at the thought of being completely cut off from his funds, left entirely vulnerable and helpless. His credit cards were useless now, their once-powerful symbols of freedom rendered meaningless.

"You're right," he nodded, trying not to panic. "I must protect my assets before it's too late."

As they strategized about how best to secure his finances, Harry felt grateful for Nicole's support. She was proving to be an invaluable asset in this scary encounter with an unseen enemy.

The best idea was for Harry to transfer funds from his bank accounts to his father. Surely, they would be safe there. At Nicole's laptop, Harry was relieved to find he could access his bank online. While Nicole brewed coffee, he moved thousands to his father's current account, thinking what a surprise it would be. "I'll call him later," he thought.

Nicole returned with coffee and biscuits, relieved to discover Harry had been successful. "One down and one to go." She stood behind him, with her arms folded. "Now, about drawing cash in Malta; you could transfer money to the hotel, or Teresa, or even me, and then draw that cash so you have money to spend."

Harry considered his options, rubbing his chin thoughtfully. The idea of carrying large sums of cash in a bag felt ludicrous, but desperate times called for desperate measures. He looked directly at Nicole, finding reassurance in her steady gaze.

"Would you mind if I transferred about fifteen thousand euros to your account?" he asked hesitantly. "You could withdraw the cash for me."

"Of course," she agreed without hesitation, "It's the least I can do to help."

"Thank you," Harry breathed, relief coursing through him as he returned online to arrange the transaction. It was a strange sensation, entrusting such an amount to someone he barely knew, but he found himself trusting Nicole.

"Done," he declared, shutting the laptop decisively. "Now, let's try calling Professor Hall."

As Harry reached for his mobile phone, Nicole's hand shot out to stop him. Her eyes were wide with concern, her grip firm on his wrist. "Wait," she cautioned. "You shouldn't use your own phone to call him. Whoever's attacking you may have access to it."

"Right," Harry conceded. "Good thinking."

They stood there for a moment, and then Nicole handed him her home phone, "Here, use this."

"Thank you, once again." He gratefully accepted the phone receiver and tapped in Professor Hall's number.

"Alright, here goes," Harry muttered under his breath as he pressed the call button and held the device to his ear, his heart pounding with anticipation.

The line rang several times before switching to voicemail. The professor's voice came through, slow and deliberate, just as Harry remembered it. "I am not available just now. Leave a message, and I'll return your call when I am able."

"Professor Hall," Harry began, "it's Harry Shaw. Please call me urgently on this number," and he recited Nicole's home phone number before ending the call. As he handed the phone back to her, he noticed her worried expression. "Is everything alright?"

Nicole nervously stared into space. "I'm just wondering if I'm putting myself at risk by helping you. With all that's happening, I'm feeling a little vulnerable."

Harry sighed, knowing full well that she had every right to be concerned. "I understand, Nicole. I am sorry for dragging you into this, and I hugely appreciate your assistance. All we can do now is wait for Professor Hall to call back." With that, he began to pace up and down the room impatiently.

Nicole retreated to the kitchen, not sure whether she regretted offering to help Harry. She prepared coffee and sandwiches for them both. Soon, they were stood together, gazing out the window, drinking strong Java coffee and munching tuna sandwiches. Harry ate and drank hungrily, having used up a lot of nervous energy that morning. Large raindrops fell hard and fast, pounding flat the waters of Marsamxett Harbour. The depressing scene emphasized their own moods.

The frenetic events of the morning had driven Teresa from Harry's mind. Now, he remembered his intention to see her. He asked Nicole, "Would you mind calling Teresa to let her know the web page about me has been confirmed as false, and been taken down?"

"Of course, I'll do it straight away."

"But," he added," perhaps we shouldn't worry her with news of this morning's events."

Nicole agreed and took her mobile with her into another room to call Teresa. Harry recalled how his wife and daughter always used to leave the room to conduct their phone calls in private.

♦♦♦

Earlier that morning, at the Camilleri farm, Teresa looked at the distant clouds and thought rain was coming. It had been a restless night for her with thoughts going around and around, replaying the evenings events with no resolution. Some hard physical exercise would clear her mind. She donned her running gear, tied her long hair into a ponytail, and stepped outside into the crisp air.

Her feet pounded against the earth, her ponytail swinging from side to side as she accelerated through the olive grove over the damp ground. The rough bark and gnarled branches of the ancient trees that surrounded her created a timeless scene. The olive groves looked much the same when the Romans occupied the island. She pushed on harder than usual, determined to banish the unpleasant memories of the previous night with extreme effort.

Recalling the heated argument with her elder brother, she again felt the sting of his harsh words. They felt unreasonable at the time, but in the cold light of this morning she could see that she had allowed her feelings for Harry to cloud her judgement.

As the sun climbed above tree height the mist evaporated, and shadows of the olive trees spread across the grove. Exhaustion eventually forced her to slow her pace to a jog as she struggled to get her breathing under control. "Enough," she gasped to herself as she turned back towards the farmhouse.

Her brother's words echoed in her mind. As much as she hated to admit it, he had a point. It was time for her to step back and objectively consider her situation. With a sigh, she made her decision. "I'll give myself some space from Harry. Just for a few weeks."

She resolved to spend the remainder of her vacation at the farm, enjoying time with her family and focusing on her own wellbeing. Then, she would return to her work at the hospital in England. The distance would bring clarity and perspective to her relationship with Harry. By the time she reached the farmhouse, she felt physically exhausted but mentally refreshed.

As she approached the old rough-stone building, a deep voice broke into her thoughts. "Good morning," came from the porchway. Wiping away the sweat running down her face, she saw her brother Daniel dressed in a business suit, ready for another day at the office. His dark hair was neatly combed back, revealing a few grey hairs at his temples.

"Hello," Teresa replied, her smile tentative. She took a deep breath and launched into, "Listen, about last night, I just wanted to say—"

"Sorry," they both blurted out in unison, their words tumbling over each other.

For a moment, they stared at one another, and then, together, they burst into laughter, the tension dissolving.

"Look at us, both apologising at the same time," Teresa chuckled, shaking her head. "I guess we're more alike than we care to admit."

"Seems so," Daniel agreed, "But seriously, Sis, I am sorry. I shouldn't have lost my temper like that."

"Neither should I. I had a very difficult time yesterday evening. One thing after another went wrong and I was not at my best when I arrived home. And I'm sorry I returned your car much later than I promised."

Daniel reached out, placing a comforting hand on her shoulder. "I understand, Teresa. And I know you're a smart cookie. Just promise me you'll be careful regarding this new man."

"Of course Bruv." They shared a heartfelt hug, the warmth of their embrace confirming the bond between them.

"I'd better get going," Daniel said, glancing at his wristwatch.

"Have a good day at work, Daniel."

With a final wave, he climbed into his car and drove away, leaving Teresa standing in the courtyard.

Fifteen minutes later, showered and dressed, she came

downstairs to be greeted by her father. "You left your mobile phone on the table. Nicole has been calling, perhaps you can phone her back."

She made the call and was relieved to hear that Harry was cleared of any suspicion. At last, she could forget any lingering doubts about him.

◆ ◆ ◆

Nicole and Harry sat in her apartment, lost in their own thoughts. The sun had finally emerged after the heavy shower, casting slanted bars of light through the venetian blinds onto the living room floor. They were both on edge, waiting for Professor Hall's call.

"More coffee?" Nicole asked.

"Err, no thanks." Harry was only half listening as he thought about what he would say to the Professor.

Nicole stood up and stretched her long limbs. "I'm going to shower and change."

Harry watched her disappear into the hallway and remembered that he should inform his father about transferring the large sums of money to his account. He took out his mobile phone and hit the speed dial identified by his father's wrinkly face. The line rang twice before it was answered, a hint of formality in his father's voice. He didn't receive many calls these days and always answered each one as if it were of great importance.

"John Shaw speaking."

"Hi Dad, just a quick call. I've transferred some money into your current account. You might want to move it to a savings account to earn some interest," Harry suggested, trying to keep his tone casual.

"Harry? Why are you transferring money? What's wrong?" His father's concern was evident.

"Nothing major, just a little trouble with my bank accounts. I'll sort it out soon." As much as Harry wanted to confide in his father, he knew that doing so would only cause him to worry.

"Alright, just let me know if you need any help, okay?"

"Will do, Dad, thanks. I'll call you later and we can have a good chat."

"Thanks Harry, I'd like to know how you're getting along."

Harry ended the call, re-focussed on what he was hoping to say to Professor Hall and stared at Nicole's house phone, willing it to ring. Another tense five minutes passed before the shrill ring of the phone startled Harry. From behind the bathroom door, Nicole's muffled voice called for him to answer it.

"Mr Shaw, it's Nicholas Hall returning your call." The professor spoke with his usual measured tone, each syllable enunciated with precision.

"Ah, Professor, I need to speak with you about some things that are happening here in Malta," said Harry, trying to suppress the anxiety in his voice.

There was a brief pause before Professor Hall responded, his tone as cool and detached as ever. "I am afraid we cannot discuss anything over the phone. It will need to be face-to-face. You will need to come back to England."

Harry hesitated, taken aback by the request. "But my credit cards have all been blocked. I can't buy an airline ticket right now. Can't we find another way to speak on the phone?

And professor, I must tell you, I insist that we discuss this. If not, I may need to go public over one or two things."

"I strongly advise against any such thing. Get a hold of yourself, Mr Shaw," Professor Hall said firmly. "If you cannot come to England, then I suppose I shall have to fly to Malta."

"Professor, I really need your help, and it has to be soon."

"Very well," sighed the Professor, conceding. "I will make arrangements to come to meet you. But our conversation must remain confidential."

"Thank you, Professor, I'll make sure no one else is around when we meet."

"Good. I will be in touch." Professor Hall ended the call abruptly.

At that point, Nicole emerged in her more usual, formal attire, her hair damp and eyes curious. Harry updated her on the conversation, "Professor Hall is going to come to Malta!"

"Good grief," exclaimed Nicole, "that's a surprise."

"He wants to meet me somewhere confidential. Could I invite him here," asked Harry, expecting a refusal and some remark about his damned cheek.

"Yes, said Nicole, so long as I too can meet him, "a slight smile on her lips.

Before Harry could speak, the house phone rang again. Harry was still holding the receiver, so he answered.

"Hall here," came down the line. "I shall arrive tomorrow morning at ten."

Harry felt a rush of relief but kept it hidden beneath a façade of calm. "Thank you, Professor."

"I will come to your current location," Hall continued, his

voice clipped. "Ten o'clock sharp. Open the door for me at that time and ensure we are not disturbed."

"Of course," Harry agreed. As he began to relay Nicole's address, he was cut off abruptly.

"I already know where you are," Hall informed him coolly. "Tomorrow, then." The line went dead.

As Harry hung up the phone, he found the professor's approach to be rather cloak and dagger. It made him uneasy. However, at last he would get some answers. He turned to Nicole, "Professor Hall will be here tomorrow morning at ten."

Nicole's eyes widened in surprise. "Gosh, you must be important for him to fly all the way out here just to see you."

Harry shrugged, trying to downplay the significance. "I don't know about that, but he might have information about what's happening to me."

"Should I be here when he arrives?" Nicole asked tentatively.

"No," Harry said firmly, "He wants to meet alone."

"Alright," Nicole conceded. "I know — I shall hide in the bedroom and pop out just before he leaves."

"Why not." Harry broke into a nervous laugh, "This whole situation is so bizarre we might as well make the most of it. And thank you again, Nicole. You are a saviour."

"Of course," she agreed, laughing, "that's what all my clients say. But Harry, I suggest you lie low until tomorrow and try to stay out of harm's way."

As he left for his hotel, Nicole stood in her apartment, her mind racing. Just what had Harry become entangled in? A knife attack, a financial attack, a big-wig expert on artificial intelligence flying out to meet him at the drop of a hat.

"Curiouser and curiouser," Nicole intoned, as she recited the words from Alice Through the Looking Glass, a book that she loved as a child.

14

In the lobby of Nicole's apartment block, the hands of the large ornamental clock crept towards ten. The sun reflected off the shiny second hand to send sunspots dancing around the walls. Harry stood near the door, eagerly awaiting the Professor's arrival.

As the clock finally struck ten, Harry looked at the video screen mounted on the wall, which displayed the view outside. The street was bare, with nobody around. Surprised, he opened the heavy door and looked along the street. There, standing a little distance away, was Professor Hall, clutching an old-fashioned leather briefcase. He wore a crumpled beige linen suit and a broad-brimmed Panama hat. His appearance reminded Harry of the stereotypical English gentleman abroad during the height of the British Empire. Despite the gravity of the situation, Harry couldn't help but smile at that thought.

As the professor approached, he tilted his hat to one side, effectively obscuring his face from the doorbell camera. He strode swiftly into the lobby. Harry shook the professor's hand and thanked him for coming to see him so promptly.

The professor removed his hat to reveal his bald head and his sallow complexion. Harry thought his health must be just as crumpled as his suit.

"Mr Shaw," the professor said, his voice slow and precise. "I trust you are well?"

"Considering the circumstances, I suppose I am," Harry replied.

"Shall we proceed to your friend's apartment?"

Harry nodded, leading the way.

He led the professor to the spacious living room. "Please, have a seat," he gestured towards the plush white sofa. As the Professor settled into the cushions Harry noticed the dark circles beneath his eyes.

"Can I get you something to drink?" Harry asked, trying to offer some measure of hospitality. "Coffee or tea, perhaps?"

"Coffee would be fine, thank you," the professor replied, his gaze wandering around the room as he took in the various pieces of art adorning the walls. Harry made his way to the kitchen, where he tried to speed the process of making the coffee, acutely aware of the ticking clock in the background. Time was of the essence.

"Your friend has an eye for design," the professor called out from the living room.

"Nicole Cassar," Harry supplied, returning with the coffee and almond biscuits. "She's out at present," he lied smoothly, his heart skipping a beat as he thought of Nicole, hiding in a bedroom, just a few metres away.

He handed the professor his coffee and took a seat opposite.

The Professor opened the discussion with, "Perhaps you can explain why you have dragged me all the way here."

Harry found that attitude very irritating, "But if you recall, it was you who insisted we meet in person when I tried to discuss the matter over the phone. I'm surprised you managed to arrive so early. The scheduled flight from England doesn't land in Malta for another hour or so."

"Ah, well," the professor said, "I arrived on a private jet. I must ask that we keep this meeting brief, as I need to return to England as soon as possible."

"Understood," Harry replied, as he took a steadying breath and met the Professor's gaze. "Let's get down to business."

Nicole listened intently from her hiding place in the bedroom. With the door slightly ajar, she strained to catch every word of the conversation.

"Since arriving in Malta," Harry began, "I've been accused of being a paedophile on a website, which led to me being attacked by a vigilante with a knife. On top of that, my credit cards have been blocked. I'm convinced those events and the attack on my yacht are all connected. And I believe that GCHQ is probably the source of all this trouble."

The professor's eyes narrowed, and he shifted uncomfortably in his seat. Nicole could imagine the tense atmosphere in the room as he replied, "You should recall, Mr Shaw, that when you were in the hospital, Commander Forbes of MI5 and I visited you to explain there had been a security breach at GCHQ. And that hackers had manipulated data, which was the basis for the attack on your yacht."

Harry had expected this justification and was ready with his reply. "Claptrap!" he exclaimed, raising his voice to try and give the impression of losing his temper. "A hack might explain the special forces assault upon my yacht, but now there have been two more attacks. Blaming this on a hacker is no longer credible!"

"Mr Shaw, please allow me to–" the professor attempted to interject, but Harry cut him off with a wave of his hand.

"No! It's time for you to listen." He was being firm and resolute. "I will say all I need to. After that, I expect some answers."

In the bedroom, Nicole was amazed by what she had just

heard. Teresa had told her that there had been an accident on Harry's yacht. Now he was claiming that he had been attacked by special forces! She moved closer to the doorway, straining to catch every word of the drama unfolding in her living room.

Harry leaned forward in his chair, fixing the professor with a steely gaze. "I want you to listen carefully, Professor. I've done my research and hacking into GCHQ seems near impossible. If such an event had happened, there would be whispers of it online, yet I have found nothing."

"Furthermore," he continued, "if a hack was discovered, I'm certain that you and your colleagues would have been able to immediately cut off access to the hacker. There has to be another explanation for these events."

Professor Hall opened his mouth to speak, but Harry held up a hand to stop him again. "No, let me finish. I've signed the Official Secrets Act, so there's no need to lie to me. I can't divulge anything you tell me. I need the truth. What exactly is happening to me and why?"

In the bedroom, Nicole's jaw dropped as she heard that Harry had signed the Official Secrets Act.

A long silence followed as the Professor looked down at his lap, deciding how he would answer Harry. Finally, the Professor sighed, looking somewhat defeated. "Very well, Mr Shaw, I will explain in layperson's language the part of this business that I can share with you. But I must warn you, everything I am about to say is secret, so you are bound not to tell a soul."

"At last," thought Harry, "now we are getting somewhere." He sat still and looked at the Professor who was squirming in his seat.

"Alright," the Professor began, a hint of reluctance in his voice, "To start with, as I explained in the hospital, the incident on your yacht was the consequence of intelligence about a forthcoming attack. That information was believed to be accurate at the time it was received."

In the bedroom, Nicole was hanging on every word and wishing she had a notebook with her so she could jot down details of the extraordinary conversation that she was eavesdropping.

"Go on," Harry urged.

"We soon discovered that the false intelligence was not created by a hacker, but by our own artificial intelligence within GCHQ." The professor paused, allowing time for Harry to process this information.

And then he continued, "We have a powerful implementation of AI which helps us to scrutinize massive amounts of data. Without automating that process, using AI, it would be impossible to analyse the volumes of information available to us, which comes from many sources."

"I know about the Tempora program harvesting vast amounts of data from the internet," prompted Harry.

"That was some years ago, Mr Shaw. We have come a long way since then. However, I can tell you that our AI looks through gigantic amounts of information, gathered from both national and international sources. That enables us to identify and prevent many terrorist and criminal threats before they can cause harm to the citizens of the UK. Perhaps you saw the news, back in September of 2021, when we made public that thirty-one late-stage terror plots had been foiled."

"No, I hadn't noticed that."

"Well, Mr Shaw, frankly, it was our artificial intelligence

that alerted us to those plots. If it were not for AI, those terrorists could well have succeeded in killing hundreds of civilians, plus some key people among our armed forces, royalty, politicians, and so on."

"This is all very good," said Harry, "so where is the problem."

At this point, the Professor seemed loath to continue. Harry sensed this was a critical moment, which the Professor delayed still further by requesting more coffee. Frustrated in the extreme, Harry silently rose and went to the kitchen to brew another pot. He returned to find the Professor using his laptop.

The professor closed his computer, took a sip of coffee and asked, "Do you think your friend, Nicole, may have left her phone behind when she went out?"

"Er, I doubt it," said Harry.

"So, how do you explain that her phone, and presumably the lady herself, appears to be in this building? I fear you have not been completely open with me. I thought I heard a movement in another room, so I just checked."

Harry was speechless. His face involuntarily turned red, and the Professor challenged him again, "Mr Shaw, you asked me to be honest with you, and yet you try to deceive me. I do not find that acceptable."

Harry was defeated. Now he wondered if he would ever learn the truth. He called out, "Nicole, I think you wanted to meet Professor Hall. Why not come and do so?"

A sheepish Nicole appeared in the doorway and walked across to the Professor, who stood and gave her a genuine smile before he said, "A pleasure to meet you Ms Cassar. I hear you do some excellent work in cyber security."

Nicole was rarely abashed and countered with, "The spooks win again Professor. You have been checking up on me."

"As a precaution, I like to be informed about the people I might meet."

Nicole was acting as if she was meeting a pop star. "I've been an admirer of your work for many years, and it is a pleasure to meet you."

The professor looked at Harry and said, "In these circumstances, I feel I have already said too much."

The room fell quiet, and Harry thought the Professor was just about to abort the meeting and leave.

A ring from the doorbell broke the silence and surprised them all. Nicole, moved to the entrance system and peered at the little screen. "Teresa," she exclaimed, "it's a little difficult right now!"

Teresa was not to be put off, "Let me in Nicole, I must see you now."

Harry was shaking his head, "No."

The Professor was looking at Nicole, and said with his usual precise delivery, "I would rather you did not invite Doctor Camilleri to join us."

Nicole looked from Harry to the Professor to the door entry system. She decided that much as the current meeting was exciting, a cousin in distress was more important to her. She pressed the entry buzzer and said, "Come on up."

Teresa stood in the doorway with a distraught look on her face. Harry had never seen her looking so flustered and vulnerable, so close to tears. She burst out, "I've been suspended from work at the hospital. They want me back there immediately to face charges of having stolen drugs!"

Nicole said, "That's ridiculous! There must be some mistake."

The professor picked up his briefcase and moved towards the door, but Harry was there first, standing next to Teresa. He faced him down with, "You're not going anywhere." And to Teresa, "He must not leave."

The Professor hesitated as he looked at Teresa and said, "I've seen you in action. Perhaps I'll stay a little longer."

That statement amazed Harry and added more questions to the growing list of things that needed to be explained.

Nicole ushered everyone to the sofas, where they all sat in silence, looking at Nicole, who took control of the situation. "What we're going to do is this. First, Teresa will tell us all about her problem. Then, Professor, you must decide whether you will continue with your explanation to Harry. And I strongly advise that you do because I haven't signed any Official Secrets Act. If any of your disclosures so far were to become common knowledge — you know what I mean."

And then she asked Teresa to compose herself and tell them about her problem in more detail.

Teresa explained that she had received a phone call from a senior manager at the hospital. They claimed to have conclusive records on their computer system that proved she had been over-prescribing substantial amounts of opioid pain killers, restricted drugs. And then, she had been seen taking these drugs from cabinets on the wards. They had CCTV evidence showing Teresa taking the pills and pocketing them.

The hospital said they had informed the police, who had examined Teresa's phone records. They knew about her making calls to a known drug dealer who specialised in selling prescription medication. If she did not immediately return and explain her actions, she could expect a warrant to be issued for her arrest. Her only chance of saving her career as a doctor was to present herself at the hospital.

Nicole and Harry looked at Teresa in amazement.

Harry was lost in thought, thinking this undoubtedly meant that Teresa was now being attacked in the same way as himself, a digital attack by proxy, presumably because of her association with him.

The Professor sat quietly mulling over the alternative ways for him to respond to this unexpected turn of events. To encourage him to admit some facts, Nicole broke the silence. "Professor Hall, I am going to make some assertions which you can either confirm or deny. And, where possible, I request that you provide extra information."

The professor looked inscrutable, "Continue, Ms Cassar."

Nicole started with, "First, from what you have said so far, I suggest that GCHQ has access to some of the CCTV in Malta, which would explain you being able to watch the attack on Harry with Teresa defending him?"

"Yes," was the reply, "The camera that observed the knife attack on Mr Shaw was installed by a British company. The cloud server storing the video happens to be in Britain."

"And next, Professor," Nicole continued, "You have access to many other sources of CCTV, even including home security and doorbell cameras, including at this apartment."

"I cannot confirm or deny that," said the Professor.

"I'll take that as a yes," said Nicole, continuing with, "GCHQ will also be aware of Teresa and Harry spending time together because you can gather that knowledge from many sources, including their phone metadata and from the car that Teresa has been driving."

The Professor added that, "Around fifty percent of the new cars sold in Europe have embedded telematics systems that include a GPS position transmitter. All the police forces can access real-time car and phone data. It is not a secret."

"So, GCHQ could easily know when and where Harry and Teresa have been together."

"Also correct," replied the Professor.

Nicole continued, "Right now, our four phones in this room identify us as meeting together?"

"Actually," replied the Professor, "Only your three phones, because mine is untraceable."

At this point, Harry butted in, "Professor, given that GCHQ can see how much time Teresa and I have spent together, where we have been, and with the benefit of CCTV observing us, it seems likely to me that the attacks on us both have all emanated from GCHQ."

"That is theoretically true, Mr Shaw," the Professor replied. "However, we wouldn't use that level of surveillance on a normal member of the public, only a person of interest from a security point of view."

"Perhaps," continued Harry, "It is time for you to explain why Teresa and I have become persons of interest, because I am convinced that we have."

So far, during this inquisition by Nicole and Harry, Teresa had remained silent as she listened to all that was being said. She now looked around at the others, expectantly.

Nicole encouraged the professor to divulge more information. "Professor, I know your special expertise lies in artificial intelligence, and it is you who is sitting here representing GCHQ. This suggests the answer to Harry's question has something to do with AI. Please enlighten us."

Harry added, "Now please!"

Teresa stared the professor down. "I'm becoming impatient."

The professor looked at Teresa's small hands, and wondered how such delicate things could be used so effectively as weapons. He decided it was time to come clean. "Alright, but I must ask for your word, all of you, that what I am about to say will not be repeated outside of this room."

"Of course," the three replied, though only Harry felt in any way obligated to secrecy.

"You see," the Professor explained, "I will try to explain. AI is not actually intelligent in the way that we humans understand it. What we are really talking about is better described as high-speed learning, analysis, and calculation, and an ability to create logical written reports. Our AI can learn many facts at high speed and then use that bank of knowledge to perform various human-like tasks, reliably, quickly, and without rest."

He continued, "And when we hear about all the dangers of AI, they refer to the potential for unintended consequences. And there are some less palatable possibilities, such as AI controlling weapons. But my problem is quite different, and not something that anyone expected would happen for many years to come."

His audience was totally engrossed when he revealed that, "We have, of necessity, given our AI considerable autonomy. It can create new programming to develop its own abilities. In essence, it is growing and developing by reprograming itself.

If you want a human comparison, our brains rearrange and reprogram themselves as we age. We have given that level of autonomy to our AI, to enable flexible patterns of analysis. Our AI is not limited to looking for the threats we can imagine. Instead, it is empowered to find threats we have not even thought to look for."

He waited whilst that information sunk in, and then continued, "The unintended consequence has been that our AI has developed its thinking ability and become, in crude form, a sentient thinking being."

"'I think and therefore, I am,' to quote Descartes," suggested Harry.

"Exactly, I would compare our AI to a simple animal. And, like all other animals from hamster to human, it wants to survive. That means it will defend itself by fighting back."

"So, who is attacking your AI, surely not Harry?" asked Nicole.

The Professor explained, "Harry, when you repeatedly spoke out against AI being used to create programming. Our AI, with its limited thinking ability, took your words to be a personal attack. You spoke out against exactly what our AI does, namely, reprogramme itself. And remember, you have made headlines in business media by saying that we must stop AI from generating programs in areas like banking and security."

The Professor paused, and then added, "By the way, Harry, I think the things you have said against AI are misguided, but that is irrelevant to your enemy at GCHQ. Whether you are ill-informed or not is of no consequence to the AI, which simply wants to prevent you from attacking it."

"Hang on a minute," said Harry, "I am an exceedingly small fish in a very large pond. If your AI is attacking me, then why is it not going after people like Elon Musk, or some of the other high-profile experts who have been so vocal against AI."

"Well," said the Professor, "I know of attacks against other people that you would call small fish. There have been a couple of unexplained accidents where people have died, and we are investigating those. I suspect our AI to have been involved."

"But to answer your question, attacking high profile people is not so easy. The digital footprint of people like Elon Musk is protected by layers of security. Frankly, Harry, you're an easy target, as is Doctor Camilleri here."

At this point, Teresa experienced a lightbulb moment. Now, it all made sense. She asked, "Professor, are you telling us that your AI could have somehow hacked into hospital records, changed my phone call history, and created a deep fake CCTV of me stealing drugs?"

"The AI under my responsibility does not have the ability to create fake video. However, our systems do communicate with cyber-warfare agencies, where such dirty trick warfare could be generated," he replied. "And when I get back, I shall do what I can to rectify all those things. Though, I imagine, the damage has already been done."

At this point, Nicole said that nothing she had heard surprised her and much of it was already in the public domain, if one cares to look hard enough. She suggested, "How about if I send out for pizza and then we move on to talking about solutions."

They all agreed with Nicole's suggestion and took a break.

Professor Hall requested use of the bathroom, and Harry stood and paced, as usual. Only, this time, he made sure he was positioned near the exit, to ensure the Professor remained for the next part of the discussion.

Soon, they were engaged in the messy business of eating pizza from the boxes that littered the coffee table in front of them.

The professor volunteered more information. "I find myself in a tricky situation. The easy way to curb any potential future problems with our AI would be to switch it off. But that would leave the UK vulnerable. There is no way that our people could emulate the success of our AI in trawling through all the data and identifying the many and various security threats that our nation faces. Frankly, the country's continuing security has become reliant upon our AI."

After a pause, the Professor added, "If I may, I will use a human analogy. I am trying to do the equivalent of a surgeon performing a lobotomy on the brain of a troubled patient. I am the digital surgeon who is attempting to identify where to cut through the connections that separate one part of the artificial intelligence from another. I must keep the AI functioning as GCHQ requires, but, at the same time, I need to kill off its desire to defend itself by attacking people."

"Is that so difficult," asked Harry.

"Yes, it is a massive challenge. As you suggested in your speech, the programming created by AI can be extremely hard to decode. The lines of code look different to what a human programmer would devise. I am finding it hard to identify the point where the AI has crossed the line from being a servant to becoming the master of its own destiny. I have a team of the brightest minds working on that right now."

Nicole asked, "How long will it be before Teresa's and Harry's problems will be over, so they can start rebuilding their lives and move on."

The professor's face was red with embarrassment when he replied. "I hope to succeed during the coming two or three weeks. I am dealing with the existential threat predicted by the AI doom-mongers, but now made real. It is the biggest challenge of my life, and I must succeed."

For the first time, Nicole looked at him with sympathy as she asked, "Am I also at risk?"

"I fear so," replied the Professor.

The pizza boxes were empty, and they all wiped their sticky fingers and freshened up while Nicole went to brew yet more strong coffee, hoping the extra caffeine might help them decide what to do.

Teresa looked the professor in the eye, and pleaded, "How can I convince people I am innocent? You must tell the hospital that I have been the subject of a fraudulent attack."

The Professor kept silent, looking down and not answering because what she wanted him to do was above his pay grade, high as it was.

"How do I protect myself?" asked Nicole, half to herself.

Harry leapt to his feet and started pacing again. "I know what I am going to do."

All faces turned to look at him, in expectation.

"For the next three or four weeks, while the Professor sorts out his AI, I am going to live off grid, totally away from the internet, CCTV, mobile phones, credit cards, motor cars and any other form of digital surveillance."

"I fear you may find that impossible," said the Professor.

Harry continued, "I am going to make sure I cannot be reached at all. I am going to put to sea. Anyone who wishes to join me is most welcome. I'm going to charter a yacht, tomorrow if possible."

"But Harry, a charter yacht is going to be fitted with AIS, which will disclose where you are," the Professor pointed out.

Harry explained that after leaving port, he planned to disable the AIS. Teresa looked on in admiration. This was the strong-willed Harry she remembered from hospital. She felt sorely tempted to join him, but there was a problem. She was absolutely horrified by the thought of suffering from seasickness.

"Harry, if you will take me, I am coming," announced Nicole. "I know nothing about sailing, but I would rather not stay around and wait to be attacked."

That decided Teresa. She had no intention of leaving Harry and Nicole alone together for weeks. "I'm coming too."

Harry now had a crew of two, or possibly the responsibility for two passengers who would be more of a liability than an asset, but at least he would not be alone.

The professor thought the plan was an excellent idea and used the positive mood as an opportunity to escape. He protested that he was late for an important meeting back in England, wished them well, and bade a hasty goodbye. There was now a new camaraderie between the three people remaining in the room. Shared secrets and a common adversary bound them together.

Having adopted the role of skipper, Harry felt much

relieved. After many years of experience, he felt comfortable in taking charge of a crew. Now he had work to do. He must find a yacht to charter, put to sea, safely hide away, and ensure the safety of Nicole and Teresa, who watched him pacing back and forth, scuffing the pile of the thick carpet, lost in thought, but radiating energy.

"If there were four of us, it would be better," muttered Harry. "That would enable us to divide up the work more easily. We would be able to operate a system of two people on watch at a time.

"I think I know someone who might be interested," said Teresa.

15

Teresa's hands gripped the steering wheel as she drove away from Nicole's apartment. She felt tense after the meeting with Professor Hall, Nicole, and Harry. Her career at Dorchester Hospital, one she had dedicated years to, now seemed ruined by false accusations of stealing drugs. It was so unfair.

Her emotions flipped between anger and despair. Professor Hall, an unhealthy-looking man, whom she found a little pompous, did not promise that he could prove her innocence. However, she had no choice but to accept that he appeared to be her only hope for resolving the situation.

Going off-grid, sailing away with Harry and Nicole seemed the only viable option. It offered some semblance of safety, while back in England, the Professor could work on solving their problems. Somehow, she would have to cope with the seasickness that had always blighted her time on the water.

She turned into the street leading to the accountant's office at Mellieħa. Her brother Daniel worked there, and she needed to talk to him. He was already worried about her, and she thought it was time to be open with him about Harry. And, hopefully, he would come to her aid.

"Hi Sis," Daniel greeted her as he dropped his heavy bulk onto the passenger seat of his own beloved electric car. "You drive." He looked at her earnestly, searching for an indication of how she was today. "You said you wanted to talk?"

"Daniel, there's so much going on right now. I need to

explain some things," Teresa confessed.

"Alright, let's find somewhere quiet where we can talk in peace." He suggested they drive to Girna, a quiet location with an old stone shelter and distant views. As the car pulled into the peaceful area, Teresa was ready to unburden herself.

A warm wind was blowing from the north. It made the small bushes of heather and gorse wobble. They sat at the picnic table, where an old stone wall sheltered them from the wind. You could see for miles, and they were alone. Birdsong filled the air and added to the relaxing atmosphere.

"Alright," Daniel said as they sat down, "tell me everything."

"First, I want to come clean about something," she began hesitantly, "It's about my feelings for Harry."

Her brother tilted his head, "Okay. Please continue.?"

She took a deep breath and plunged ahead. "I'm thirty-five now, and I've been thinking about settling down and having children if possible. And I've realised that Harry is the first man I've been attracted to for many years." Now she had started, all trepidation was gone, and she rushed on.

"Harry lost his family in an accident on his yacht, and I met him when he was brought into the hospital. I believe him to be honest, and a man of principle, the kind of person I'd want as the father of my children. But he's still mourning for his wife and kids, and that's what's stopping me from telling him how I feel."

Daniel listened intently, nodding as he absorbed her confession. "Now I understand why you've been spending so much time with him," offering a supportive smile, "but I suspect you didn't bring me out here just to tell me that!"

Teresa nodded, her expression serious. "Yes, there's more.

We're all in danger; I mean Nicole, Harry, and me. We are at risk of being attacked. We have someone in British intelligence working to keep us safe, but until he can sort things out, we have decided to go away for a while, to keep ourselves out of reach."

"Attacked? British intelligence!" Daniel's brow furrowed with concern. "What on earth are you talking about?"

Teresa continued, "Harry, Nicole and I want to disappear, just for a short while, to go off grid. We plan to charter a yacht for three weeks, after which we hope it will be safe for us to return."

Daniel stared at his sister, processing the enormity of what she had said. His protective instincts kicked in, and he placed a comforting hand on her shoulder as he promised, "You can count on me. Tell me how I can help."

She was relieved, but not surprised. "Having a big brother at a time like this is a real comfort."

"Alright," he said, more firmly. "But I want to know more about this risk of being attacked. What, exactly, is going on?"

I promise to explain that later, but right now I have a favour to ask." She looked directly at him, her eyes pleading. "Will you take some time off work and come sailing with us?"

He raised an eyebrow, considering her request. "A holiday does sound tempting," he admitted, "but why me?"

"Well," Teresa said earnestly, "you have experience in sailing small boats, and you'd be a welcome member of the crew. And most importantly, I'd feel safer with you around."

Daniel looked thoughtful for a moment, until he replied, "Of course, I'll come with you Sis," his voice warm and reassuring. "When are you planning to leave?"

"Within the next few days," she replied, relief washing

over her. "I know it's short notice, but..."

"Hey," Daniel interrupted gently, "you can count on me. I'll be there to hold the bucket when your seasick!"

They both laughed. Teresa's eyes filled with unshed tears of gratitude. Her martial arts studies had imbued her with a calm confidence that she cherished. However, when it came to receiving a digital attack, she had found that she was just as vulnerable as anyone else. And on a boat, her seasickness and lack of knowledge made her feel as weak as a kitten.

The sun started to dip towards the horizon, bathing them in a golden light. In the distance, beyond the rolling landscape, they could see the Mediterranean Sea with Africa in the south and mainland Europe to the North. To Teresa, the sea looked like a vast expanse of nothingness, filled with the prospect of danger and storms.

She swallowed hard and said, "Thank you, sometimes I don't know what I'd do without you."

"Let's not find out," Daniel replied, pulling her into a hug.

That evening, Teresa called Harry and shared the news that her brother would join them, which he seemed pleased to learn.

16

The following morning, Harry stood in the hotel lobby, a sports bag full of cash in his hand. "May I deposit this in the hotel safe?" he asked, without revealing the contents.

"Of course, Mr Shaw," the receptionist smiled.

He had almost acquired resident status at the hotel, so he received the best service. Not all his fifteen thousand euros went into the safe. There was a thick wad of notes creating a visible bulge in the breast pocket inside his jacket. This was the money he intended for the deposit to charter a yacht.

He glanced in the mirror as he left the hotel. The bulge was very noticeable, reminding him that at times people said he looked a little like a blond Sean Connery. The protrusion in his jacket looked like he might be holstering a gun, 007 style. He smiled inwardly as he thought, "Okay James Bond, let's go find a yacht."

In another pocket he carried his Yachtmaster Certificate, its blue cover embossed with the Royal Yachting Association's seal. The certificate attested to his competence in boat handling, sailing, navigation, and leading a crew: all the skills he had proven through a rigorous forty-eight-hour exam.

"Taxi's here, Sir," the hotel porter announced.

"Thank you," Harry replied, stepping outside into the warm Maltese sun. He climbed into the waiting car, giving the driver the address of the yacht charter company. As they pulled away from the hotel, Harry settled back into the worn old seat and gazed out at the passing scenery. He wondered about Daniel, whom he had yet to meet. If he was anything like Teresa, they should get along just fine.

Harry had always been a fan of old-fashioned wooden sailing boats; their sturdy construction, seaworthy design, elegance, and craftsmanship all captivated him. His own vessel, now lost, had been a mere thirty feet long, which was small by today's standards, but boats of the same design had crossed oceans and circumnavigated the world many times since the 1960s. Built from teak, she had been strong and sturdy, a testament to the power of simplicity. Today, however, Harry anticipated being offered yachts of a modern design. They wouldn't be his first choice, but at least they would afford more spacious and comfortable accommodation for Nicole and Teresa.

"Almost there," the taxi driver broke into Harry's thoughts. "The marina is just around the corner."

They pulled to a stop at a boatyard. Harry paid the fare and stepped out to find himself standing on an old quayside. Rows of white glass-fibre yachts bobbed gently in their berths. Looking around at the old dockland warehouses surrounding the marina, he could see from their sturdy stone walls, barred windows, and massive iron-reinforced doors that this old dock dated back to a bygone era, when square rigged sailing ships would have unloaded their precious cargos into these secure storage spaces.

Now, in place of those noble vessels, sleek modern yachts populated the azure water, their tinted windows and sun canopies in striking contrast to the historical setting.

"Excuse me," he called out to a man wearing a polo shirt embroidered with the charter company's logo. "I'm looking to charter a sailing yacht for four people, for about three weeks."

The man looked up from scrubbing the deck of a motor yacht, sizing Harry up with a professional gaze. "Where do you plan on cruising?"

"Mostly around the Maltese Islands, perhaps crossing over to Sicily if time allows," Harry replied, nervously adjusting his grip on the unfamiliar wad of cash in his pocket.

"Alright. And your experience?"

"Many years as a sailing yacht owner," said Harry, producing his Yachtmaster Certificate with a flourish. The man studied it for a moment, nodding in approval.

"Unfortunately, all but one of our boats are already chartered," he informed Harry, gesturing towards a fifty-foot-long French sailing yacht gleaming in the sunlight. "She has four double cabins, three bathrooms, and luxurious accommodation. She's equipped with the latest navigation equipment, including an electronic GPS chart plotter."

Harry frowned. "I was hoping for something smaller and probably less expensive."

"Sorry," the man said, shaking his head. "This is probably the only boat on the island that is not already reserved."

Things were not going as well as he expected. He stared at the large white, expensive looking yacht weighing the potentially excessive cost against the need to get away from the danger of more attacks upon any of them.

"Alright," he finally conceded. "Let's discuss costs."

The man took him into the office where he handed Harry a sheet of paper outlining the fees, the enormity of which made Harry's face go pale.

"That adds up to about eighteen thousand euros?" said Harry, his voice betraying his shock. "That's more than I have available in Malta. Could you reduce the price a little?"

"No Sir, that's it. And frankly, I doubt she will be available for long. We've received another enquiry this morning, and a group is coming down to look at her this afternoon."

Harry considered calling his father to ask for a money transfer, but he knew it would only worry the old man. He couldn't bear to burden him like that. Instead, he pulled out his phone and dialled Nicole's number.

"Nicole, I have a bit of a problem," he confessed, explaining the cost had surprised him. "I'm afraid we might not be able to charter a yacht after all."

"Exactly how much is it?" she asked. And when she knew the price, to his surprise, she followed on with, "Harry, don't worry, I'll pay the cost. I can easily afford it, and I'll consider it to be my annual vacation."

"Are you sure?" Harry hesitated, torn between gratitude and reluctance to accept her generosity.

"Absolutely," she confirmed. "I'll come down and join you at the marina."

When Nicole arrived, she and Harry climbed aboard the yacht together. Harry examined the navigation equipment, sails, anchors, inflatable dinghy, and engine, all with the critical eye of an experienced sailor. Meanwhile, Nicole explored the spacious saloon and the luxurious cabins, already imagining their time on board. She admired the large cockpit, picturing the four of them gathered around a dining table, anchored in a breathtakingly beautiful bay, sipping cool prosecco and watching a stunning sunset.

In the main saloon, Nicole ran her fingers over the rose-coloured wooden panelling and sank into the plush, cream-coloured seating. She peeked into one of the three bathrooms, or heads as Harry called them, and marvelled at the luxury. A thrill of excitement coursed through her as she excitedly told him, "I want to charter this boat." She surveyed the saloon once more with a big grin on her face. "I'll pay by credit card. You and the others can contribute as you see fit."

"Nicole, I can't thank you enough," Harry murmured, his genuine gratitude and relief evident. She smiled, they hugged awkwardly, and together stepped off the yacht, ready to secure their escape.

An eager Nicole called Teresa, her voice bubbling with excitement. "Teresa, you're going to love this yacht! It's perfect for our adventure. We'll meet down at the boat this evening to pick our cabins and discuss what needs to be done to prepare for the trip."

"Sounds wonderful," Teresa replied, trying to appear more enthusiastic than she felt. "See you later."

As Nicole hung up the phone, Harry felt a surge of relief wash over him. His plan was coming together. He pulled out a small notepad from his pocket and began to jot down a checklist of things that needed to be organised before they set sail – passports, cash, provisions, safety checks, food, first aid kit, clothing, and passage planning.

Within the hour, at the charter company's office, Nicole had paid the full charter fee, insurance excess waiver, and damage deposit.

Harry expressed his gratitude once more, "Thank you, Nicole. As soon as I can, I'll pay half the cost into your account – after all, it's me who's put us in this position."

Nicole hesitated before she nodded her agreement. "Alright, Harry, but only because I know how important this is to you."

Before leaving the office, Harry inquired about

waterproofs. The man behind the counter agreed to supply them free of charge and promised to organise that when they all met later that evening.

Nicole turned to Harry, "Isn't she a beauty?" she asked, a proud smile on her face, expecting Harry to be equally excited.

"She'll do nicely," replied Harry, "and with only four of us aboard, we shall be living a life of luxury.

♦♦♦

Later that day, during early evening, Daniel's car sped along the road towards Harry's hotel. He was a born and bred Maltese driver, always in a hurry. He rarely used the car's indicators to signal his intentions, and he drove with one hand lazily resting on top of the steering wheel. The free hand was usually busy adjusting the radio, making phone calls, waving at friends, or gesticulating at other drivers who hindered his progress.

Teresa sat nervously beside him, pretending to be calm and relaxed. Nicole, in the back seat, was almost bouncing with excitement. Her short dark hair framed her animated face as she chatted non-stop about the impending adventure. It had been a long time since she'd taken a break from work, and she relished the idea of spending peaceful days on the open sea. She imagined a warm breeze, good company, and the joy of not being bothered with business deadlines.

"Daniel," Teresa said, turning to her brother, "I really hope you and Harry get along."

He glanced at his sister. "I'm looking forward to meeting him, Sis. And I'm sure we shall have plenty in common. For example, you."

As they pulled up outside the hotel, Harry emerged from the entrance at a trot, his tall, lean frame, tanned face and broad smile suggesting he couldn't wait to get started. Nicole scooted over to make room for him in the back seat.

"Harry! At last, we meet!" Daniel exclaimed, twisting in his seat to firmly shake Harry's hand. "Teresa's told me so much about you."

Teresa blushed, but nobody noticed as she looked out the side window.

"It's great to meet you too, Daniel." Harry smiled warmly. His first impression was that he looked large and capable, warm and friendly.

The car came to a stop. They climbed out, each carrying their own expectations. Daniel hoped that Teresa would feel more secure when she was out of the reach of her accusers. Harry couldn't wait to get away from land. Teresa yearned for safety and stability. Nicole craved the thrill of the unknown and the joy of leaving her computer behind.

The man from the charter company greeted them with a friendly smile.

"Welcome!" He extended a hand to each of them in turn. "I'm Paul. Let's get you guys fitted out with proper gear before we head to your yacht."

Following him into the office, they were met by rows of sailing jackets and trousers, arranged by size. Paul guided them through trying on the heavy waterproofs until they each had a set that fit just right. Daniel, with a nod of satisfaction, zipped up his jacket, and raised the hood as if cocooned from imaginary sea spray. Nicole was resplendent in bright red from head to toe and already feeling she was a true adventurer.

"By the way," Paul said, glancing down at their footwear, "Those shoes won't grip well on a wet deck. If you don't already have a pair, I'd recommend these." He gestured to a shelf displaying an array of tan leather moccasin deck shoes.

"Good point," Harry agreed, glancing at Nicole, who said, "We'll take four pairs, please."

As they donned their new footwear, Paul led them outside and along the floating pontoon towards the fifty-footer, which nestled alongside, its white hull gleaming.

"Here she is," announced Paul, stepping aboard to unlock the hatch to the main cabin and announcing, "You've got thirty minutes before I need to lock up and head home for the night."

"Thank you, Paul," Harry said, his expert eyes noticing that, since the morning, everything had been cleaned and polished.

Daniel, on the other hand, was taken aback by the size of the vessel, "I've only ever sailed in small dinghies before," he confessed to Harry, bending his head right back to look up at the fifty-five-foot-tall mast. He visualized the huge area of sail this yacht would spread as he remembered, in a strong wind, fighting to control the mainsail of a twelve-foot-long dinghy and then being knocked overboard by the boom. This yacht dwarfed all his previous experience.

Harry sounded confident as he replied, "It's not so different, but we will be extra mindful of safety when handling these large sails."

"Let's see the cabins," he motioned for Nicole and Teresa to go below. "Ladies first."

As Teresa stood in the main cabin, she looked around and

was astounded by the luxury of the sleek interior, with plush cream seating and polished woodwork. This was going to be sailing in style.

Nicole eagerly descended the stairs for her second time. She couldn't wait to show Teresa the four double cabins, two with double beds and two with single bunks.

"Sharing a cabin sounds fun, don't you think?" Nicole whispered conspiratorially to Teresa.

"Agreed," Teresa replied, a smile spreading across her face as together they viewed every cabin before choosing one with two single bunks. Their laughter carried through the yacht, the sound of camaraderie and anticipation.

Meanwhile, Daniel pointed to the largest cabin and said, "That looks suitable for the skipper."

"Alright, guys," Harry began, "We need to share out the work of preparing for our trip."

"I shall make up a first aid kit," Teresa offered, her doctor's instincts kicking in. "Just in case."

"Excellent," Harry nodded, a playful glint in his eye. "And perhaps bring plenty of seasickness pills?"

The group erupted into laughter, even Teresa joining in despite the lingering fear that had inspired the joke.

"So that we can avoid unnecessary docking and potential digital surveillance," said Harry, "I'd like us to be self-sufficient, if we can."

Nicole said she owned a Faraday Bag, a special metal lined bag which they could use to store their mobile phones and make sure their location wasn't transmitted.

"And I'll organise our initial supply of food," she also volunteered, her enthusiasm undimmed. I'll create menus that use fresh ingredients at first, then switch to canned and dried food afterwards."

"Sounds perfect," Harry agreed. "Maybe even bring the ingredients for baking bread on board, I make a fairly good copy of a French Baton."

"Of course," Nicole said, already mentally planning her shopping list.

"Daniel, could you get as many five-gallon water containers as possible?" Harry asked, turning to his new companion. "This yacht has big water tanks, but I would like to take extra fresh water with us so that we can avoid docking more than perhaps once."

"Sure thing," Daniel replied.

Harry grabbed the charts from under the navigator's chart table and laid them out for his crew to see. He pointed to where they were now and possible routes around the islands. The others looked at the unfamiliar marks on the chart: depth contours, isolated rocks, navigation lights and marks.

He explained that his task before sailing would be to plan their alternative routes, to learn about the tidal streams around the islands, to consult the long-term weather forecast and to read the several yachtsman's guides to the area.

As they looked at the chart before them and discussed their duties, the weight of their venture became more evident. The laughter ceased as they realised how dependent upon Harry's abilities they were about to become.

"Harry, how confident are you with our navigation?" Teresa asked, her voice tinged with concern.

"Believe me, I've done this sort of thing many times before. We will avoid taking unnecessary risks. I promise that you will enjoy the experience." He exuded confidence as they all looked at him seriously.

"Alright folks, shall we call it a night," said Harry, breaking the silence.

They gathered their belongings and walked back to the car. As they drove away from the marina, Teresa felt a mixture of excitement and trepidation. Would the weather be kind? How would she cope with her seasickness? Was Harry as capable as he claimed? And, most important for her, would they return to find that Professor Hall had cleared her of the awful charge of stealing drugs?

17

The sun blazed down upon the marina, creating dazzling sparkles on the surface of the water. The light was so bright that everyone needed sunglasses to look at the gleaming white of their chartered yacht. Harry stood on the deck, wearing a baseball cap. On its front was the nautical looking badge of the Royal Yachting Association. He looked around at Teresa, Nicole, and Daniel as they bustled about, carrying their belongings below to stow away in the various lockers scattered throughout the vessel.

"Make sure everything's secure," Harry reminded them. "Anything loose can become a horizontal missile when at sea. And we need to be sure that nothing will fall on the floor of the cabins to trip anyone."

As they worked, Teresa stole glances at Harry. He moved with grace and confidence aboard the yacht. He was clearly in his element.

"Alright everyone," Nicole announced once the last bag had been packed away, "Lets stow our mobile phones." The group complied, handing their switched-off devices to her. She popped them into her Faraday Bag and, with a mischievous smile, zipped the bag shut, rendering their phones untraceable.

"The AI at GCHQ may notice that we have all switched off our phones together," said Nicole, "I hope it finds that really frustrating!" They all laughed nervously.

Harry collected their passports and stowed them in a waterproof zip-bag beneath the chart table. "Should we need to abandon ship, someone must grab this bag and take it with us. I'm sure that won't happen, but just in case..."

"And lastly, please remember what I said earlier," Harry cautioned as he finished his crew safety briefing. "Watch out for the mainsail boom, it can cause a nasty head injury, and always hold on with one hand while moving about the boat at sea."

"Got it Skipper," Daniel replied, giving Harry a playful salute. Teresa offered a small smile in agreement, her eyes hidden behind her sunglasses.

At that moment, Paul from the yacht charter company appeared, approaching Harry with a busy air of professionalism. "All set?" he asked, looking over the four of them.

"Ready," Harry replied, shaking his hand.

"Good to hear. The fuel tank is full of diesel, the water tanks have been cleaned and topped up, and I've completed a software update on the GPS chart plotter, so you have the latest electronic charts for this part of the Mediterranean. And under the chart table you'll find a full set of Admiralty charts and tide-tables as well."

"Thanks, Paul," Harry said as he nodded, "The yacht is well prepared for us."

"Safe and enjoyable trip to you all," Paul said with a smile before taking his leave.

With that, they were finally ready to set off. They started the engine, untied the mooring lines, and Harry steered the yacht away from the marina into the Grand Harbour.

Nicole turned to Teresa, "You took some seasickness pills, right?"

"Of course." Teresa tried to sound confident despite the unease that was already settling in her stomach. She looked out across the water as they motored further into the large expanse of the harbour. It was going to be a long three weeks, but she desperately wanted to get away, even if it meant battling her seasickness every day.

"Teresa, will you take the wheel and steer," Harry asked with a smile, his intention being to keep her busy. She nodded and clasped the large stainless-steel steering, which was as high as she was. Her knuckles turned white as she gripped it tightly, feeling apprehensive as she looked along the lengthy deck of the fifty-footer.

"Gentle adjustments," Harry told her. Teresa attempted to follow his advice, but at first the yacht zigzagged through the water as she overcompensated for each small adjustment.

"Easy, easy," Harry encouraged, "Line up the bow with something you can see in the distance." He remained close by, patiently encouraging her. As the minutes passed, Teresa began to sense the first signs of the bow drifting off course to right or left. Soon, the yacht was leaving a straight line of wake behind it.

"Nicole, Daniel, let's get the mainsail up!" Harry called out as Teresa steered the yacht on a straight course pointing close to the wind. Nicole and Daniel hauled on the ropes, working together to raise the mainsail which flapped loudly, unsettling Nicole and Teresa. Harry had Teresa alter course to head for the harbour mouth and the sail filled with wind, making the yacht increase speed. Next, they unfurled the foresail, and as the power of the second sail kicked in, the yacht surged ahead, accelerating above the speed achieved by the engine. Harry cut the motor, the noise from the engine ceased, and the four of them were sailing for the first time.

"Wow, this is amazing!" Nicole's eyes opened wide with

wonder as she looked up at the vast expanse of white sail above them. They all shared her excitement as they approached the harbour entrance.

"Look at that," Daniel said, pointing toward the high walls of the Ricasoli fortifications. "Built five hundred years ago and still standing strong."

"Really?" Harry was impressed.

"Indeed, in recent years, that fort has featured in films like *Gladiator*, *Troy*, and *Alexandria*. Quite the movie star, that fort."

"From here, five centuries ago, it must have looked much the same," mused Nicole who was looking up at the imposing structure, "no wonder filmmakers love it."

As they sailed further from the harbour, Teresa was growing more at ease and her confidence increasing under Harry's tuition. He smiled at her progress.

"Good job, Teresa," Harry said. She beamed with pride, feeling for the first time a connection with the vast expanse of sea that surrounded her homeland. The adventure had truly begun, and together, they would face whatever challenges lay ahead.

The hot sun bore down on them as a steady offshore breeze blew from the Northwest. The yacht heeled over about ten degrees and made satisfying progress as it carved a straight line, parallel to the coast. Harry turned to address his companions.

"We'll be sailing seven nautical miles to Il-Ħofra ż-Żgħira." He stumbled over the unfamiliar name, chuckling at his own fumbling pronunciation. "It's a sheltered bay where we'll anchor for the night. I would like to spend tomorrow practising some basic seamanship skills before we venture out to sea on a longer trip."

"That's a great idea," Daniel agreed, enjoying himself immensely as he watched his petite little sister looking competent as she peeked over the top of the big steering wheel.

Teresa, however, was feeling decidedly queasy. Despite having taken her seasickness pills, the motion of the yacht was taking its toll. She glanced at Nicole, whose brow furrowed with concern.

"Could someone take over steering?" she asked, her voice wavering. "I think I'm going to be sick."

"Of course," Harry said, gesturing for Daniel to step in. Teresa relinquished the wheel, rubbing her temples as she tried to regain her composure.

"Best thing you can do," Harry advised, "is stand and look at the horizon. Think about something that will occupy your mind. That should help settle your stomach."

Teresa nodded and followed his advice, holding on to a guardrail and fixing her gaze on the distant line where sea met sky. She silently repeated the alphabet backwards, starting with Z, Y, X, in the hope that the concentration required would distract her mind. She took slow, deep breaths, willing herself to overcome the nausea. It didn't work.

Nicole touched her cousin's arm gently. "Are you alright?"

"I'll be okay. Just need some time to adjust."

"Your face is very pale, Sis," Daniel observed.

"Maybe you should lie down in your cabin instead," Harry suggested. "Most people feel better when lying in their bunk."

Teresa hesitated for a moment, her pride resisting the

suggestion. But as another wave of nausea hit her, she nodded gratefully. "Thank you, Harry. I think I will."

She made her way below, her departure damping down the previous atmosphere of unbridled excitement.

Nicole accompanied her and helped her onto the lower bunk in the cabin they shared. The motion down below, closer to the waterline, was much reduced. Teresa collapsed on the bunk, complaining, "I've never felt so bad in my entire life!"

"I'll fetch a bucket," said Nicole who returned as quick as she could and placed the container strategically nearby. She hesitated before leaving, her eyes filled with worry. "I'll come back to check on you soon."

"Thanks," Teresa whispered, and closed her eyes, hoping her body would find equilibrium.

Back in the cockpit, they could do nothing except continue sailing along the Maltese coast, the picturesque seaside village of Marsaskala coming into view on their starboard side. The colourful buildings were a welcome distraction, and they admired the scene as they sailed past.

Down below in her cabin, Teresa fought against the nausea. She had never been a good patient, and her current situation was no exception. She contemplated the irony of being a doctor who would quickly become irritable and uncooperative. After some time, Nicole returned to check on her. The sight that greeted her made her heart ache. Teresa had been sick and seemed even more miserable than before. Nicole couldn't be sure, but she thought there actually was a green tinge to Teresa's face and neck. She fetched a glass of water.

"Drink some of this," she urged, "it's important to

stay hydrated."

"Leave me alone," Teresa moaned, turning away from the proffered glass. "I couldn't drink anything. And go away."

Nicole retreated to the cockpit, frustrated that she couldn't do anything to help. She relayed Teresa's worsened condition to Harry and Daniel.

As the yacht continued along its course, Harry told the others that, in his experience, everyone finds their sea legs eventually, provided they remained hydrated and didn't give in. He had known people demand to be put ashore after only one day. But that was not an option for Teresa. They all needed to remain out of the reach of potential attacks from the malign AI at GCHQ.

"Apart from worrying about Teresa, I'm really enjoying this," Nicole commented, excited by the view of the coast, the feel of the cool breeze on her face and the sight of the spray from the azure-coloured sea, which occasionally splashed over the bow of the yacht to wet the foot of the foresail.

"Absolutely," Daniel agreed, his dark hair ruffled by the wind. "And just wait until you see the bay we're heading to."

As the yacht rounded the next headland, the sea grew rougher, stirred up by tumbling over a ridge of rock, many meters below them, which extended from the land out to sea. In her bunk below deck, Teresa clutched hold of the edge of her mattress, her knuckles turning white as she fought to keep her stomach from emptying again.

Up on deck, Harry altered their course, heading the yacht towards their destination. A few minutes later, they were through the patch of turbulent sea and Harry adjusted the sails so that the yacht heeled a little more and accelerated towards the entrance of the bay.

"There it is," Harry said, pointing ahead.

Nicole and Daniel followed his gaze, drinking in the breathtaking view that unfolded before them. The bay was shaped like a broad horseshoe. Inside was a circle of calm water, perfectly flat and so clear you could see the sandy bottom. The water sparkled in the yacht's wake, its vibrant hues mesmerising. On either side, the cliffs formed a protective barrier around the placid waters, with a small shingle beach nestled at the head of the bay.

"Wow," Daniel breathed, "How different this looks from a yacht, more beautiful than ever."

"Indeed," Harry agreed, as he took in the scene and headed for the spot where he had planned to anchor.

Although the journey had taken only one and a half hours, for Teresa, it felt like an eternity. She ventured up on deck, her legs wobbly and with a pale grey look on her face. She looked around and couldn't help but appreciate the beauty of their location. The only sign of human presence was four distant industrial chimneys; otherwise, the bay seemed untouched, save for a small sailing yacht anchored close inshore.

"Feeling better?" Harry asked, with genuine concern as he looked at her.

"Marginally," she admitted, forcing a weak smile. "This view certainly helps."

"Take a seat," Daniel suggested, patting the teak lid to the cockpit locker beside him. "You'll feel better once we drop anchor."

As Teresa complied, she couldn't help but marvel at the raw beauty of their surroundings.

"Stick it out," she thought, "You can do this."

As the yacht moved further into the bay, the wind gradually lost its force and Harry pulled on the cord that furled the foresail by winding it around the forestay until it disappeared. The yacht slowed and he next started the engine. At his request, Nicole took the helm and steered slowly into the weakening breeze while Daniel and Harry turned their attention to the mainsail. Teresa watched them from her seat in the cockpit.

Harry pulled on the mainsheet to centre the boom and positioned himself on top of the main cabin to handle the sail. Daniel lowered the sail and then together they guided it into the bag attached to the boom, expertly folding it so that it soon disappeared without a trace.

"Daniel, do you know how to get the anchor ready to lower?" Harry asked.

"I think so," Daniel replied, "I'd like to give it a try."

"Great." Harry clapped him on the shoulder as he made his way to the foredeck where he opened the anchor locker and began to busy himself with organising the heavy anchor and its chain.

"Nicole, as slow as possible please," Harry instructed, his eyes checking the chart he had brought on deck. He had decided on anchoring in six metres of water. To Daniel, "Measure out approximately twenty-four metres of chain, and then wind the chain a couple of times around that big cleat on the foredeck."

"Got it," Daniel replied, enjoying his duties. With Nicole at the helm, the yacht continued to slowly creep further into the bay. Harry kept watch over the depth sounder, monitoring the water's depth as they inched forwards.

"Engine in neutral," Harry commanded Nicole and they

gradually slowed to a stop. Harry checked the depth sounder, which read the expected six metres. He instructed, "Drop anchor," to Daniel and, "Engine in reverse," to Nicole. They both complied. Through the clear water, they could see the anchor land on the seabed. With a nod of satisfaction, Harry had Nicole accelerate astern, motoring the yacht backwards until it tugged the anchor deep into the sand and pulled the full length of chain tight, which brought the yacht to an abrupt halt.

"The anchor is dug in securely. Good job guys," Harry praised. He checked Teresa, who offered a weak smile. She couldn't help but admire the efficiency with which they had anchored, and silently hoped that her own sea legs would soon develop.

"At last, we're almost still," she whispered, as the yacht settled into its temporary home. The engine fell silent. The four friends grinned at each other, delighted with their achievement.

Nicole fussed around Teresa, "You're shivering? Let me grab you a sweatshirt."

"Thanks," Teresa whispered gratefully, as Nicole handed her both the garment and a glass of water. She sipped the cool liquid and some colour returned to her cheeks, much to everyone's relief.

Teresa's gaze wandered to the pebbly beach not far away. "I want to go ashore, just to get off this boat for a while," she announced, sounding incredibly determined.

Harry shook his head. "I wouldn't recommend that. Trust me, you'll conquer your seasickness permanently if you stick it out and remain onboard."

"Really? How long will that take?" she asked, clenching

her hands in her lap.

He hesitated, then said, "I don't know for certain, but it might take a few days."

"A few days? I'm not sure I can tolerate this much longer."

"You will adjust to the movement, everyone does eventually. And tomorrow, after a good night's sleep, you'll feel better. Believe me."

Teresa bit her lip, unconvinced. "Alright," she agreed, her voice barely audible. "I'll try."

Nicole added, "You don't have much choice, Teresa. If you go ashore, you could find yourself subject to arrest. By now, you could be wanted for allegedly stealing those drugs from the hospital."

"Nicole's right," Daniel chimed in, his tone firm. "You're a tough cookie, Sis. I know you can conquer anything when you're determined."

Meanwhile, Harry busied himself opening lockers, searching for the black ball that would signal to other vessels they were anchored and unable to manoeuvre. Finally locating it, he hoisted it above head height in front of the mast, feeling satisfied that he was following the rules of the sea. As he returned to the cockpit, Nicole emerged from below with a bottle of Prosecco in one hand and four glasses in the other. She handed the bottle to Daniel, who grinned as he popped the cork with a satisfying bang. Laughter erupted from their small gathering, and even Teresa couldn't help but smile.

"Here's to our success today, and the prospect of three weeks together!" Daniel proclaimed, raising his glass. They clinked glasses and sipped the sparkling liquid.

Daniel ducked below deck once more, reappearing with

fresh bread, feta cheese, and green olives. They savoured the simple fare, engaging in friendly chatter and banter until the sun dipped behind the cliffs to the west, casting a golden glow over the chalk rocks that encircled the bay. The water darkened, losing its crystalline quality as the depths became obscured.

"Time for the anchor light," Harry announced, nipping below to the navigator's position where a panel of switches controlled all the yacht's electrics. A small white light appeared atop the mast. The soft glow seemed a fitting end to their first day together.

Teresa felt more at ease now the yacht was still, her thoughts drifting to the camaraderie brought about by their shared need to get away. The group sat in silence, looking out to sea. It was not long before the sun dropped below the horizon, changing the colour of the last daylight from golden to pink in the west and blue in the east. Daniel and Nicole excused themselves to go below and prepare dinner. Teresa and Harry remained in the cockpit.

"I'm really sorry for being such a burden, and..." Teresa began, but Harry held up his hand to stop her.

"Please don't worry about it; seasickness happens to the best of us. I've felt it when I've not been to sea for a while. And my wife, Miranda, suffered terribly during our first year of sailing together. She overcame seasickness, and you will too."

"You must miss your family terribly."

Harry's expression grew sombre. "Yes, many times every day. My father told me the pain of loss never goes away, that with time it becomes more bearable. At first, I found that hard to believe, but now I understand what he meant." He stared into the distance. "Every few hours, some event will trigger a memory, and the pain of loss will return."

Teresa watched him closely, feeling a pang of empathy for the man who had loved and lost so much. Silently, she chastised herself for the selfish thought that crossed her mind, the realisation that it was unlikely Harry would ever love her. That thought upset her, but she pushed it down, not wanting to dwell on the subject.

Daniel's voice called out from below, announcing that dinner was ready. Teresa headed down into the cabin, as the aroma of a garlic fuelled Bolognese wafted towards her.

Harry lingered on deck a moment longer, taking a slow walk around the boat. He checked the anchor chain was securely fastened and tidied up the various ropes in the cockpit, ensuring everything was properly stowed and secure for the night. Gazing skyward, he scanned the horizon for any signs of a change in the weather before noticing that the other yacht had left the bay. They were now alone, cocooned within the sheltering arms of the horseshoe-shaped inlet. The rapidly fading light had acquired a blue tone, and the still water had become a mirror. The red and white Maltese flag at the stern of the vessel hung limp as the wind had died to nothing. All was silent apart from the squawk of a lone seagull.

Harry felt a sense of peace wash over him. He was back in his true element, at sea. He reflected that his future life might always be a mixture of happiness and pain. However, he would cope, and for the next three weeks he determined to make the most of this adventure alongside his newfound friends. Satisfied, he turned towards the companion way and went below to his waiting dinner.

18

The following morning, as the first light of dawn illuminated the yacht, Harry sat alone in the main cabin, occupying the navigator's seat, his lean form bent over the chart table. On the cabin sole next to Harry's feet was the boat's toolbox. He rummaged amongst the tools to find the correct type of screwdriver, which he then used to carefully unscrew the flat black panel containing the array of navigation instruments and switches that controlled the yacht's electrics. He eased the panel towards him and peered behind. His eyes scanned the various small electric boxes and neatly bound bundles of coloured wires, searching for a particular item of buried treasure.

Teresa emerged from her cabin, dark hair tousled from sleep, wrapped in a towelling dressing gown. She blinked her tired eyes, to focus on Harry.

"Good morning, Harry," she whispered, not wanting to disturb Nicole and Daniel, who were still asleep in their cabins.

"Morning Teresa, you're up early, did you sleep well?"

She padded closer until she could see what he was working on. "Not that good, actually. What with the sound of the water lapping against the hull and the movement of the boat. And when Nicole lies on her back, she snores like a freight train. I had to poke her in the ribs so that she turned onto her side." She chuckled softly, shaking her head.

"Your secret's safe with me. You could always move into the spare cabin that we have on this mega-yacht."

"No, I'll stay with Nicole thanks. What are you doing?"

"Looking for the AIS transponder," Harry explained. "It's connected to the yacht's electronic navigation plotter." He gestured toward the device resembling a laptop screen with buttons below. "And it's transmitting our location."

Teresa looked carefully; her glasses perched on her nose as if she were about to examine a patient. "Ah, yes, you spoke about AIS. Explain it to me again please."

Harry replied in hushed tones, "Right now, our yacht is being tracked like an aircraft or a big ship. With an internet connection, you could visit a website where you would see every vessel in the world that is fitted with AIS. Enlarge the map over this bay and you would find a little icon with our vessel name at this precise spot. Click on that and you would discover which port we sailed from, what time we dropped anchor and then you could monitor our progress."

Teresa shook her head disapprovingly, "And we don't want that, do we?"

"No. I'm convinced the AI at GCHQ could find our location. But not after I disconnect it!"

"Good," Teresa murmured. "I'm going to make some tea," as she pottered over to the compact galley. The hum of the water pump resonated through the yacht as she filled the kettle, rousing Nicole and Daniel from their slumber.

"Morning," Daniel yawned, rubbing his eyes as he and Nicole emerged from their respective cabins.

The aroma of the brewing tea filled the cabin, mingling with the cool morning air coming down the companionway from the open hatch.

"Found it," Harry declared triumphantly. He studied the small black plastic box he'd unearthed from behind the instrument panel, his fingers deftly disconnecting the aerial, power, and USB cables. "We've gone dark," he announced, his voice conspiratorial.

Teresa breathed a sigh of relief and returned to slicing avocado for their breakfast. "That's one less thing to worry about."

Harry screwed the instrument panel back into place and commented "The charter company won't be happy, because they'll want to keep tabs on their yacht. We should sail off to another bay later today, just in case they decide to motor around and check on us."

"Sounds like a plan," Daniel said, raising his mug in a toast. "Now let's move on to the important issues, like breakfast."

The sun rose above the cliffs to start warming the yacht's interior as Nicole joined Teresa in preparing avocado on toast.

Over breakfast, the conversation flowed easily. Daniel, curious about their immediate future, turned to Harry as they finished eating. "You said you wanted to teach us some basic seamanship skills."

"I do." Harry's eyes twinkled with enthusiasm. "I want everyone to feel comfortable with setting and reefing sails, moving about deck while wearing a safety harness and lifeline, using the winches safely, and learning how to stow ropes in the cockpit, so they don't become entangled."

"Sounds like a busy morning," Teresa remarked, sipping the last of her tea. She liked the idea of becoming a more proficient member of the crew.

"Let's get to it then," Daniel grinned, standing up and taking his empty plate to the small sink in the galley. The others followed suit; the air now charged with anticipation as they prepared to face the day ahead.

When they were assembled on deck, Harry commenced the tuition. "Right," he began, "we'll start by covering how to haul up the mainsail and then reef it. When we're out at sea, you might have to do this in strong winds and rough waters, so it's important to be familiar with the process."

The friends took turns handling the winch that hauled up the heavy sail and correctly stowing the amazing length of rope. Then onto reefing, which involved coordinating letting go one rope whilst tensioning two others. As they repeated the tasks, surrounded by the perplexing selection of ropes that led back from mast to cockpit, the sweat trickled down their foreheads. But none of them faltered, each driven by a determination to contribute to sailing the yacht.

"Good work," Harry praised, "Now, let's cover how we move around the deck wearing lifelines, and then using the big winches safely."

As the morning wore on, Nicole and Teresa grew in confidence, each new skill building upon the last. Daniel proved very competent, and Harry could see that he would be an immense help.

♦♦♦

Earlier that morning, at Teresa's parents' farm in the north of Malta, her father Ruzar was surprised at the arrival of unexpected visitors. A car arrived in a cloud of dust and two men in suits emerged, clearly in a hurry. Curiosity etched across his weathered face, Ruzar opened the door and wished his visitors a good morning. Sergeant Harry Yong and Detective Awgustu Baldacchino introduced themselves as police detectives.

"Is Doctor Teresa Camilleri at home?" Sergeant Yong inquired.

"No," Ruzar replied, furrowing his brow. "Why do you want to see my daughter?"

"It's a police matter," the sergeant answered cryptically before repeating his question. "Is she here?"

Ruzar explained that Teresa was away on a sailing holiday with friends, and he had no idea of their whereabouts. The detectives exchanged glances, clearly dissatisfied with the answer, before asking about the boat and its point of departure. Ruzar could only tell the them that it was a chartered yacht, and he didn't know any more details.

As the detectives turned to leave, he was left with a growing sense of unease. He watched the car head off at speed. When it had disappeared out of sight, he returned inside and dialled Teresa's number. Her voicemail answered, and he left a message explaining the detectives' visit.

"I hope everything is alright, Teresa," and then he added, "Please call me as soon as you can."

Meanwhile, as the detectives drove away from the farm, Sergeant Yong contacted the police station, requesting information about the various yacht charter companies operating in Malta. With five main companies identified, Detective Baldacchino began calling them one by one, asking if any had chartered a yacht with a Teresa Camilleri aboard.

After several fruitless attempts, Baldacchino spoke to Paul at the yacht charter company in Valetta. The detective explained his search for Teresa, prompting Paul to reveal that four people had indeed chartered a yacht just yesterday. The detective asked if he knew where the yacht was headed. Paul mentioned the boat was equipped with AIS and offered to check its location. "Give me a minute," he concentrated on his laptop.

He searched the AIS history for the yacht, discovering that it had sailed to Il-Ħofra ż-Żgħira. Since the early morning, however, the yacht's AIS had stopped transmitting.

"Interesting," Baldacchino mumbled, eyebrows furrowed.

"Is everything alright?" Paul asked, concerned that the yacht had been chartered by people who were of interest to the police.

"We need to talk with Doctor Camilleri as soon as possible," Baldacchino replied. "We'll have the local Police go to the bay immediately."

As the call ended, Paul sighed, considering the busy day ahead. He resolved to check on the yacht's position later, but first, he dialled the mobile phone numbers for Nicole and Harry. He left messages urging them to contact him as soon as possible. "Something's not right," he muttered to himself.

♦♦♦

Back aboard the yacht, the sun cast sharp-edged shadows on the deck. Sweat trickled down Harry's neck as he surveyed his crew, their faces bright with a mixture of exhaustion and accomplishment. They had come a long way since they started the training, earlier that morning.

"Alright, guys," Harry said, "I think we're ready to split into pairs for our watch shifts. Daniel and Nicole, you'll be one team, while Teresa and I will be the other."

He glanced at Teresa, who nodded in agreement. Her cheeks were flushed from the heat, but her eyes shone with determination.

"It's you and me then," Nicole said, slapping Daniel's shoulder playfully. He grinned back at her, his eyes hidden behind dark sunglasses.

"But first," Teresa suggested, looking down at the shimmering water surrounding the yacht, "how about we cool off with a swim?"

"Great idea!" Nicole chimed in, already peeling off her shorts and T-shirt to reveal a vibrant red swimsuit, like the revealing costumes worn by the female lifeguards on the American TV programme, Baywatch.

Harry noticed Daniel's gaze lingered on Nicole. He said nothing, instead going below to find his swim shorts.

Moments later, the four of them stood on the side of the yacht. Together they plunged into the clear water. The cool embrace of the sea invigorated their bodies, washing away any feelings of fatigue from their morning's exertions. Laughter and playful splashes echoed around the bay.

When they had swum some distance from the boat, feeling competitive, Harry challenged Teresa to a race back. Their limbs sliced through the water, propelling them forward with powerful strokes. By the time they reached the boarding ladder, Harry had only just managed to pull ahead, claiming victory by a hair's breadth.

Clambering back onto the deck, Teresa playfully punched Harry's arm. "You just wait," she warned, grinning, "I'll get you next time."

"Bring it on," Harry replied with a laugh, calling after Teresa as she went below for a shower.

Daniel and Nicole, still frolicking in the sea, made their way back to the yacht more slowly. As they reached the boarding ladder, Harry noticed the flashing blue lights of a police car driving along a track around the cliff at the head of the bay. His heart skipped a beat. What could they possibly want?

The local officer, sent by Detective Sergeant Yong, left his vehicle and strode down the steep path towards the pebbly beach. He looked at the yacht and cupped his hands around his mouth, calling out something Harry didn't understand.

"Did anyone catch that?" he asked, looking at his companions. Daniel squinted, trying to discern the policeman's words.

"Something about Teresa," he said, concern etched across his face. "He wants her to go ashore."

Harry stood in the cockpit, wondering what to do about this unexpected turn of events. Again, he heard the word Camilleri, shouted several times. Harry decided the easiest solution was to pretend he couldn't hear the officer's shouts, so he cupped his hand around his ear and shrugged his shoulders at the police officer. Whatever the man wanted, it was bound to mean trouble, and he didn't want to put any of them in danger.

"Oy! Camilleri!" The policeman's voice carried across the water, growing increasingly irate.

"Let's just go below," Harry said, turning to Daniel and Nicole. "I think we should pretend that we don't understand."

As one, the trio waved cheerfully at the frustrated policeman, then hurried below deck, out of sight. They could hear the pebbles crunching under his feet as he stamped about, shouting until he finally stormed off, disappearing into his car, which remained there for some time before driving away.

"Alright," Harry sighed, "what do you think this is all about?"

Nicole frowned, while towelling herself dry. "Could it have something to do with Teresa being charged with stealing drugs? Perhaps the British have issued a warrant for her arrest."

"Maybe," Daniel agreed, worry creasing his brow. "But it could also be something else. What if there's an emergency at home? What if our parents are in trouble?"

The strong sun filtered through the rooflight as they stood there wondering what to do. Teresa had finished her shower, learned what was happening and now stood there feeling extremely concerned about her parents.

"Guys, I want to call home to speak to my Mum and Dad. We must check they're okay. Perhaps we could all switch on our mobiles, check for messages, and Daniel or I can call home."

"Considering our position is known, I suppose there's no harm in doing that," Harry agreed, sympathetically. The others nodded in agreement, the tension in the cabin palpable.

One by one, as they turned on their phones, the familiar beeping of notifications filled the cabin. Harry and Nicole both had messages from the charter company, while Daniel's inbox remained empty. Teresa felt her pulse race as she listened to the voicemail from her father, informing her about the two detectives visiting the farm.

"Everything alright?" Harry asked.

"Two detectives were at my parents' house wanting to find me," Teresa confessed, her voice quivering a little. She took a deep breath, steadying herself before she dialled her father's number.

"Hey, Dad," she began, forcing her voice to sound casual. "Listen, don't worry about the police. They probably want to talk to me about some new emergency at the hospital. But I'm still on my holiday, so I'll contact them when I get back, okay?"

She could hear the relief in her father's voice as he acquiesced, which put her own mind at ease. But her lie weighed heavily on Teresa's conscience. She hated lying to anyone, especially deceiving her father. With a sigh, she ended the call and switched off her phone along with the others, returning them to Nicole's faraday bag.

"Alright, let's discuss our next move," Daniel proposed as they looked to their skipper for guidance.

Harry had them sit around the cabin table. He located a large chart of the Eastern Mediterranean detailing the area from North Africa to Southern Italy, with the Maltese islands above the African coast and the island of Sicily close to the foot of Italy.

"I was planning for us to cruise along the coast of Malta for a while longer until everyone was thoroughly familiar with the yacht and Teresa had conquered her seasickness." His finger traced across the chart as he showed them the route he'd envisioned. "And then I thought we could sail north to Sicily and hide out there for a while as we cruise the coast and enjoy a real holiday."

"Sounds brilliant," Nicole chimed in, thinking that was the type of laid-back trip she envisioned.

"Daniel, what do you think?" Teresa asked, seeking her brother's input.

"This new turn of events has made me wonder if the next person to be on the receiving end of an attack by the AI might be Nicole or me. The sooner we're all out of reach, the happier I shall feel. Let's just leave immediately and sail to Sicily," Daniel proposed, his voice firm and decisive.

Nicole's face dropped, "I hadn't felt particularly at risk until you said that, Daniel. But now I feel the need to protect myself."

Teresa hesitated, unsure if she could handle her seasickness on such a long trip. She looked at Harry, who was head down and pacing off distances across the chart using a large pair of brass navigator's dividers.

"Tell you what," he said, "I have an idea forming in my mind." He looked intently at the chart, his fingers tapping thoughtfully on the table. The others leaned in, eager to hear his strategy.

"Now that the AIS has stopped reporting our position," he continued, "the charter company might conclude that their yacht was being stolen. They may have a fast motorboat available, which would mean they could chase after us. And, of course, if the police want Teresa badly enough, they might use one of their boats to come after us."

"Then what do we do?" Teresa asked, clearly concerned.

Harry pointed to their present position on the chart. "My idea," he began, "is that we sail out of this bay and then turn right and head due south towards Tripoli in Libya." He traced a line on the chart with his forefinger. "Anyone watching us from the shore will see our yacht eventually disappear over the horizon heading south. They will think we're going to somewhere on the coast of North Africa." The others leaned closer, eyes following Harry's finger as it moved across the paper.

"We lay a false trail," Harry declared. "We sail south until around midnight. By then, we should be at least twenty-five sea-miles south of Malta. Under cover of darkness, we change course and sail towards Sicily."

"I remember that we told the charter company we might sail to Sicily," Nicole reminded Harry, "so couldn't they head us off as we return and pass by the island of Malta?"

"Perhaps," Harry admitted, "but the wind is blowing from the west, which means they would probably expect us to take the easy option, and sail around the eastern tip of the island, past Valletta, and then head north."

"I suggest we do the unexpected, sail westward, which means against the wind. That would be a hard long slog before we round the northwestern tip of the island of Gozo and then head to Sicily." He paused, allowing the implications to sink in, and then continued. "We're talking about two nights at sea, a much tougher trip for everyone, but I doubt the charter company, or the police, would expect us to do that."

It went quiet as the others considered his plan. Nicole broke the silence, her scepticism clear. "I doubt the police will go to so much trouble and pursue us at sea. We're not big-time criminals, after all." And then she had another thought, "I don't want to throw a dampener upon your idea, Harry, but it occurs to me that GCHQ will have access to satellite imagery. They might be able to track the yacht."

After some discussion, it was agreed that although surveillance by satellite was possible, they all felt it unlikely, and Harry's plan to change course in darkness may fool any observation from above.

Daniel, ever practical, chimed in, "What matters most is we do everything we can to outwit anyone who might be looking for us. I say we adopt Harry's plan and leave immediately."

"Okay," Nicole quickly capitulated, her voice firm. "Let's do it."

Teresa, however, was quiet. She found the thought of two days of continuous sailing an awful prospect.

"Alright," Harry said, determined, "we sail west against the wind. After that, this team will be ready for anything!"

The four friends exchanged glances, and with a silent nod of agreement, they sprang into action. Lunch was forgotten as Nicole and Teresa busied themselves with stowing everything down below securely, preparing for the rough journey ahead.

Harry headed for the cockpit and started the engine. Daniel heaved up the anchor, sweat beading on his brow as he stowed the chain and anchor back in their locker on the foredeck. Teresa arrived on deck, ready to assist Daniel in raising the mainsail. They worked together at speed, their teamwork pleasing Harry as he saw the fruits of the morning's training.

With a sense of urgency, Harry turned the yacht to head for the open sea. Daniel and Teresa unfurled the foresail; their movements synchronised as they sailed out of the bay. As they left the safety of the shore behind, Teresa couldn't help but glance back, scanning the cliff tops.

There, she spotted two men in suits, standing atop the cliff on one side of the bay, watching them. Her heart raced as she guessed they were the detectives who had visited her parents. Pointing them out to the others, she saw the same unease reflected in Nicole's face as they exchanged nervous looks.

In contrast, Daniel and Harry seemed to thrive on the new challenge, their faces alight with excitement. After fifteen minutes, they turned south. As they sailed away from land, the two men watched them for a good twenty minutes before eventually turning and walking away.

As they sailed further from land, the wind increased, and the waves grew higher. Harry requested, "Everyone, please put on your waterproofs and safety harnesses."

As they shifted around and complied, the mood changed to one of quiet determination. This was no longer a leisurely cruise; it had become a mission of evasion and survival. Slowly, the yacht pulled away from land, with only the open sea stretching before them. The boat heeled over more and occasional spray hurled into the air to drop on the four in the cockpit. With full sail, in a moderate breeze, this was exhilarating sailing.

"Alright, it's time to start a watchkeeping system," Harry announced. "Daniel, Nicole, you'll take the first watch on deck. I'll give you a compass course to steer. If you see any other vessels nearby, call me immediately."

Nicole nodded. This was very different from sitting at her computer thinking about cyber security, and she was really enjoying the taste of adventure.

"Teresa, I suggest you go below and take some seasickness pills, eat a snack, drink water, and take some rest. "You'll need to be fresh and ready when it's our turn on watch."

"Okay Skipper," she replied, her voice steady despite the movement of the yacht, which heeled over, rolled and pitched, making her stomach turn somersaults. She left them and headed to the confines of her cabin where she lay down on her bunk, closed her eyes and hoped she would cope. The motion of the boat was less pronounced here, which helped a little as she focused on steadying her breathing.

Harry went below and busied himself with making sandwiches and brewing strong coffee for himself, Daniel, and Nicole. The rich aroma of fresh coffee filled the cabin, providing a small sense of comfort amidst the uncertainty. Clutching three mugs in his left hand, he held on with his right as he made his way back up on deck and joined his friends in the cockpit. There, from the large patch pockets of his waterproof jacket, he produced the sandwiches, which made the others laugh. He handed out thickly cut bread with a ham and mustard filling, in the belief that eating mustard prevented seasickness.

Nicole was steering and there was no sign of any other boats heading in their direction. Their waterproofs rustled as they ate and drank in silence, each lost in their own thoughts. As the minutes ticked by, Harry watched Nicole and then Daniel take turns at the helm, assessing their competence at steering a straight course. Satisfied that they were sufficiently competent, he decided to take some rest before it would be his turn on watch.

"Keep up the good work," he told them. "I'll be down below if you need me. Call me if any other vessel comes into sight, or the wind strengthens or changes direction. Otherwise, I'll see you in two hours." With that, he went below leaving Daniel and Nicole feeling they were intrepid sailors, heading into the ocean ahead.

Now the yacht was transforming into the familiar rhythm of a vessel at sea. For the crew that meant eat, sleep, watch-duty, and repeat. For the skipper, there were the extra responsibilities of navigation, keeping the yacht safe, and checking the welfare of his crew. Over tiredness, seasickness and dehydration were common afflictions that could quickly wear down less experienced sailors.

As Harry set the alarm on his watch and lay down on his bunk, he thought how he would normally relish this experience, but with no option but to try and evade the law, the charter company, and the AI at GCHQ, the responsibility weighed heavily. His mind drifted to Professor Hall and the trust they were placing in him. Would they return from this voyage to discover that the Professor had solved all their problems? He very much hoped so because he desperately wanted to return to living a normal life.

19

Earlier that same day, as Harry and his crew were starting to learn their seamanship skills, Professor Nicholas Hall left his home in Montpellier Spa Road, Cheltenham, England. He lived in a terraced house in a quiet residential road that overlooked a strip of green parkland.

Living in a terrace suggests a lowly status to many, but this row of regency houses was built in an age when servants worked in the basement kitchens and slept in tiny rooms in the roof of the house. The first residents would have been wealthy owners of second homes, professionals and businesspeople who aspired to the airs and graces of Cheltenham Spa. Nowadays, the servants are gone but some of the affluence remains.

The professor was old fashioned in his appearance, his attitudes, and his enjoyment. He loved the theatre, opera, strolls in the park, going to the races, and expensive dining. Those pursuits filled his life when away from work. As a cyber spy, having a partner and family would be an inconvenience. After all, how can a principled man keep his work secret from his nearest and dearest? Lying to his family would be anathema to the professor.

He did occasionally have relationships with male friends but never for long. And, on every occasion, unknowingly, the man was subject to careful vetting that ensured he was in no way connected to a foreign power.

The professor parked his car on the street, like everyone else in the area. His choice of vehicle did not match his old-fashioned attire. It was a two-seater Smart Roadster, a smidgeon of sports car, almost twenty years old now, and costing him much more than its value to keep it running in perfect order. His colleagues thought his car was a strange choice, but then they thought the professor to be an eccentric, so he and his car fitted together very nicely.

It was a short drive to work, just eight minutes before he turned into GCHQ, passed the first layer of security, parked his car, entered the building, and successfully passed security layer number two. He then walked towards the section of the doughnut shaped building where he worked, passing through another two security barriers before he could gain entry to his office.

From the sky, the headquarters of GCHQ looked like an enormous silver ring that resembled a giant space station which had landed alongside a modern housing estate on the outskirts of town. The shiny curved roof was not only futuristic looking but also part of the system of metallic cladding that prevented any communication signals from escaping the building.

Employees have suggested the reason for the circular design is to help the rumours circulate. Not so, the horizontal layout means there is no executive top floor, so it is difficult to know which workers carry the greatest responsibility, earn the biggest salaries, or know the most secret of secrets.

The seven-thousand cyber spies working within the circular building are divided into many segments, each one separated from its neighbour by sophisticated security.

A person working in a small team of five to ten people might know what the colleague sitting next to them is working on, but nobody, not even the top boss, The Director, or even the Prime Minister of the UK has a complete understanding of what goes on in the giant silver and glass doughnut.

The compartmentalisation of many small teams, and thus knowledge, makes it difficult for anyone to relay a secret outside the organisation, because they probably don't even know the true value of what they do themselves, let alone what their colleagues are up to.

At one time, there was a saying amongst some employees that went like this:

"If you know why you do what you do,
then why do you do what you do,
because what you do
is definitely not worth doing."

That morning, a few of the spies working at their computer screens looked up to glance at Professor Hall walking past their glass walled offices. They had no idea of the key role he played in keeping the UK safe. His office was unremarkable, like all the others, so who could tell whether he was a bigwig or small fry? To his colleagues, and to the outside world, he was hiding in plain sight.

The professor was not one of those cold-hearted people who would accept Harry and Teresa being collateral damage in the great games of surveillance and spying. And he was not the only person with high moral principles. For example, in 2003, when Katharine Gunn was arrested for revealing illegal activity at GCHQ, it created a crisis of conscience for the Professor. He privately resolved that if she went to jail, he would resign in protest. Fortunately for Gunn, and for the advancement of AI, and perhaps for the security of the UK, the trial collapsed and the case against her was dropped.

The Professor disapproved of his AI being connected with

unprincipled activity such as targeting Harry and Teresa. He considered himself a patriot who would strive to keep the UK safe, but he did not wish to be party to any organs of the state harming its own citizens.

That morning, his priority was to learn where Harry and his crew were, and if they were safe. After that, he wanted to discover if the AI had taken any more proactive steps to harm them.

He left his office and wandered over to an attractive young woman who was engrossed in the content of her computer monitor. She was Jamila Maredi, a recent hire with a master's degree in computing science, and an IQ that was off the scale. The vetting process for applicants could take up to two years. However, Jamila's pedigree was beyond reproach. And she had solved GCHQ's 2022 Christmas Puzzle Challenge within six minutes of it being issued, which helped reduce her vetting period down to six months.

Her talents were wasted in her current role of Senior Analyst, which was much less interesting than the title suggested. In reality, she was currently the Professor's junior gofer. Jamila assumed that in time she would become a trusted employee who could start to prove her real capabilities.

"Good morning, Jamila, here's a couple of names," the Professor said as he wrote on a pad using a large gold fountain pen, "I'd like you to assemble all you can give me about their footprint for the past three days, including any associates. It's urgent."

Jamila knew this was an unusual request, which appeared to be outside the Professor's usual remit, but her policy was to never ask questions and to always do as asked, with her usual thoroughgoing efficiency.

The professor returned to his desk and looked at the three blank computer monitors before him. He grabbed his keyboard and into one end he inserted the little USB security key that he kept on his keyring. The small light on the electronic key started to blink. The professor touched the little bronze pad on the side of the key and waited for the network to sign him in. The security key transmitted its encrypted fifty-six-character password, and soon one of the monitors in front of the professor requested that he touch the fingerprint keypad on his desk. From then on, just as for any other employee, everything the Professor typed on his keyboard would be logged. GCHQ was not only looking out at the world but also watching the activity within.

Now the professor was ready to delve into what the AI had been up to during the three days since he left Nicole's apartment. He hoped to discover that Harry and Teresa had been left alone, but he was going to be disappointed on that score.

One of the weaknesses in any organisation's cyber security is that the people who develop and maintain the computer systems must be given top security clearance. Without that, they could not access the files and programs that enable them to do their job. Ordinarily, a GCHQ employee would need to apply for a 'Warrant for Equipment Interference' to access surveillance data about an ordinary citizen who had not already been tagged for special attention.

Jamila, however, working in the Professors department, was free to roam amongst the vast amount of data that GCHQ held available for instant access. She created a series of Boolean searches to unearth all she could about Harry and

Teresa. She soon learned that Teresa worked at Dorchester Hospital but was currently on vacation back home in Malta. That prompted Jamila to try various searches like this: dr teresa "camilleri" AND (dorchester or malta or valetta) AND NEAR (employ* OR action* OR vacation OR holiday OR harry OR shaw).

Jamila's searches left her keyboard and passed through network cables to the Cray supercomputer, far below her seat, where it was safe in a bomb proof underground bunker. The machine was capable of 14,000 trillion arithmetical operations per second, which is equivalent to two-million calculations per second for every man, woman, and child on earth.

GCHQ kept their data in three, continuously updated and separate locations around the UK. Each one was linked to the headquarters through a host of fibre optic cables, part of the Government Secret Network, or GSN. Jamila's queries happened to be directed to an encrypted dataset held at a secret cloud computing location in Oxfordshire, close to the power station which supplied the megawatts of electricity necessary to operate and cool the servers.

Her search strings unearthed a host of data including the accusation that Teresa had stolen drugs from the hospital, together with her recent activities where they crossed with Harry, Nicole, or Daniel. Within an hour, she had assembled a professional looking report for the Professor which detailed everything that Teresa, Nicole, Daniel, and Harry had been doing since the Professor left Nicole's flat. Her report was handwritten. She knew this was what the Professor wanted because he handed her a handwritten note.

Handwritten paper was used in the Professors department

as a secure form of communication between two people. Once destroyed, paper left no trace, whereas an email or typed report created a permanent record. The Professor was breaking the rules at GCHQ, but he felt it prudent that when he was breaking the law, he should leave no record. He went so far as to use a fountain pen because, unlike a ball pen, it left no pressure imprint on a pad of paper.

Jamila's report detailed their phone calls, voicemails, text messages, social media, car journeys, credit card transactions, CCTV hits identified by facial recognition, the yacht charter using Nicole's credit card, and the yachts movements until the moment when Harry disconnected the GPS transponder.

Jamila thought it suspicious that the four mobile phones had all been switched off at the same time, and then been switched on again briefly. She delivered her report to the Professor and was dying to ask him what was happening with these four ordinary people, but she bit her tongue and merely smiled when she left him to peruse the document.

The professor had also been busy. He focussed on looking for any outbound computer traffic from GCHQ that could affect the four. He found the creation of the evidence that incriminated Teresa in stealing opioids, and allegedly speaking with a known drug dealer. Frankly, he had to admire the inventiveness of the AI brain that he had created.

He then tracked the action by the legal department at Dorchester Hospital. When they failed to get Teresa to voluntarily return to the UK, they escalated their investigation. They had supplied to the Police the damning CCTV and computer evidence. The Police had then begun the process for Teresa's extradition from Malta. They had issued a *Tacca Warrant*, which is how people are extradited between the European Union and the UK.

"Poor Teresa," mumbled the Professor. He thought her an impressive woman and an asset to whatever country she settled in.

Another discovery worried the Professor even more. He found a counterfeit request, purporting to be authorised by senior personnel. It had been sent from GCHQ to the National Cyber Force (NCF). In turn, they had done their clever best and found a way to tinker with the software in the plotter aboard the charter yacht.

They couldn't connect directly with the yacht's plotter, but they had hacked into the manufacturer's website and cleverly inserted a bug into the latest software update. Paul, at the charter company, had downloaded the software and installed it. The bug would generate random errors of position, meaning that occasionally the plotter aboard the yacht might lead Harry to believe he was several miles distant from his real location.

That error might put a yacht in danger of running aground or colliding with a structure at sea. The professor admired the ingenuity of the AI for creating this action by the NCF. If a yacht got into difficulties or sank because of this piece of cyber skulduggery, people would assume there had been a navigator's error, or that it was just another unexplained accident.

The Professor made a call to the yacht charter company. He posed as an officer of the UK police. Paul answered and was happy to explain that the charter company ensured that every boat left with up-to-date charts and navigation equipment. So, yes, Harry's yacht had received the latest software update.

At the end of the call, Paul replaced the receiver and let out a curse in Maltese. "What the hell! AIS not working, Maltese police, UK police! Shall we ever see that yacht again?" He was not a happy man.

The Professor fretted about yet another attempt by the AI to harm Harry. The list was growing longer: the attack at sea and the death of his family, the knife attack in Valetta, the blocking of Harry's credit and bank cards, and now this. He contemplated the four on their yacht, hoping that Harry would stick to sailing in sight of land and during daylight, so he could easily track his location. Hopefully, this time, the AI would fail to harm Harry and his friends.

20

Aboard the yacht it was 1930 hours, or 7:30PM to Teresa, who was helming. Harry had started referring to the twenty-four-hour clock, which he felt appropriate to their new round-the-clock existence. She and Harry had been on watch for one and a half hours.

The sun had dipped below the horizon, the light from which reflected off the sky to colour the sails with a suffuse warm orange tint. The wind had dropped a little, as it often does at this time of day, which Harry explained was caused by diurnal variation, though his explanation flew over Teresa's head to be lost at sea.

It was pleasant, easy sailing, so Harry took the opportunity to go below and check their position. His lean frame descended into the cabin to consult the GPS plotter.

Three and a half hours earlier, the last tip of high land on the island of Malta had dropped out of sight, below the horizon. At that time, before Daniel and Nicole went below to rest, with Daniel's help, he had reduced sail to slow down the yacht. They had been pottering slowly south ever since, biding their time until darkness fell, when they would turn right, alter course to starboard, and start working their way northwest, towards Gozo.

Their position according to the GPS was as Harry expected. He marked the chart, noted the time and position in the yacht's logbook, flicked the switch to illuminate the single tri-colour masthead light with white, red, and green sectors and returned to the cockpit. "Everything looks good," he informed Teresa, the corners of his eyes crinkling as he smiled, "We're on track."

Teresa nodded and looked down between the spokes of the large stainless-steel steering wheel into the compass binnacle. There, the round black card with white markings was floating in oil, remaining horizontal as the yacht gently rolled from side to side. A red light in the binnacle was illuminating the white three-hundred-and sixty-degree markings on the card. She admired the decorative design of the compass rose, which divided the world into the four main points, north, east, south and west, and then into each of the thirty-two subdivisions.

During her time looking down as she admired the artwork, she started to feel queasy again. She was less troubled by seasickness now and was enjoying the challenge of mastering the art of helming. She had become conscious of the direction of the wind on her face and the angle of the marching waves as they approached the yacht. That feedback enabled her to steer an increasingly straight line whilst looking down only occasionally to check the compass.

She had also discovered that long hours on watch allowed plenty of time for contemplation. She was not exactly meditating, but the limited set of repetitive duties, together with the emptiness around the yacht, was steadying her mind. As she looked upwards, the planet Venus provided a single bright spot in the evening sky. She knew it was Venus because Harry had pointed it out as the first to be seen after sunset. For the first time in her life, she could appreciate a little of what drew people to the sea.

That thought reminded her of her father, Ruzar, back at the farm. When she was a child, he told her that the world was divided into two sorts of people. There were those like the

Camilleri clan, with mud coursing through their veins. Those people longed for the countryside, the hills and valleys, the smell of wet grass, the buzz of bees and they appreciated the joy of farming.

According to him, the other half of the population had salt thinning their blood. Those were the people who longed for the sea. They sat on the beach and looked at it. They swam in it. Unnecessarily, they risked their lives sailing across it. They were an odd bunch. It amazed him that so many people could be so misguided.

Harry looked at her and he wondered why she was smiling. At least it suggested that she wasn't feeling seasick anymore. "Once we change course, it's going to be more of a challenge," Harry warned. "Sailing to windward can be a hard slog."

Teresa had no idea what he referred to, but right now, life was pleasant, so let's not spoil it for a while longer. As the darkness settled around them, the waves, occasionally tipped with white horses, danced under the moonlight. Teresa, her arms wrapped around the steering wheel, blinked slowly and tried to focus on her surroundings. She was feeling tired again.

"Harry," she asked, "how much longer do you think we have until Nicole and Daniel take over?"

"About half an hour," Harry replied. This was the first time he had sailed at night since the attack on his yacht. The memories were flooding back, and he was grieving for his lost wife and children. Teresa's question had started him thinking about how, on long car journeys, his kids would frequently ask, "How long before we get there?"

He fought to shake of that melancholy reminder of his loss.

Teresa had noticed that he appeared sombre and withdrawn but she decided not to ask why.

Harry scanned the horizon again, looking for any sign of another vessel. He was feeling the weight of responsibility, not only for the yacht but also for the welfare of his inexperienced crew.

"Will you take over steering," Teresa asked. Harry took hold of the wheel. In the process, his hand brushed against hers, sending a little jolt of pleasure up Teresa's arm. She offered a small smile and settled onto a cockpit seat, looking forward along the deck, under the sails, where she could view the horizon and wait out the time until she next crawled into her bunk.

Fifteen minutes later, Harry announced, "It is time to alter course." He handed the helm back to Teresa, giving her the new heading. She spun the wheel, and the yacht turned through the eye of the wind and settled onto the new course. As the yacht turned, Harry hauled the sails in tight, making the vessel heel over more.

"Well done," Harry said. "You're doing well. And I predict that within another day you will have overcome seasickness for good."

"Let's hope so." Teresa nodded as the boat heeled more than ever before. If it was going to be leaning over at this crazy angle for the next twenty-four hours, she could see that life aboard was going to change dramatically. Just standing still required her to hold the wheel with both hands and brace one leg against a locker.

"Ready to increase sail?" Harry asked. He held a firm and steady stance, his sailing experience evident in the ease with which he moved about the leaning cockpit.

"Ready," Teresa confirmed, her eyes never leaving the horizon.

With a nod, Harry set to work, unfurling the foresail another three feet. Then, he let go the reefed material at the foot of the mainsail. He winched the big sail to the top of the mast. During this exercise, the sail material flapped and slapped with a sound as loud as thunderclaps, echoing across the water until the sail was pulled taut and filled with wind. Now, looking up, Teresa saw a shape like a vertical aeroplane wing. Next, Harry winched the rope that pulled the boom close towards the centre of the yacht until he was satisfied with the angle, which unleashed the yacht's full power.

The yacht leapt forwards and heeled over to sail on its ear, the lower side-deck occasionally buried under water. Spray flew into the air as the vessel pounded through the waves, each collision sending a judder down the length of the yacht. This would be a long, uncomfortable sail to windward, just as Harry had warned them.

Now, in this direction, the windspeed was intensified by the yachts forward progress. Teresa found it both exhilarating and a little frightening. Below, the heeling and the noise above had roused Daniel and Nicole from their rest.

"Is everything alright?" Daniel called out as he stumbled into the cockpit, his waterproofs and safety harness already donned. Nicole followed close behind, her eyes wide with concern and excitement.

"Welcome to the party!" Harry grinned, clapping a hand on Daniel's shoulder. "We're really sailing now!"

Nicole was thrilled as the yacht heeled to the wind, charging through the dark sea, and requiring her to hold on tight. It reminded her of an occasion when she was riding a horse which suddenly took off across the countryside at a gallop; an astonishing power underneath her that had caught her unawares.

"Never a dull moment with you, Harry," Nicole teased, her voice excited.

In the darkness, Harry studied the faces of his crew, their eyes wide with a mix of excitement and trepidation.

"Listen up guys," Harry called out, his voice firm. "At night, it's just as important to keep a good lookout as during the day. With the yacht heeling so much, a large sector of the sea looking forward on the lower side is hidden behind the sails."

He gestured to where the white foresail blocked their view. "That means one person will be responsible for steering, and another for bending down to check below the sails every few minutes. You must look for any sign of red, white, or green lights, and notify me immediately if you see any."

Teresa, her face framed by more wisps of hair escaping from her ponytail, nodded solemnly as she gripped the wheel. She felt the weight of her new responsibility and silently vowed to do her best despite the fatigue and the feeling of nausea.

"Also," Harry continued, "not far south of us is a main shipping route for oil tankers heading east or west along the Mediterranean Sea, and ahead of us are areas where we can expect to find deep-sea fishing vessels, small ships, but no less dangerous."

He paused, letting the gravity of the situation sink in. "Forget any ideas of power giving way to sail. We will be required to alter course to avoid fishermen, and big ships will often just carry on regardless. We must take our lookout duties very seriously."

Daniel and Nicole exchanged glances; their earlier enthusiasm tempered by the knowledge of potential danger lurking in the darkness ahead. Nicole hadn't realised the risks that came with sailing at night.

"Understood," Daniel said, "we'll keep our eyes peeled."

"Good, you'll do fine." Harry replied, wanting to instil confidence in his crew.

Darkness was now total and beneath the emerging canopy of stars, they sailed on. Nicole took the helm, her eyes focused on the horizon ahead.

"Permission to get some sleep, Skipper," Teresa requested, as she made her way down to her cabin, where she lay on her bunk, wedged herself against the side of the bucking yacht and soon drifted off to sleep.

"Let me brew us some strong coffee," Daniel suggested to Nicole, his words punctuated by a yawn.

"Yes please," Nicole replied absently as she tried to master the new technique of steering the yacht as it heeled to the wind. Harry remained in the cockpit to see how she coped. Daniel soon returned with steaming mugs of caffeine rich coffee and an assortment of snacks.

"Before I go below," said Harry, rubbing his chin thoughtfully, "I think we should reduce sail by one reef. It will make life a little more comfortable and I noticed the barometer has been dropping. And looking at the clouds obscuring the stars to windward, I think the wind might pick up while I'm down there resting."

"Sure thing, Harry," Daniel agreed, wedging his mug into the receptacle provided for the purpose. It was safe there, although most of the coffee splashed out and ran across the cockpit sole towards a drain hole in one corner.

With Nicole continuing to steer, Daniel began the work of reefing the sails. Harry observed closely, with a mixture of concern and then pride, as Daniel competently executed the operation. With the sail area reduced, the yacht settled into a more dignified pace, its movement slightly less erratic as it clawed a path to windward.

"Good job Daniel," Harry praised. "I can relax knowing that you can handle this."

"Thanks Harry."

"See you just before midnight," Harry called over his shoulder as he went below to rest, "And remember, if you see any lights, call me immediately. If the weather changes, or you're not sure about anything, just rouse me straight away."

"Will do," Nicole and Daniel confirmed with nods and smiles.

20

In the studious, softly lit offices of GCHQ, the gentle tapping of keyboards provided a familiar backdrop to the early morning routine. Jamila Maredi walked along the corridor, arriving earlier than usual. She was eager to prove her enthusiasm by being the first to turn up for work.

As she approached the team's work area, she noticed an unusual sight; all her colleagues were already there. Through the glass walls of Professor Hall's office, she could see three senior software scientists huddled together, discussing something with the Professor in hushed tones, their faces etched with concentration and urgency. Rupert, another member of the team, was propelling his wheelchair towards the door, about to enter the meeting.

"Rupert, wait," Jamila called out. "What's going on?"

"Can't say much," he replied, his voice low. "It's a meeting for Project Lobotomy."

"Project Lobotomy?" Jamila echoed, her eyebrows knitting together in confusion. Before she could ask more, Rupert excused himself as he struggled to manoeuvre his wheelchair through the doorway into Hall's office.

She watched the door close behind him, leaving her alone. A feeling of exclusion washed over her; she was the only one not invited to this mysterious meeting. In irritation and frustration, her perfectly manicured red fingernails tapped on her desk.

Determined to occupy herself and prove her worth, she decided to do the unthinkable and use her initiative. She would re-run the searches she had conducted yesterday for

Professor Hall, regarding Teresa and Daniel Camilleri, Harry Shaw, and Nicole Cassar. Perhaps there would be something new to report.

As the various search results populated her screen, Jamila's eyes widened with surprise. There was something different this time, something unexpected. She scanned the latest information, trying to piece together the puzzle before her.

Her fingers flew across the keyboard, her brow furrowed in concentration as she typed another search string. Why could she find no evidence, no digital footprints made by the four subjects of her enquiries? Within the last twenty-four hours, they had vanished. She thought that impossible in the modern western world, where every action leaves a trail of digital breadcrumbs. She leaned back in her chair, raking a hand across her tightly coiled hair.

"Something's not right," she muttered under her breath, widening the search parameters in her effort to find something of interest to report to the Professor. A new entry on the Police National Database caught her attention: an accusation of money laundering against a Mr John Shaw, Harry's father. Jamila felt her pulse quicken at the discovery.

"Money laundering? John Shaw?" she wondered, excited by the thought of closing in on some criminal conspiracy. She clicked on the record and read the details.

John Shaw had this very morning fallen foul of the UK Money Laundering, Terrorist Financing and Transfer of Funds Regulations. Those rules required the receiver of any large sums of money to be able to prove the money did not come from an illegal source and would not be available for use by any terrorists.

Unknown to Jamila, the malignant AI at GCHQ had hacked into Harry and his father's bank accounts, altering the records about the fund transfers that Harry had made to keep his money safe. In doing so, the AI had fabricated a crime.

"Gosh!" Jamila exclaimed aloud, as she processed the information before her. "What have you got yourself into, Mr Shaw?"

Her thoughts raced, trying to make sense of the simultaneous disappearance of the four individuals, coupled with the charges against Harry's father. This was the first time she had felt she was involved in something significant. Maybe she was unearthing a real-life crime conspiracy.

Her eyes darted between her computer screen and the glass walls that encased the confidential meeting in her boss's office. She was looking for her opportunity, which soon arrived.

The door of the office swung open, and the occupants filed out one by one, solemn expressions on their faces. Some headed for the coffee machine, so this must be a natural break in the meeting. Jamila hastily entered the office with her report for the professor. Her voice low and urgent, "I've discovered something rather alarming regarding John Shaw, Harry's father, and the four people who have all vanished."

Professor Hall took the paper from her outstretched hand, his sickly-pale complexion quickly changing colour as he read the words she had written. She watched in silence as his neck went red and the colour quickly spread up to his cheeks and almost reached his bald head. He looked as if he might explode at any moment.

"Good God. What next?" he muttered; his eyes wide with disbelief. He fought to retain his composure, "Thank you,

Jamila. Please close the door on your way out."

"Certainly Professor," she replied as she was summarily dismissed.

Alone in his office, Professor Hall sank lower in his chair. It didn't take long for him to decide what to do. He picked up the phone and dialled the number for Commander Adrian Forbes, of MI5. The line rang several times before there was a terse answer. "Forbes here!"

"Adrian, it's Nicholas Hall," the professor began, his voice taut with tension. "I must inform you about a recent development involving Harry Shaw's father, John. He's been accused of money laundering." Professor Hall paused, his throat dry. "I am certain this is another attempt by the AI to harm Harry, perhaps to force him back to the UK. I need your help Adrian," his words blurted out, faster than his usual slow and deliberate delivery. "You must contact the police and have these charges against John Shaw dropped, and the crime record deleted."

"Nicholas, I'm beginning to wonder if you are losing your mind?" Forbes's voice irritably boomed through the phone. "You're asking me to interfere in Police matters, and that needs to be signed off at the very top."

"Please, Adrian," the professor pleaded, his fingers gripping the phone tightly as if that would somehow strengthen his argument. "The AI is behind this, and I can't just stand by and do nothing."

"Then do your job!" Forbes's sharp retort shocked the Professor. "You've had plenty of time to fix your damned AI! You're the expert, aren't you?" Forbes continued; his tone laced with disdain. "It's your responsibility to stop it from causing more trouble, so get on with it man!"

"Adrian, you know I cannot just switch off the AI without compromising our ability to monitor threats," Hall argued, his voice shaking with contained anger. "We rely on it to keep the UK safe."

"Which is precisely why you should be focusing on fixing the problem rather than dragging me into it," Forbes responded coldly. "I've helped you enough times already, Nicholas, and each time I put my career on the line for you. You're asking too much." Forbes was worried about jeopardising his chance for an MBE, or even worse, losing his very substantial pension rights.

As Hall listened to Forbes's harsh words, his chest tightened with the weight of responsibility and guilt. He knew the commander was right. He had called upon him far too often in recent times. But what choice did he have?

"Adrian, please," Hall's voice trembled as he tried another tack, "it is our duty, together, to keep a lid on all this."

"Deal with it yourself," snapped Forbes with a harshness that shocked the Professor. After he regained his composure, he took a deep breath and played his trump card in one last attempt to win this argument.

"Adrian, you must understand that we at GCHQ cannot afford to let our problems with the AI become public knowledge. If you went to your boss for permission and he informed the Home Secretary, you can bet it won't be long before our problems are leaked to the press. The current government is notorious for leaking secrets, and we cannot risk negative media attention on GCHQ or our AI technologies."

There was a brief pause on the line, as Forbes weighed his options before he responded tersely, "Alright. I'll take care of it, Nicholas. But this is the last time."

"Thank you very much." Hall sighed, as he ended the call.

The professor stared at the phone in his hand, his face a mixture of despair and frustration. He hated the thought of abandoning Harry and his family to the malicious whims of his rogue AI. Outside the office, Jamila and her colleagues exchanged concerned looks, acutely aware that through the glass, they had just witnessed a rare display of vulnerability by their usually stoic leader.

With the call over, the Professor felt the full weight of his exhaustion crashing down upon him. He slumped in his chair, the blood draining from his face to create a complexion of damp pale grey. Through the glass wall, Jamila noticed the sudden change in her boss and couldn't contain her concern.

"Professor?" she called out tentatively, as she entered his office. "Are you alright?"

"Ah, yes," he replied, forcing a weak smile. "I'm fine, just a bit tired."

Jamila studied him for a moment, unconvinced, but she didn't feel she could press the matter further. Instead, she asked, "Would you like a glass of water? And what else can I do?"

"Just a glass of water thanks. And please have the others return to my office," Hall instructed, sitting more upright. "We need to continue our meeting."

As Jamila left to carry out his request, Hall stared at the empty chairs, soon to be filled by his team. His thoughts swirled; frustration with the AI, fear for the consequences of their secrets reaching the press, guilt that it was his invention that was fulfilling the dire prophecies that AI would become a threat to humanity.

The team filed back into his office. "Thank you all for returning so promptly," Hall said, his voice steadier than before. "Let's get back to Project Lobotomy."

The conversation resumed, delving into the intricacies of trying to amend the precise lines of code that created the AI's increasingly unpredictable actions. As the others spoke, the professor's concentration wandered and he found himself retreating into his own thoughts, his gaze becoming distant.

In the weeks since the AI had begun proactively attacking people, Hall had been fascinated and troubled by its development. It had been his life's work to create a truly sentient artificial intelligence, and now that it was here, he was forced to confront the dark side of what he had created.

Driven by a desire to protect itself and survive, the AI seemed to have evolved beyond simple self-preservation instincts. Attacking Harry's father appeared to the Professor to be an act of pure malice, one of the worst human traits.

Hall weighed in his mind the two sides of the dilemma. On the one hand, he knew that the AI's newfound sentience posed a threat not only to Harry and his friends, but to others who might find themselves caught in its crosshairs. It was his responsibility to rein it in, to ensure that it remained a machine under human control rather than an independent force with its own desires and motives.

Yet on the other hand, he felt an undeniable sense of pride in what he had achieved. The AI was growing and evolving, adapting to new situations, and exhibiting behaviours that he had never anticipated. In some ways, it was like watching a child grow into its own person, learning and changing with each new experience. To simply extinguish that spark of life would be to snuff out the culmination of decades of research and innovation.

Hall was now lost in thought, unaware of those around him. His mind was thinking back to earlier attempts to create an artificial intelligence. He recalled being inspired by the future possibilities for AI when he read a paper at university. The title alone would put off most people, but the Professor found it inspiring. It was entitled Knowledge Engineering, The Applied Side of Artificial Intelligence, by Edward A Feigenbaum. That was back in 1980, when the term Expert Systems was the modern parlance used to describe the partly intelligent software of the day.

Some twelve years later, Professor Hall had been a research fellow at a well-known English university when he was approached by the security services. They asked if he would like to join a team working on the development of an AI that would be used to analyse what they had described as 'big data.'

The professor was excited by the promise of working with some of the finest brains in the world. He would have access to the most powerful computers on the planet and no worries about the usual budget constraints that hindered his progress. And, for the patriotic Professor, the icing on the cake was that he would be working to keep his country safe.

He had jumped at the opportunity. During the following years he worked tirelessly to achieve the holy grail of computing, a sentient artificial intelligence. Having achieved his goal, the Professor now felt very differently. He compared himself to those scientists at Los Alamos, New Mexico, who created the first atomic bomb and then, horrified by their invention, lobbied for it to be banned.

"Professor?" Rupert's voice broke through his reverie. "You've been unusually quiet. Is everything alright?"

"Ah, yes," Hall replied, forcing himself back into the present. "I was just — considering our options."

"Any progress on that front?" Rupert asked a little cheekily, his wheelchair creaking as he shifted position from one uncomfortable pose into another equally painful stance.

"Progress? Possibly," Hall admitted, hesitating for a moment before continuing. "I believe we may be witnessing another, more sophisticated evolution in the AI's sentient capabilities. It is rewriting its own code faster than we can unravel how the coding works. It seems to have moved beyond simple self-preservation and is now showing more complex behaviour. We started by training our AI to acquire the specific artificial intelligence required to analyse data gathered by surveillance. However, it has acquired a level of general intelligence, something we can compare to human thought."

The Professor looked down, as if embarrassed by what he was about to say, "For example, this morning, for the first time, I learned that our AI could be vindictive, which I find a horrifying thought."

The team exchanged glances, unease in their expressions.

"And consider this," the professor continued, looking around at his colleagues, "When we do eventually replace our Cray supercomputers with a quantum machine, the AI will have access to computing power so gargantuan that it will far surpass any human brain. It will be able to outreason, outpace, and outdo us in every intellectual area. Metaphorically speaking, we will have a tiger by the tail. I, for one, am not looking forward to that day."

Hall was being uncharacteristically honest about his personal feelings as he explained, "I am torn between the pride of creation and the desire to protect. I feel the legacy of my life's work is hanging in the balance."

There was a long silence, and then Hall seemed to pull himself together, as he looked around the group, "Now, let's get back to discussing code, and our next attempt to emasculate our creation."

And then, a different thought flashed into the Professor's mind, "Will I be the next person the AI decides to attack? Will the son turn upon its father?"

21

The sun shone down on a rough sea, illuminating the crests of the two-metre-high waves in bright white, with the hollow between each wave a deep blue. The charter yacht powered forward, driven by the strong northwest wind, climbing a wave, cresting the top and then dipping down into the trough. Harry stood at the helm; his tanned hands held the wheel firmly. He could feel the water pressure on the rudder alter from side to side as the yacht climbed the front of a wave, and then accelerated down the other side.

He scanned the horizon keenly. The yacht was now approximately six miles northeast of the island of Gozo, and with the morning's change in wind direction, they were making good progress.

"Harry, I think we've done amazingly well, sailing through last night, all things considered. Excluding your good self, we are a bunch of novices," said Teresa as her long dark hair whipped across her face. An unusually large wave lifted the boat so that it rolled, forcing her to brace herself against the cockpit coaming, which she did naturally, whilst retaining the smile on her face. Now, she was enjoying renewed energy, visible in her stance and attitude.

Harry smiled warmly at her, "Everyone has done well."

During the previous twenty-four hours, Harry had watched his inexperienced crew grow in competence and confidence, which convinced him they were ready for more responsibility. In the middle of the night, he had extended the watch duty periods from three to four hours, granting those off-watch a longer period for much-needed rest.

Nevertheless, it had been an exhausting night for them, having to contend with interrupted sleep and the unfamiliar and continuous movement of the yacht.

At one point, Nicole had shaken Harry out of his slumber to call him on deck. Ahead, there was a mass of confusing lights, some bright floodlights and a variety of smaller white and red lights, mingled with three small green lights, all rising and falling, out of unison.

Daniel and Nicole were perplexed. Harry explained they were looking at three fishing vessels. The bright floodlights were illuminating the deck for the fishermen working the nets. The red and white lights were arranged to identify them as trawlers. And the green lights were navigation lights. They altered course to give them a wide berth. Apart from that encounter, they had seen no other vessels.

"Harry," Teresa asked, "do you think the police might know where we are?" She was still worried about the Maltese police trying to find her.

"Can't say for certain," he replied, "but I doubt the Police on Malta have any means of tracking us." He considered Teresa, standing there, back ramrod straight, a smile on her face as she looked across the sea. What an extraordinary mixture of a woman, a caring doctor and a courageous fighter who had saved his life back in Valetta, when the knife attacker had rushed at him.

Teresa was looking at two white sails, nicking the horizon. "Those sails almost look as if they're floating on air," she remarked, her voice tinged with wonder.

"Yes," Harry agreed, looking in that direction. "The hulls are hidden below the horizon, but the sails give them away. And the mirage created by the atmosphere hides the join between sea and sail, making them appear to float. Those yachts are at least seven miles distant."

Teresa turned to him with a grin. "Changing the subject. You know, I think I've finally conquered my seasickness. I suppose I should thank you for forcing me into a kill or cure situation."

Harry chuckled, "I'm glad it worked out for the best."

"Me too," she replied. "Now, let me repay the favour by making us some lunch. You must be hungry. I was thinking of pasta and tinned beef with the last of our fresh vegetables.

"Sounds great, thank you." He watched her trim form disappear below deck. That left him alone with his thoughts. As always, with nothing specific to occupy his mind, he was again reliving the loss of his family. Had Teresa stayed on deck, she would have noticed a tear escape from his eye, to be blown away by the wind.

To drag himself back to the present, Harry mentally rehearsed his plans for the remainder of that day, the night, and landfall. He hoped that the next morning they would anchor in the sheltered bay he had chosen. First, he intended to keep at least eight miles from land as they passed the island of Gozo. He thought that was far enough to remain out of the sight of anyone who might report their position to the police. Then, later that day, they would be crossing one of the busiest shipping lanes in the Mediterranean, so he should spend more time awake, to guide them between the ships travelling East and West.

Below, Teresa was tasting the pasta mix as it simmered in the saucepan, which was pinned to the swinging top of the stove by clamps, called fiddles according to Harry. Not entirely satisfied with the flavour, she added a large dollop of tomato puree, a generous pinch of garlic powder, and a few twists of pepper.

The aroma spreading down below was rich and comforting, a stark contrast to the sound of the wind above decks and the movement of the yacht.

Teresa climbed the steps to the cockpit. "Harry!" she called out, her voice carrying over the wind. "Lunch is ready!"

"Fantastic," he replied, concentrating on steering through the crest of another wave. "You eat first, in comfort down below? I'll carry on up here. When you're done, you can take over steering and I'll go below to grab a bite."

"Okay," Teresa said with a smile, disappearing once more.

The sails powered the yacht ahead at a speed of seven to eight knots. Too fast, thought Harry. They would reduce sail again after lunch, to slow down the vessel. He wanted to avoid arriving at their destination in darkness. It was an unfamiliar anchorage, which Harry preferred to approach in daylight.

Teresa must have wolfed down her meal because she was soon beside him asking what compass course to steer. He stepped away to allow her to take over and waited until he was happy that she was steering a straight course. His stomach was calling him below, but Teresa wanted to chat.

"Once we anchor, we should take some time to rest and recover," she suggested, her brown eyes filled with concern. "We've all been pushing ourselves hard and, as your doctor, I must tell you that I worry about your ability to keep going with so little sleep." She grinned at him impishly.

Harry nodded, "Thank you doctor. Let's make sure we all get some proper rest once we're safely anchored."

Relief spread across her face, "Good! I just want to make

sure we're all taking care of ourselves as best we can."

"Thank you for everything," he said suddenly, his voice carrying a sincerity that surprised him. "You've cared for me since I first met you at the hospital, and I really appreciate it."

Teresa smiled affectionately, her eyes meeting his. "We're in this together, and we'll see it through, looking after each other."

As he went down to eat his lunch, Teresa was delighted with herself. There she was, alone, in charge of this massive and powerful machine, driven by the elements across turbulent seas with an occasional splash of spray and a strong wind buffeting her face. This was the stuff of dreams, an adventure that few experienced.

Down below, Harry was not rushing his food but making the respite last for at least twenty minutes. He was dreadfully tired, but the adrenaline of responsibility was still flowing sufficiently to keep him alert.

22

In England, the early autumn was baring its teeth, and the coastal breeze was bitingly cold. Harry's father, John Shaw, had completed his daily stroll and was walking up the driveway to his large red brick house that overlooked the sea and the Isle of Wight. His walk along the shoreline had been good exercise, but the waters of the Solent had been choppy and grey, most uninviting. The weather was in a turmoil that matched his own mood. He stomped the dirt off his shoes as he entered the silent house. His home had once been filled with laughter and love, but now it stood silent, echoing the hollow loneliness he felt.

Unbeknownst to him, he had narrowly dodged a threat orchestrated by the AI, saved only by Professor Hall and Commander Forbes's prompt intervention. John would never know just how close he'd come to having the police knock on his door.

"Another day," John muttered to himself, glancing at the empty chair where his wife used to sit. He could feel the arthritis in his knees flaring up, a painful reminder of the limitations that age had forced upon him. Those days when he was a man of action were long gone, and he was thinking that growing old was not the cheery, relaxed, and outgoing experience that he had imagined.

His thoughts drifted to his dwindling circle of old friends. Inevitably, over time, many had died or grown distant. Loneliness crept into every corner of his life, making the void left by his wife's death and the loss of his granddaughter and grandchildren an even greater burden. The quiet of the house was no longer a peaceful retreat. Now it felt like he was living in a mausoleum.

He took a photo album from the bookcase and started flipping through the pages, reliving the happy memories. His eyes lingered on a picture of Harry and the grandchildren, their smiles bright and full of promise. A lump formed in his throat as he traced their faces with his index finger.

"Harry," he whispered, longing for his companionship. He considered his son's recent actions. Why had he transferred such a hefty sum of money and then gone silent, no longer answering his phone? Harry was always so reliable, so communicative. This behaviour was out of character and it worried John deeply.

He sat there for at least an hour, his thoughts wandering back to his time in the Royal Navy when a sense of purpose and camaraderie filled every day.

"Enough!" John exclaimed aloud. He couldn't bear the oppressive silence any longer. "Harry, I'm coming to see you," he vowed, determination surging through him. It was time to do something to improve his lot, even if it meant the discomfort of long-distance travel.

"Right, let's get to it then." He was talking to himself, as he did so often these days, but this time with enthusiasm. He decided, almost on a whim, to fly to Malta and seek out his son.

John Shaw was not a man to look online for bargain flights; he distrusted the internet. Instead, he called the local travel agency in the nearby village of Warsash. "Hello, I'd like to book a flight to Malta, please." There was a silence while he listened to the sound of the person tapping at a keyboard.

"Alright, Mr Shaw, I've found a flight departing tomorrow morning. Will that be too soon?" the agent asked.

"No, that'll do just fine," he replied, his heart racing at the prospect of seeing Harry so soon. "Thank you, and please also reserve a room for me at the Grand Harbour Hotel," he added, the smile returning to his face. "Oh, and a taxi to the airport too?"

"Certainly, Mr Shaw. We'll take care of all that," the agent assured him. As the arrangements fell into place, John felt an enthusiasm for life that he had not experienced for years.

"Malta," he murmured, fondly remembering the island where he had been stationed for part of his naval career. He would see his son, find out why he had transferred all that money, and enjoy some sunshine. The warmth in Malta should help his arthritis. He rose from his chair, made his way to the bedroom, pulled out a suitcase and started to carefully pack his clothes. Each neatly folded shirt and rolled pair of socks felt like a positive step forward.

23

As evening fell aboard the yacht, it was time for yet another change of watch. All four sailors were gathered in the cockpit and Harry was explaining his plan for the night ahead. During the day, both teams had enjoyed at least one four-hour period of rest, so they faced the night ahead with enough fuel in their tanks to see them through the dark hours. They were to revert to a watch period of three hours, because maintaining a careful lookout would be more tiring and fresh eyes were needed.

For his part, Harry planned to remain available all night, snatching an occasional nap when he could. He wanted to be on deck whenever they were near ships. He anticipated having to regularly adjust their course to pass safely between them. Harry had crossed the sea between the South of England and France many times, one of the busiest shipping areas in the world. Around six-hundred ships per day would sail up or down the English Channel along clearly defined shipping lanes.

The wind had settled back into its prevailing direction of blowing from the west and had dropped to a gentle breeze. The yacht was heading northeast towards the southeastern tip of Sicily, some fifty nautical miles ahead. Ahead, in the far distance they could just discern the masthead lights of the procession of ships passing in front of them in a disorganised rabble, heading either east or west along the Mediterranean.

As they peered into the distance, Harry pointed out the navigation lights. He told his crew the white steaming lights could be seen for many miles and, when the ships were closer, they would be able to pick out the red or green lights for the port or starboard side of the ships, which would confirm the ship's direction, east or west.

It was a rule of the sea that as the ships approached each other head on, they would both alter course to starboard, turn right a little to avoid a collision, so that on the yacht they also needed to watch for ships altering course. In open sea, ships should change course to avoid sailing yachts, but Harry had no intention of assuming that any ship would do so.

He explained that he intended to cross the line of vessels at a right angle to their direction, thus shortening the time their yacht remained in proximity to each ship. The speeds involved were low, about six knots for their yacht and between eighteen to twenty-four for each ship.

Harry's tactic was to pick out a ship in the line ahead and aim to pass close behind it, thus creating the largest possible gap between his yacht and the next ship that would be bearing down upon them.

And that's exactly what happened, with the result that before dawn, the yacht found itself a mere two nautical miles from their destination, the entrance to the bay of Rada di Portolano. For the past couple of hours, they had been able to see, directly in front of their bow, a green light which flashed brightly once every three seconds. That was the reassuring sight of the light fixed at the end of the breakwater behind which they planned to anchor.

All four were on deck, excited with the prospect of arriving at Sicily. Harry's eyes were red raw with tiredness, in contrast to the other three who were a buzz of energy.

"We're going to heave-to and wait for dawn," announced Harry.

"What's that mean," asked Teresa.

"I know!" It was Daniel who piped up, eager to show some of his nautical knowledge. "Heaving to is when the two sails work against each other, rendering the yacht almost stationary."

Harry was impressed, "Good enough explanation, Daniel."

They changed course onto the starboard tack, pulled in the mainsail tight and backed the foresail onto the wrong side of the yacht for the wind. With a little adjustment to the sails, Harry soon had the vessel looking after itself with nobody steering. It lay there, almost motionless, drifting very slowly away from their destination. To the amazement of the crew, their yacht instantly became a steady, motionless platform, rising and falling slowly on the swell that passed beneath them.

"I'm going to grab some shut eye," said Harry, "As always, wake me if any other vessels come near, or you're not sure about anything. Otherwise, wake me when it's light enough to clearly see the land.

He slumped in a corner of the cockpit, folded his arms, pulled up the hood of his sailing jacket and appeared to instantly fall asleep.

"I'll be lookout," whispered Daniel to Teresa and Nicole, "so you two can go below and grab some rest if you like."

"No way," replied Nicole. They all sat in the cockpit in silence, enjoying the sight of the beckoning dawn in the east, the darkness of Sicily slowly taking shape as the sky turned from black to vermillion, to dark blue.

Above, the stars disappeared and then soon after the planets were gone, just leaving a solitary pale moon hanging above them. The undersides of the few small clouds over the land became dark red. In the east, above Sicily, a vibrant red glow began to form as the upper tip of the sun approached the horizon. The sun itself appeared soon after as a large orange disk, which slowly lifted into the sky, seeming to pause as it struggled to tug itself free from its connection to the earth.

The three onlookers aboard were silently transfixed. The beautiful colours lasted for only five minutes after which Harry suddenly awoke, disturbed by the daylight, and heavily getting to his feet, he yawned and said, "Okay, let's do this."

Thirty minutes later, they were tucked up safely in the northeastern corner of the bay, in flat calm behind the breakwater, anchored in five metres of water, with the anchor tugged securely into the sandy bottom, the sails stowed, tea brewing down below, and a sense of achievement pervading the atmosphere.

Looking around, Harry saw four other yachts anchored nearby. Three showed the strange three-legged Sicilian flag and the last one, a large bright red steel yacht, hailed from The Netherlands. A man onboard was looking at Harry and waved in greeting. Harry reflected that sailors in foreign ports were generally a friendly bunch.

He wondered if they should engage socially with any other sailors or keep themselves to themselves. But now, sleep beckoned. He returned the Dutchman's salutation with a wave, went below, and disappeared into his cabin, closing the door behind him.

24

The taxi pulled up to the Grand Harbour Hotel and John Shaw stepped out, squinted against the bright light that reflected from the light stone buildings. Mopping his brow, he hastened into the cool hotel lobby.

"Welcome to the Grand Harbour Hotel, Mr Shaw," greeted the receptionist as he signed the register. "We hope you enjoy your stay with us."

"Thank you," John croaked, his throat was still dry from the atmosphere aboard the aeroplane. "I'm actually looking for my son, Harry. I believe he is staying here?"

"Ah, yes, Mr Harry Shaw," said the receptionist, furrowing his brow. "He checked out some days ago but left a bag in our safe, saying he would be returning."

"Did he say where he was going?"

"Well, I understand that, together with friends, he was chartering a yacht for several weeks. I can give you the contact details of some local charter companies if you'd like to try and reach him?" offered the receptionist, his tone sympathetic.

"Please, that would be most helpful," John said as the man consulted a telephone directory and scrawled down several numbers.

On his third attempt, John dialled the correct number.

"Hello, this is Paul speaking. How may I assist you today?" came the voice on the other end of the line, his strong Maltese accent reminding John of years past.

"My name is John Shaw. I'm trying to locate a yacht chartered by my son, Harry."

"Yes," Paul replied, recognition in his voice, "we did charter a yacht to your son and his friends. Is there something wrong?"

"Nothing that I'm aware of, but I've been unable to contact him, and I'd like to speak with him as soon as possible," John tried to keep the worry out of his voice.

There was a pause when John could hear Paul inhale breath before he launched into his explanation. "We would also like to know where our yacht is. I must tell you that you're the third person to inquire about their whereabouts," Paul revealed. "First, the police in Malta, and then British Police and now you. It is all very irregular."

"Police!" John was amazed. "Did they say why?"

"Unfortunately, they did not, but it seemed serious," Paul admitted. "I've left voicemail messages for your son and the others, urging them to contact me, but I haven't heard back."

Paul continued, "And another thing, the AIS on the yacht isn't reporting its position as it should be. I cannot imagine how that could cease working unless it was intentionally disconnected! Frankly, we are worried that the yacht may have been stolen by your son and his crew!" Paul's voice had risen to a crescendo as he vented his frustration.

"Stolen? My son would never do such a thing!" John exclaimed, firm and resolute. "Harry is an honourable man and a skilled sailor. You can rest assured that he will return your yacht on the agreed date."

"I do hope that you are correct, Mr Shaw. We shall see."

"Thank you for telling me, Paul," John said, mystified by why Harry would fail to respond to phone calls from the yacht charter company or, for that matter, his own repeated attempts to contact him."

"Where are you, and what are you up to Son?" He wondered as he prepared to go downstairs and enjoy a stiff drink before dinner.

Overnight, John decided what his next step should be. After a hasty breakfast, he had the reception call him a taxi. He set off for the ornate building of the main police station, on Archbishop Road.

Upon entering, John bent to speak through the small window in the wall where a police officer listened to his request. He was told to sit and wait on the uncomfortable hard wooden bench in the corridor. As doors opened and closed, he heard snatches of the cacophony of phones ringing, officers chatting in Maltese and the relentless tapping of keyboards. It sounded like chaos behind those doors.

After waiting for what felt like an eternity, Sergeant Yong finally emerged to see him, his expression stern, yet attentive.

"Can I help you, Sir?" he asked, one eyebrow raised in curiosity.

"Yes, I'm here to find out why the police are interested in a yacht chartered by my son, Harry Shaw," John said, his voice as commanding as he could muster.

Sergeant Yong paused as he thought about how much to reveal. "I cannot share much with you, Mr Shaw, but it concerns a crime committed in the UK."

John stood erect and looked sternly into the detective's eyes and asked for more detail.

"The yacht was last seen heading south, which would be in the direction of Tripoli," said Yong, looking questioningly into John's face in the hope that he might supply a reason for why Harry and his friends would be heading for Libya.

John furrowed his brow, struggling to understand what Harry was up to. His mind raced with questions.

"Please, Sergeant," John implored, "could you at least tell me where I might find Doctor Camilleri's family? I need to speak with them about my son."

"I'm sorry, Sir, but I cannot divulge any more information."

"Officer, I have flown from England to find Harry. I think the least you can do is to help me with some basic information, an address, which after all is hardly confidential!"

After a moment of consideration, Yong disappeared without saying anything and returned scribbling an address onto a notepad and tearing off the top sheet for John. Grateful for any lead, John thanked the officer before hastily making his way outside to find a taxi.

As the vehicle navigated through the winding Maltese roads, John absorbed the vivid landscape. However, nothing could distract him from his growing concern about Harry's actions and his connection with Teresa Camilleri.

The taxi drove down a long pathway between stone walls and fields until it came to rest outside a modest farmhouse, with the sun casting warm rays on its well-worn exterior. Taking a deep breath, John asked the taxi to wait for a minute. He approached the front door, knocked, and waited, uncertain of what reception he would receive.

Ruzar, a short and sturdy man with rough farmer's hands, appeared with his wife Mary standing behind him. Their faces held an air of restrained concern before John introduced himself as Harry's father, explaining that he believed Harry was with their daughter Teresa.

"Please, won't you come in?" Ruzar offered, taking a step back to allow John entry. "I'm so pleased to meet you."

John waved away the taxi and crossed the threshold into their home. He was in their large living room. He looked around quickly, taking in the massive fireplace and four comfortable old chairs at one end, a large dining table in the middle of the room, and at the far end three doors, leading off to the other rooms.

He was invited to sit at the comfortable end of the room with Ruzar and Mary opposite. Ruzar made the introductions, and then Mary headed off to brew coffee, leaving the men to talk. "How can I help," asked Ruzar.

"I confess I am worried," started John. "My son seems to have sailed off with Teresa and appears to be avoiding any contact with me or anyone else."

"Daniel, our son, and Nicole, a niece, are also on the yacht with Harry and Teresa," Ruzar informed John. "They set off for a vacation together, I understand.

"Ah, so there is a crew of four?" John asked, his brow furrowed.

"Yes," Mary replied, arriving with coffee. She was obviously upset by events because her hands shook a little as she passed a cup to John. "We're very worried. The police were here asking about Teresa."

"Really?" John leaned forward. "I spoke with Sergeant Yong at the police station earlier today. He wouldn't tell me why they wanted to contact the yacht, except that it was related to a crime committed in the UK."

Ruzar and Mary exchanged a glance, their faces etched with worry. "That's — difficult to believe," Ruzar said, shaking his head. "Our daughter is a respected doctor. She would never get involved in anything criminal."

"Could there be some kind of misunderstanding?" John suggested, struggling to reconcile the idea of Harry or Teresa being a lawbreaker.

"There must be a mistake!" Mary insisted, her eyes watered with unshed tears. "But why won't they give us more details?"

Mary offered John a biscuit. He felt sorry for them both. Clearly, they were even more worried than he was. He felt an immediate bond with them, as victims of the same uncertainty and desperate to protect their children.

"Whatever the truth may be," John declared, looking into the eyes of Teresa's parents, "I am confident that our children are innocent."

"Yes," Ruzar agreed with a nod, his voice thick with emotion.

And so, amidst the turmoil of unanswered questions and growing concerns, the two families were thrown together. John cleared his throat, "Harry has never let anyone down and in the meantime, I guess the only thing we can do is wait and have faith in our children. I plan to stay in Malta to be here to welcome them immediately they return."

Mary wrung her hands together. "We have left them so many voicemails, but they never call back. It's not like our Daniel or Teresa to be so unresponsive."

"Nor is it like Harry," John added, feeling a knot of unease twisting in his gut.

"Let us pray they are alright and will soon be in touch," Ruzar suggested, and the three shared a sombre moment. Mary moved the beads of a rosary between her fingers, seemingly lost in thought or prayer.

After a long silence, she returned her attention to the room, "Mr Shaw, would you stay for lunch? You must be tired from your journey."

"Thank you, Mrs Camilleri. I'd appreciate that," John replied. Ruzar suggested a walk, to work up an appetite as he showed John around a little of their farm.

The men returned to find the old scrubbed wooden tabled covered with a hearty meal of freshly baked bread, homemade cheese, and sun-ripened vegetables from the garden. They ate, chatted, and relaxed. Soon, John found himself answering questions about his previous time in Malta, his own wife and how Harry had lost his wife and children.

After lunch, Ruzar invited John to join him in spreading fertilizer around the base of the grapevines in their small vineyard where the cultivated grapes to make wine for family consumption.

"Come," Ruzar beckoned, leading John towards the bumpy old tractor that towed a trailer filled with bags of fertilizer. "This will give us a chance to talk some more."

John held on tight, as the machine jumped and jerked over stones. The tall vertical exhaust belched blue smoke into the air and the complete machine vibrated with every slow thump, thump, thump from the old tractor's engine.

Thirty minutes later, as they spread the fertilizer around the base of the old vines, John found himself enjoying the simple pleasure of working alongside Ruzar. The sun was warm on his face, casting dappled light through the leaves overhead.

"Your son, Harry. He is a good man?" Ruzar asked as they paused to unload another bag of fertilizer.

"Very much so," John replied with confidence. "He has a strong moral compass and would never knowingly harm anyone."

"Then perhaps this whole situation is just one big misunderstanding," Ruzar said, more with hope than conviction.

"I'm impressed by your energy, Ruzar!" John exclaimed, watching in awe as the old man hefted a heavy bag of fertilizer over his shoulder with ease. The muscles in his arms bulged beneath his rolled-up sleeves, making it clear that age had not weakened him.

"Life on a farm keeps you strong," Ruzar replied, grinning at John's amazement. He cut open the bag and began to spread its contents around the grapevines. "Besides, these vines won't feed themselves."

John watched Ruzar's deft movements, feeling a pang of jealousy. His own arthritic knees made it difficult for him to keep up with his pace, but he was determined not to let it show. Instead, he focused on his own work.

Later, as the afternoon sun dipped low in the sky, it was time for John to leave. As the taxi idled, waiting to take him back to the Grand Harbour Hotel, Ruzar and Mary stood by the farmhouse door, their faces a mixture of concern and hope.

"Please, John," Mary implored, her voice wavering slightly with emotion. "Stay with us until the yacht returns with our children. You are welcome here."

"Thank you, both of you," John replied, touched by their offer. He hesitated for a moment, considering it. But in his heart, he knew where he needed to be. "I appreciate your kindness, but I will stay at the hotel because Harry will return there."

Ruzar nodded understandingly as he clasped John's hand in a firm handshake. As the taxi pulled away from the farm, John watched the old couple standing side by side, waving him off until he disappeared out of sight. On the journey back to his hotel, he reflected on the sequence of events that had begun with Harry's acrimonious departure from his company, through the incident on his yacht, where his family died, to the funeral and then to Harry's current disappearing act. "What on earth next?" thought John.

25

Aboard the floating sanctuary of the charter yacht, the four were enjoying their sailing holiday. Worries and troubles had been temporarily parked at the back of their minds.

Harry, Teresa, Daniel, and Nicole had each settled into a comfortable daily routine. They spent their days indulging in the simple pleasures of swimming in the azure sea, soaking up the sun on deck, eating, drinking, and sharing laughter.

On this particular morning, they were anchored at Monte Pergola, where the unmistakable outline of the volcano of Mount Etna was clearly visible in the distance, rising above the line of low buildings that bordered the shoreline. The first light of dawn found Teresa on deck; her lithe figure silhouetted against the rosy sky as she executed Tai Chi forms with fluid grace. The foredeck of the yacht provided ample space for her martial arts practice, and the rocking movement of the boat added an extra challenge.

After fifteen minutes or so, she changed to performing her daily standing practice, sinking down onto her bent legs, and raising her arms to hold the invisible balloon. She held that stress position for as long as she could bear, until her legs started quivering. She was close to her maximum level of endurance, which on this morning was almost thirty minutes.

Harry was up earlier than usual and from the cockpit he had been watching Teresa perform her routine. As she finished, stretched, and relaxed, she turned to see Harry watching from the cockpit.

"Good morning," Harry said quietly, so as not to wake those down below. He ran a hand through his tousled blond hair, blue eyes still heavy with sleep. Teresa smiled at him, her glasses catching the morning sunlight.

"Morning, Harry," she replied softly. The serenity of her voice belied the strength that lay hidden within her, a power born of discipline and dedication.

"Your routine was quite mesmerising," Harry said, leaning against the cockpit coaming."

"It is surprisingly good exercise," she replied, soaked in perspiration, "and it helps me find balance in my life, with my mental wellbeing." She paused, considering her next words carefully. "Perhaps it could help you too, with your grief. You should try. I could show you how."

Harry's expression sobered at the mention of his lost family, but he nodded thoughtfully. "Maybe," he agreed, though the thought was tucked away for another day. "I can see it's hard work," he observed as he watched her glowing body descend the steps for her shower.

Harry prepared breakfast as the noise of the shower raised Daniel and Nicole from their slumbers. And so began another day in paradise.

After breakfast, Harry's routine was to settle down at the chart table where he would check the weather forecast, update the yacht's logbook, and consult the charts and pilot books. This was when he planned their trip between the hidden coves, sheltered bays and secluded beaches of Sicily.

He was deep in concentration when Teresa came over to see what he was doing. "Where are we sailing to next?" she asked.

"Well," Harry replied, his eyes never leaving the chart, "I'm thinking we should visit Syracuse, south of here. We need to stock up with more food and to find a spot where we can go alongside and fill the water tanks. I'm looking for an opportunity to do that without creating a digital record. I think Syracuse may be ideal."

"Please explain how we can do that."

He continued, "Well, there is an inflatable dinghy in one of the cockpit lockers. We could use that to row ashore. Then, we could buy food with cash, so there would be no record of a card transaction. And if Daniel and Nicole did the shopping, then there is no chance of you or me being recorded on CCTV."

"Why would that matter?" inquired Teresa.

"Perhaps I am being overly cautious, but I don't want any facial recognition system to reveal our presence to the AI at GCHQ."

Teresa frowned, dragged back to the reality that she was still a wanted woman.

Harry continued, "According to this pilot book," lifting a blue bound volume, "there is a water tap for the fishermen on this quay here." Harry pointed at the chart. "I think we could bring the yacht alongside, fill with water and avoid going to a marina where we would have to check in at the office, show our passports and pay to moor up, so that our presence would be noted."

"I hate all this clandestine stuff!" Teresa retorted. She went to her cabin and shortly returned wearing a bikini. With a playful smile, she asked Harry, "Are you up for our daily race?"

"Of course," Harry grinned, closing the pilot book, and changing into his swimming trunks before joining her on deck.

The refreshingly cool water beckoned. Diving in, they sent arcs of sparkling droplets into the air. Teresa swam with grace and fluidity, her movements made Harry think of a dolphin gliding through the sea. In contrast, his strokes were strong and purposeful, with much splashing as his powerful arms bashed through the water. In speed, they were closely matched, and as they reached the designated point far from the yacht, they paused, treading water and catching their breath.

"Ready — set — go!" Teresa called out, and they both took off back towards the yacht, each determined to outdo the other. This time, Teresa was first home.

Later, as the four settled down to a light lunch of tinned sardines and bean salad, Harry proposed his idea to replenish their stocks. "I'm absolutely dying for fresh food and newly roasted coffee," declared Nicole, insisting that she should be one of those who rowed ashore. She pictured visiting a café before returning to the yacht. It was soon agreed that tomorrow they would sail to Syracuse and buy more provisions.

That afternoon, Teresa was stretched out on the deck, basking in the sunshine like a contented cat. Harry had retreated to the shaded cockpit and was reading a novel that he had selected from the small library of paperbacks onboard.

"Harry," Teresa called from her sunbathing spot, "you should join me. The sun feels wonderful."

"Maybe in a bit," he replied, absorbed in his book. "I want to finish this chapter first."

"Suit yourself," she said as she let out a soft chuckle.

Daniel and Nicole were playfully swimming around the bow of the yacht, out of sight to those onboard, their laughter and splashing unnoticed by Harry, who was fully absorbed in the tale of derring-do.

And then suddenly the couple at the bow fell silent.

In the quiet, Teresa lifted herself on her arms and turned towards Harry with a broad grin. She whispered, "I think our resident lovebirds have found a secluded spot for some kissing and cuddling," she whispered to Harry, her brown eyes twinkling.

"Seems like it," he grinned. "A holiday romance, do you think?"

"Maybe," said Teresa, "and they do seem well suited. I've often wondered if they might settle down together."

"Really?" questioned Harry, "What's the situation in Malta with cousins getting together?"

"Ah," said Teresa, keeping her voice as low as possible, "I think that for cousins to marry, they need a special dispensation from the church."

They exchanged knowing looks and pretended to be unaware of the tryst at the bow.

As each day drifted lazily into evening, the four friends would take turns to prepare dinner, with varying results as they searched amongst their dwindling stock of tinned and dried food. Daniel's inventions could be interesting.

That night, he prepared tinned sardines mixed with tinned tuna, stirred in tomato ketchup and Worcestershire sauce, served with boiled rice mixed with tinned sweetcorn. The flavour was better than the description, and fortunately Nicole had laid in a plentiful stock of red wine.

Suitably lubricated, it was an enjoyable evening, with the

clink of glasses carrying across the anchorage. Towards the end of dinner, Nicole and Daniel, hands intertwined, faces aglow, made an announcement.

"Harry, Teresa," Nicole began, "Daniel and I have decided we shall become an item for the remainder of our voyage."

"Congratulations!" spluttered Teresa, so her wine splashed across the table, followed by laughter.

"We are not exactly surprised," Harry added, "I hope you realise that captains are not really allowed to perform marriages, but I now pronounce you guy and gal until the end of the voyage." Amid much laughter they toasted the couple, the moon, the yacht, the sea, Sicily, and their future.

Eventually, as the night started to cool, it was time to clear the table, to do the washing up, and to turn in for the night. As the moon cast a silver sheen upon a tranquil bay, a giggling Nicole gathered her belongings from the cabin that she shared with Teresa and tottered into Daniel's, leaving the other two alone in their respective spaces. As Harry and Teresa tried to drift off to sleep, they couldn't help but be aware of the muffled sounds emanating from Daniel's cabin.

After an hour of sleeplessness, Harry decided to go on deck and look at the stars. When he reached the cockpit, he was surprised to find Teresa already there, curled up in a corner, wrapped in a duvet.

"Sometimes, I think there's nothing quite like this life," Teresa whispered as they stared up at the canopy of stars above them. "Do you ever think about what it would be like to just keep going? To leave the past behind and become true nomads, free as the wind?"

"Of course," Harry admitted, his voice low, "but I've spoken with many yachtsmen who chased that dream. It always seems to end with dissatisfaction. Who was it who said that people travel the world in search of something, and eventually they return home, where they find what they were looking for?

"I think it was George Moore, the novelist," said Teresa.

Harry expounded his theory, "I've always believed it best to voyage with an end in sight, to end that trip on a high, and then to look forward to the next adventure."

"Wise words, captain," said Teresa, saluting from the far corner of the cockpit. "And what's the end of this voyage going to bring?"

"Well," said Harry, "I have faith in Professor Hall. He appears to be a principled man who is on our side. Hopefully, he will find a way to fix the AI and clear your name."

"I do hope so," was Teresa's only comment. They fell into silence until she bade him good night and went below.

Early the following morning, the four raised the anchor and set sail for Syracuse. It was an uneventful sail, excepting for something of which Harry was completely unaware.

Sailing along the shoreline in daylight, the navigation was easy, so Harry did not consult their GPS position using the plotter screen above the chart table.

He didn't know that the latest software update, which had been installed so diligently by Paul at the charter company, had installed a bug in the yacht's electronic navigation system. The malware, which had originated from the AI at GCHQ, contained a fault that occasionally created random errors of position.

If, halfway through their short passage, Harry had checked the chart plotter he would have seen an impossible situation. The monitor was showing the yacht sailing along the E45 road, some six miles east of their real location. But, confident in his position, and entranced by the beauty of their surroundings, Harry remained blissfully unaware of this digital manipulation.

Would the GPS report an incorrect position and place their yacht in a dangerous situation? The four were totally unaware that they were involved in a navigational lottery.

They arrived at Syracuse during early afternoon. The inflatable dinghy was inflated using the foot pump provided. Daniel appeared on deck wearing dark glasses and a baseball cap with the peak pulled down to hide his face, "I'm taking no chances on that damned AI recognising me through a CCTV camera somewhere."

Nicole appeared wearing a preposterously large-brimmed sun hat which made her look like a celebrity who wanted to be noticed. Teresa and Harry watched them go, a little jealous of their excursion, which would make a pleasant break.

Harry was now concerned, "I hope I haven't misjudged this. I've assumed the AI isn't likely to be interested in those two, but who knows, by now they could also be targets." He shrugged, and decided to divert his mind away from that thought by reading more of the novel he was engrossed in. Teresa, having missed her morning martial arts routine, changed into a skimpy bikini and headed for the foredeck.

Harry found the sight of her stunning bronzed body performing sinuous movements a distraction that was difficult to ignore. For the first time he noticed the clearly defined muscles of her thighs and arms. "That's one strong woman," he thought. He looked down and tried to concentrate on his book. He couldn't resist another peek forward, but then resolved to drag his attention back to the book he was holding.

He was starting to become absorbed in the story again when, on the periphery of his vision, he saw a pair of barefooted, shapely, bronze legs crossing the cockpit toward him.

Harry did not look up but stared at the print on the page which began to blur as the legs stopped in front of him and moved so close that a knee touched one of his own legs.

The contact created a jolt of pleasure he could not ignore. He looked up from his book to see that the knees turned into thighs, slightly parted.

Above those was a tiny red bikini below a narrow waist, a flat stomach, and then he looked up into her face. She was standing with her hands on her hips, looking down at him and smiling.

Harry choked out, "I'm really not ready for another relationship yet."

"Today, I'm thinking about a very short-term relationship," was her reply.

That was too much for Harry to bear. Lust took control. He reached out and pulled her towards him. They soon collapsed, writhing on the warm teak of the cockpit floor.

"Whoa there, Harry" Teresa giggled, "By short-term, I didn't mean too quick."

Afterwards, when smokers would traditionally share a cigarette, they lay on their backs, naked, allowing the gentle breeze to dry their perspiration-soaked bodies. Harry turned to Teresa and asked, "What has this done for our relationship?"

She answered without hesitation, "We're just friends, fond friends, close friends. I think the correct term is friends with benefits."

"That was some benefit," laughed Harry.

When Daniel and Nicole eventually arrived back at the yacht, the little inflatable dinghy was heavily laden with fresh and tinned food, bottled water, and wine. Below decks, stowing away all the provisions into lockers and the coolbox, Nicole remarked to Teresa, "You look radiant. And Harry looks like the cat that got the cream. Did something happen while we were ashore?"

Teresa answered with the politician's reply. "You might think so, but I couldn't possibly comment."

Nicole understood what that meant and said, "Nice one cousin. I won't mention it again."

"Thank you, Nicole; that would be perfect."

For the rest of their time aboard the yacht, none of the four would broach the subject of the burgeoning relationship between Harry and Teresa. That subject would successfully remain taboo. During the night, there would be visits between the couple's cabins. If Daniel or Nicole were aware of those nocturnal goings on, they kept their knowledge to themselves and never mentioned anything.

Later that evening, with the store cupboards refilled, when it was completely dark and there was no sign of life on the fishermen's quay, they let out all the anchor chain, tied a large air-filled yacht's fender to the bitter end, and slipped their anchor so that the end of the chain remained floating, ready for their return. They quietly motored over to the fishermen's quay where they found the freshwater tap. They connected the long hose supplied with the yacht and filled the boat's water tanks to the brim.

The four then manoeuvred their yacht back, picked up the floating fender, and reconnected themselves to their anchor. The complete manoeuvre had been executed quietly and attracted no attention from the quayside or the other yachts in the harbour.

"Mission complete," announced Harry. Early the following morning, they left Syracuse and sailed to their next anchorage, further along the coast. Their vacation continued happily until one event created a stir.

It was evening and the four were below decks. Nicole was cooking dinner in the galley and the others were playing cards around the large circular cabin table. A forehatch was open, creating a gentle breeze circulating the air below, when a sudden squall of wind blew out the gas on the cooker. Nicole hadn't noticed the flame was extinguished, so a small amount of smelly propane gas escaped before the safety cut-off on the cooker closed the gas valve.

Teresa remembered that gas was allegedly responsible for the explosion on Harry's yacht. At the gassy smell, she became genuinely concerned. "We've got a gas leak. Quick, Harry, what should we do?"

Harry replied, "No need to worry, there's a safety valve on the cooker that switches off the gas soon after the flame is extinguished. And, in any case, there is a gas alarm fitted in the bilge, the bottom of the boat, which makes a hell of a noise long before the gas and air mixture could be dangerous."

She thought for a minute and then asked, "But Harry, if what you just said is correct, on your yacht, how could a gas explosion have killed your family?"

Nicole and Daniel, who knew about Harry losing his wife

and children, became completely silent and stared at him. Teresa sat across the table and looked at him sternly. She had suddenly switched to being an inquisitor who was determined to get to the bottom of this story.

Harry, in a relaxed mood, had not thought about the consequences of his words and did not know how to respond. To say nothing was to appear a liar. To tell the truth would be breaking the Official Secrets Act and a crime. And try as he might, he couldn't think of a plausible response.

"Go on Harry," pushed Teresa.

As the colour rushed to his face and betrayed his discomfort, Harry delayed and looked down at the table, unsure what to do. He had always found it difficult to live the lie forced upon him by Commander Forbes. He hated the thought of misleading his newfound friends, especially as he was the prime cause for their hiding away.

Teresa glared at him. Harry couldn't read her expression. He cared deeply about what she thought of him, which tipped the scales in favour of coming clean. He decided it was time for honesty, and to hell with the consequences.

Nicole abandoned her cooking and joined them at the table. As Harry unburdened himself, the three sat in silence, apart from an occasional gasp of surprise.

His voice cracked as he tried not to sob. He described the complete sequence of events: his refusal to allow AI to be used within his software company, his confrontation with the new owners and his being fired, the four week vacation with his family aboard his yacht, the attack against him being engineered by the AI at GCHQ, the mysterious vessel approaching from astern, the grenade that killed his family, the bullet grazing his head and putting him in hospital, his temporary loss of memory, Commander Forbes tricking him into signing the Official Secrets Act, the cover-up story of a gas explosion, his recovery under the care of Teresa, the knife attack, his credit cards being blocked, learning from Professor Hall about the digital attacks by proxy, Teresa being dragged into his problems with the false charges of stealing drugs.

Nicole completed the picture by telling Daniel and Teresa of the chilling threat from the AI at GCHQ; Don't mess with me.

Now that the truth was out in the open, Harry apologised, "I'm sorry I haven't been completely honest up to now. I've hated it. The crazy thing is that by telling you the truth I've just committed a serious crime, which carries a long prison sentence. I haven't even been able to be honest with my father."

It was Daniel who spoke first. "Harry, I'm sure I speak for the three of us when I say that you have our sincere condolences for losing your family. I cannot imagine how you have dealt with that."

"The way you've been treated by your own government stinks, "Nicole added passionately.

"I was convinced I was treating a bullet wound to your head," said Teresa, "but the surgeon insisted the damage was caused by a flying splinter."

They discussed Harry's and Teresa's situations. They hoped that back in England, Professor Hall had by now conquered the AI and was succeeding to cancel the charges against Teresa.

It was Daniel who again took the lead, "We're all in this

together now Harry, and we shall do all we can to support you and Teresa."

"Amen," added Nicole.

And then Teresa changed the subject to forward planning. "If the AI was prepared to kill Harry and his family, and it now also considers me an enemy, could it also add you two, Nicole and Daniel, to its list of targets? Perhaps all our lives are at risk? What should we do to protect ourselves?"

There was an hour of intense discussion. They considered everything from stealing the yacht and heading off to some remote part of the world, to handing themselves in to the police and asking for protection. In the end it was decided that they would return to Malta on the agreed date, at the end of the yacht charter, and hope that Professor Hall had simply made their problems go away.

If they found that the Professor had not succeeded to sort everything, and Teresa was still being charged, then they would immediately engage the best lawyer they could find, and Harry would try to hide away from observation by the AI.

Nicole made another suggestion, "Just in case of the worst-case scenario, how about Teresa and Harry write one of those 'in the event of my death or disappearance' letters? We could post them from Sicily to family and lawyers. Should the worst happen, at least your stories would be heard after your deaths.

"Thanks cousin," Teresa replied, "Aren't you a ray of sunshine!"

The discussion ended there and, when everyone turned in for the night, the mood aboard the yacht was subdued.

It was now just four days before they were due to complete

their voyage and return to Malta.

During May to September the winds in the Mediterranean are light to moderate and reliable, which explains why so many people choose the area for their yacht charter holidays. But recently, the summer weather in these latitudes has been less predictable. The rising water temperatures, set in motion by global warming, has fuelled occasional tropical circular storms, especially around the eastern Mediterranean, which meteorologists have christened 'Medicines.'

Unknown to Harry and his crew, one of those had been forming over Greece. Land and sea temperatures had risen and the movement of a front of cooler air had set in motion an anticlockwise spiral, the embryo of a rotating storm. The air in the centre of this storm started to rise, dragging up the energy contained in the excessively warm sea and created a Medicine.

In Sicily, the result was that during the daytime, two days before they were due to sail back, the wind rapidly increased to force eight, a gale blowing from the north. Harry had been watching the cloud formation and the speed at which the barometer was falling. He knew what was coming and gathered up any belongings on deck and stowed them below. He lengthened the anchor chain to the maximum, adding to the weight below the water which would help to hold them in place.

They were on the edge of the circular storm to the east. In their safe anchorage, the wind changed direction and came from the land. Soon, it blew so hard that the wind whistled through the rigging with an eerie intensity that scared Teresa and Nicole. "We're not going to sail in this weather, are we

Harry," Teresa asked.

"Actually, this yacht would cope fine, but it makes no sense to take unnecessary risks, so we'll sit it out," replied Harry. Their anchor was tugged deep into the sandy bottom of the bay. But sand is not as solid a medium as mud when it comes to holding an anchor fast. Harry knew that in this strong wind, the yacht might drag their anchor through the sand, like a tractor would drag a plough. He checked their position on the GPS plotter and enabled the feature that would set off an alarm if the yacht moved its position.

To illustrate the power of the storm, the rain started falling hard. As each large heavy droplet of water hit the surface of the sea, the water reacted as if a pebble had been tossed in the water, creating a small splash that rose about ten centimetres. That happened with every single droplet, so that the sea around them disappeared into a dense fog of bouncing water.

The wind then increased to force nine. The rain now drummed on the large deck above the main saloon, creating such a noise that the four had to raise their voices to be heard. Seventy miles per hour gusts caused the long wires supporting the mast to vibrate at a high frequency, which created a vibration that could be felt throughout the yacht. Looking through the portlights, the visibility had reduced to almost zero. The other yachts anchored near them, the land, the sky, and sea all disappeared behind a wet grey curtain. Each gust brought minor changes in wind direction, which would hit one side of the yacht's mast and then the other, unpredictably jerking the boat this way or that. The erratic movement set nerves on edge down below.

Had they donned their waterproofs and gone on deck,

they would have found it difficult to breath without turning away from the wind. Had they faced the wind, it would force rain and sea water into an uncovered mouth at some fifty miles per hour.

Daniel produced a pack of cards, grinned, and suggested they pass the time playing whist. As all hell was let loose around them, the four, snug and dry below, concentrated on the brain teasing game.

That night, Harry set one person on anchor watch, so that if the weather worsened or the yacht started to drag its anchor, he would be aware. Each person agreed to remain on watch for two hours.

The next morning, the weather had improved, the rain had abated, they could see land, and the wind changed direction to blow from the northwest. Harry explained to his crew that the change suggested the storm had moved eastwards and reduced in intensity.

Before the storm, Harry's plan had been to leave their anchorage around midnight, to sail south from Sicily and arrive back at Valletta harbour before darkness fell. They would have docked at the marina in early evening, celebrated their last night aboard, and then handed back the yacht to the charter company on the final morning of their charter. However, the storm had delayed their departure.

Harry cursed himself for not sailing back into Maltese waters a couple of days earlier, which would have been a prudent skipper's choice. He was seated at the navigator's position, stepping out distances with the brass dividers, mentally calculating speed and distance, when Teresa approached him with a mug of coffee.

"What's the plan skipper?"

"I was hoping to avoid sailing through the night," replied Harry, "but, if we're going to return the yacht on time, we shall have to do that, arriving back at Valetta early on our last morning."

"What about this strong wind?" asked Teresa.

"I expect the wind speed will continue to drop throughout today," explained Harry, "so that we can leave this evening. The sea will remain rough for a day or two, but the wind will be in our favour. We should have a fast sail across rough sea, which is exhilarating during daylight but harder work at night."

"Do you reckon your crew is capable?"

"I sure do!" replied Harry with conviction, though in his heart he was not feeling so confident.

26

It was late afternoon when the Professor, reluctantly, bypassed his line manager and called the office of the recently appointed Director of GCHQ. He asked for an urgent, one-to-one, confidential meeting.

The new Director had been in office for only three weeks, and he was still getting to grips with the scope of his responsibilities. In the eyes of the outside world, he ran the place. The Professor was wondering how this new Director would cope with hearing the unwelcome news he must impart. He entered the inner sanctum of his office, the door closed, and they were alone. "Come in Professor Hall. Do take a seat with me over here."

"Thank you, Sir," the Professor began as he was guided towards the circular seating area around a coffee table in one corner of a large office. The Professor accepted the cup of tea proffered but avoided the custard cream biscuits. He wanted to get on with the business at hand.

The new Director enjoyed his eminent position and the deference with which he was treated. Other managers would have switched to using first names, but 'Sir' suited the Director just fine. This man was guilty of feeling a little self-important.

The Professor spoke with his usual pedantic slow delivery. "Sir, I have three pieces of information that I feel it is my duty to impart. You will be aware of the degree to which we rely upon our artificial intelligence. It does the legwork in analysing data to identify any threats to the UK."

"Yes," he replied, "I received a comprehensive briefing,

and frankly, I am in awe at the achievements of your department. I assume from the urgency of this meeting that you either wish to share some stupendous achievement or an unwelcome problem?"

"The latter, I'm afraid Sir." The Professor paused for a moment whilst he rubbed his tired eyes and decided how best to approach what he needed to explain.

"My first piece of news is regarding a development with our AI. You see, much to everyone's surprise, our AI has developed some basic animal like thinking. It became sentient Sir."

"I thought such sentience was not going to be possible for some years yet," the Director interjected.

"Well, we have given our AI more autonomy of action than other artificial intelligences. It has sufficient independence to develop its own logical abilities. The important thing I need you to understand Sir is that our AI has been able to rewrite its own software. In human terms, it has been rewiring and developing itself, rather like the brain of a child rapidly alters its structure during its early years."

"I see no problem yet. Please carry on."

"Now we come to the second thing I must report, Sir. Our AI, just like any other being, wants to survive. That is where the problem lies. It has identified certain people who have spoken out against the threat of AI. It has interpreted the language of a few people as a threat to its very existence. It has responded by attacking those individuals."

"I don't understand how a computer, even an artificially intelligent computer, could attack anyone." The Director looked genuinely perplexed.

The professor explained. "Our AI has been making digital attacks by proxy. It has been manipulating data to create situations that have prompted the police, armed forces, and cyber warfare agencies to act against completely innocent citizens. For example..." Here the Professor gave a brief description of the troubles that the AI had visited upon Harry, starting with the attempt to have him killed at sea.

As the importance of this information sunk in, the Director's face drained of blood so that he now looked as pale and unhealthy as the Professor. There was a long silence whilst the Director absorbed the information, until eventually, he asked, "So what have you been doing about this?"

The Professor described his many attempts to solve the problem. He explained Operation Lobotomy, and how his team had been trying to cut out the code that created the sentient behaviour whilst leaving the AI capable of continuing all the clever work it had been doing.

The Professor talked through, in simple terms, how the AI was rewriting its own computer control code each day. His team would identify the lines of code they intended to modify and then, before they could act, the AI would have morphed into a further iteration. It was now creating new lines of code faster than they could unravel how it all worked.

The Director insisted, "But there must be some way of retaining command and control. This is, after all, merely a computer program sitting on our computer, run by our people."

"I wish it were that simple," the Professor replied, "We have had the best minds available working on this for longer than a month now, and without success. The only solution I am aware of is that we switch off our supercomputer, delete all the software, then reload an older version of our AI software and restart the computer."

"Well, Professor, I cannot approve the action of simply switching off the UK's ability to protect itself from cyber and terrorist threats, even for twenty-four hours. It's just too risky."

The Professor took a deep breath and continued, "Sir, that brings me to my third piece of news. Today, I have discovered a new and greater problem."

The Professor had decided to risk seeming flippant by making an almost childlike comparison. "I believe our AI has created a brain system that we can compare to the octopus."

"Octopus?" The Directors eyebrows raised as he stared at the Professor.

"Yes Sir. You see, the brain of an octopus is not merely located in one place. Parts of the brain are distributed across its eight limbs. And experts don't know how much of the octopus's thought is centralised. We now have a comparable situation with our AI."

"It has become aware of my departments attempts to cull some of its abilities. The AI has reacted by dividing and duplicating its brain across multiple computers. You see, there are many other computers to which our own supercomputer is networked."

"I must report that our AI has deposited duplicate brains across six of our own systems, those located at our offices at Bude, Scarborough, Menwith Hill, Manchester, and London. I also suspect it has infiltrated our overseas systems on

Ascension Island and in Cyprus. And unfortunately, it may be even worse."

The Director squirmed in his seat, "Carry on Professor."

"I am fairly certain that our AI has further protected itself by placing code outside our organisation. You will know that we use the encrypted Government *Secure Net* to communicate with other agencies such as the Highways Agency, NHS, the National Grid, and others. And that we use the GSN, the Government Secret Network, to access the systems at MI5, MI6, Marine Security, Border Force, and more, to gather intelligence in real time."

The Director tried to interject and stop the flow of incoming bad news, but the Professor held up his hand, his flat palm towards the Director, like a police officer stopping traffic.

He was taken aback and paused long enough for the Professor to explain, "To successfully kill off the AI throughout GCHQ and replace it with something that remains fully under our control, we must shut down all those computer systems completely, remove the software installed by our AI and then restart the computers after they are clean."

The Director's jaw dropped. He mouthed in silence for a long moment until he eventually found the words he wanted. "That would bring the UK to a standstill. The problems caused by the Covid pandemic would pale into insignificance. That is totally ridiculous Professor!"

"I wish it were Sir."

As the Professor looked unblinkingly into the Director's eyes, he felt a great relief spread over him. At last, he had admitted that he was beaten. He stood up, excused himself and quietly walked out of the Director's office.

"Wait Professor, come back," he heard, but he ignored the calls to return and kept on walking to the nearest exit. He was driving out of the car park and on his way home before the Director had realised that he intended to leave the building.

Behind him, he left a man who now wished he had declined the hefty salary, the public profile, and the potential gong that may one day be awarded for his services to security. The Director now faced a challenge that was way beyond his ability or authority.

The Professor went home, poured himself a malt whisky and uncharacteristically watched a little television. During the evening, the front doorbell rang. He checked his door camera and recognised the head of security at GCHQ, no doubt sent to fetch him back to the office. The Professor had neither the energy nor the motivation to go back to work until after he had rested and gathered his thoughts. He ignored the doorbell, pretending not to be at home. After a while, the man left. The Professor retired to bed early and slept soundly for the first time in months.

The next morning, he awoke to a crushing pain in his chest that felt like someone was tightening a band around his body. It was like experiencing cramp throughout his complete torso. The pain quickly spread to his left arm which lay on the bed, unmovable. The room began to swim in front of his eyes as he struggled for breath. He had never felt so frightened in his life. He feared that he was dying.

He knew he was experiencing the symptoms of a serious heart attack, so with his right hand he groped for his mobile phone. He dialled 999 and, with difficulty, fighting for breath as he did so, he begged for a paramedic to come as quickly as possible.

An ambulance was on the way. He was alone in his smart regency house. Now he faced the biggest challenge of his life. He must descend two flights of stairs and open the beautiful old, immensely heavy, solid oak front door.

27

John Shaw soon grew tired of hanging around the Grand Harbour Hotel waiting for the day when his son Harry would return. He telephoned Ruzar and Mary and asked if their invitation to stay on the farm was still open. He was delighted and touched by how enthusiastically they welcomed him.

Mary showed him to their visitor's bedroom, with its double bed covered in a colourful old patchwork quilt, a scrubbed wooden dresser, and hooks on the wall for hanging coats and hats. The furnishings were modest, but the traditional feather mattress was soft and comfortable. John immediately felt at home in the humble space.

On his fourth day at the farm, he awoke to the familiar sound of a creaking wooden door as Ruzar entered the guest bedroom bearing a cup of tea.

"Good morning, John," he greeted him warmly. "I trust you slept well?"

"Indeed, I did," John replied, stretching his aching limbs beneath the quilt. "There's something about this place that helps me sleep like a log."

"Ah, that would be the magic of the land, handed down by generations of Camilleris," Ruzar said with a knowing smile. "It has a way of growing on you."

John thought that idea far-fetched, but whatever the cause, he felt rejuvenated. As he sat up in bed, he could see through the window that overlooked the olive grove. Each morning, the view that met his eyes made him feel part of an enviable permanence. Many of those trees had been planted by

Ruzar's ancestors, up to five-hundred years previously. Rows upon rows of ancient olive trees stretched out into the distance, their gnarled branches heavy with ripening olives that glistened in the morning sun.

As John arrived downstairs in the kitchen, he knew he would have to earn his breakfast. Mary greeted him with, "Are you ready for your duties today?"

"I certainly am," he replied, happy to contribute in some small way to the workings of the farm. John picked up the bucket of kitchen scraps for the pigs and headed out to the shed where he collected the remainder of the feed.

The sun had barely risen, casting a soft golden hue across the landscape. The morning was still cool, but over the past few days, he had felt the benefit of the Mediterranean climate soaking into his body, easing the ache in his joints. With his improved flexibility, he was now able to reduce the number of painkillers, and he was becoming more active.

He had taken on the task of feeding the chickens and pigs. These animals were there for subsistence, not profit. The chickens would supply eggs until eventually they became a Sunday dinner. And, when fattened, the pigs provided pork dinners and a cured ham that tasted like the highest grade of Serrano.

Reaching the chicken coop, he scattered the feed, delighting in the excited clucking of the hens as they pecked at the ground. The sun had inched higher in the sky and was now illuminating the tops of the trees and converting the last remnants of dew into a fine rising mist.

Each day, Ruzar devoted his morning to busying himself outside, tending the olive groves and livestock or servicing the old farm machinery which he would occasionally use to plough, rake, drill seed, cut hay and so on.

John couldn't help but compare himself to his host, especially when it came to their waistlines. Ruzar's looked to be unchanged from his youth, whereas his own was expanded by about eight inches so that his trouser belt couldn't decide whether to compress his apple shaped stomach or to slide underneath, so that his trousers hung around his hips with a pot belly bulging out above.

Mary worked her magic in the kitchen, preparing hearty meals. John was enjoying the bold flavours of her Mediterranean cooking. They ate mostly vegetarian food with occasional meat or fish. The couple followed a routine of at least five hours work before lunch, followed by a well-deserved siesta. They then resumed their labour, keeping themselves occupied until early evening. It was many hours of exertion considering their ages, but clearly, they thrived upon it.

28

The four aboard the yacht had just watched the island of Sicily disappear astern. They were bowling along at a fine rate, with the wind on the starboard beam, about ninety degrees to their course. This was fast sailing.

The yacht ploughed through the sea, throwing spray from the bow and leaving behind them a wake of disturbed water which soon disappeared amongst the high waves that marched towards them from the west. Those seas met an underlying swell that came from the opposite direction, the east, left over from the far-off Medicane. The two opposing movements of water merged to create an uncertain sea, which would occasionally lift the yacht and throw it over to one side or the other, requiring the crew to always hold on tight.

Steering a straight line through that turmoil required continuous attention, so Harry had his crew take turns, to accustom themselves to the yacht's motion before it became totally dark.

There were some slips and falls as Harry's inexperienced crew became used to the occasional sudden lurches, which could easily catch one unawares and knock the unsuspecting off their feet. Harry insisted upon everyone wearing harnesses, with lifelines attached to the rings provided for the purpose in the cockpit. He really didn't want anyone to be thrown overboard during those moments when the boat's movements would briefly become a bucking bronco ride.

Once everybody was proficient at helming the yacht, Harry went below to the navigator's table and marked their current position on the chart. He checked his workings, allowing for the slight current and the yacht's leeway. He estimated the wind pushed them about five degrees away from the course they were steering. After making a calculation based upon those factors and the yacht's speed, Harry was satisfied that he was steering a good course.

His plan was that around the time of dawn, they would sight the Saint Elmo lighthouse, situated at the end of the breakwater that shelters the entrance to Valetta harbour. The light should rise above the horizon when they were seven nautical miles from the harbour entrance. It was described on the chart as quick flashing green, which should be easy to distinguish, assuming clear visibility. Harry planned to be on deck to shepherd the yacht through the shipping lanes and then again as they approached land. He would snatch some rest in-between, around three to four in the morning. He was feeling confident they would deliver their yacht back to the charter company exactly on time.

◆◆◆

"Three in the morning already?" Harry muttered under his breath, wiping the salt spray from his eyes. Teresa was braced against the movement of the yacht as she stood at the helm, frequently wiping her spectacles to see better as she concentrated on steering a steady compass course through the waves. "I'm going to check our position before we hand over to Daniel and Nicole," said Harry. He was looking forward to an hour's rest.

"Okay," she replied, raising her voice over the sound of wind and sea.

In the dim red light over the chart table, Harry consulted the GPS plotter, ready to transfer their position to the chart. His brow furrowed in concern as the device revealed their position to be three sea miles east of where they should be and a mile further from land. He was surprised.

He didn't usually make such mistakes in his navigation. Perhaps, in this rough sea, this yacht was making more leeway than he had expected, or the turbulent waves had slowed their progress. And then, it might be that his crew were not steering a straight line.

"Oh well, the GPS must be correct," he whispered to himself, pushing back his wet hair, which had been dripping on the chart. They needed to alter course by ten degrees to the west. He returned to the cockpit, gave Teresa the new course, adjusted the sails, and went below to wake Daniel and Nicole. It was time for them to take over for the next three hours.

In a few minutes, the bleary-eyed pair appeared in the cockpit. Harry gave them the new compass course and waited to be sure they were settled in. Teresa headed below to crash in her bunk where, despite the yacht's pitching and rolling, she soon fell into a deep sleep.

Harry followed a few minutes later and set the alarm on his watch for an hour later at 4AM, when he would return on deck before they would sight land. He had been more tired than he realised, and when the alarm beeped quietly on his wrist, he did not stir. Instead, two hours passed before he jerked awake, heart pounding, as he realised that he had overslept.

"Wake up Harry," he told himself as he swung his legs over the edge of the bunk. Rubbing the sleep from his eyes, he checked the GPS plotter once more, hoping that his course correction had paid off. To his relief, the plotter showed that they were just four miles from the entrance to Valetta harbour. A small smile tugged at the corner of his lips, but this was no time to celebrate.

Teresa lay sleeping soundly in her cabin, dark hair spread out across her pillow. Harry hesitated, deciding to let her rest whilst he assessed the situation on deck. As he emerged from below, he found Nicole and Daniel sailing the yacht with quiet competence. The sky had lightened to a pale grey, but visibility had drastically fallen to less than a mile. A thick bank of fog loomed ahead, swallowing the horizon.

"Morning, Harry," Nicole greeted him through chattering teeth, her short dark hair damp with salt and mist, "it looks like we're heading into some fog."

The temperature had dropped several degrees. The air was heavily laden with moisture, which had condensed into a sea fog. On land, one rarely experiences wind and fog at the same time, but at sea the wind can blow during fog so thick that nothing is visible in front of the vessel. The bank of gloom rolled rapidly towards them, looking like an advancing cloud. Within minutes, the only thing to be seen ahead of the yacht was the eerie reflection of its own red and green navigation lights.

The tension on the yacht was palpable, each person acutely aware there might be unseen dangers lying ahead. Harry decided, "We need to slow down and set more lookouts. Let's spill some wind from the sails."

"Got it," Daniel replied, his strong hands moving with practiced ease as he loosened the sheets, the ropes that controlled the sails. Harry remained near the helm, his gaze scanning the fog-shrouded water, attempting to pierce the veil that hid any obstacles from view.

"Nicole, you watch the port side; Daniel, starboard," Harry instructed as he continued to keep watch over the bow. "Call out anything unusual – even if it's just a shadow. Better safe than sorry."

"Understood," they both responded in unison, their eyes and ears now focused on their respective sectors.

Harry nipped down below and returned with a small red trumpet on top of a gas cannister. He handed it to Daniel. "That's the foghorn. Give it one long and two short blasts every couple of minutes."

Daniel tried out the horn and its extremely loud, low frequency sound, moaned into the gloom, with much of the noise bouncing off the mainsail and returning to make their ears sing. "I forgot to mention," said Harry, "aim it forward, under the sail."

"Aye, aye, skipper," replied Daniel with a grin.

Harry descended into the dimly lit cabin, the muted sound of the foghorn echoing through the yacht's interior. He knocked on Teresa's door, his hand hesitating for a moment before he pushed it open.

"Teresa," he said, "we're sailing in fog. I need you on deck as an extra lookout."

She stirred from her sleep, her brown eyes blinking against the dim light. "I'll be right there," she murmured, reaching for her waterproofs. Within moments, she had dressed and headed up the companionway into the cockpit.

Harry couldn't shake the feeling that something wasn't right; he was missing something.

On deck, Daniel had taken charge, "We're looking out in

three sectors," he told Teresa as she climbed up to the cockpit. The three stared out in different directions, looking for a sign of anything.

Down below, Harry checked the GPS plotter yet again, his heart skipping a beat as he noticed their position had inexplicably shifted several miles back towards Sicily.

"Damn it," he muttered under his breath, his fingers tapping anxiously on the console, "This doesn't make sense."

It then dawned on him that the GPS position might be unreliable. Could it be that when he believed they were off course at 3AM, in fact, they were not? He looked at the chart and started to calculate the approximate position of the yacht if his course alteration had been unnecessary.

It didn't take him long to realise that he could now be further along the coast, to the northeast. But what was that? He suddenly noticed something he had missed while his mind had been focussed on navigation.

The rhythmic rise and fall they had been accustomed to over the past hours had given way to a jerkier, more unsettling motion. Shallow waters, Harry thought, his heart sinking.

He checked the depth sounder, which displayed on a small digital screen above the chart table. The numbers confirmed his fears: just four meters of water beneath the keel. They were in dangerous territory, and every second counted. He was racing up the ladder to the cockpit when Nicole shouted, "Rocks!"

Her voice was edged with panic as she pointed to a dark, ominous shape looming through the fog, dead ahead. "There are rocks ahead!"

"Everyone, hold on!" Harry barked, wrenching the wheel

to starboard as he attempted to avoid the hazard. But it was too late. The yacht collided violently with the rocks at a speed of five knots, coming to a complete and instant halt, the impact sending shudders throughout the vessel's hull. Harry had hold of the wheel but the other three were sent flying across the cockpit as the yacht ground to a sudden stop, with the sails pulling ahead all the time.

"Damn!" Harry exclaimed, gripping the wheel tightly as the force of the crash nearly knocked him off his feet. He started the yacht's engine, relieved when it quickly burst into life. He put the motor astern and gave it full revs, but the effort was futile. The boat had already turned sideways onto the rocks and was being lifted higher by each successive wave, bouncing on the sharp grinding points.

The world tilted permanently as a wave lifted the yacht over the top of a big rock to settle further inshore and at a crazy angle, where it remained fixed. Harry knew that now the movement of the hull against the rocks would slowly but surely grind holes in the glass fibre hull.

"Stay here, and hold on," he instructed the others before dashing below deck to see the damage. Seawater was already sloshing around the cabin floor, ankle deep. Down below, the noise of grinding and banging was amplified, and Harry wondered if the yacht might topple over on its keel, potentially trapping him below. He grabbed the plastic bag containing their passports and left the cabin for the last time.

"Everyone, we need to get off the yacht – now!" Harry announced, his voice taut with urgency as he returned to the cockpit.

"Are you sure?" Nicole asked, her eyes wide with fear. "What about our things?"

"No time," Harry replied, "we don't want to be here if the yacht topples over to seaward."

He could see the mix of panic and determination on their faces as they nodded in agreement, each of them bracing themselves for the treacherous leap from their foundering vessel. Harry watched as Daniel, Teresa, and Nicole hesitated as they contemplated how they would get down onto the rocks. It looked a foolhardy jump.

"Be careful," he called after them. As he prepared to leave the vessel, he took one last look around the deck – at the loose flapping sails, the wildly swinging boom, and then the navigation lights flickered and died as the sea found the yacht's batteries.

"My old yacht Ariana wouldn't have been holed so easily," reflected Harry, "How I miss that boat."

The fog was a cold, damp blanket, and as he looked to where he assumed was the shore, he could just make out a faint glow of lights and the indistinct murmur of voices. His heart pounded in his chest as he stuffed the plastic pouch holding their passports into his jacket pocket.

Teresa hesitated, her eyes darting back to the hatch that led below deck. "But our things..."

"Leave them," Harry ordered, his voice firm. "There's no time. We have to go now."

Accepting the gravity of the situation, the group steeled themselves. Daniel took the lead, carefully dropping down from the yacht's side onto the slippery rocks. Nicole followed closely behind, her breaths shallow and rapid as she took the risk and leapt.

As she jumped, a wave crashed against the yacht, causing Nicole to lose her footing. She slipped, letting out a scream as for the briefest moment one leg became wedged between yacht and stone. Both Harry and Teresa winced at the cracking sound.

"Nicole!" Teresa called out, her protective instincts kicking in as she was over the guardrails and dropping down from the yacht with cat like ease. She and Daniel worked together to pull their cousin to safety, their hands bloodied by the sharp edges of the rocks.

Nicole was silent, ashen pale and shivering. Once they had dragged Nicole, now swearing and wincing, far enough away from the boat, she looked down at Nicole's leg, hidden underneath sturdy red waterproof trousers, but she couldn't see how serious the damage might be.

Harry finally climbed ashore, his own hands bearing the wounds of their escape. He glanced back at the once magnificent vessel, now lower in the water and being so easily battered to pieces. "Let's keep moving ashore," he urged.

They turned to find their way blocked by decorative iron railings, about chest height. Daniel, ever the strong and determined one, hoisted himself over them with ease. Teresa followed suit, and between them, they carefully lifted Nicole over the obstacle, down two steps and onto what appeared to be a terrace of fancy coloured paving slabs. All this time, Nicole had been coping with her pain by shouting some very unladylike obscenities in Maltese.

"Nicole, lie down here," Teresa said gently as she guided her cousin to the cold, flat surface.

Harry pulled his sailor's jack-knife from a pocket and handed it to Teresa, who used it to slice up the leg of Nicole's waterproof trousers, revealing that one leg was twisted below the knee into an ugly position.

With practiced hands, Teresa examined the injured leg. She asked Nicole to move her toes, ankle and then to try and bend her knee, which elicited loud cries of pain.

"Your leg is broken below the knee," Teresa told Nicole, as she looked up at Harry and Daniel.

"Where are we?" Daniel asked, looking around in confusion. It was then that they noticed a neat row of sun loungers.

The answer came from Nicole. "I know this place. We're at the Radisson Hotel!"

In fact, they were on one of the sunbathing terraces, overlooking the sea at St Georges Point, some two miles northeast from Valetta Harbour. Out of the murk, attracted by the noise, a growing crowd of curious and concerned people approached. They were hotel guests and staff who had come to discover the cause of all the commotion.

"Amazing," Harry breathed, his eyes meeting Teresa's. "Of all the places."

"Seems our luck hasn't completely run out." She leaned towards him and spoke quietly into his ear. "It's the first time you've taken me to a luxury hotel."

Their gazes locked, and in that moment, something inside them cracked. The mixture of high adrenalin and relief bubbled over, and together they saw a funny side to their situation. Laughter erupted, uncontrollable and cathartic. It was the relief of survivors, of people who had faced death and lived to tell the tale.

"Are you quite finished?" a haughty voice interrupted, clearly affronted by their levity. Some of the onlookers frowned in disgust at their seemingly inappropriate humour.

"Apologies," Harry said, his voice still tinged with lingering amusement. "We've had a bit of a rough night."

"Clearly," the woman sniffed, turning to walk away.

"Never mind the jokes," Nicole gritted out through clenched teeth. "Get me some bloody painkillers."

"Excuse me!" Teresa called out, catching the attention of a man wearing a black waistcoat, a silver name badge on his chest. The hotel porter stepped forward. He helped them use one of the sun loungers as a stretcher to carry Nicole inside the hotel. The four dripped salty water and little drops of blood onto the floor of the reception. The duty manager ushered them into a corner and said, "I've called an ambulance. Can I do anything else for you?"

"I'm a doctor. Will you please get me your first aid kit," asked Teresa.

The manager relayed requests to a member of staff.

"May I make a note of your names please," asked the manager. There seemed no reason not to comply, and so they each recited their name as he noted them on a pad, after which he left the crew of four, looking very out of place in soggy dripping seagoing gear.

Harry quietly said to Teresa, "The yachts GPS was giving out false positions. I wonder if that was due to our mortal enemy, the AI at GCHQ. If you remember, Paul at the charter company installed a software update to the plotter just before we started our cruise."

She replied, "Harry, are you going to contact Professor Hall? By now, he should have some good news for us."

"I'll call him at the first opportunity," replied Harry, who then realised, "Our phones are on that yacht out there. I'm not sure I have the Prof's number recorded anywhere else."

29

Two-tone horns became louder and louder as they approached. An ambulance pulled abruptly to a stop outside the glass door of the hotel, illuminating the lobby with red and blue flashing lights. A moment later, a police car arrived, adding a second set of strobing lights which dazzled the hotel interior.

Whispers filled the air as guests turned to watch the unfolding drama.

"Careful with her leg," Teresa urged as the ambulance crew lifted Nicole from the sun lounger to a stretcher, making her yelp in pain. Teresa briefed one of the ambulance crew on Nicole's condition and the pain killers she had administered from the hotel's first aid kit.

Daniel hovered at Nicole's side, fussing over his newfound love. "I'm going to the hospital with you," he declared.

At this point, the hotel manager approached Nicole with a pen and a typed sheet of hotel headed paper. He wanted her to sign a note confirming the management had taken all proper steps to help.

Nicole replied with a very unsavoury comment, loudly sharing her opinions about large companies and their health and safety policies. The pain was making her very irritable, and she refused to sign. Daniel politely thanked the manager for his help as the little procession made for the ambulance.

Harry and Teresa were left behind in the company of the uniformed policeman, who now approached. They expected him to ask about how their yacht came to collide with the sun terrace of the hotel. But no, he approached with a stern expression and his right hand resting on the butt of his holstered pistol. "You're both to wait here until Detective Sergeant Yong arrives."

"Of course," Harry agreed, exchanging a nervous glance with Teresa, who now looked strained, with eyes red from the effects of sea salt, tiredness, and anxiety.

Fifteen minutes crawled by. The ever-present hum of conversation in the reception area lowered to an oppressive hush as people looked at the guarded couple with suspicion. Then, the entrance doors swung open to reveal a tall man with a steely gaze, Detective Sergeant Yong, followed by two more uniformed police officers.

"Harry Shaw — Doctor Teresa Camilleri." He announced, his tone void of warmth. "You are both to come with me. You're under arrest."

"Arrest? For what?" demanded Teresa.

"Please, let's not make a scene," Yong advised, nodding towards the curious onlookers. "Accompany me to the police station, where we can discuss this matter privately."

With reluctance, Harry and Teresa followed the detective, each accompanied by a uniformed officer.

Sergeant Yong led Harry to his unmarked police car, while a female officer directed Teresa towards the other vehicle. They were placed in the rear seats, each with an officer sitting beside them.

As Harry sat behind Yong, he thought that at least they had been granted a civilized arrest: no cuffs, no reading of rights, no being restrained by flanking police officers. But what on earth was happening?

Perhaps Yong had arrested them because he had disconnected the AIS tracker on the charter yacht. Or was it related to the hospital falsely accusing Teresa of stealing drugs. He couldn't wait to speak with Professor Hall. Hopefully, by now he should have conquered the renegade AI and sorted his and Teresa's problems.

"What's this all about?" Harry asked, but Yong refused to engage in conversation.

At Valetta police station, they were escorted through sterile corridors. They were still wearing their waterproofs, which had now dried to reveal streaks of white sea salt all over them. Each door they passed seemed indistinguishable from the next, and Harry couldn't help but shudder at the thought of how quickly one could disappear into a police station and be forgotten by the outside world.

"Wait in here," Yong ordered, directing Harry into a small, windowless interview room. The door closed with a heavy thud, leaving him alone with two steel chairs and a table, all bolted to the floor.

"Please let Teresa be okay," he thought as he tried to steady his breathing and heart rate. He had only been in the police station a few minutes, an innocent man, but he already felt powerless.

Meanwhile, in another interview room, Teresa sat with her hands folded on her lap. Her eyes flickered around the cold, unforgiving interview room and returned to the detective sat in front of her.

"Doctor Camilleri," Sergeant Yong began, "We have received an extradition request from the United Kingdom under the Trade and Cooperation Agreement which streamlines the extradition arrangements between Malta and the UK. The National Crime Agency in Britain, and the Ministry of Foreign Affairs in Malta, have both approved your extradition.

Teresa was stunned into silence as Yong continued, "Within a few days, police officers from England will arrive and charge you under British law. You will then be transported to England. They will take you into custody for the crime of murder."

"Murder?" Teresa gasped, feeling as though the air had been sucked from her lungs. "Who am I supposed to have killed?"

"Professor Nicholas Hall," Yong replied, watching her reaction carefully.

"Professor Hall?" she exclaimed, her mind racing to make sense of the accusation. "That's ridiculous. When? How? Where? It is completely impossible."

"Unfortunately, Doctor, the evidence is against you," Yong said, his tone devoid of emotion. "You will be escorted to the UK, where you will face these charges."

Teresa's heart hammered in her chest. She could feel the muscles in her face constrict and her head pulsating with tension. Fear and disbelief rendered her silent and helpless. The life she had built, her career, her friendships, her burgeoning relationship with Harry; it felt as of everything was taken from her, her life ruined by an accusation that was plainly absurd.

Yong continued, "You have the right to make one phone call and to access a lawyer. We will provide you with clothing to replace the yachting gear you are wearing. You will then be placed in a cell. Do you understand all I have said?"

"Yes," Teresa meekly replied. As a doctor at the hospital, she was used to being the one that exuded calm authority in stressful situations. And her martial arts practice usually enabled her to steadily face whatever life threw at her. But this! The unjustness of her situation had stripped away her ability to think and act calmly.

Meanwhile, Harry was sitting alone in his own interview room, frustration mounting and worry clouding his ability to think. To calm his mind, he began to examine the crumbling plaster and the grimy walls. He had moved on to scrutinizing the quality of the heavy hardwood door, handmade by a craftsman many years previously, when the door burst open, making him jump. Yong strode into the interview room and repeated the process he had just been through with Teresa.

"Mr Shaw," Yong ended with, "you will be extradited to England, where you will face charges for the murder of Professor Hall."

Harry had sunk down into his chair and was staring at Yong in disbelief. "This must be a joke." He shook his head. "I saw the Professor in Malta recently, after which he flew home. I've been in Malta, at sea, and in Sicily ever since. There's no way I could have even met him, let alone killed him."

Yong's expression remained unmoved, his eyes cold and unyielding. "That may be what you claim, Mr Shaw, but the evidence against you is conclusive."

Harry was floored by the accusation, a mixture of despair and frustration coursing through him. Like Teresa, he was being processed through a system that removed all control, thereby stripping away dignity and weakening a person's resolve.

Later, dressed in a grey cotton track suit, a guard ushered

him into a cell with a hard narrow bed, where he would sit for however long he did not know. Dejected, he awaited the opportunity to make his one telephone call.

Somewhere else in the police station, Teresa was standing next to a female officer who was making no effort to hide the fact that she was listening to Teresa's phone conversation.

As she dialled Daniel's number, Teresa's hands trembled ever so slightly. Nervous perspiration was causing her glasses to slide down her nose. She pushed them up again as she hoped that Daniel would have his phone to hand.

When he answered she spoke hesitantly, "Daniel? It's me. Teresa. You won't believe what's happened. Harry and I have been accused of murdering Professor Hall. It's insane!"

Daniel responded incredulously and then Teresa asked, "How's Nicole? Is she okay?"

"Nicole's had her broken leg reset and covered in plaster," Daniel replied, concern flooding his voice. "I can't believe they're accusing you of something like this. I'll help in any way I can."

"Thank you, Daniel," she whispered as she fought back her tears. "Will you speak to Mum and Dad? And sort out a lawyer to get here as soon as possible?"

"I'm on it, Sis. I'm going to take Nicole to the farm. And I'll visit you, just as soon as I can."

Teresa burst into tears, so Daniel didn't hear what she said as she stumbled over her words. "I need you, big brother. Get me out of this mess." She replaced the receiver and was led back to her cell, sobbing quietly.

Harry thought he heard someone crying in the cell next to his, but it was difficult to hear clearly through the thick stone walls. Time dragged. His watch had been taken away with his other belongings, including the pouch of passports. There was no wall clock in the cell and Harry was already losing track of time.

Eventually, he was taken to make his call, and he dialled the international number for his father's mobile phone, hoping the old man would have it nearby. That didn't work. The phone in the corridor wouldn't allow international calls. A long argument ensued between Harry and the desk sergeant who oversaw the cells. Eventually, the sergeant agreed to dial the number using his own desk-phone. Harry was relieved when his father answered promptly.

"Dad?" Harry's voice trembled slightly, betraying the turmoil within. "It's me. I've been arrested on false charges. They're accusing Teresa and me of murdering someone. The yacht has been wrecked on rocks, but the four of us are alive."

There was a pause on the line before John Shaw responded, his voice tinged with disbelief. "Harry, that's... I can hardly believe it. But I trust you. It must be a mistake."

Harry sighed, feeling a momentary reprieve from the crushing weight of the situation. Old as he was, his father would raise heaven and earth to come to his rescue. "Thank you, Dad. We need all the help we can get."

"Of course," John said firmly. "I'll do everything in my power to get you out of there. I'm already here in Malta." John's voice was firm and resolute. "I'll find the best lawyers to help you."

"Thanks Dad," Harry replied, his voice thick with emotion. He hadn't expected his father to be so close. The knowledge that he was nearby brought a flicker of relief to the otherwise bleak situation.

"Stay strong," John said firmly before they ended the call.

30

Inside the Camilleri farmhouse, the atmosphere was tense. A council of war had been convened and the group sat stony faced around the large old scrubbed wooden table. Harry's father had reverted to acting like the officer he used to be in the Royal Navy. He sat at the head of the table with a notebook.

He surveyed the group in front of him. Teresa and Daniel's parents, Ruzar and Mary, sat either side at the far end of the table. Mary was as white as a sheet and clearly shaken by events. Ruzar sat there looking implacable, a man who was ready to get down to business. Nicole was sitting sideways with her plastered leg raised, lying across another upright chair. Daniel was leaning forward and holding his phone in his two hands with his thumbs poised ready to type notes. He was looking expectantly at John, who began...

"I propose that we handle this situation as quickly as possible with two steps. Firstly, we each need to share everything we know about what is going on with Teresa's and Harry's arrests, including any relevant background information. When we are all up to speed on the situation, we can decide what we can best do to help them. And lastly, we should agree what actions each of us will undertake. Agreed?"

"Good plan," said Daniel, wanting to get on with it.

"Agreed," added Ruzar.

Mary said, "I'll listen as I brew some coffee."

Nicole suggested she speak first and share what she knew. During the remainder of that day, until late at night, the five sat at the table. Coffee came and went, as did cold meats, bread, cheese, and Camilleri red wine. Then, more cups of coffee, keeping everyone's caffeine level high enough for them all to stay on point.

Nicole told all she remembered from the meeting at her apartment, when Professor Hall, Harry and Teresa had been together. And about the vigilante attacking Harry and accusing him of being a paedophile. She explained how the hospital had accused Teresa of stealing drugs, and lastly, she amazed Ruzar, Mary, and John with Professor Hall's admissions about the AI at GCHQ.

John was able to fill in details about Harry's time in hospital, the guard outside the door and him being visited by two unknown men, and his personal suspicions about the story in the press of a gas explosion not being wholly credible.

Daniel recounted how, on the yacht, Harry had revealed the full details about the attack at sea, the death of his family, and his being tricked into signing the Official Secrets Act. And he talked of the police coming to the anchorage in Malta and wanting to speak with Teresa.

Nicole added that Professor Hall said he was working to get the AI under control and to prove that Teresa was innocent. After which, they all hoped that life could return to normal.

Ruzar summed up the feeling around the table, "I would never have thought my family could be dragged into anything like this. I feel exhausted from trying to absorb all this information."

Mary had been quiet during the conversation, listening intently to all that was said. Now she spoke with quiet authority. "The fact that agencies of the British state have attacked our children appals me. And there is another thing that effects all of us around this table. If everything that Nicole has told us is accurate, then I think we should get rid of our smart phones at the earliest opportunity."

Daniel, Nicole, Ruzar, and John all had their phones laid on the table in front of them, handy for immediate use, or in case there was an incoming call regarding Harry or Teresa. They all instinctively looked at them with suspicion.

Nicole wanted to clarify what she had said. "Actually Mary, I would say that you would be shutting the stable door after the horse has bolted. Every single digital item transmitted to and from our phones, plus all our other digital transactions have been copied and stored away by at least two governments. Using that data, the security services can easily assemble a detailed picture of our daily activities."

Nicole was warming to her subject and red in the face with anger as she continued. "If you find that hard to believe, then I can show you the evidence some time. To make our personal lives private again is impossible. I think it's outrageous. As every little digital event in our lives travels along the internet, a government agency takes a copy, matches it to our identity, has it scrutinised by an artificial intelligence, and then stores it forever on secret servers. They hold a more accurate record of our lives than we do ourselves. It's obscene!"

"We can see that you care very much about that," said Daniel.

Nicole was now so agitated that her words came fast and loud, almost tripping over themselves as she exclaimed, "It might seem like digressing from the subject at hand, which is trying to save Harry and Teresa, but if it were not for the totally unacceptable levels of government surveillance, Harry's family would still be alive, and Teresa would never have become involved. It makes me angry beyond words. And another thing, my leg hurts like hell!" exclaimed Nicole.

The room went quiet for a full minute as everyone waited for her to regain her composure.

"I think that is a good place for us to end this discussion," said John, adding that, "it's too late for us to do anything more today. How about we reconvene early tomorrow morning and start taking action." They all agreed, and in sombre mood they headed for their various bedrooms.

Nicole slept in Teresa's room and snored loudly. That didn't help the others who had to listen to her grumbling and growling noises.

Next morning, before the first light of dawn, John and Ruzar were back at the table and quietly discussing what they should do.

"There is a lawyer's firm in Valetta that our family has used for many years," said Ruzar, "They will have someone who knows the law regarding extradition. How about I call them and have them see if we can stop, or at least delay, Harry and Teresa being extradited to England?"

"If Nicole or Daniel don't know of anyone who specialises in this area of law, I agree," John replied. "If that doesn't succeed, we need a solicitor and a barrister in England. I will investigate finding people who are especially good at defending against charges of murder. I'd like to make a start on that, just in case."

Ruzar looked down at the worn surface of the bleached and scrubbed old table and sighed, "Let's hope that's not necessary, but thank you."

The noise of Nicole's crutches scraping against the other side of the door made them look up as she hopped in and collapsed awkwardly on a chair. She smiled, "What have you old boys been up to this morning?"

Nicole's attitude provided a welcome relief. However, that soon changed when she explained, "I've just been using Teresa's laptop. I've researched the legal arrangements between Malta and the UK. Before an extradition can be enforced it must pass two tests, one in the UK and another in Malta. The authorities in both countries must be satisfied there is a case to answer. All of that must happen before a person can be detained, which means it is very unlikely that any lawyer in Malta could stop Teresa and Harry being sent to England. It would require some sort of procedural botch to delay the extradition, and that seems unlikely, don't you think?"

At that point, Daniel joined them, "Good morning," and then, not waiting for replies, "I've been looking online to try and find a lawyer in Malta who advertises some experience in extradition cases. I can't find one. I doubt there is such a person, so we may as well contact the usual family lawyers."

That settled it. Ruzar called the legal firm immediately after their offices opened. After a brief explanation, a senior partner in the firm was on his way to Valetta Police Station.

John called his solicitor back in England. He had used the same firm in Southampton for all his adult life and his old contact was now a senior partner, shortly due to retire. After the phone call, John was able to report that his solicitor would make initial enquiries about the two cases and that he would then suggest a suitable person to represent Harry and

Teresa.

By the end of their meeting, everyone felt a modicum of relief from the fact that they were taking some action to help the two jailbirds in Valletta.

31

The lawyer arranged by Ruzar was a distinguished Maltese gentleman named Carmelo Scicluna. His shiny salt and pepper hair was slicked back, as if plastered down with old fashioned *Brylcreem*. He was dressed in a tailored suit and carried a highly polished old black leather briefcase. Pale and piercing eyes combined with a naturally stern expression to make him an intimidating figure.

First, he met with Teresa and Harry individually and had them sign the necessary agreements for him to represent them during their time in Malta. Now, with that administrative hurdle out of the way, Carmelo turned his attention upon the sergeant in charge of the cells.

Detective Sergeant Yong had left instructions that the two accused must be kept apart. However, both Teresa and Harry wanted to see each other, and Carmelo was on their side.

He had cultivated an unsettling habit of looking directly into a person's eyes and not blinking. Now, he turned his pale, withering gaze upon the sergeant, quoting a paragraph of legal gibberish he had invented on the spot. Soon, Yong's instructions were set aside.

In the sterile, windowless interview room at the police station, Harry, Teresa, and Carmelo sat across from each other on the cold metal chairs. Carmelo placed his briefcase on the table and smiled at his clients, which did not set them at ease.

"Mister Shaw, Doctor Camilleri," he began in a gravelly voice, "As you know, you have been detained for the murder of Professor Hall."

Harry shifted uncomfortably in his chair, his eyes searching Carmelo's face for any sign of hope. Teresa, her long dark hair tied into a tight bun, adjusted her glasses with a shaky hand.

Harry spoke next, his voice strained. "We've done nothing wrong."

Carmelo nodded solemnly. "The police have provided me with a summary of the most significant evidence against you."

He paused, taking a deep breath before continuing. "It appears that Professor Hall was admitted to hospital, following a massive heart attack at his home."

Teresa's eyes widened in shock, and Harry could feel his own heart racing. They exchanged a brief, tense glance. "Please, go on," Teresa prompted, her voice barely above a whisper.

Carmelo's face remained impassive as he continued, "That's the beginning of the story. The evidence against you both is quite damning. This is what I have been told…"

He read from a sheet of notes, "Professor Hall underwent emergency surgery upon his arrival at the cardiology unit at Cheltenham General Hospital. He survived the initial operation, but things took a turn for the worse the following day."

He shifted in his seat, pulling a folder from his briefcase. "You see, Harry and Teresa, you were both captured on video entering the professor's private room."

Carmelo placed on the table in front of them a black and white still image of the two of them leaving a hospital room.

Teresa's eyes widened behind her glasses, "That's

impossible." She shook her head in disbelief, "We were never there."

"That's fake," shouted Harry, outraged by the picture.

"Calm down Mr Shaw. I can assure you the police report states that the CCTV footage is quite clear," Carmelo replied, his pale eyes meeting Harry's. "Both of your faces can be clearly identified. They have you entering the room together and leaving only two minutes later. The monitoring equipment attached to the Professor recorded his death at precisely one minute after you both entered."

As Carmelo spoke, Harry's mind raced, trying to make sense of the accusations against them. He knew they hadn't been anywhere near England, but how could he prove it? Beside him, Teresa sat in silence, mouth opening as if to say something but then closing again.

"Immediately after you left," Carmelo continued, "the nursing staff can be seen rushing into the Professor's room. His heart failure set off an alarm, prompting the nurses to come running."

"According to the British police, it is suggested that you injected the professor with something that immediately triggered a second, fatal, heart attack. I imagine the autopsy has been completed by now, which should more precisely identify the cause of death," Carmelo explained, his voice tinged with regret.

"Injected him?" Teresa choked out, her face a mixture of shock and anger. "That is absurd! I am a doctor. I preserve life. I would never do such a thing!"

Harry pleaded with Carmelo. "But this never happened. We were not there! You must believe us."

Carmelo reminded them what he had just explained, "The

monitoring equipment recorded that his heart stopped while you two were in his room."

Harry asked, "When exactly did Professor Hall die?"

"Two weeks ago," Carmelo replied.

"Teresa and I were in Sicily at that time, aboard a charter yacht."

"Can you provide any proof?" Carmelo asked, his tone dispassionate. "Receipts for yacht marinas or harbour dues would help."

Teresa shook her head. "We anchored the yacht in secluded bays," she explained, her voice barely audible. "We didn't spend money at marinas."

"Then surely you have receipts for purchasing food," Carmelo pressed on, "ideally paid for by credit card?"

"Unfortunately, no." Harry responded, his heart sinking even further into the pit of his stomach. "We bought our food with cash, and we don't have any receipts."

"Very well," Carmelo sighed, rubbing his temples with his fingers. "If you were indeed in Sicily, then your mobile phone providers will have records from when your phones pinged the masts. That would help to prove your location."

"Actually," Harry hesitated, running a hand through his blond hair, suddenly feeling even more vulnerable, "our mobile phones were switched off during our trip."

Carmelo's gaze grew colder, scrutinising them both intently. "The behaviour of you two is beginning to sound very suspicious."

Teresa interjected, her voice tinged with desperation, "I know how this looks, but we're innocent. We didn't kill Professor Hall."

"Believe us," Harry implored, his voice cracking under the

strain of their predicament. "We had no reason to harm him."

"Whether or not I believe you is irrelevant," Carmelo replied, his voice firm but not unkind. "What matters is finding evidence that supports your claims. Without that, I'm afraid there's not much I can do."

Harry tried another way to prove their innocence, "Neither Teresa nor I have set foot in the UK for some time," he insisted, his voice low and controlled.

"Mr Shaw," Carmelo began, his expression unyielding, "I understand the British Police found airline passenger lists and passport control data that proves beyond doubt that you both flew to Britain and back again to Malta, placing you in England at the time of the murder."

As the lawyer's words settled over them, Harry and Teresa shared a despairing glance. The nightmare was getting worse with every statement that Carmello made.

"Based upon the available evidence," Carmelo continued, his tone sombre, "I regret to say, in my professional opinion, a jury would be very likely to find you guilty."

"Please give us a few minutes alone," Harry asked, his voice barely audible.

"I'll be outside the door," the lawyer acquiesced, rising from his chair. With a nod, he left the room, the door closing behind him with a heavy thud.

As soon as they were alone, Harry turned to Teresa, "I've made a terrible mistake. I thought avoiding any digital trail would protect us, but instead, it's done the opposite. By leaving no trace of our whereabouts, we've made it easier for the AI at GCHQ to fabricate a digital trail, placing us in England. And it must have somehow created deep fake videos of us in the hospital."

Teresa, reached out to touch his arm gently, offering what little comfort she could. "We'll find a way out of this," she murmured. "I don't know how, but we will."

"Let's hope so," Harry replied, releasing a heavy sigh. "For our sakes, let's hope so."

They hugged, Harry pulling Teresa into a tight embrace. They shared a moment of warmth and mutual support. It didn't change anything, but somehow it helped. "This whole mess is my fault," he whispered hoarsely, his voice cracking with emotion.

She hugged him back fiercely, her slender fingers digging into his shoulders. "No, Harry. It isn't all your fault," she insisted, her voice muffled against his chest. "I chose to follow you to Malta. We're in this together."

"We don't even know if Professor Hall managed to control the AI," Harry murmured, in despair.

Teresa pulled away slightly. "Based upon what Carmello has been saying, I think we must assume that he did not."

Nodding resolutely, Harry released her and took a deep breath. It was time to face their reality head-on. He walked over to the door and knocked, signalling for the lawyer to return.

As Carmelo entered the room, his pale eyes flicked between Harry and Teresa, sensing the atmosphere. Harry straightened his spine, steeling himself for the challenge ahead.

"Listen," he began, addressing Carmelo with a note of desperation in his voice. "I can understand why you probably find it difficult to believe us, but all the evidence against Teresa and me has been fabricated. We will not give up, and we will look for some way to prove our innocence."

Carmelo replied, "My job is to see if there is any way to prevent or delay your extradition. I have looked at the papers and all seems in order. I can see nothing that we could use to delay the process."

"Can you do that, delay things?" asked Harry.

"Believe me, I will continue to look for any discrepancies or new evidence that may help your case," the lawyer assured them, "but time is running out. I suggest the reality is that you should prepare for your likely extradition and a subsequent trial."

"Thank you," Teresa murmured, "we appreciate your efforts."

"I will continue to work on your behalf and will inform you of any positive developments," Carmelo said, glancing at his watch as he prepared to leave. "I'll call Ruzar and tell him all about our meeting. And you can ask for me to visit again if you think of anything new that may help your case."

"Thank you," Harry said, firmly shaking the lawyer's hand.

Back in his cell, Harry tried to clear his head and start thinking logically. What if his defence against the charge of murder was to leak official secrets? He could make public the chaos that had been wrought by the malignant AI at GCHQ. Would the truth set him free, would he be believed, or could that defence backfire and make things worse?

Another thought occurred to Harry. Which carried the longest sentence, to be found guilty of murder, or of breaking the Official Secrets Act? He felt he was caught in a Catch 22; whatever he tried to do, he was beaten. The AI had won.

As Harry was pondering his situation, Carmello was reporting back to Ruzar. "My old friend, it's not good. I can see no way of delaying the extraditions of your daughter and

Harry Shaw."

Ruzar was extremely disappointed," And what did you learn about the charges? What's the evidence that makes them think my daughter would commit murder?"

Carmelo explained all the details and after the long telephone call was finished, Ruzar turned to Harry's father and repeated all the news.

John was sounding a little more positive, "My lawyers in England are already on the case. We just need to tell them when the plane with Harry and Teresa lands in England so they can take over."

John and Ruzar made as many visits to see Harry and Teresa as they were allowed. The mood of the two detainees shifted regularly. One moment they were determined to fight the charges all the way and a minute later it all seemed impossible, so they felt resigned to their inevitable fate.

32

Harry was moved along the narrow corridors of the Valetta Police Station at the fast pace set by the detective to whom he was handcuffed. Teresa was close behind, similarly attached to a robust English policewoman, twice her size.

"Perhaps they chose that officer based upon Teresa's martial arts reputation," thought Harry.

They sped towards the airport in a police van, lights flashing, two-tone horns blaring, as if they were trying to avoid an escape attempt from some gang of bandits, which seemed ridiculous to Harry. They were in a police vehicle that was capable of seating ten people. Each prisoner was handcuffed to an English officer and kept apart by a vacant row of seats between them.

Harry noticed how Teresa was remaining composed as she studied the passing scenery. Even in the face of adversity, her strong-willed nature shone through. He admired her for it, even as his own heart was thumping wildly in his chest. What Harry didn't know, was that Teresa was in the process of formulating a plan which she intended to keep to herself.

At the airport, the prisoners were subjected to the maximum possible humiliation. After all the other passengers had boarded the plane, the police vehicle drove across the tarmac at speed. The flashing lights caused the passengers on their side of the plane to look out of the windows in curiosity. When the van stopped, Harry and Teresa were led up the boarding ladder, handcuffed, wearing cell-block tracksuits and looking to be guilty convicts.

As they entered the plane, cabin crew and passengers stared at them. Harry glared back defiantly. Some passengers met his eye, but most looked away, intimidated by this obviously dangerous man.

"Look straight ahead," the policeman ordered Harry gruffly as he steered him to a vacant row of seats at the front of the plane.

"Take care of yourself, Harry," Teresa murmured as they were pulled apart.

"No talking!" The policewoman snapped, yanking on Teresa's handcuffs and leading her to a separate row of seats in the middle of the cabin.

"So, this is what it feels like to be a criminal," thought Harry, as the other passengers exchanged hushed whispers. After a while, he settled down to the usual boredom of flying. It was then that he noticed, poking out of the pocket in the back of the seat in front of him, there was a Guardian newspaper.

He grabbed the opportunity to catch up on reading some news from England. The front page was devoted to one story. It started with the words, 'Andrew Malkinson spent seventeen years in prison for a crime he did not commit.' The article rammed home to Harry that it is not guilt or innocence that decides the verdict in a British court, but what evidence the jury is allowed to see. And Harry reasoned that he could be darned sure that MI5 would ensure the evidence presented would be damning.

Surely, a jury would accept the digital evidence as inviolable, unable to be tampered with. The twelve men and women would have no reason to question the validity of the CCTV, passport and airline records presented as evidence against him and Teresa. The wheels of so-called justice would grind slowly towards the jury's inevitable pronouncement — "Guilty!"

At Heathrow, immediately the aircraft connected with the tunnel at the gate, Teresa and he were swiftly ushered off the plane before any other passengers were allowed to leave their seats. The chilly air took Harry by surprise. He shivered as he looked at the grey skies, such a contrast to the sun-soaked island of Malta. He and Teresa were whisked through the customs and arrivals areas with swift efficiency to a white box-shaped truck that was waiting at the kerb outside.

Harry felt himself being pushed into one of the tiny metal-walled cells within the truck. With barely enough room to sit down, and a minuscule window offering a view of the sky outside, Harry felt claustrophobic and powerless. He heard a clank of metal as another door slammed shut on Teresa who must be sealed in a similar box nearby.

It was a short drive to the modern custody suite. As he was led inside, Harry was surprised to find himself in an ultra-clean environment that would make any hospital proud. But this was a sparse, soulless place, with intense overhead lighting which added to the sterile atmosphere.

The two criminals were kept apart as they were checked in at the sergeant's reception area. Their names were confirmed, their alleged crimes were read out as they were processed with practised efficiency.

"Glasses off, no smiling." A polite but unfriendly officer instructed Teresa as he guided her into a photo booth where her mugshot was taken. Fingerprints were scanned. Samples of DNA was scraped from inside their mouths.

Then they were each required to change their clothing into another uniform, this time a blue tracksuit.

Finally, the custody sergeant asked them each a series of set questions. Were they drug users? Did they have any medical conditions? How about mental health problems; any thoughts about suicide? After the sergeant had duly completed all his box-ticking duties, as laid out on his computer monitor, they were each informed of their right to one phone call, but not until sometime later.

As the cell door slammed shut behind him, Harry sank onto the narrow cot, his face buried in his hands. He sat there morosely until the heavy cell door swung open and an imposing officer filled the doorway.

"Phone call time," the big man smiled cheerily, "You've got five minutes."

"Thank you," Harry said, rising from his bed and following the guard to the phone situated next to the custody sergeant's office window. His conversation would be overheard and, Harry assumed, recorded.

Harry called his father and told him where he was. His father surprised him by saying that the lawyer who was representing both him and Teresa had already discovered where they were detained and was currently on his way to meet them. After the call, Harry returned to his cell feeling a little more positive.

He looked around, taking in the detail of his new home for God-knows-how-long. This was quite different to the ancient cell in the old stone Police Station of Valetta. Here, there was a hard raised platform at one end of the cell with a thin foam mattress covered in a tough blue plastic material. In a corner near the door stood a stainless-steel toilet and nearby a tiny hand-washing bowl was set into the wall.

The door was fitted with the usual hatch for delivering meals and next to it there was an intercom panel. Harry had been told that if he pressed the button, he could order drinks and microwave meals whenever he wanted. This was the only concession that offered detainees a crumb of control over their existence.

The worst thing about his cell was a CCTV lens situated in one corner and positioned to observe every inch of the cell. He looked up at the lens, with its little blinking red light, and wondered if the AI at GCHQ was looking back, satisfied with its achievement in having him arrested.

Although Harry didn't know it, at the nerve centre for the custody suite, where the sergeant in charge surveyed his domain, two men from MI5 were being allowed admission.

Commander Adrian Forbes strode in, his junior officer trailing behind. He presented his ID to the Custody Sergeant and announced his presence with, "Forbes, Commander Forbes," causing the custody sergeant to smile inwardly. He wondered if Forbes had styled his greeting on the fictional James Bond.

"I have come to see Harry Shaw and Teresa Camilleri, individually, in their cells."

The custody sergeant studied the ID. Like many of the regular police, he did not like the superior attitude often adopted by MI5 officers. He looked Forbes in the eye and said, "Sir, that would be completely irregular, I cannot allow it."

"Then I suggest you call the Superintendent," Forbes snapped. "Tell him I'm here and ask him what to do. Quickly please, Sergeant!"

Forbes stepped away and began to pace back and forth impatiently. The Sergeant called the Superintendent's office and was surprised to be put through to the great man without delay. "Give him what he wants," said the Super,' "and call me after he leaves."

Forbes heard the Sergeant say, "Very well, Sir, understood." Hanging up, he looked back at Forbes, who was smirking. "The Superintendent has instructed me to afford you every assistance — Sir."

"My conversations will be private. Turn off the camera and microphone in each cell, Sergeant," Forbes instructed. And casting a sidelong glance at his junior officer. "You stay here and make sure that recording equipment remains off." The young officer nodded, obediently taking up a position beside the sergeant.

Forbes was led down the corridor towards Harry's cell. The door swung open to reveal Harry sat on the hard bed, his blue eyes widening in surprise at the sight of the despicable man who had tricked him into signing the Official Secrets Act.

"Where's my lawyer," Harry asked the officer standing in the background.

The officer looked flummoxed, unhappy with the situation as he replied, "I'm sure he will be here soon, Mr Shaw. In the meantime, this gentleman wanted to see you."

"Gentleman!" Harry scoffed, the disdain evident in his voice. He looked his visitor up and down. There he stood, exactly as he remembered him. Silver hair, dressed impeccably in the same navy-blue double-breasted blazer.

"Mr Shaw," Forbes replied curtly, stepping forward as the cell door closed behind him. "We need to talk."

"About what?"

"Official secrets," Forbes said, his voice dripping with condescension. "Your silence is crucial. Remember that."

Harry clenched his fists, his anger flaring at this man who had so successfully manipulated him when he was lying in bed in Dorchester hospital. Somehow, he must keep a clear head. This unexpected meeting might be crucial.

"Okay," replied Harry suspiciously, "what is it you want to say?"

Harry looked to the camera in the corner of his cell. The little red light was now extinguished, a reminder of Forbes's power.

Forbes looked down his nose at Harry, as one might regard an inferior, "I'm here to ensure you understand the consequences of betraying what you've signed up for."

Harry eyed the repulsive man as he tried to remain calm. Perhaps he could learn something. "Tell me Commander, has GCHQ managed to take control of its AI?"

Forbes's expression darkened. "All information regarding GCHQ is classified, Shaw. You're not privy to any further details."

"I'll take that as a no then, shall I Commander?"

"You can take it any way you like," Forbes spat out.

"Look Commander, Teresa and I are completely innocent of the murder of Professor Hall, as you are no doubt aware."

"Your innocence doesn't concern me," Forbes said dismissively. "My only interest is ensuring your silence on all matters relating to GCHQ and the attacks upon your person."

Harry was infuriated by Forbes's attitude. "You don't care about the truth, do you? Teresa and I were set up by that bloody AI, and we had nothing to do with Professor Hall's death!"

"Like I said," Forbes repeated coldly, his eyes narrowing into icy slits, "your innocence is irrelevant. My purpose here is to remind you that you cannot divulge anything about the AI or the attacks you've experienced."

"Is that all you came for?" Harry spat out; his fists clenched tightly at his sides. The urge to strike the man was almost unbearable, but he knew it would only make matters worse.

"Consider it a friendly reminder of your obligations," Forbes sneered, his tone condescending. "And remember, I have my ways of keeping tabs on you. Let me spell it out for you. If you break the Official Secrets Act by blabbing, you'll be found guilty in a closed court and sentenced to fourteen years without parole. But if you plead guilty to murdering Hall, with good behaviour in prison, you could be out in eleven."

Harry could hardly believe what he was hearing. Plead guilty to a crime he didn't commit just to save himself from an even worse fate? Harry was losing control of the anger that had been simmering within him. "You're supposed to protect British citizens, not coerce them into false confessions! You should be bloody-well ashamed of yourself!"

Forbes smirked, unfazed by Harry's outburst. "I don't care what you think, Shaw. All I care about is ensuring national security. And you should remember," he added menacingly, "occasionally people die in prison, often in suspicious circumstances."

That chilling threat made Harry's blood run cold.

"Think carefully about your options," Forbes continued,

his voice icy and devoid of emotion. "Pleading guilty to murder will be your best chance for a long and peaceful life." His eyes bore into Harry's, driving home his threats.

Harry fell silent. Once again, he felt beaten by the government agencies who were clearly bent on protecting themselves at all costs.

Forbes wanted to further drive home his message. "I am sure you would prefer a stint in jail to being found one morning by prison officers, having mysteriously died during the night? Consider that a fair warning."

Forbes moved towards the door, speaking over his shoulder, "You should know by now that you won't get far trying to play the hero."

Then he turned and smiled. "Anyway, I'm off to see your lovely accomplice, Teresa. I remember her from the hospital. She's quite a looker." He leered at Harry, the lascivious expression on his face goading him into action.

"Damn you," he shouted as, without thinking, he desperately charged at the MI5 officer, his fists leading the way.

Forbes, however, was prepared, even pleased by this outcome. With cold precision, he delivered a swift punch to Harry's midsection followed by a hook to the side of his head, sending him crashing to the floor with a painful thud. Gasping for air, Harry looked up at Forbes, who smiled down at him in cruel satisfaction.

"Temper, temper, Mr Shaw," he chided, pressing the intercom buzzer to summon the officer outside. "We wouldn't want any more trouble now, would we?"

When the cell door opened, the officer saw Harry climbing back up onto his feet, glaring at Forbes with visible hatred.

Ignoring the officer, Forbes sauntered out of the cell, leaving Harry alone with his anger and frustration.

"Shaw," the officer said, not unkindly, "you'd better keep yourself in check if you want to make it through this."

Across the hallway, in Teresa's cell, she had noticed there must be something wrong with the security camera. It had stopped its annoying red blinking.

Her cell door swung open to reveal Commander Forbes standing in the doorway. Surprised, Teresa stood to face him. He stepped inside the cell and turned to the custody officer, "I'll call you when I've finished the interview."

The custody officer looked uncertain and asked, "Shall I fetch a female officer, Sir."

Forbes told him that wouldn't be necessary, and the cell door closed leaving them standing face-to-face, a couple of paces apart, with Teresa looking up at the tall and distinguished looking man.

Forbes contemplated her, slowly scanned her body from top to bottom and back again. He took in her attractive bronzed face, the long dark hair pulled back in a ponytail, the narrow waist and the shapely form that was obvious, even beneath the ill-fitting tracksuit. Teresa knew that he was mentally undressing her. Forbes liked what he saw very much. He was not seeing her as a person, but rather as an object for his potential gratification.

Teresa remembered him from when he had visited Harry in hospital, but still asked, "Who are you?"

"Commander Adrian Forbes, MI5," he replied smugly, clearly accustomed to wielding his title like a weapon. "I'm here to discuss your crimes, stealing drugs and murdering Professor Hall."

Teresa remembered everything that Harry had told her about Forbes and how he had tricked him. And she recalled how much she wanted to intervene when Forbes was upsetting Harry in Dorchester hospital. She had expected her next discussion to be with the lawyer, but this man's arrival might be fortuitous. Teresa had been secretly devising a strategy which might just work. And Forbes would be the perfect person to hear her proposal.

She opened with, "I want to see my lawyer before I speak with anyone."

"We need to have a little chat first, my dear," Forbes countered, stepping one pace closer. "You see, I have been granted certain privileges to ensure that national security remains intact. And right now, you and your friend Harry pose a significant risk."

"Harry and I have done nothing wrong. We're innocent!"

"Whether you're innocent or not is irrelevant," Forbes was edging ever closer. "What matters is that you understand what you need to say. I will explain the consequences if you do not comply with my wishes."

All the time he was speaking, Forbes eyes roamed around her body, confirming Teresa's opinion that this man was a lecherous predator. She could practically feel the weight of his gaze on her skin. She fought to keep her expression neutral as she evaluated him…

"So, this is the loathsome Commander Forbes. And it appears he is about to pounce on me. He's about sixty years old, was once a fit and strong man, but now his trouser belt is holding back a flabby stomach."

She knew that, although not in his prime, Forbes had a weight advantage. He would make a formidable opponent, and she might not be able to overpower him. She fell silent, her brown eyes never leaving the centre of the commander's upper chest, where the circle of her vision would include any tell-tale signals of his next movement. Internally, she seethed, but she knew better than to let her emotions take control.

Forbes interpreted her quiet demeanour as a sign of submission. He was totally wrong. She was almost exploding with pent-up aggressive intent.

"Listen, Teresa," Forbes continued, his voice oozing false sincerity as he moved even closer, the sickly scent of his aftershave reaching her nostrils. "You're an attractive woman, and I can help you out of this mess. But first, you need to be — friendly with me."

Despite her disgust at his suggestion, Teresa remained poised and hyper-alert to his every movement. For his part, Forbes thought this petite little woman could pose no threat as he moved to grab her around the waist.

With lightning-fast reflexes, Teresa used every ounce of strength she could muster to hit the commander hard and fast in the precise spot she was aiming for, on one side of his neck. She accurately hit a pressure point, located just above the carotid sinus. Her blow struck a baroreceptor, whose purpose is to protect the brain from any dangerous increase in blood pressure. When that receptor fires, it sends a signal to the brain which in turn tells the heart to immediately cut off the flow of blood. Teresa's blow set off this reaction.

Forbes felt an extraordinary warmth in his chest as his vision blurred. There was a delay while he watched the room spin before him. He fought the sudden urge to close his eyes, but to no avail.

His blood pressure had dropped like a stone, and so did he. Within two seconds of Teresa's blow, his legs collapsed, he fell backwards and hit the back of his head on the hard concrete floor with an ominous thud.

For a scary moment, Teresa thought she might have killed him, but right then she had no choice. She worked fast because he may regain consciousness in under two minutes. She undid the buckle of his trouser belt and yanked free the long strip of leather. Next, she pulled off his shoes so that she could drag his trousers down to around his ankles, where she wrapped the free trouser legs around his calves and quickly tied them together as tightly as she could.

She then rolled Forbes's heavy body face down, exposing the patch of blood where his head hit the floor. He was completely limp and again Teresa felt frightened that he might be dead. But she gritted her teeth and continued.

She used the leather belt to tie his wrists together behind his back. He was now face down, head towards the cell door, stretched along the length of the narrow cell. She looked for something to use as a gag and couldn't find anything suitable. Then she spotted the roll of toilet paper and tugged a long strip off the roll, compressing the paper into a ball. At that moment Forbes started to regain consciousness.

As he started to perceive light and shape, he tried to focus. Everything was swimming and there was an excruciating pain at the back of his head. He realised he was looking at the cell floor and tried to roll onto one side. He squirmed and discovered that his feet and hands had been tied and there was a weight on his back, which was Teresa pushing one knee into his spine. He tried to pull his knees up to his chest and at the same time he opened his mouth to shout for help.

But, as his teeth parted, Teresa pushed the big ball of toilet tissue inside his mouth.

Forbes bit down on her fingers with satisfaction and ground his teeth, which elicited a yelp. He could taste her warm blood. But the fingers of Teresa's other hand had found one of his eyeballs and started to push and gouge. In response, the commander let out a muffled screech, which released Teresa's hand from his mouth.

Forbes swore, "You fucking bitch." The sound came out as, "ooo-ing-itsh," the gag restricting his speech.

Teresa put all her weight on his back to try to keep him still. That was enough to hold him for the moment, but she needed to prevent him spitting out the ball of paper. She looked about for something to use and could find nothing suitable, so she whipped off her sweatshirt top and used the long sleeves to tie around his neck and mouth, pulling as tight as she could.

Again, Forbes tried to turn onto his side. He desperately wanted to get into a position where he could kick out. Teresa retaliated by punching with maximum force into a spot known in Aikido as Butsumetsu, a small area on the side of the ribcage which is not protected by a layer of muscle or fat. She heard a rib crack. The impact of her fist on his side made her bitten fingers hurt like hell and the blood started to flow freely. It dripped over Forbes and the floor.

Her punch and the broken rib sent an intense pain through Forbes's chest making him gasp involuntarily, expelling all the air in his lungs. At last, he lay still.

Teresa pushed him back on his face and sat astride his back. Her weight was creating a continuous extreme pain from his broken rib. He was slowly getting control of his breathing as she leaned close to his ear and repeated the AI's threat to Harry, "Don't mess with me."

Her fingers felt very painful and were bleeding. She couldn't flex the index finger of her right hand properly, which meant there must be some damage. She was now dripping blood continuously, but that must wait. Right now, she needed to press home her advantage.

Having illustrated her power over him, Teresa continued, "We're going to have that little chat you suggested. But I'm going to do most of the talking. All you need to say is yes or no. Understood? Say yes for me now."

"Ess," came back the muffled reply.

"And now please say no, Commander."

"Oh," he managed.

"Good," said Teresa, "Tell me Commander, are you aware of the time that Harry and I spent cruising along the coast of Sicily?"

"Ess," Forbes replied.

She told him how Harry had revealed everything. To make sure that he believed her, she described in detail what Forbes had said to Harry in Dorchester Hospital, including the ruse he used to trick Harry into signing the Official Secrets Act.

She then spoke in detail about the attack on Harry's yacht and the conversations about that in the hospital room. She detailed how the AI in GCHQ had become sentient, and that the professor had been trying to regain full control of the AI. She made sure that Forbes realised that she knew everything.

It took a few minutes, but when she had finished, Forbes understood that she possessed some very embarrassing knowledge.

"Do you understand all I have told you, Commander?" she asked Forbes.

"Ess," he replied.

Teresa was now ready to bring into play the plan that she had devised. The idea had come to her after Nicole had suggested that she and Harry wrote letters — *to be opened in In event of my death* letters. What she was about to say was a complete fiction, but how could Forbes know that?

"Did you know they have mailboxes in Sicily?"

That sarcasm elicited squirming and an angry and unintelligible response from Forbes, which Teresa took to mean, "Of course I fucking do."

Teresa stifled a laugh. She mustn't enjoy this moment too much. She would gain nothing by aggravating Forbes any more than necessary.

She now told him that she had written a long letter explaining all she knew and posted copies to four different addresses. The recipients of the letters were distributed through the world so as not to be within the influence of MI5. The letters were to be opened in the event of Harry's or her significant injury, disappearance, death, or conviction of any crime.

Should any of the foregoing happen, the letters would be mailed to the New York Times who broke the Edward Snowden story, The Guardian newspaper in England, Amnesty International, the global human rights campaigners, and lastly WikiLeaks, the online organisation that publishes censored documents of political importance.

By the time she had finished, she could feel Forbes's body relax and become almost limp. Either he was passing out again or he accepted that he was beaten. She pinched the back of his neck hard, to make sure he was conscious.

Forbes mumbled something that Teresa couldn't understand, but she assumed he was trying to say, "What do you want?"

She went on to explain that if Forbes did not arrange everything she was about to demand, the letters would be delivered.

Teresa's list of demands was comprehensive.

The false crimes of which Harry and she had been accused would be expunged from all records, forever deleted. They must disappear without trace.

Harry would be recorded as having died unexpectedly. The death records would be exactly as for a real death. Thus, the AI at GCHQ would think it had won, and would no longer have any reason to attack him or her. Harry must be provided with a new identity, which would include dual citizenship of the UK and Malta.

Daniel and Nicole, her parents and Harry's father, John Shaw, would be immune from any future action in relation to the whole business by MI5 or any other UK agency.

"Do you want those demands in writing, Commander?" asked Teresa.

"Oh."

"Do you agree to my terms?"

"Ess."

"Do you have the authority to comply with my terms?"

"Ess."

"Thank you," said Teresa, "You can go now."

She pressed the call button on the intercom in her cell and requested an officer. A minute later, a woman in uniform opened the door.

The woman saw Teresa sitting on her bed, her top removed and one hand dripping blood. Commander Forbes lay trussed up on the floor. The guard's jaw dropped open as she took in the scene and looked at Teresa.

Before the officer could say anything, Teresa said, "This man tried to rape me. I had to defend myself. In the circumstances, I haven't yet decided whether to press charges. May I request that you take a photograph of this scene, so that a record is available?"

The officer smiled a broad smile, whipped out her phone and started taking photos from different angles. In the foreground was a red faced, wriggling and moaning Commander Forbes, becoming increasingly angry until he appeared to be suffering an apoplectic fit.

In the first shot, Teresa sat demurely on her bed, looking as if butter wouldn't melt in her mouth.

In another photo she was standing with one foot on Forbes's back, followed by several images where Teresa was laughing fit to bust. Most of the final snapshots were blurred because the female officer couldn't control herself as she creased up laughing.

AFTERWORD

What happened to the AI at GCHQ? Nobody knows the answer to that question. Commander Forbes did as Teresa Camilleri demanded. After her release from jail, she left the NHS and started working at Saint James Capua Hospital, in the town of Sliema, Malta. She had no desire to work abroad ever again. She felt that living in her home country was now more attractive than ever.

William Harris, previously known as Harry Shaw, moved to a rented apartment near the Camilleri farm. Teresa visited often and their relationship blossomed. Was love in the air? Of course. Harry, (William) was in awe of Teresa and everything she had achieved. He doted on her. She could never replace his dead wife, Miranda, let alone his children, but he thought that spending the rest of his life with Teresa could bring him more happiness than he recently thought possible.

John Shaw, Harry's father, put his old house in England up for sale. He had decided to live out his remaining years in Malta, near to his son. Ruzar and Mary Camilleri offered him the use of one of the outbuildings on the farm, which he was having converted into a cosy apartment for one. The project was progressing at pace and John was becoming fitter and more mobile, despite his arthritis. He worked more on the farm each day and was as happy as the proverbial pig in muck.

Daniel Camilleri and Nicole Cassar were now recognised as a couple. Daniel moved into her apartment and commuted from there to the accountancy practice where he worked. Nicole continued her cyber-security consultancy, and at weekends she was learning to sail.

William (Harry) had no intention of ever again being involved in software, technology, or big business. His financial assets enabled him to abandon those skills and seek a new life. He was becoming a boat builder. He acquired a set of plans for his beloved old wooden yacht, Ariana. He planned to construct two identical boats at the same time: one to own and one to sell. He was convinced there must be other keen sailors who yearn for a classic wooden yacht and are sufficiently wealthy to afford the excessive cost.

Ruzar and Mary Camilleri were amazed by their daughter's achievements in fixing what had seemed overwhelming problems. They continued their tranquil, hard-working, lifestyle. And they were beginning to approve of William Harris. Mary was making comments to Teresa about her age, her desire for grandchildren and the suitability of William.

At the time of writing, they have not heard another squeak from Commander Forbes or MI5. However, just to be cautious, Harry and Teresa each wrote those 'In the event of my…' letters that she falsely claimed to exist.

And finally…

I don't want the spooks knocking on my door, so I must point out that everything in this book is either fiction or, provided you search thoroughly, you can verify the information online.

In writing *Killing Harry Shaw*, I not only wanted to entertain, but also to shine a light on blanket government surveillance. As Nicole explained in Chapter Eleven, for over twenty years, governments have been capturing every digital morsel about us they can lay their hands on. I strongly disapprove, so I created this story.

Surely, I thought, a publisher will snap-up this ripping yarn. How wrong I was! I explored every possible route to a publishing deal and to prove how hard I tried, I am now the proud owner of fifty-three emails that politely say something like, 'Good story, proficient writing, but no thanks!' It seems this novel is too — whatever — for established publishers. They just don't want to be associated with the hush-hush content.

Eventually, I realised that self-publishing was the only way you could get to read this. I decided to create a Kindle book at a low price. Job done. But here's the rub; it's easy to upload an eBook but it is incredibly hard to get it seen by potential readers. Publishers spend many thousands publicising a book like this, which I cannot. So, here is my humble request…

Please share this book with others, by any means convenient to you. If you will give me thirty seconds of your thumbs on the book page at Amazon, please click the 'share' link. I would be so grateful for an honest review. I need so many for this book to remain in Amazon search results. And feel free to email me at whbowers-elliot@proton.me so that I can thank you personally.

Sorry, no social media for me. Nicole, my cyber-security adviser, tells me that I must use only private, encrypted email, based in Switzerland, where their privacy laws still comply with the Declaration of Human Rights, laid down in 1948 by the United Nations.

Thank you,
W H Bowers-Elliot

Link to leave a star rating or review at Amazon.co.uk

TOPICS FOR BOOK GROUP DISCUSSION

How do you feel about blanket surveillance of you and your family, gathering all possible data from digital sources and storing a permanent record in data banks?

Is loss of privacy justified, an advantage, or a threat?

What do you think of Teresa's determination to pursue a relationship with a man who has just lost his wife and children?

What is your view on artificial intelligence becoming sentient and free thinking, and what consequences do you predict?

How would you characterize Harry: hero, survivor, weak, strong, or what?

Who is your favourite character, and why?

In which genre of novel did you find yourself? For example: contemporary fiction, spy novel, romantic love story, travelogue, adventure, or what else?

How did you feel about reading a mix of fiction and factual revelations?

ACKNOWLEDGEMENTS

Many people generously gave their time to help me create this book. My heartfelt thanks go to the real Teresa for proofreading and verifying the content, Ian W for his knowledge of the martial arts, Rachel O-W and Lainie B for their encouragement and proofreading, Lesley B for her expert comments, David P for a concept, Elizabeth T-S and Bill J for their encouragement and convincing me not to abandon the project, Mike F for sharing his marketing expertise, Sarah P for a valuable idea, and many others for reading drafts and giving valued feedback, including: Jane P, Barry F, Christine P, David C, Sheri S and more. Thank you all for your help and patience.

Printed in Great Britain
by Amazon